DÉJÀ VU

With one hand still taking support from Sean's shoulder, Christian hooked the thumb of the other into the waistband of his shorts and began to slide it down over his slim hips. Sean turned hastily to face the other way, almost sending him pitching forward into the tub.

"No need to be shy," he reminded her humorously. "There's nothing there that you haven't seen before."

"That was a long time ago," she answered, still not turning around. "I've forgotten."

Forgotten? About his most delicate parts? *"Touché,* darling," he muttered. She really knew how to aim below the belt. He stepped in, and eased himself painfully into the warm water.

She turned towards him, and with the cool efficiency of a hospital matron, proceeded to lather up a large bath sponge and apply it to his chest. The first touch of her fingers was electrifying.

He eyed her covertly, wondering if she was suffering the same overwhelming déjà vu that he was. Her shuttered face gave no indication of this. His pride was piqued. There she was, sponging him down with the detachment she would hold for the family dog, and there he was, his whole being so awake, so stimulated by her touch and her memory.

"That should do it." She got up off her knees and tossed him a towel. He rose and began to modestly wrap it around his waist. This time, instead of turning away, she let her hazel eyes move slowly along his body, concentrating on his midsection.

"Just refreshing my memory," she informed him laconically.

MESMERIZED

Simona Taylor

ARABESQUE
BET
BOOKS

BET Publications, LLC.
www.msbet.com
www.arabesquebooks.com

*Dedicated to my parents, Trevor and Cynthia,
for filling my home, my life, and my heart with books.*

ARABESQUE BOOKS are published by

BET Publications, LLC
c/o BET BOOKS
One BET Plaza
1900 W Place NE
Washington, D.C. 20018-1211

First Printing: January, 2000

10 9 8 7 6 5 4 3 2 1
Printed in the United States of America

Prologue

The men worked fast, as they had been instructed. Six months of training in the grueling Middle-Eastern heat, at the hands of a small international group of experts in terrorism and mayhem, had taught them to enter the bank, make their lethal deposit with as little fuss as possible, and leave without a trace.

The bomb was a lot smaller than one would have expected, considering the amount of damage it was designed to cause. Its digital works counted away the seconds, the minutes and the hours silently, with neither a tick nor a click. It was hidden in such a way that the bank's employees, when they arrived to work in the morning, would never notice it, even if they chose to visit the deserted room in which it lay. Its anonymous shape and color blended seamlessly with the rows of laminated cabinets and metal files.

The men were far from the vaults, far from the money, but that didn't matter; money was not what they were after. As a matter of fact, their location made things easier for them, as the bank's security system was designed to protect its assets, rather than the file graveyard that stood forgotten in the bowels of the building.

They left as swiftly as they had come, not even turning to glance at the security guards, who, for a price, had agreed to look the other way. Like swiftly shifting shadows, they separated as they stepped once again into the quiet city streets. Each took a different path. There was no need for conversation, no need to meet again, not for many days.

As they parted, each felt a sense of satisfaction; they had done an excellent job, and they were sure to be commended. Do it fast, and do it right; that had been their injunction, and they had obeyed. The Prophetess would be pleased.

One

The world ground to a halt. Everything had stopped moving, everyone had stopped talking, and there was no sound except a high-pitched ringing in Sean's ears, and no sensation except the bands of pain around her chest that reminded her she'd better let out the breath that she'd sucked in sharply the minute she'd turned to shake hands with Christian Devane.

It couldn't be him. Not here, not now. Surely the tall dark man who was clasping her hand with the cordial disinterest of a total stranger couldn't be the man she'd stood up at their engagement dinner six years ago, vowing that she never wanted to see him again. The gods could never be so cruel, so uncaring, so awfully unjust.

Standing beside the two of them, shrewd blue-gray eyes flitting from Sean's suddenly bloodless face to Christian's unrevealing one, Andrea Gooding was the first to speak. Sean could see the thin painted lips moving, but couldn't seem to get a fix on what the older woman was trying to say. She had recovered sufficiently, however, to gather that the Senior Vice President was inquiring whether she was all right.

Sean disentangled her cold hand from the strong one that held hers, and wiped it surreptitiously against the rough linen of her skirt. She knew that the shock had made it unpleasantly damp. "Fine," she murmured in answer to Gooding's question. "Tough day, that's all. I've been at my desk since dawn. . . ." Sean's voice trailed off. It sounded callow, whining about how hard she was working. As if she were doing a little personal campaigning, angling for a little recognition from one of the bosses. She decided to make the best of a bad morning and simply shut up.

Andrea nodded unconcernedly and then turned to look up at Christian with an uncharacteristically warm smile. "Well, my dear," she said, placing her smooth, manicured hand lightly on the jacketed arm, "maybe I should introduce you to the rest of the staff." She gave him a barely perceptible tug. "Shall we?"

Sean watched, dazed, as the man who had ruined her life and destroyed all of her faith in the other sex nodded politely to her, still no trace of recognition in his obsidian eyes, and followed the platinum-haired woman along the corridor. She stared after his receding back for a long time, counting her breaths—in . . . out . . . in . . . out—until her respiration returned to normal. Then she walked unsteadily to her office and sat down heavily behind her cluttered desk.

The day that had begun badly had suddenly become exponentially worse. Her desk was obscured by scattered documents, and although it was only ten-thirty, the thick curly chestnut hair that she usually kept swept up off her spice-brown forehead was beginning to wilt and fall onto her face in wisps. Deciding that her only option was to immerse herself in the documents until she was home and alone, where she could sort out her tangled thoughts at leisure, she ruffled through her documents and struggled to concentrate. There was, after all, work to be done.

Orion Methanol was a new company, American-owned and Texas-based. The owners had been attracted to the small Caribbean island of Trinidad by the wealth of natural gas and oil to be found just a few miles offshore. In the past few years, with the island's government bending over backwards to woo foreign investors in the energy business with promises of almost outrageous tax holidays, choice parcels of land and bureaucratic fast-tracking, companies such as hers were converging on the island like flies on a sticky bun.

Offered the opportunity of an overseas posting two years ago, Sean didn't have to think too long. She reflected briefly on the Brooklyn brownstone that she was renting, the elevator that was busted more often than not, and the noisy, busy streets which lay just outside, guaranteeing fractured sleep every night. She thought of the intense city heat in the summer and the feel of snow turning to sludge under her boots in the winter. Then she took Orion up on their offer, and never regretted her decision.

Her job as Public Relations Manager was exhausting but always interesting, as the dynamic organization spared no effort in getting established as a major producer of methanol in a country known in the business world as an ideal home for industrial giants.

But these past few days had been more hectic than most. The operations of the plant, which was located on the island's populous west coast, necessitated the relocation of eleven families who had been squatting dangerously close to their southwestern perimeter. The relocation process was not one that was welcomed by the families in question, as they lived there more through necessity than by choice, and leaving would mean releasing their tenuous grip on the tiny homes they had erected and the land that they had been farming for years.

Although the actual relocation was a responsibility of the Trinidadian government, it was potentially damaging to the company's image. The last thing they wanted was to appear to the locals as a huge American ogre muscling in on their land and their livelihood. In the interest of maintaining good neighborly relations, she had been called upon to organize a series of open discussions with the residents and her own company's management, so that everyone's views could be heard. The first meeting was to be held in less than a week, and it was going to take all her time and energy to pull it off right.

She popped a Hershey's almond-filled nugget into her mouth as if it were a tranquilizer, desperate to keep her focus, trying not to think of the encounter that had in a few short seconds threatened the calm and happy existence she had succeeded in establishing. If there was one thing that was guaranteed to make her feel better, it was chocolate. It was her personal addiction, her source of solace, comfort and inspiration. She unwrapped another piece, and laid it carefully on her desk. Some people chain-smoked; she chain-nibbled.

Suddenly she became aware that she was not alone, and her instincts, heightened as they were by the unnerving incident a few minutes ago, told her unerringly just who the infiltrator of her small office space was. Startled, she looked up, tugging at her errant strands of hair with long-fingered brown hands.

A tall, broad-shouldered shape filled most of the doorway. The man's finely tailored gray suit, with its clean classic lines, drew her eyes along the length of his torso and down a pair of mighty fine-looking legs. Dammit, he could still do it to her. By force of will she dragged her eyes upwards again, back across that broad chest to finally focus on the face that belonged to the body.

He appeared older, of course, and considerably better looking. Not that he hadn't been good-looking to begin with. But in their college days, adopting an attitude of disdain towards things sartorial had been *de rigueur.* The man-child that she remembered, with his unkempt hair that bordered on baby dreads, and the chin that went several nonchalant days without shaving had been replaced by a man whose smooth jaw could only have been maintained by the careful application of an expensive razor, and whose classic neatly trimmed haircut boasted the prowess of a talented barber.

And the skin! With the clarity that only a painful memory could have, she remembered how much she used to tease him about the similarity in tone and smoothness between her treasured candy and his mellow dark skin. Slap him between a giant graham cracker and a huge marshmallow, she used to tell him, and you'd have the world's biggest S'more.

Irrationally guilty at being caught gobbling candy like a child (especially by one who knew her addiction so well), and needing to remove the taunting evidence that had triggered the memory, Sean hesitated, not knowing what to do next. Eventually, she solved the problem by picking the offending piece up off the desk, slipping it into her mouth, and crunching it hastily down.

"I see you're still hooked on those things," he said casually. He hadn't moved from the doorway, but instead stood there, shoulder against the door jamb, watching her with the same inscrutable expression he had worn when Gooding had first introduced them.

He *had* recognized her! Her heart did a double somersault. Silently giving thanks to the Muse of Chocolate for not causing her to choke on the last traces of the melting nugget, she managed to look at once politely interested in and coolly disdainful of her visitor's approach. Two could play at the sangfroid game, she counseled herself. Of course he recognized her. He wasn't stupid. He'd probably chosen to feign ignorance just to rattle her. He was always good at finding ways to do that.

"Is there something I can help you with, Christian?" She had her best don't-bug-me-I'm-busy face on. It was known to daunt even the most stubborn offender.

"Maybe there is," he drawled idly, and the deep mellow

voice and unmistakable accent placed his origins squarely in the Lone Star State. Sean remembered the accent and the deep baritone well. She remembered how his voice had been one of the things that had first attracted her to him, how his lazy manner of speech had seemed so refreshing to her jaded New York ears.

Sean glanced quickly past his shoulders, hoping there was nobody in the hall behind him who could hear their conversation. The last thing she needed now was an audience, especially since she had no way of knowing how she would hold up under the strain of his presence.

Adopting a professional attitude was her only line of defense. She waited for him to speak again, but when she realized that nothing was forthcoming, she sighed, placed her light-framed glasses carefully on the desk, and focused on him. "Well?" she asked pointedly.

"You look good. More mature." He took a step into her office, and her initial instinct was to fly around the desk, shove him back out with both hands, and slam the door.

Instead, she nodded mildly. "I grew up." She held his gaze stoically. He may have had the power to hurt her a long time ago, but she was a big girl now. Things had changed—for the better.

"That you did." His gaze roved unabashedly over her face, taking in the hazel eyes that struggled to keep from showing hurt and the wide mouth that was far from smiling. His scrutiny was more than she was prepared to bear.

She blurted out in frustration, "Christian, are you going to tell me what I can do for you? Because if not, I have lots of work. . . ." She pointed to her cluttered desk, hoping that he would take the hint.

The big man eased his frame into the leather-covered visitor's chair that was closest to her desk. "I was getting to it, actually." His gaze had settled upon her lips, and she hoped he wasn't going to make a bad situation worse by saying something suggestive. But he was all business. "I was told that you'd get me settled in today. You know, take me to the bank, help me get my paperwork organized."

Sean couldn't suppress a laugh. There was no way she was leaving her desk to baby-sit a newcomer, especially not *this* particular newcomer. "You were told that? By whom?"

With a toss of his dark head he indicated the direction from which he had come. "Andrea sent me over. She said you'd help." He appeared fully aware of the discomfort he was causing, and the awareness seemed to amuse him.

He'd called their only female VP Andrea, and she was willing to bet they'd only met that morning. She remembered Gooding's proprietary attitude towards Christian when she had introduced them earlier. She had no doubt that the woman had willingly invited him to use her first name. That was the kind of man he was; he seemed to have a knack for coercing women into doing what he wanted, while allowing them to believe that it had all been their idea. A fine one with the ladies, as envious men would say. She, having suffered terribly because of his easy charm and casual flirting, had a different name for his talent, and it wasn't one she could use in polite company.

Patiently, she tried to explain that 'Andrea' was sure as hell mistaken. "I'm in Public Relations, Christian. Showing new employees around, as enjoyable as the prospect might seem, is not exactly part of my job function. Surely someone from Human Resources would be able to help you?"

The man was leaning forward on her desk, toying idly with one of her favorite office toys. It was a solid mahogany sculpture that she had brought back from her most recent trip to Guyana. It consisted of a male figurine whose feet had been narrowed to a fine point, and which balanced precariously on a round slab of wood. Across its shoulders, the figurine carried a balancing pole with a weight at each end. The sculpture had been so carefully calibrated that when pushed in any direction it would bob back and forth, sway from side to side, but never fall over or lose its balance. Tapping it and watching it spring back into an upright position was one of her favorite stress relievers. She could do with a stress reliever right now, but the one she had in mind came in a glass and was usually served on the rocks.

She waited for a response, and after the wooden character had been made to bob back and forth for some time, Christian gave it. "I don't know, Sean. I was sent to you. I've been traveling a long time. Are you going to help me or not?"

The obvious fatigue in his voice almost made her feel sorry for him, but she really had no intention of being thrown into his company at the moment. Besides, her work was still pressing. How in the hell did Andrea Gooding think she could do both at the same time?

Sean made for the door. "I . . . ah, I'd just like to have a word with Ms. Gooding. Would you like to have a seat in the waiting area?" Pointedly, she indicated the well-furnished lobby with a wave of her arm.

"Sean," he began slowly, "I've had a bitch of a flight, and the twenty-four hours that I've spent on land have been uncomfortable beyond belief. It's been one problem and hitch after another. If you don't mind, I don't think I could get up out of this chair if I tried."

"Problems? Such as . . . ?" she asked skeptically, thinking *Aw, come on. The trip couldn't really have been that bad. Don't be a baby*.

"Such as the hotel I was booked into last night saw fit to hold a party on the roof, one floor above my head. Such as I got here an hour late because they've gone and dug up half the highway to run some cable or other." He looked at her accusingly, almost as if he were holding her responsible not only for the unfortunate booking but the ill-timed roadwork as well.

He did look a little ragged around the edges, she thought almost sympathetically. Still, sympathy wasn't going to get in the way of good judgment. She was going over to Gooding to straighten everything out.

She rose to her feet, and as she did so she noted with a pang the way his dark eyes flickered along her body as she drew herself to her full height. Christian used to love her height. He hadn't been daunted by it like so many men were, but instead relished her uniqueness. Not many women got to be six feet tall. Sean was one of them. For a girl who was five and a half feet tall by age thirteen, her height had brought nothing but shyness and misery. By the time she turned seventeen, she had topped off at an even six. This she learned first to accept, and then to relish. Her height gave her a sense of power that was almost exhilarating, and her strong, fit figure and elegant limbs gave her a grace of movement that stopped many an onlooker dead in his tracks. As she left the room, she could feel the light feathery touch of his gaze along the backs of her bare legs.

The fleeting pleasure that his remembered admiration brought her did not deter her from her mission. But as she strode up the hall in the direction of Gooding's office, in hot pursuit of justice, or at least a reprieve, she was obliged to make a slight detour, as she was waylaid by a tiny but enthusiastic firebrand called Delta.

"Girl, don't tell me I really saw that great big hunk of good-looking step into your office a while ago!" Small, claw-tipped hands held onto Sean's upper arm, dragging her into the small alcove where a stainless-steel water cooler hummed idly to itself. "Don't *tell* me you got that new fella in your office and you didn't call me in to say hello!"

Delta was a bright, good-looking Jamaican woman with a sharp mind for corporate law and a sharp eye out for available men. Flighty and vivacious, her mere existence was an overstatement, and as Orion's unlikely but knowledgeable Legal Officer, the only common sense she ever showed was around the negotiating table. She had been Sean's closest friend since she came to the island; they worked closely together when necessary, and hung out together wherever possible. In a male-oriented industry such as this, they reasoned, it was a smart move for two bright, attractive women to put up a united front.

"Delta," Sean began, but the other woman cut her off.

"I hear you get to show him around. Girl, you a lucky pig. You need help?" The honey-brown eyes flashed with mischief.

"I hardly think getting to show him around is what I'd call lucky," Sean answered sardonically. "I've got work to do. Besides. . . ." she stopped. There was no real need for her girlfriend to know that she and Christian had a history, was there?

Swept up by her own little wave of lust, Delta failed to notice Sean's hesitation. She snorted. "Girl, you lost your mind? When was the last time anything looking like *that* graced these stuffy halls? When was the last time Orion hired any male under fifty?" She tossed her burgundy waist-length human hair weave out of her eyes with an extravagant gesture.

"Attractive or not," Sean explained painstakingly, "I'm busy. He may have errands to run, but he isn't running them with me." She disentangled herself from her friend and continued on her quest. "I'll talk to you when I get back, okay?" she tossed over her shoulder in an attempt to placate. Delta was much too sweet to offend.

"You can tell the Silver Dragon I'm willing to take over the task, if she's looking for a replacement for you!" the incorrigible Delta yelled after her. Sean pretended she hadn't heard, and kept on going.

"Ms. Gooding," she began before she was properly in the doorway, "the new Operations Manager is in my office. . . ."

Andrea Gooding looked at her as if she were informing her that the sky was blue this morning. "Yes, I know. I sent him to you." She was a woman who had fought hard to make it to VP in an environment where men called the shots, and as such, wasn't averse to being as unbending as any male executive.

Privately, Sean thought that Gooding's striking resemblance to Margaret Thatcher didn't end with superficial appearances. The smoothly coifed hair, in such contrast to her own stubborn, out-of control waves only made Sean feel more disheveled, and therefore at a negotiating disadvantage.

Nonetheless, she pressed on determinedly. "He said you told him I was to take him around?" She hoped that Gooding would tell her she was mistaken.

"Yes. I did. Be a dear and help him settle in, will you?"

Gooding was one of those managers who saw the Public Relations function as that of a glorified hostess. There was nothing that could be done to change that opinion, but Sean tried, even though she knew the battle was already lost. "Isn't it a Human Resources function?"

"Human Resources is in a Divisional meeting." She gave a smile like a hairline crack in cement.

Sean took another stab at it. "Office Services?"

"There's a brownout down on the site, Sean. Most of the Office Services staff are there, trying to get the generators up and running." Gooding set her pen down and leaned slightly towards Sean, resting her elbows on the desk. "I don't have to tell you what an important employee he is. The Company has a vested interest, a very *large* interest, in ensuring that he settles down as fast as possible."

Gooding didn't have to make herself any clearer. Orion was on a tight schedule, competition in the petrochemical world was stiff, and if one producer failed to deliver, there were a number of others just waiting in the sidelines to snap up the customers. And they were behind schedule; the man whose shoes Christian had been chosen to fill had been given his walking papers quite a while ago.

Carlos Fabregas had turned out to be a surprising disappointment to the company. He had seemed so stable when he had been hired last year, when construction had first begun. He had been a dashingly handsome man of thirty-eight, with fifteen years of experience in the Persian Gulf petrochemical sector, and his downfall on the job had been due not to a lack of knowledge, but to a fondness for alcohol which had led to stupid, dangerous and costly mistakes.

It was only a matter of months before it became apparent that things were going terribly wrong. Whether he had been seduced by the insidiously enticing nightlife of the island, or whether he had arrived with his own demons in tow, not even those close to him ever found out. But Carlos soon started coming to work tired, disheveled, and hung over. At first, his charm and good looks allowed him to talk his way out of almost any self-induced trouble, but business was business, and his charmed existence did not last.

He had chosen a profession that was not suited to his reckless personality; how he had managed to survive so long and rise so far was anybody's guess. Carlos's job was one of the most crucial in the company: he was responsible not only for all the work that went on at the plant, but for the safety and welfare of the hundreds of temporary workers who were building it. As soon as it became evident that even his work was suffering, Carlos was discretely put on a plane for New York.

He had not gone happily; his dismissal, although just

by any standards, had been met with protests, stubborn resistance, and finally, loud, almost incoherent threats that one day he would get even with everyone involved in his downfall.

"This new man is very important to the Company's success," Gooding was saying, "and we have no doubt that his performance is predicated on his being comfortable, and making the transition from his old home to his new one as smoothly as possible. Of course," she added silkily, "*you* of all people would know just how important the performance of the person who fills this position is to us all."

Sean's face stung. Leave it to Gooding to refer, even obliquely, to the role that Sean herself had played in the dismissal of Carlos Fabregas. His eventual downfall had come about largely on the strength of her testimony regarding his inability to continue to serve the company as he should.

For some inexplicable reason, she'd always sensed a fine undercurrent of resentment from Gooding over the circumstances that led to Carlos's dismissal. There seemed to be no reason for it, unless of course, since Carlos had fallen directly under Gooding's Vice Presidential purview, the woman had resented Sean's encroachment on what she obviously saw as her own personal turf. Sean shook her head. The less she reflected upon that particular unpleasantness, the better.

But, as unlikable as Gooding was, she was right. Christian's presence could mean life or death to Orion, and she, as an employee, should be happy to ensure that he settled in as fast as possible, the better to grasp the helm of their operations and begin to pull the Company up out of the mud in which it had been mired. The position had been a tough one to fill. Months had dragged by, and staff had become anxious, as every month's delay was costing the company millions. But a hasty choice could be as dangerous as none at all, as the business, like all energy-based businesses, was one in which there was stiff competition. Rival companies were not above planting a mole at Orion, especially in such a crucial position where a potential saboteur could do irreparable damage. Many were interviewed. None were chosen. Finally, there was talk around the plant that the head office back in Texas had head-hunted a young whiz kid from one of the U.S. giants, and that this engineering miracle was supposed to turn things around and get the project back on stream.

Employees had spoken with reverence in the corridors about the new wonder who would halt the losses that they were incurring. What Sean had never for a moment considered, though, was that the new man they were whispering about would be Christian.

She regarded Gooding solemnly. The older woman was right. It was in the best interests of the company that he settle down as fast as possible. But why did the facilitator have to be her?

Gooding was speaking again, and Sean struggled to focus. "Be a nice girl," she was saying. "It won't take more than a few hours. Unless of course you have a problem with helping the company out of a tight spot . . . ?"

Talk about being backed up against a wall! Sean couldn't answer. Letting Gooding, or anyone else for that matter, know that this was not the first time she and Christian had met, would only lead to more complex problems. She realized that Christian had been right in pretending not to recognize her.

In mute response to the woman's question, Sean shook her head. Without another word, Andrea Gooding returned her attention to her work.

Ain't that just the way, Sean griped. Good old Public Relations, the general dogsbody of professions. Whenever a job needed to be done that defied classification, PR would do it. Defeated, she stalked back into her office to find the man she had loved and then rejected still apparently fascinated by her mahogany balancing figurine.

She was embarrassed to admit that she had been defeated in her attempt to have him shunted onto somebody else, but work was work. She moved around behind her desk again. "Uh, shall we get going?" She tried to sound pleasant and not look too longingly at her pile of papers.

The smile that he threw her was one of relief, tinged with an unmistakable glimmer of triumph. He rose to his feet. "I'll try not to make it too onerous for you," he promised solemnly. "I haven't forgotten how loathsome you find my company."

Sean shrugged and began gathering her things from her desk. She refused to be baited, and besides, past experience had taught her, very painfully, that his promises were worth less than a three-dollar bill.

She slung her black, locally crafted leather handbag onto her shoulder, skirted the table and made for the door, taking such long strides that he was obliged to hasten to fall into step. As he did so, she noted that the three-inch heels she perversely wore to accentuate her height made her just about an inch taller than he was. The small, if artificial advantage satisfied her immensely.

"We'll do the bank first," she told him.

"No problem," he said.

"One would have thought," he observed sourly, "that in an island climate like this one, the residents would have done away with the uncomfortable formality of a business suit."

They were standing in line, waiting for a free teller at the counter that inexplicably lumped the sale and purchase of foreign exchange, credit card inquiries and new accounts all into one. It was pretty close to the end of the month, so the bank was hopping. The crowds seemed to be growing thicker by the minute.

Sean fought to suppress a malicious smile as her long-lashed hazel eyes took in the fine beads of sweat that broke out on his forehead like a constellation, running out of his neat razor-marked hairline and down his face, to be stopped only by a pair of thick black brows. Her gaze fell to the heavy herringbone knit gray jacket, solid bone-white long-sleeved shirt and silk tie that were causing him so much distress.

So he was uncomfortable. Good.

He had complained about her driving on the way over, saying that if her driving had been reckless in New York, driving with the locals had definitely not improved it. After a few minutes of irritated woman-handling of the company Volvo's delicate controls, during which she considered telling him just what she thought of men who criticized her driving, she solved the problem by sweetly explaining that when in Trinidad, one drove as the Trinidadians drove. Besides, she taunted, if they were going to be catapulted into eternity with the screeching of brakes and the grinding of metal, what pleasanter place could they have chosen than under the bright Caribbean sun? This last comment had the desired effect of shutting him up for a full ten minutes. For this small mercy, she was grateful.

Now he was starting up again. She should have known. Blessed silence wasn't something that lasted very long, even in hallowed financial halls such as these. And although she had vowed to say as little to the man as possible during their enforced proximity, she had to admit that he was in obvious distress. Out of some kind of latent girl-scout kindness, she grudgingly offered a word of advice.

"I'm afraid that most of the time you really will have to wear a suit, except when you're down on the plant. After all, business is business, and formal dress codes are pretty much the same in any Westernized country, island or not. But for what it's worth, it's not the cut of the suit that's causing you so much agony, it's the material. Maybe you should think about investing in a few lightweight summer blends."

One dark sweaty eyebrow arched, and its owner regarded her as if she were a complete moron. "I think I know about the comparative benefits of summer blends and winter blends, Sean," he said in the voice of one whose intellect had been unfairly questioned. "But when you land in a strange country and find that somehow the airline has managed to miss-send your luggage to the freaking Cayman Islands, of all places, and when the shipping company informs you that the rest of your belongings won't be arriving in the country for another six days or so because of a union work-to-rule, you just have to make do with what you've got." He turned his face frontward and crossed his arms with an injured air.

Things were getting better and better, she thought gleefully. He had probably been wearing the suit since he left JFK airport, in full winter, the day before. She wondered idly if he'd had the foresight to pack anything in his carry-on luggage, a T-shirt or a pair of jeans, perhaps. A change of underwear. This last made her glance at the solid thighs that were encased in uncomfortable (but, she had to admit, flattering) wool pants. She was unable to keep from grinning. If he hadn't remembered this small but crucial item, then his discomfort was probably a hell of a lot more than he was letting on.

Now, if she had been in his place, and Lord knows she had, dozens of times, she'd have packed enough in her carry-on for at least two days: clothes, toothbrush and toothpaste, comfortable shoes, even a few of her own personal addiction, Hershey bars, just in case her overseas destination had never heard of them.

But Christian had always been impulsive. His brilliance in engineering had somehow failed to transfer itself to his personal life. He was not the kind of person who would have thought of anything so logical. Far from it; he lived by the seat of his pants, sailing from one adventure to another, consequences be damned. She used to worry about him and his youthful high jinks, promising him that he'd wind up arrested, stranded in a desert, or mangled and broken at the bottom of some cliff before he was thirty.

Well, she'd been wrong. He seemed to have done pretty well for himself, so she guessed that a day in grubby clothes would be a minor inconvenience to a man like him. She shrugged off his plight. She hoped he itched.

Christian turned to face her, no doubt reading a flicker of resentment on her face. "Seeing me again like this has been a pretty nasty surprise for you, hasn't it?" he asked softly. He stood a little closer than was necessary, even taking into account the confined space and long lines.

Thrown off guard by his perception and concern, she opened her mouth to respond, and found that there was nothing that she could say. A nasty surprise? An understatement if there ever was one. She thought she had shaken off the dust of their disastrous love affair long, long ago. Never mind she still kept every photo they'd ever taken together, and every once in a while she tugged them out from the farthest reaches of her closet to thumb through them and sigh. Never mind she'd found herself in the arms of other men during the intervening years, some of them very nice men, she had to admit, but every so often, a treacherous thought would flit through her mind. . . . *Christian used to touch me like that, just like that, but somehow when he did my head would reel because of all the tiny firecrackers he would send shooting off in my brain.* Nasty surprise? A horrible shock would be closer to the mark. Why him? Why now? Of all the methanol plants in all the little islands in the world, he had to walk into hers.

With an uncanny ability to step in at the most inappropriate moment, thus saving her by the proverbial bell, the bank clerk saw no fitter time to interrupt, asking how she could help. Before Sean could decide whether to answer Christian honestly or shield herself with a lie, his attention was turned from her and focused on the girl behind the counter. As she watched, she witnessed a phenomenon that she had been all too familiar with six years ago.

The clerk, a young smooth-skinned East Indian girl with glossy black hair that cascaded down to her waist, turned her sloe-black eyes towards Christian's. As she did so, she flinched, jolted by the heady male attractiveness that seemed to surround Christian like an aura. Her carmine lips curved involuntarily into a smile that was much warmer than was required by the demands of her job.

Christian responded with a smile of his own, the kind of smile that Sean had wished, in vain, could be reserved only for her. Sean couldn't prevent herself from rolling her eyes upwards. Hardly a gesture worthy of a mature woman of the nineties, but fortunately, the two of them would have been too preoccupied to notice if she'd leaped up onto the counter and begun juggling deposit slips.

A small brass name tag bearing the bank's logo proclaimed the clerk's name to be Naimah. "Can I help?" she breathed, her black eyes holding Christian's fast.

"Maybe you can, Naimah," he began, and pulled a sheaf of personal documents from his briefcase.

There he went again, leaping to the first-name stage without so much as a by-your-leave. Irritated, Sean sucked her teeth. And to think she was almost beginning to warm up to him for a moment there! He didn't deserve her warmth, didn't deserve her sympathy or her understanding. She'd learned that years ago. Seething, she watched as he detailed his request to the pretty, smiling girl, voice and gesture seeming to convey needs that went beyond finance.

Sean stared at the broad, solid back, which had now turned slightly as if to shield her from the transaction, and wondered what would happen if she whacked him squarely between the shoulder blades with her purse. Lord knew he deserved to be thumped, and thumped good.

The dark thoughts that fluttered across her mind on devils' wings were answered by an eardrum-splitting roar that came from all sides. A brilliant flash glowed red, then yellow, then excruciatingly white at the backs of her retinas.

It was like something in a bad movie, where reality was and yet was not. The walls, the people, everything, rose up around her, was sucked up, or thrown up into the air, in the grip of a wild tornado.

She realized with ludicrous clarity that Christian was in her arms, thrown there by a force that hit them like a wall, tossing them violently backwards. As she fought for the air that had been ruthlessly torn from her lungs, she found that her arms were empty, and that he wasn't there anymore. She lurched desperately, reaching out for him and feeling nothing. At that moment, having him back in her arms again, and holding onto him while the insanity raged all around, was the most important thing in her existence.

But there was no up, no down, and nobody beside her, not for miles around. There was only a jarring blare in her skull that wouldn't rest until she acknowledged it. No pain, just a noise that was becoming part of her, like a new organ. Like a tumor. Wrapped in the thick blanket of gray dust, blinded by it, surrounded by nothing but space, Sean floated.

Two

The first thing Christian heard was the screams. They were ghostly, inhuman screams that rose up out of the seventh circle of hell to whip and swirl around him. To his shock, he saw that it was already night—how long had he been unconscious? The blackness that cloaked him was impenetrable. Then, as he struggled to peer through the darkness, blinking hard to remove the grit that scoured his eyeballs, he realized that the frightening blackness was caused by the cloud of dust that billowed like a foul belch from a dragon's mouth.

His next thought was of Sean. He remembered being catapulted into her by some ungodly force. He remembered her desperate fingers as they clawed at him, trying to hang onto him in the chaos. Then she was gone.

He had to find her in this godawful mess. She had to be somewhere close by. He tried to turn his head, but the lancing pain that shot through his skull and down his spine put paid to that effort. He was hurt, dammit.

Gingerly, he freed one hand from the rubble and did a slow and painful self-examination. He ran his fingers along his face, skimming the jawbone lightly, glad that it seemed intact. As he continued upwards, along his nose-bridge and along his forehead, his fingers encountered a sticky warmth.

He was bleeding. Heavily. From his skull. He groaned;

this wasn't good. At least he was conscious, and that was proof enough that the damage couldn't be all that bad. He tried again to look around him, but the pain slapped him down.

Wiggle your toes, Devane. He tried, and he was sure that he was indeed moving his feet. But his feet felt like they were miles away, and there was no way of telling whether the slight twitch below the ankles wasn't a figment of his befuddled imagination.

On his left, there was a stirring, more muffled cries, and then a loud grunt of pain. Someone was getting to their feet right next to him. "Sean!" The call died on his dry lips, and he tasted pulverized mortar, soot and grime. He flicked his swollen tongue out and tried again. "Sean!"

There was a grating, scraping sound, and then a heavily booted foot hit him full in the face as some panicked victim scrambled over his prone body. The footsteps continued on, their owner oblivious to everything except the need for escape.

"Sean!" His frightened cry was reduced to a whimper, as the energy that his shouts had taken from him left him drained. For the first time he wondered if she had heard him, or if she could hear anything. He remembered the force of the eruption, and hoped desperately that she wasn't lying crushed under some huge chunk of cement.

The idea was unthinkable. He forced it from his mind. She wasn't dead. For Chrissakes, she was just standing next to him a moment ago, with that look on her face, the same look she always got whenever she caught him smiling at a pretty girl. She'd been pouting, pissed off . . . why was it that he always pissed her off like that? He never meant to, but he did all the same.

But that was a long time ago, he reminded himself. Years. A lifetime. He'd only met her again this morning.

Walked into his first day on a new job and run straight into her in the hallway. Her with her sexy mouth and smooth spicy skin. And that look of horror when she saw him, recognized who he was. Her with her Hershey's Nuggets, with the almonds. No, she couldn't be dead.

The untenable prospect caused him to try once again to get to his feet, but as he gathered up his forces, trying to lift his aching body up off the ground that it seemed plastered to, he realized why he couldn't move. A large portion of countertop—*that's right,* he remembered he'd been standing at the counter when this all started—was lying across his midsection. It prevented him from looking down and seeing his feet, and more importantly, prevented him from getting up and looking for his woman.

Then, as if he'd wished her there, she was next to him. A dusty apparition, crawling low on the ground, on her hands and knees. He felt her hands make contact with his chest, felt her fingers skitter up to his face in an attempt to identify him by touch. Even in the cursed darkness, he knew it was her.

"Baby," he gasped. He sent up a free-floating prayer of thanks, hoping that it would rise out of the devastated building, rise up into the universe, until it met a target that would listen and accept his gratitude as that of a man who had had his most sincere wish answered. She's alive. She's all right. *Thank You.*

"Chris," Sean panted with the effort of speaking. "Are you okay?"

He heard the concern, and it warmed him, almost making his injuries not matter anymore. Almost, but not quite. "No, not okay." Then he added, regretfully, "Hurt."

"Bad?" The anxiety had returned to her voice.

"I'm afraid so. I can't get up."

There was silence, then he heard her grunting, and felt the huge slab that lay across his chest budge just an inch. She was trying to move it all by herself. It was impossible, but Sean was never the kind of woman who understood the word.

"Don't do it, Sean. Get out. Get help."

She shook her head. "No. Not without you."

He heard the sound of her breath escape through gritted teeth as she grasped the slab again and tugged. It shifted a few more inches, but with a frustrated grunt she let it fall from her hands, and it slammed into his chest with excruciating force. He was unable to prevent the howl of agony from escaping his lips.

She was back on her knees beside him in a second, clasping both her hands to his face. "Chris, Chris, I'm so sorry!" Then she felt the wet blood that trickled down his face and stopped. "You're bleeding!"

His instinctive nod hurt like hell, so he stopped it abruptly. "Yes. You can't get me out alone, baby. Go find someone. Get someone to help us."

"No! I'm not leaving you!" He'd forgotten how stubborn she could be. He felt her hands along his sides again, grasping at the laminated countertop, pulling, tugging. He squeezed his eyes tight, bracing for the moment when her arms would fail at their task and let go of the slab. He didn't think he could stand it slamming back onto him a second time.

But they say that in times of great danger, people can achieve the impossible. Whether it was a sudden rush of adrenaline, or the assisting hand of an angel, Christian would never know, but, amazingly, with superhuman force, Sean shifted it, grunting like a Sumo wrestler, then shoved it, hard, and it lifted off his chest and landed next to him with a crash.

For the first time he was able to fully inhale, now that his chest was unrestricted. He did so, to hell with the pain, sucking deeply. In spite of all the dust and grit, the lungful of air was blessed. He lay back, trying to gather his strength before he attempted to sit up.

It occurred to him that he had not, before now, wondered what could have caused such devastation. His eyes had become accustomed to the clouded darkness, and he glanced around him. There was destruction everywhere he looked. With his mind still clouded by pain, he decided that the building had simply collapsed. Total structural failure. With an engineer's disdain for shoddy workmanship, he commented contemptuously, "Who the hell designed this thing anyway?"

"What?" Sean was confused.

"The building. It's collapsed. Whoever designed this piece of crap should be shot."

When she spoke next, it was in the gentle tones that one reserved for a sick child. "Chris," she hesitated, then pressed on, "I think it was a bomb."

The rational part of him accepted this to be the more reasonable explanation. He digested it for a short moment. "Does this happen here often?" he managed to joke weakly.

Even in the darkness, he knew she was smiling. That was his Sean. Courage under fire. "This is my first time."

"Mine too." Then he was serious again. "How do we get out of here?"

She slid her hands gently under his torso. "We go out together. Come, let me help you."

He submitted to her gentle insistence. With some struggling, she managed to get him first to sit up, then onto his feet. He did his damnedest not to let her know how much the effort hurt.

"Lean on me," she suggested.

He didn't have much of a choice. Although he had determined that he had suffered no spinal injuries, he knew that it would have been impossible for him to stand on his own. He braced his aching body against her solid one, feeling her arms around his, confident and strong and reflected briefly that he *knew* there was a reason why a tall woman was good to have around.

Slowly, painfully, they inched forward. Somewhere in the distance there was a glimmer of pale light. It was either an open doorway or a hole that had been blasted into the wall. Whatever it was, it looked like as good a place to head for as any.

They had only progressed a few yards when they stumbled over something soft. The jolt of the impact sent Christian pitching forward, lurching out of Sean's arms. He fell with a thud that rattled his very bones. Then he looked down at the horror that lay beneath him.

It was the pretty clerk who had tried to serve him earlier, the one who had smiled at him with her glossy red mouth, who had flashed her bright black eyes at him with honest feminine appreciation.

Now those black eyes were wide, staring unseeingly into a space into which he couldn't reach. And the eyes, the smooth coffee skin, the silken black hair, all were covered with a thin film of gray dust. Knowing that seeking a pulse would be useless, he put out an exploring hand to touch her cool cheek, and as he did so, the pretty young face fell limply to one side. Her neck had been broken.

In spite of his injuries, the awful encounter drove Christian to his feet without any assistance. An awful cry escaped his lips.

"God," Sean breathed behind him.

"Yes," he agreed. He stood staring at her for a long time, unsure of what to do next. Then he felt Sean's fingers nudging him gently in his side.

"Let's go, Chris. We have to get out of here."

He didn't budge. The dead eyes held his, imprisoning him.

"Chris!" Sean insisted, the pitch of her voice rising. He could hear the urgency in her tone, but couldn't respond.

"I don't know if we should leave her. . . ." It was ridiculous, he knew, but he felt as if there was something he should be doing.

"Chris, you've been hit on the head. You need a doctor. And the rest of this building could go anytime. We can't help her." Then, is if she were offering a consolation prize to a fractious child, she added: "There may be more people farther down who are still . . . still alive. Who we can help. But we have to keep moving."

She slid her strong hand under his armpits and attempted to get him to lean on her again, drawing him away. "Come." He let himself be led, glad that she could be strong while he was feeling so weak. But even as they progressed, and as the light that was their goal grew brighter, promising salvation, he felt that there was something from deep within him, some kind of innocence that was mirrored in the eyes of the dead girl, that he would be leaving behind with her, never to be recovered.

The light pierced Sean's eyes, burning into her skull, sending blood-red waves across her retinas. Although it hurt to look at it, she was happy for the light, any kind of light, because for a while there she had been sure she would never see light again.

Hospital sounds and hospital smells were everywhere. Sean hated hospitals, the stink of suffering and death. The walls were imbued with the fear of getting old and infirm, and with the even greater fear that one might never get the chance to. This one was made even worse by the chaos, the ambulances screeching up outside to deliver the wounded, only to peel back out of the hospital gates to return to the site of the bombing.

There she was again, back in a hospital, waiting. The last time, her pain had not been physical, but it had been real all the same. Less than two weeks into her first trip

home since she'd taken up her assignment in Trinidad,
tragedy had sunk its claws into her family.

She remembered another poorly lit corridor in another
hospital back in the States, larger but no less chaotic. She
remembered racing from ward to ward, her fear that she
would be too late, making the nurse's detailed directions
blur in her memory. She'd just received a call at her office
that her father had been rushed to the hospital by the
EMS with a searing pain in his abdomen.

Her mother had complained for days that he'd been
nursing a pain he'd refused to do anything about. He
was a stoic, silent man who never admitted to any emotions, fears or frailties. His adamant refusal to seek help
had been his undoing. By the time his gurney barreled
into the emergency room, he was dead of peritonitis.

She hadn't reached his bedside in time. Under any circumstances, this would have been painful enough, but
Sean's desperation to see him before he died had been
due to more than a daughter's need to say good-bye to
a dying parent. She had wanted to do something she had
never had the guts to do while he was alive, and for that
she felt like a coward. She never had the chance to beg
him, plead with him if need be, to release her from the
promise he'd held her to for ten years.

She'd hated having his secret thrust upon her, hated
looking into her mother's trusting eyes and knowing she
was carrying around a bombshell that in her innocence
she had promised to keep hidden. And now he was dead
and Sean would be obliged to bury in her own heart the
indiscretion that her father had taken to his grave.

Sean thrust her father's image forcefully to the back
of her mind. This time, she was here to see Christian,
and judging from the shape that he was in, she was going
to need all of her resources if she were going to be of
any help to him. Close by, policemen in their somber
black and grey uniforms walked past in pairs, with military

precision. They were moving from witness to witness, asking questions, looking for answers. One of them, a young pale-skinned fellow with a thick bristle-brush moustache, recognized her as one of the victims, and nodded in acknowledgment. Sean replied with an almost imperceptible movement of the head.

Farther along there were soldiers in their army greens, stern-faced, striding up and down the halls in their heavy black boots. She'd already answered their questions, and the questions of the doctors, and the questions of the press. She didn't want to answer anyone anymore. She had questions of her own this time. Highest among them: where was Christian?

She corrected her despondent posture and moved stoically, if painfully, forward. The hospital was hot and sticky; there was no air-conditioning, and the ancient fans that dangled dangerously from the ceiling didn't even stir, which was just as well, because they looked perfectly capable of detaching themselves the minute they were set in motion, becoming deadly whirring missiles.

She was lucky; only a fool would deny that. Apart from a few bruises, she had been given the all-clear to go home by the doctors. She was fine, they assured her. A few days' bed rest and she would be as good as new. Sean received this information with a wry smile. Funny, the last thing she felt was healthy. She couldn't identify a body part that wasn't hurting.

But if she was in bad shape, Christian was a hell of a lot worse. She stood outside the door of the men's ward, staring at the flaking battleship-gray paint, the filthy smears left around the door handle by a thousand hands over years of use. The damage caused by the bomb had left every ward on the small floor filled with the lucky ones. The old-fashioned, inadequate morgue, situated at the back of the building, was filled with those who hadn't been so lucky.

Shouts, and a gurney was shoved past her and through a door that was thrown wide open by an agitated medic. Another victim. Before the forbidding doors could slam shut in her face she slipped in behind them. Ideally, the area should be kept clear of visitors, but Christian was in there, and she needed to see if he was all right.

She searched the ward with wild eyes, looking at each incumbent form, seeking out the handsome, grimy face. No luck. More scared now, she ran between the beds, calling his name. There was no answer but the anguished groans of the injured.

"What is this woman doing here!" The angry bellow came from a thickset, bearded man whose green scrub suit was liberally splashed with drying reddish stains. In a macabre way, the stains almost looked harmless, like dribbles of paint dropped there by a careless artist. The innocuous comparison only served to make them more gruesome.

"I'm looking for a man. . . ." Sean began, still casting her eyes about the room.

"Get out! Get out! This area is off limits!" He waved his hairy arms in the air, his dark brown eyes full of fire.

"But . . ." Sean began. She wasn't leaving before she found Christian.

The man was in her face in an instant, and a rough gloved hand grasped her upper arm, making her wince in pain. She was unceremoniously shoved towards the door. "We have no news for you. Get out!" Then, seeing the terror, pain and fatigue on her face, he sought to explain his actions in slightly milder tones. "We're very busy in here. This is more than we can handle. We're not equipped for this." A wave of his hand encompassed the suffering in the room. "People are dying . . ."

Nodding, Sean left voluntarily. The man had his job to do. But it still didn't help her. She had to find Christian. Where could he be? And why had nobody from her office come looking for them? Even Delta, bubblehead that she was, should have guessed that something was up by now.

But then the dishearteningly long list of things that she was supposed to help Christian do today came to her mind. After the bank, they were supposed to go to the airport to lodge an inquiry about his missing luggage. Then he was supposed to find another hotel that would satisfy him until his company lodgings were ready. The shopping. The paperwork. The visit to the U.S. Embassy. No wonder the office hadn't gone looking for them. They had no way of knowing where she and Christian had been at the time that the bomb went off. Until they didn't show up for work later, maybe even the next day, nobody would become worried. Still, they could have at least checked when they heard about the bomb on the news, just to make sure.

It was depressing, the feeling that nobody cared enough about them to come looking. Disheartened, Sean let her tired body fall into the nearest available seat, and put her hands up to cover the tears that had sprung to her eyes. She wasn't a crier; she hated tears. The last time she cried was out of hurt, not exhaustion. The last time she'd cried was six years ago, when she'd had that final crushing proof that Christian had gone back on his promise never to be unfaithful to her again. . . .

She felt a light, gentle touch on her shoulder, and looked up, startled, to see the kind eyes of the young Chinese nurse who had cleaned her wounds. The pure, honest concern in the contact made her tears spring afresh.

"You came in with the head wound?" The girl was asking. Sean had to struggle to shift her focus from the moving lips to the words that were coming out of them.

Funny how a career in medicine can sometimes reduce persons to physical conditions, rather than people with names, Sean thought, but she was too happy for the attention to voice her disapproval. "Yes!" she said eagerly. "Where is he?"

The girl held out a hand and helped her to her unsteady feet. "Come."

Sean followed her into the bowels of the building, past the crowds of relatives clamoring for information to another, smaller ward. On the farthest bed lay Christian. The Hershey-chocolate skin was, for once, a dull dishwater gray. His head had been completely shaved, and a large white bandage was wrapped around his crown, like a turban. When he saw her, he smiled past his evident pain.

"Sean." The lone word spoke volumes.

She slipped around to his side and held onto his hand. She couldn't remember ever having been so glad to see him. "Are you okay?"

He was about to shake his head, but thought better of it. "No, but I'm going to live, if that's what you mean."

"Good."

"Cracked a rib, cracked my skull." He sighed. "College football was never as bad as this."

"Does it hurt very bad?" She touched his head bandage gingerly.

He gave her a rueful smile. "Are you really asking me that question?"

"Do you think you have a concussion?"

The nurse answered for him. "A mild one. He'll be in pain, but he's not in any immediate danger. The x-rays are just fine."

Sean turned to her. "How long are you keeping him?"

The other woman sighed and fidgeted. She put her hands in her pockets, looked up at the ceiling, and sighed again. "We aren't," she answered after awhile.

Sean *knew* she wasn't hearing right. "What?"

"We aren't keeping him. We can't. Look." She put her hands up to silence any protests before she could finish speaking. "It's a madhouse out there. They brought in eleven dead. We're losing others as I speak. We don't have any beds for him. There are people coming out of surgery all the time. The wards are filled, and until we can pull the emergency services off of rescue operations so that they can begin transferring the less wounded to other hospitals on the island, we need all the beds we can get." She pointed to the aging metal cot on which Christian lay. "Including this one."

"But what if something happens to him? What if he takes a turn for the worse?" Sean was aghast.

"He'll be fine. He'll have to hit the painkillers pretty heavy for a while, but he's not in any danger. The rib won't be a problem, if he rests and lets it heal. And as I said, his head . . ."

"But he just got here! He has no place to go! He's staying in a hotel, for Chrissakes! He can't stay alone!"

The girl flickered her eyes over Christian's incumbent form. "Hasn't he got any friends who can take care of him for a few days?"

Sean shook her head emphatically. "He's new here. He just flew in yesterday. I'm the only one he knows. . . ." She trailed off as the nurse held her gaze purposefully. She struggled with the realization that was dawning. Christian, in her home? It was too much. Today, this whole day, was more than she could handle. First he walked into her life as if nothing had ever gone on between them, either good or bad, then, hours later, she was throwing her arms around him, pulling him out of a crumbling building. Now they wanted her to welcome him into her home?

Christian saw the hesitation on her face, and knew the reason behind it. He held up a hand. "It's okay, Sean. There must be a nursing home that would have me. I'll find someplace. . . ."

What was she thinking? She was overwhelmed with sudden self-loathing. What kind of person was she? Whoever he was, and whatever he had done to her in the past, he was a wounded creature, and he needed her help.

She cleared her throat. "I'll take him home with me."

The nurse nodded. "That settles it," she said with a decisive snap of her fingers, in a tone that rebuked protest from Christian. Before anyone could change their mind, she grabbed his chart from the foot of his bed and shoved it into Sean's numb hands. "Sign here."

Sean signed, acknowledging the transfer of responsibility for his well-being from the hospital to herself. Then the young woman grabbed Sean by the arm and tugged. "Come, I'll take you to a phone. You'll need to call somebody to come pick you up."

As she allowed herself to be bustled out of the room by the nurse, Sean caught a glimpse of Christian's eyes. The gratitude in them was almost enough to convince her that she had made the right decision.

Three

Authorities are still tight-lipped about the cause of yesterday morning's blast, but they have acknowledged that the explosion that killed thirteen people and left dozens wounded was no accident. Speculation is rife among the banking community that this might have been a botched attempt at a robbery. Others are unsure as to whether the incident was politically motivated. . . .

Sean clicked the remote with her thumb, and the dark, suitably solemn face of the reporter disappeared in a hiss of static. She'd been reading and hearing just as much about the blast as she wanted to.

It was on the front page of all the daily papers that lay rumpled on her lap. She stared at the jumble of full color photos, mesmerized by the extent of the damage and the awesome idea that she, Christian, and so many others had made it out of the twisted heap of rubble and exposed steel alive.

Like everyone else, she was stumped by the incident. What could possibly have been the reason for such a bombing? It was unthinkable. Trinidad was a peaceful, stable country, with an economy and political lifestyle that was the envy of the region. The island was a democracy, with a long history of peaceful elections and a level-headed, educated populace. Trinidad simply wasn't a savage wilderness. People just didn't go setting off bombs in banks.

Yet someone had. It was unbelievable. The media were full of speculation. Some bandied about the idea of drug wars between Colombian cartels who were willing to do anything necessary as they clawed their way northwards along the Caribbean archipelago. Some journalists put forward theories of private vendettas with the bank, while still others were sure that it was the work of a lone, lunatic bomber. Yet nobody seemed confident that they had hit upon the truth, and each question they raised stirred up a dozen more.

Lying on the couch, Sean stretched out fully and tossed the papers away from her. The disaster seemed to be all around her, thrown back in her face by every arm of the media. One of the stations had actually called the office in an attempt to track her down for an interview. She was grateful that her coworkers had refused to give out her address or her unlisted number.

In a bizarre example of synchronicity, as the words 'unlisted number' entered her brain, the phone at her elbow rang, scaring her out of her skin. Heart beating, she stared at it. *Please, don't let it be the news people,* she prayed. *Don't let them have tracked me down.* Gingerly, she lifted the phone out of the cradle, handling it like a live snake.

"Hello?" she waited for a reporter's brash tones to come onto the line. Instead, the voice that answered was soft, hesitant, and infinitely recognizable.

"Sean?"

Sean's spine snapped ramrod straight in her seat, even before she realized that the suddenness of the action would make her dizzy. "Mama?"

There was a pause on the other end, and then Elspeth Scott's voice came again. "Yes. It's me. How are you? Are you seriously hurt?" There was fear and worry in the gentle voice. Sean's muscles tightened around her chest. She hadn't contacted her mother to tell her about the incident.

Instead of answering, she responded with a question of her own. "How did you know something happened? Who told you?"

"The office. They called me. Are you seriously injured? Are you wounded?"

Sean fought to reduce the rising sound of panic in her mother's voice. "No, no, Mama. It was nothing. I'm fine. They shouldn't have called."

"What do you mean, they shouldn't have called?" Her mother's voice was growing higher. "I'm your *mother!*"

Sean could hear the hurt and bewilderment and hastened to correct her apparent dismissal. "No, no, Mama. I mean they shouldn't have worried you." She paused for a moment and then lied. "It was nothing serious. Believe me. We're fine."

"We?"

Sean could have bitten off her tongue. She'd unconsciously included Christian in her statement. She wondered if her mother would remember him, then dismissed the question as ridiculous. You hardly forgot the man your daughter walked out on, even if you'd never met him. "I was . . . in the bank with . . . with Christian. Christian Devane. Remember him?"

"That boy you were with in college?" Elspeth sucked air into her lungs sharply. Sean had never told her what had caused the breakup between them, but with true motherly loyalty, she had always been convinced that whatever it was that Christian had done to her only daughter, it had to have been something truly diabolical. "What's he doing there in Trinidad? He's not stalking you, is he?"

Even Sean had to stifle a bitter laugh. Stalk her? Christian had left their relationship without so much as a backward glance, no doubt quite content to shrug her off like an old football jacket and saunter calmly off to pursue the next willing conquest. Stalk her? Hardly!

"No, Ma, don't be silly. He got a job here. At Orion. He's an engineer, you know."

"I know what he is," Elspeth sniffed. "You be careful where *he's* concerned."

Sean smiled. There was certainly no chance of her not being careful around Christian. Devilish Devane, his football buddies used to call him in admiration. She had *his* number. "I will," she assured her mother confidently. "Believe me." There was, of course, no need to let her know that the man in question was asleep, at this very moment, in her spare room.

The conversation drew to a standstill, and every second that ticked by was a pinprick of pain in Sean's heart. Why, why, why were things not different? Why was it so hard to talk to the woman who had brought her into this world, and who had nurtured her until she was grown enough to take care of herself? Deep down, Sean knew the answer, and knew that their distance and strained silences were all her fault. She blinked away the ghost of a tear. It wasn't something she wanted to dwell on. Not now.

Elspeth's voice reached across the chasm of time and brought her back from her musings. "Well, I just wanted to be sure you're all right."

Awkwardly, Sean answered, "I'm fine. Thank you for calling." Even as the words left her mouth, she knew that she was responding as if to a casual acquaintance or colleague who had simply called to pay their respects.

Her mother sensed the same thing. "Well, okay," she said dully, and let the phone drop without allowing her daughter to say good-bye.

Sean let her head drop wearily against the cushions and let out a long-held breath. Would the hurt between her mother and herself ever go away? She squeezed her eyes shut, trying to listen to the rustling of the trees and the cheerful chirping of the dozens of bright tropical birds that inhabited her garden, and made herself not think about it.

The quiet comfort of her apartment, nestled in the hills of San Fernando, the island's second city, was peaceful. There was little activity outside, as hers was a residential area, and most of her neighbors had long since gone to work. Trying to focus on something happy for a change, she pictured her feathered little garden guests, the yellow-and-black keskidees and the small, round-bellied bananaquits that normally hung around for the papayas and bananas that she usually stuck along the prongs of her garden fence for them.

This morning there had been no fruity breakfast for the loudmouthed little birds; Sean just couldn't summon the energy it would require to locate a piece of fruit, unlock her side door, and make her way out to the fence. Her head hurt. Her chest, legs, back, body . . . her *everything* hurt. The painkillers they had given her as she left the hospital the evening before weren't worth squat. And if she was feeling lousy, she didn't want to be in Christian's shoes. . . .

The thought of him propelled her to her feet. He'd been sleeping when she'd woken, but it was after eleven now. He should be stirring. She limped slowly and painfully to the door of the guest room and tapped lightly on it.

Silence. No answer. Gently, praying that the door did not give in to its tendency to squeak, she nudged it open and stuck her head into the room.

A large shape lay on the bed in a tangle of sheets. His tossing and turning, audible through the walls that separated the two bedrooms, were evidence of the tormented night that he had spent. Several times she had heard him cry out, and knew that it was the memory of a pair of black unseeing eyes that was causing his agony. She'd wanted to run to him, more than once, but something had kept her glued to her own bed, her own damp twisted sheets, and her own miserable memories.

Part of what had prevented her from going to comfort him was her own fatigue, and her own pain. Another part was her fear, the fear of having to touch him, even to lay a comforting hand on a sore, bruised shoulder, in the intimacy of the night. It would be more than her own ragged emotions could handle. He might be in pain, but she'd been through a lot herself.

But the tiniest part, though, the shameful reason for not offering comfort, was her remembered resentment of the smile that had passed between Christian and the bank clerk twenty-four hours ago. She'd been angry at him for flirting, and angry at her for flirting back. Even in death, the girl had left enough of an imprint on his mind to have him crying out in the night.

Sean was disgusted with herself even for admitting it. She hadn't gone to comfort him because she'd been jealous. Jealous of a dead girl.

"You make me sick, Scott," she hissed through her teeth, and stepped into the room.

Through the fragile veil of troubled sleep, he heard her, and stirred, but didn't awaken. She stood at his bedside, looking at him. Watching him sleep had always been one of her favorite activities. Why not? There had been many empty nights when she had passed the time doing just that. Christian was a man who could fall asleep anywhere if necessary. She used to tease him that he could sleep on his feet like a horse. She, on the other hand, was a classic insomniac, and had run the gamut of sleep aids, from warm milk to boring novels, from late-night TV to bedding down with her head at the foot of the bed and her feet at the head. No dice.

Sometimes he would wake up and catch her staring. He used to smile groggily, and say, "Can't sleep again?" At her sheepish admission, he would throw back the sheets and open his arms, and offer her a dose of Devane's Own Patented Sleep Aid. His 'cure' for her insomnia usually consisted of a back rub that started out with the most honorable of intentions but degenerated— or advanced—into a sensual massage that usually left her panting, with sleep suddenly the farthest thing from her mind.

Then he would make love to her, swiftly. There was none of the prolonged, languorous exploration that they usually both preferred. His intention was solely to bring her to a sudden sharp climax that would send the tension draining out of her muscles better than any back rub, and quickly put any problem that might be gnawing at her out of her mind. On those occasions they coupled with an abrasive intensity that left them at once exhausted and invigorated. Sleep always came easily after that.

It had been so good. He had done things for her that no man had done before, or, if she were honest, had done since. She, an undergraduate pursuing a degree in communications, was used to nothing more spectacular than the sophomoric fumblings of boys on campus. He, a handful of years older, would shed the disguise of a serious postgraduate student in Engineering, which he wore successfully by day, to become the impulsive, passionate, hungry lover that she knew by night.

He had made her final year at college a memorable one, filled it with promises of forever. He'd describe to her, in such detail, exactly what their future would be. In his earnest moments, he outlined his plans for their home, right down to the repayment terms on the mortgage they would obtain, and the nice comfortable research job he would get so he could stay close to home, close to her. In his more euphoric moments he would

name their future children, tell her that their names
would all begin with an S, after their mother.

Fool that she was, she'd fallen for it. She wept on the
day that he presented her with a small ring. The speck
of clear stone at the center had been so tiny that she'd
had to take his word that it was a diamond. He was slightly
abashed at its small size, but on a post-grad scholarship,
it had been all he could afford. Although she assured
him, quite truthfully, that she didn't mind, not one bit,
he was full of promises that he'd get her a bigger, brighter
one as soon as they were done studying and he had a
full-time job. She'd bought all his promises. And, God
help her, she'd bought all his lies.

Watching him as he slept now, Sean took advantage of
his unawareness to let her eyes run along his face, past
the heavy-lidded eyes with their coal-black lashes, down
the long nose, to the full, ridged lips. Since she was 'introduced' to him yesterday morning, she hadn't dared to
fully look at him. Didn't want any of her confused
thoughts to become readable to his sharp eyes. Now she
could see that he had grown up. Gone was the boyish
softness that once touched his face. In its place was the
rugged handsomeness of a man.

His body, too, had changed. The young man she had
known, and loved so very deeply, had been slender, with
long smooth limbs and a slightly gangly appearance, the
kind that suggested that even at twenty-five he still had
quite a bit of growing left to do. The tangled sheets had
fallen away in places, leaving a considerable expanse of
dark flesh exposed, and as far as she could see, his body
had fulfilled that promise. The slenderness had been replaced by solidity and strength; the limbs were heavier,
the chest deeper. Involuntarily, Sean let the tip of her
pink tongue flick against her own lips. There was no
doubting that this was a very attractive man. Even asleep,

and in a disheveled condition, he looked pretty damn good.

The unconscious gesture of desire was replaced by a sneer. She was willing to bet ten bucks to a nickel that this new maturing had stopped at his face and body. Christian was the kind of man that never grew up, especially where women were concerned. It was in his nature, this love of women. It was the kind of love that led him to stare in unabashed appreciation at the swish of a passing skirt, the kind of love that led him to exchange every flirtatious glance with one of his own. She'd borne the brunt of his nature once too often to believe that he could ever shuck it off like an old skin. His nature made him a tremendous lover, but, as she found out just in the nick of time, it also made him lousy husband material.

"Like what you see?" the soft deep voice brought her crashing back to reality. She felt the color rise to her face. She'd been so deep in thought that she hadn't noticed him open his eyes. How embarrassing!

She tried to act as if nothing untoward had been crossing her mind. "I just dropped by to see if you're awake."

"I'm awake *now.*" The black-black eyes regarded her intently.

She leaned forward to plump up his pillows, and as she did so, her breasts brushed lightly against his face. She pulled back as if she had received an electric shock. "Did you sleep well?" She asked the patently stupid question to cover up her confusion, even though she already knew the negative answer.

"No," he said abruptly. His eyes clouded over, and he turned his head to face the wall.

"I . . . stupid question," she apologized. Propelled by genuine concern, she perched on the edge of his bed and laid a hand on his brow, lightly, doing her best not to come into contact with his bandaged wound. "How's the pain?"

He winced expressively. "Pretty bad."

"Can I get you some painkillers?"

He seemed to consider it for a moment.

"Don't be macho about it," she advised him, knowing what he could be like. "If you're in pain, take painkillers. There's no shame in that."

"It isn't that." Her palm was still resting lightly on his forehead, and he reached up to encircle her wrist with one of his hands. Thinking that he objected to her having the audacity to touch him like that, she withdrew her hand sharply. But he stopped her, the bracelet formed by his fingers drawing tighter, and firmly put her hand back against his forehead. He let his thumb move back and forth lightly against the suddenly quickening pulse point that ran close to her skin.

"It's not a macho thing, Sean," he was saying. "It's just that the drugs, well, they might do what they're designed to do, but they make my mind a little woolly. And when I don't have full control of my thoughts, they tend to . . . stray. Then this whole flood of images come, and I can't hold them back. I don't have the strength. If I take any more of those pills, I don't know who—or what—I'll meet the next time I fall asleep."

Sean listened with compassion. She knew exactly what he was talking about. In the dark of the night, she, too, had been forced to listen to a replay of that awful reverberating blast, the screams of horror, shock and pain, and the anguished cries of the lost and injured as they climbed over each other in their effort to escape from that hellish hole where everything was dust. The face of the pretty little Indian girl flashed across her mind again, not the dead, unresponsive face, but the bright, vibrant one of a few moments before. Again, the shame of her uncharitable, unreasonable jealousy mocked her. She hung her head.

"You understand," he said slowly. It was not a question.

"Yes. I see her face, too. But her name, I can't . . . it was. . . ."

"Naimah," he supplied sadly, as if he'd lost a close friend. "She was Naimah."

This time Sean didn't answer.

"Maybe I'll take a few of those later," he offered, in the tone of one who intended to do no such thing, but who was willing to mouth the words in an attempt to placate.

"Maybe later, then," she agreed, humoring him.

"Who could have done this?" The question had the anguished sound of a child wondering aloud why God let bad things happen to good people. "Who caused all those innocent people to die?"

Like a mother desperate to offer a reasonable explanation to her little boy's pained query, Sean wished she had an answer for him. She shook her head. "Nobody knows."

"The police . . . ?"

"No. Nothing yet. They're still looking."

"I hope they find someone. And when they do, I hope. . . ." he trailed off as the tremor in his voice became an emotionally laden quiver.

Sean understood, and shared the need for vengeance. In spite of her compassionate nature, she herself fervently hoped that the perpetrators of the vicious act of terrorism would be made to suffer. Such deep-seated, vengeful emotions weren't something she liked to admit to, even to herself, and certainly not to him.

They were quiet for a while. Sean's eyes searched the room as her mind searched for something to say, anything that would dispel the pall that shrouded them. "You can stay as long as you need to, you know. I won't mind."

"Okay."

"Really, I won't."

"Thanks."

In truth, she minded terribly. Not because her resentment of what had passed between them made her too
bitter to extend a little hospitality, but because his presence made her afraid. Very afraid. Even as he was now,
injured, with limited mobility, he was a threat. The fact
that he existed, so alive and so virile, and that he seemed
to be fulfilling the vast potential that he had always
shown, was a threat to the decision she'd made long ago
never again to let him make her want him as much as
she had. And there was so much that was left unfinished,
never any closure, never any sense that the past would
lie still if it were to be buried.

In an effort to make light of the potentially dangerous
situation, she stroked the scalp that the nurses had completely shaved the night before. "Smooth as a baby's
butt." She put a grin on her face. "When was the last
time you got yourself such a fine haircut?"

"I don't think even the army barber could have done
me in like this." He smiled ruefully and gingerly patted
his naked skull.

Her eyes widened. "You were in the army?" She hadn't
known that. But then again, she was sure that there were
quite a few things about him that she didn't know. The
idea of that caused a slight pang.

He shrugged. "Oh, yeah. I signed up, on an impulse,
I guess, a few months after . . ." he stopped short.

Just a few months after you left me, she knew that that was
what he was going to say. She let her hand fall to her
side. He looked embarrassed.

"Just a few months after I finished my Master's."

"But why the army?" Somehow, the young man she
had known just didn't seem like the type to submit to
the discipline that such a career must have placed on
him. "You were a scholarship holder. You were the darling of the department. When you got out, you could
have had any job you wanted."

He shrugged. "I guess I had a little maturing to do. The army helped."

She could accept that, and waited for him to go on.

"It was just what I needed. I got to see the world; they sent me on postings all over Western Africa. I got to make a difference."

"So why'd you leave?"

"I kind of got fed up of building bridges for other people to come along and blow up. Call it professional vanity."

He'd always been bent on using his wonderful brain to do something valuable. That had been one thing that shone through, past his immaturity, and past his frequent bouts of boyish bravado. Christian had always known that he was gifted, and had always been determined to use his gift to do something that would matter. She admired that in him. For some weird reason, she was proud of him. "And now you run factories."

"And now I run factories."

The room was quiet again.

He was the first to speak up. "So how 'bout a nice warm bath?"

She jerked her head in the direction of the adjacent guest bathroom. "You've got a bathroom all to yourself." She rose to her feet. "You be my guest. Since you haven't got any luggage, I'll get you a bathrobe. At least that's clean. Later, I'll run out to one of the shops nearby and see if I can find you some clothes, at least until your luggage turns up at the airport. You can get a pretty good deal on Levi's down at. . . ."

He raised a hand. "What I meant was, I need a bath. Could you help me?"

Her face registered her shock. "You mean you want me to bathe you? Why?"

"I'm injured," he responded, his face very serious.

"You must be joking. If you like, I'll help you across

the room. I'll even fill the tub for you. But I will *not* be helping you into it!" Her? See him without his clothes after all these years? Touch him? He wasn't serious.

"I'm serious," he told her, but he was doing his best to suppress the wide stupid grin that was playing on his face. "My ribs are in agony. It's awful. What if . . ." his sexy mouth took on a little-boy pout that was designed to manipulate, "what if I bend over to look for the soap and one of my ribs goes and pokes through my chest? What if my head wound starts acting up and I pass out in the tub? You'd come in an hour later and find me floating. Then you'd be sorry."

She pursed her lips. "The nurse last night said there was nothing wrong with your head or your ribs that a little bed rest wouldn't cure. You aren't in any danger from a little tub of water." There was *no* way. . . .

He sighed long and hard. "Oh, well. If you *really* want to take the chance. . . ." He made no move to get up. Instead, he rolled his eyes up to the ceiling, waiting for her to cave in.

Cave in she did. "Fine," she said grudgingly. She knew when she had lost a battle. "I'll go get the water running."

"You're a saint," he said to her receding back.

Sean only grunted.

Christian watched the gentle sway of her rounded bottom as she left the room. His mind might still be a little muddy from the drugs, but not so much that he couldn't notice what a fine sexy woman Sean had grown into. Sure, as a student, back when they were together, she'd been something to look at, but not like now. She was just a little kid then, a half-opened flower with more promise than anything else.

He listened to the sound of the water running as she

filled the guest bathtub. Okay, so maybe he'd exaggerated
about his inability to bathe himself, but it was an opportunity too good to miss. He wasn't exactly lying; he *was*
in pain. And he would need a little help to get up out
of bed and into the bathroom. So what was a little bath
between friends?

There was a time, though, when they had been more
than friends. There was a time when he had put a ring
on her finger. It was a cheap ring, but it had been a ring
nonetheless. He had never told her, but he'd hocked the
sax his father had given him seven years before, in order
to scare up the cash. It was a lousy third of a carat, with
no clarity to shout about, but he'd offered it to her with
all the love he could find in his immature boy's heart.

He remembered promising her he'd get her a new one,
a real ring, not the kind that a boy with a crush on the
prom queen would buy with his pocket money. She'd
brushed his sheepish protests away with a hundred tender
kisses, and told him *don't you dare, this is the ring you gave
me, and this is the ring I'll treasure. It doesn't have to be a big
one, it doesn't matter what size it is, as long as it says you love
me.*

It was a lovely memory. But it was tainted by another,
more painful one. His eyes clouded with the image of
himself, all dressed up in the new suit that he'd begged
his brother, a successful dentist, to buy him. The first suit
he ever wore that wasn't off the rack. You didn't wear a
cheap suit when you introduced your fiancée to your parents, did you?

Even though she never showed. Even though she left
you waiting in the restaurant with your mother and father, who had flown in from Houston just to meet their
daughter-in-law to be, waiting and racking your brain
for excuses for her tardiness, as she was first half an
hour late, then an hour, then two.

After he accompanied his mother and father back to

the airport, face burning with shame, heart cold and leaden, he'd rushed over to her tawdry little undergrad dorm room, and she refused to let him in. He stood in the hallway in tears, as coeds passed and snickered at his plight, while he pleaded, first loudly and angrily, then softly and brokenly, for her to let him in so they could talk about it.

What was there to talk about? she'd asked through the door. *Why should I talk about the fact that you can't afford to buy yourself a new suit, and we can't afford to get ourselves a place big enough for both of us, and yet you have lease papers in your drawer, Chris, lease documents four months old, for an apartment on the other side of the city? An apartment you're paying for. An apartment with a woman in it. Why would I want to talk about that?*

He knew with a sinking feeling that he should never have left those documents where she could have found them. He should have stashed them with a college buddy, rented a small safety deposit box, anything. Anything that would have kept her from finding out about Elsa and the apartment.

That's not how it is, he tried to convince her. *You don't understand.* If only she would let him in, then he would be able to touch her, and she could look into his eyes, and believe.

I understand more than you think, she told him. *I understand that all the pleading for you to give up your other women was a waste of breath. I understand that you can't keep your promises. You don't deserve my love.*

Then a tiny object was shoved under her door, tossed through a crack like a penny. *Here,* she told him. *Take back your stupid ring. Give it to* her.

Now, listening to the gurgle of water gushing into the tub in the bathroom next door, Christian wondered where all of his anger had gone. Because, dammit, he'd been furious at her. Her rejection of him, through a locked door, had been like a kick in the groin. It hit him at the very seat of his masculinity, wounded his pride.

He left her dorm in a rage so great that even the memory of it surprised him. When he'd stormed his way to the edge of the campus he'd drawn back his arm and flung away the ring as far as he could. The force he had put into that over-arm toss would have won him an easy touchdown on the football field, and it was enough to send the cursed object arcing out of his sight. He never saw where it fell, and didn't care to; it was probably lying in some gutter or drain right now, covered with six years of silt and muck. Days later, when he had calmed down enough to speak coherently, he persuaded the men's store to take back the damn suit. He never went back to the pawnshop for his sax.

He was glad that they took classes on separate campuses; there was little chance of them ever bumping into each other by accident. But still he studiously avoided all the places they used to go to together. His favorite bagel shop. The tennis court where they had met the year before. The dry cleaners. The little Ma and Pa market where they got three percent off with their student IDs.

His anger was enough to prevent him from ever approaching her, even though in the depth of him he knew that if only he could get her to listen, beg her for another chance to explain, he'd be able to talk her into forgiving him. Beg her to take him back. Convince her that he was sorry for all the times he'd hurt her, and all the times he'd promised that he was through with his dalliances, through with those dumb little girls that meant nothing to him, but who he just couldn't seem to resist. And most importantly, explain to her about Elsa.

But he never gave himself the chance. He held onto his anger, and guarded it jealously. In being angry at her for refusing to listen to another in a long line of apologies, he was able to divert his mind from the gnawing knowledge that he'd brought this all on himself, by being juvenile and unworthy of her trust. The anger led him away from her and into the army, and it wasn't until years later that he searched himself and found that he wasn't angry anymore. But by then, it was too late.

"It's time." Her voice, so close to his side, startled him. He looked up at her, surprised. He had been so deep in their past that he hadn't even heard her re-enter the room. She held out her long arms. "Come. I'll help you across the floor."

At first he was ashamed of his little ruse, and wanted to confess that he'd perhaps gone a little overboard in his insistence that he needed help in the tub. *Just help me out of bed,* he wanted to tell her, *and get me as far as the bathroom door. I'll take care of the rest.*

But then he felt the strength and softness of her arms as she eased him into a sitting position, and smelled the honeyed shampoo that clung to her hair as she helped him to his feet, and he was lost in the wonder of her. His pain was forgotten as they made their slow pilgrimage across the soft carpeted floor. The stiffness of his joints, and the thickness of the bandages that constricted his chest were a source of embarrassment to him. He felt like an old man. He wanted to be his usual self for this beautiful woman, young and strong and virile, but his injuries had made him an old man. It wasn't fair.

They were standing at the side of the tub. He could smell the soft fragrance of the bath oil that she had added to the water as it wafted upwards in waves of steam. Chamomile and Ylang-Ylang. Her signature soap hadn't changed. In response, his nostrils flared. She'd remembered how he liked his baths, soapy, hot, with a scent that soothed his soul. He was willing to bet good money that it was exactly the temperature he preferred.

She hemmed and hawed for a while, then spoke. "You can . . . get undressed now."

There wasn't much to remove. His last conscious act the night before had been the removal of the filthy suit that had plagued him for more than forty-eight hours. He planned to burn that thing as soon as he had the chance. All he was wearing now were his shorts, and, well, he wasn't planning on saving those either, not after the kind of day they'd been through.

With one hand still taking support from Sean's shoulder, he hooked the thumb of the other into the waistband of the offending garment and began to slide it down over his slim hips.

With a squeak, Sean turned hastily to face the other way, almost sending him pitching forward into the tub.

"No need to be shy," he reminded her humorously. "There's nothing there that you haven't seen before." Then the devil in him made him add "at close quarters."

"That was a long time ago," she answered, still not turning around. "I've forgotten."

Forgotten? About his most delicate parts? Now *there's* something a man really wanted to hear. "*Touché*, darling," he muttered. She really knew how to aim below the belt. Tossing aside the pair of shorts, he stepped in, and eased himself painfully into the warm water. He'd been right—she'd remembered his preferred temperature. "You can turn around now," he sighed. "Your modesty is assured."

She turned towards him, and with the cool efficiency of a hospital matron, proceeded to lather up a large bath sponge and apply it to his chest. The first touch of her fingers was electrifying. So much so that he felt a quiver of pleasure skitter across his skin, radiating outwards, causing his nipples to tauten. His mind may have forgotten the power of her touch, but his body hadn't. It warmed under her fingers, and suddenly every inch of him became supercharged, supersensitive.

He remembered the old claw-footed enamel tub he had had in his drafty postgrad apartment. He remembered how, once they got into it together, the draftiness just never seemed to matter. The tub had been old-fashioned, barely big enough to accommodate him alone, but somehow they managed to squeeze in there together, with her straddling his hips, wrapping her long long legs around him, and letting drops of warm water dribble from her fingers onto his lips.

They'd taken a lot of baths together. Whether they got out of the tub any cleaner than they were when they got in was debatable, but when they climbed out again one thing was always certain: the water was stone cold, and most of it was splashed all over that bathroom floor, soaking through to the apartment of the unfortunate student beneath them.

He eyed her covertly, wondering if she was suffering the same overwhelming déjà-vu that he was. Her shuttered face gave no indication of this. Carefully she avoided the thick band of rubberized material that constricted his chest, holding his ribs in place as they healed. His pride was piqued. There she was, sponging him down with the detachment she would hold for the family dog, and there he was, his whole being so awake, so stimulated by her touch and her memory, that he was eternally grateful for the thick suds that floated on the surface of the water, hiding his obvious, painful arousal.

"That should do it." She got up off her knees with insulting equanimity and tossed him a towel that she tugged down from a rack. He rose and began to modestly wrap it around his waist. This time, the scamp seemed to be perfectly aware that she'd hit him where it hurt, and decided to press home that advantage. Instead of turning away as she had done when he'd gotten into the bath, she leaned her long frame against the bathroom sink, tilted back on her elbows and let her hazel eyes move slowly along his body. Quite a large portion of her examination was concentrated on his midsection.

"Just refreshing my memory," she informed him laconically.

Admitting to himself that she'd nicely turned the tables on him, he tucked the end of the towel savagely into his waist. The bad part was that he was honestly going to have to ask her to help him back to the bed. Christian glanced out through the bathroom door to the bed, which sat an impossible ten yards away, and then glanced back at the smirking Sean, and made up his mind that he'd make it back into bed alone if he broke another rib doing it.

He turned to begin on his harrowing cross-carpet journey when a loud banging on the front door caused both of them to jump with surprise. The banging continued without letup, as if the perpetrator of the noise was being hounded by werewolves and was desperate to be let in.

"Well, seeing that I have a doorbell, and seeing that it's prominently placed right by the door, that banging could only come from one person." Sean gave a half-irritated, half-amused smile. She skirted him and moved toward the door. For a fleeting moment, Christian felt an irrational wave of panic that once she went out, she wouldn't be back, and then he'd be all alone. He put that bit of lunacy down to a residual effect of the painkillers.

"Here," she said, tossing a large fluffy object at him as she left. "You can wear this until I have time to go to the mall for some clothes for you." Then she was gone.

Propped up against the doorframe, he examined what she'd thrown him. It was a bathrobe, a big spongy maroon one with a gold crest embroidered on the breast pocket. It wasn't a woman's robe, and he could have sworn that it smelled slightly of tobacco, cigars, maybe. For no sensible reason, that bothered him. Who did the robe belong to? Was it her lover? Or, worse yet, *one of* her lovers? Jealousy didn't come naturally to him, like it seemed to have come to her when they were together. He was never one to put too much stock into the implications of fidelity or the lack thereof, which, he was man enough to admit, had been the cause of all the problems between them in the first place. But now, years later, and after only having met her one day before, he was tasting the sting of the lash, and it wasn't pretty.

He comforted himself with the fact that the robe smelled vaguely musty, as if it had been hanging in the closet for a few months, and therefore implied that the owner might be long gone. Or, probably, that he'd simply abandoned the formality of wearing robes around her apartment. It wasn't an alternative that he liked to contemplate.

He was just in the act of easing one shoulder into the sleeve, which was proving to be a bit of a tight fit, when he heard a pair of female voices in the hall outside of his bedroom. One he identified easily as Sean's calm, dry tones, the other was high-pitched and excited.

"Where is he? Are you okay? Did the bomb make a lot of noise? Did it really send you flying? Did your whole life flash before your eyes? Did he get stitches? I heard it was the Venezuelans who planted the bomb. I just know they're after our oil. When are you back to work? Can I park in your spot 'til you come back? Is he in there?"

Christian listened, incredulous. The woman was firing questions at Sean with a tommy-gun. To her credit, Sean wasn't even attempting to answer. The high squeaking grew closer very fast, and before he could react, the door was thrown open and he was standing face to face with a stick of dynamite in a long red wig.

"Hi!" the stick of dynamite squeaked loudly, and she thrust out her tiny hand to be shaken. "I'm Delta." Her Jamaican accent was vigorous, in sharp contrast to the more melodious Trinidadian accents that he'd heard so far.

"Hi," he answered, hastily tugging together the gaping folds of the robe in order to shield himself from the quick inventory being taken of his body parts by an amazing pair of mascaraed eyes. "I'm Christian."

"Nice to meet you Chris," she said familiarly. She was so small that she had to tilt back her head to look up at him. He had to admit that the effect was rather charming. "I see the hospital has you sporting the Michael Jordan look," she said, pointing at his shaved head, unabashed.

Instinctively, his hand flew to touch his smooth skull gingerly. It wasn't something he liked being reminded of. It would take at least a week before he could boast of so much as a sprinkling of stubble.

"Don't worry about it," she waved his discomfort away cheerily. "They got nurses in there that shave people for kicks. You go in with a busted knee, they'd still shave your head. No worries, man."

"No worries," he echoed, and wondered what to do next. Sean, damn her, seemed to be enjoying his predicament immensely, and was standing just a few feet behind Delta, grinning idiotically.

Delta was unaware of any undercurrents between them, which was a surprise to Christian, as the air between him and Sean was all but lit up with firecrackers. Her eyes dropped to the tight bandages that peeked out the top of his robe. "Broke some ribs?" she asked with ghoulish interest.

Christian was almost sorry to have to disappoint her. "Just one, and it's just cracked, not broken."

"Need help getting back to bed?" Without even waiting for an answer, she slipped in under his armpit and heaved. It was like an ant trying to lift a rubber tree plant.

"I'll tell you what," the other devil-woman said from across the room. "You help him get settled, and I'll pop out to the mall and pick up a few bits of clothes for Christian. He lost all his luggage. You'll keep him company while I'm gone, dear?"

Christian's jaw dropped. She wasn't serious! He tried desperately to signal to her that maybe she should reconsider, but the frantic widening of his eyes seemed to be lost on her.

Delta seemed to like the idea just fine. "No worries, gal. I can manage with him just fine. You take your time."

"I will," Sean smiled, and with that, she fled, leaving him home and alone . . . with a madwoman.

Sean hauled an armful of packages out the back door of the car and kicked it shut. Shopping for Christian had been a blast, not because she enjoyed performing such domestic tasks for men, but because she was buoyed from store to store by the memory of the look on Christian's face when she'd flounced off and left him alone with Delta in his bedroom. The look of panic that had flickered across his face had been priceless.

Delta was a great girl; that she would have been the first to admit. But people who didn't know her found her a little hard to take at first. The girl showed no mercy, and knew no boundaries. Sean was sure that by the time she got back, Delta would have Christian showing her his x-rays.

Besides, it was good to be away from the house, what with the kind of pressure that was building up inside it, between them. That bath! Touching him with all that warm soapy water clinging to his chest! By the time she was done with him, her blood was running hotter than the bathwater.

Not that she'd ever admit anything so incriminating, and certainly not to him! She'd done a pretty good job screwing her deadpan face into place. She patted herself on the back on that account. Hard as it was, she was sure she'd managed to keep the flood of memories forcefully in the back of her mind with the rest of her cluttered souvenirs, where they belonged. She'd never admit to the confusing flurry of feelings that were now assailing her, not even under torture. Stretch her on a rack and all you'd get when you were done would be a taller victim. No confession would be forthcoming.

She had to put her parcels down onto the stone step that led to her front door in order to extricate her key and unlock that large brass lock that was more ornamental than anything else. As she shouldered her purchases once again, she smiled. No doubt Christian would be happy to have himself some clean clothes once again. She chortled evilly to herself at the idea of him, inside, trapped like a rat in a borrowed dressing gown with nothing under it, with Delta there stripping away his eardrums with her pointed questions and her strident voice. *Sean,* she congratulated herself, *you're nasty, girl!*

The laughter stopped her dead in the foyer. High breathy squeaks were joined by deep baritone booms. Dumbfounded, Sean staggered to the living room, to find her good buddy curled up on the couch, short slim legs tucked under her pretty little butt, and Christian, also on the couch, dressing gown discretely pulled shut, long hairy legs stuck straight out before him. Each had a glass in their hand. The amber liquid in which clinking blocks of ice floated was not Kool-Aid.

Christian was the first to see her. He raised his glass. For the first time since she'd seen him, he wore a broad, delighted grin. "Sean! Hey, baby, you're back!"

Sean refused to acknowledge the obvious statement. She just stood there with her hostess-smile on her face. What was he doing sprawled all over her living room? Wasn't he supposed to be sick?

Christian was undaunted. "Your friend Delta was just filling me in on all the Orion office gossip," he explained jovially. "For a small company, you guys really got some soap-opera action going on. Did you hear the one about the Accounts Receivable clerk and the . . ."

"I think I'll just put your clothes on your bed," Sean interrupted tightly. "You can get dressed . . . whenever you feel like it."

"Cool." Christian made no move to get up. "Thanks." The ice in his glass made a tiny tinkling sound as he lifted it to his lips.

Delta beamed.

Sean laid his new Levi's, T-shirts and underwear on the bed. Her jaw was clenched so tight she was afraid she'd crack a filling. Trust him. No, correction . . . don't trust him. Don't trust him near any female under fifty. There was something about the dratted man that had every woman he met melting like plasticine in the sun, and it wasn't a pretty sight. Overt flirtation never was, especially not coming from him.

Of course, if she were woman enough to admit it, it had been all her fault. She'd thought she was being so smart, leaving him alone in an uncomfortable situation. But he'd gotten one up on her very nicely, thank you. Who did she have to blame but herself?

She'd have to remember to be very careful where Christian was concerned. Wherever he was, things happened. Whenever she made plans concerning him, they backfired. That was his blessing.

But it was her curse.

Four

There was a shout and a muffled thump. Even through the walls that separated the two bedrooms, Sean knew that Christian was in trouble. She leapt out of her bed which, in spite of the lateness of the hour, had offered no rest, and groped through the darkness. She was having a lousy night; each time she crossed the chasm between waking and sleep she seemed to be yanked forcibly backwards in a subliminal motion that echoed the force with which the bomb had lifted her off her feet and thrown her. If she was having such a miserable night, fraught with vivid memories of their ordeal, she had no doubt that Christian was suffering the same fate.

"Chris?" she asked softly, genuine concern in her voice. Her heart thumped deep in her chest, and the dread left her with a feeling of nausea. The sound could only have meant one thing: in the middle of his tossing and turning, he had fallen out of bed.

She was right. As she barreled into the room she was just in time to see his black silhouette haul itself gingerly to its feet. She lost no time in reaching his side. "Chris, come, let me help you," she soothed, grasping his upper arm.

He took hold of her hand and cast it away with a snarl. "I don't need you to help me, dammit. Go away. What do you think I am? An invalid?"

Sean thought it wiser not to admit that an invalid was exactly what she *did* think he was, so she said nothing. He hauled himself heavily into bed, unable to conceal a grimace of pain. She wished there was something she could do, but instead stood there helplessly, afraid to suffer another rebuff.

"Last time I fell out of bed," he confessed sheepishly, "I was seven. That time, I was being chased by the bogeyman."

"And this time?" she asked gently, knowing from personal experience just what the answer would be.

"This time," he hesitated, embarrassed to admit to his anguish. But then he drew a breath and went on. "This time, the bogeyman went 'boom.'"

She moved towards him, fueled by a special understanding of his pain. Her own nights were filled with loud noises, screams and crashes. Each time she closed her eyes she knew that she was opening herself up to a dark world where there were only frantic shouts, where people were willing to crawl over the quick and dead to get to safety. The backs of her closed eyelids were a movie screen where the same horror flick ran, a private showing for her alone.

It seemed that Christian, against his will, had been given season tickets to the same damned screening. She could almost hear the thumping of his panicked heartbeat, and his breathing, rasping in and out through his open mouth, was an echo of her own. Sympathy filled her. He probably felt that he was alone in this, that he was the only one suffering when the lights went out. Maybe he needed to know that she was being haunted by the same demons. Maybe if they both admitted their fears aloud, they could work on exorcising them together.

"I know," she began. "I know what you feel, because I feel it, too. I know what you see, because when I close my eyes. . . ." To her horror, she sensed rather than felt the wide shoulders begin to heave.

"All those people," he said in a voice filled with pain and guilt. "All those people crying. And dying. And that girl. We never did a thing for any of them. We got ourselves up and walked away from all that. Why didn't I stop and help someone? I've had training. I've saved lives before. Why didn't I do something this time? Three years in the army, and I couldn't do a damn thing."

Her arms reached up around him of their own accord. His bare skin was clammy under her fingers. "Chris," she pleaded with him to be rational. "You *couldn't* do anything! You were wounded. You were bleeding from the head. *And* you had a chunk of countertop on your chest. Don't you remember? Have you forgotten how heavy it was? Why are you blaming yourself? You aren't Superman."

His head was turned away from her, as if he wasn't even listening. She reached out to forcibly turn his face to her, and to her horror felt the dampness of tears. "Chris, don't!" she pleaded. "It's not your fault. Why are you doing this to yourself?"

"It's *someone's* fault!" he raged. "And nobody seems to be doing anything about it. Somebody meant to destroy, and they've gotten away with it. They've touched hundreds of lives, and nobody seems to care. And all I have left is a nightmare that's playing over and over in my head and won't go away."

Sean wished that there was something more she could do. She'd never seen him look so disheartened, even during their worst arguments. She let her cool lips run lightly along his brow. The bandages that encircled his head were rough to the touch and smelled of iodine. "Don't say that, Chris. You've got your life left. And your health. You'll be okay in a few days. A lot of people who were in there with us don't have that luxury."

She felt the tension in his body drain away under her touch. She continued her light soothing kisses along his forehead, and splayed her hands across his back, stroking him with the slow gentle rhythm that one would use to comfort a child. In response, the heaving of his chest stilled, and his own arms drew up around her back. As her arms tightened around him, she felt the hardness of his chest pressing against her soft breasts, and was suddenly yanked backwards into another time and place.

This niche in her mind was filled with memories of its own, some joyful beyond imagination, some painful beyond belief, none mediocre. Visions of the two of them, making love as if they had invented it, swirled around her. It had been good between them. There was no denying that. But it had also been bad—very bad. *He* had tried to deny that, and failed.

The remembered pain almost made her withdraw, but an inner voice whispered that what was going on right now, and right here in the present had nothing to do with his infidelities and the anguish he had caused her. This was something far separate, remote from everything they had had and lost. This time there was no naive college senior, and no bright young grad-school flirt. This time there were only two frightened hurting people who had peered into hell and lived to be haunted by the experience.

She sighed, expelling a gust of pent-up emotion. *Forget what was,* she reminded herself, *at least for now.* She submitted to his light, questing kiss like a martyr, convincing herself that she could be big enough to allow him this one concession. But when his probing tongue parted her lips and slipped inside, curious, searching, she felt a familiar but long-forgotten warmth welling up inside her.

Her mouth opened under the increasing force of his, moistening, lips swelling, like an unfolding blossom. The arms that had wrapped around her, seeking comfort, now roamed along her back, stroking, skimming lightly over her bruises, careful not to hurt. Then they slid around to her front, molding themselves to her waist, exerting the lightest of pressure.

Was she mad? It had only been a matter of days since she'd met him again. He'd been under her roof less than seventy-two hours. Surely she couldn't have found her way into his bed? She felt a rush of moral confusion and guilt. She knew what was happening between them, and knew exactly what was going to happen next if either one or the other didn't put a stop to it.

She wasn't used to this headlong fall into such a sudden intimate experience. Sure, they'd been together before, hundreds of times, but that was long, long ago, in a galaxy far, far away. This was the present, and she wasn't sure if going any farther was the right thing to do.

A traitorous, anti-feminist thought hit her. What kind of woman would he think she was, giving in like this? Assuaging her needs was all well and good, but for some stupid, indiscernible reason, his opinion of her mattered. She didn't want him to think she just . . . did this when it pleased her. Her spine stiffened.

Chris seemed to sense her resistance, however, and his hands grasped her arms securely, "Please," he whispered into her mouth, "let me . . . I need this. Don't turn me away."

Her mind lurched. The last thing she wanted was to turn him away. Not if he needed her. Not when she needed him as much as she did. She hesitated, for less than a second, and then her resistance rolled away from her like a heavy burden. She surrendered her mouth to him again. His opinion of her be damned—they were grown-ups. They both wanted this. Let the consequences fall where they may.

"Sean. . . ." he began to say something, but seemed

to think better of it, and took control of her willing mouth once again.

As the now-awakened desire began to pulse within her, Sean reached down and grasped his hands by the wrists and drew them upwards to press them against her breasts. His response was a deep-throated groan. He cupped her breasts, trying to cover each one completely with a large hand. When he grew tired of the limited contact offered by the thin cotton tank top that she wore, he lifted it up, pulling his head back from hers only long enough to allow him to tug the offending garment over her head and toss it overboard. He pulled ineffectively at her cotton boxer shorts. From his recumbent position, there was little that he could do to help prize them off. She pushed his hands away and quickly did what he'd been trying to accomplish with such difficulty. Her shorts joined the tank top on the floor.

Now only her bare skin was exposed to his touch. He peered into the darkness, as eager to see the smooth brown curves as he was to touch them. "Damn the dark," he grunted.

Her only response was to firmly place his hands where they'd been before, conveying to him with her fingers that sometimes the sense of touch could be even more pleasing than the sense of sight.

He ran his thumbs along the sharp points of her nipples, causing her breath to come in staccato gasps. She felt him dip his head, felt the smoothness of his scalp brush her shoulder, and then was unable to stop the startled jerk of her torso towards him as his tongue flicked out at the taut, painful peaks.

He knew her weakness. There was a time when, after they had been fighting, he always sought to iron out their differences by making love. The more rational of the two, she had always resisted, preferring discussion to love-play. But time and again, her resistance was always reduced to naught by the touch of his warm, wet, talented tongue against her breasts.

This time was no different. As he intensified his assault on her agitated skin, she felt any last shred of doubt fall away, replaced by a flood of warm moisture between her legs.

With the ease of practice and the knowledge of what made her tick, he instinctively sought out her fluid heat with his fingers, bringing a rasp into her voice as she began, incoherently, to ask what the hell he thought he was doing.

He didn't remove his fingers, but in answer to her drunken question he coaxed her into lying fully on his bed. He lowered himself next to her and she heard him grunt as a spasm of pain coursed through him.

She jerked upright, tearing her hips away from the torment that his large hands were wreaking on her sensitive, slippery flesh. "Chris, you're hurt. This is stupid. We shouldn't be doing this. . . ." To her own ears, her voice was slurred with longing.

He seemed to be making a tremendous effort to master his pain, but stubbornly, refused to acknowledge the wisdom of her words. "I'm okay. Don't stop now, Sean. You can't stop now. . . . I want this. *You* want this." As proof, he brought his fingers, wet with her musky scent, to her face and gently ran them along her lips.

The smell of her own arousal hit her hard. Involuntarily, she flicked her tongue out like a cat, and the taste of her hunger only caused the heated flood inside her to increase. "I'll hurt you," Sanity protested.

"I don't care," Desire answered hoarsely. He nudged one of her legs, trying to urge her to straddle him. "You stay on top. I can't move around much but . . ." he laughed softly, "from what I remember, that won't be a problem for you."

She flushed at the reminder of the enthusiasm with

which she had always approached sexual experimentation with him. Obediently, she moved to hover over him. With her legs tight around his waist, she was able to lean into him, her pelvis making full contact with the hard ridge that pressed up from his groin, begging for her attention.

If she had had any objections before, she couldn't remember what they were. Placing one hand on his solid chest to steady her, she sought him with the other, coaxing the thick pulsing column out of the shorts that he slept in. As she did so, she felt him shudder. For some reason, his helplessness aroused her even more. His dependence on her to please him without causing pain was almost a reversal of traditional man-woman roles, in which such vulnerability was the legacy of woman. It made her feel like so many persons at once: protector, aggressor, lover, nurse.

She eased him into her, slowly, drawing out his delicious penetration, wanting it to last. At the point of entrance she felt herself resist, just a little, as she always did, some deep element of her being laying a barrier in the way of an invasion by another being. But as she coaxed him past that tight ring of protest, she felt a ripple of sweetness flow upwards and outwards, suffusing her. She heard and felt him sigh deeply.

The strong masculine hands that had been wreaking unholy havoc with the super-sensitive skin of her breasts dropped to grip her hips and began to cajole her into a slow, easy rhythm. "Sean, honey," he breathed, "you don't know how good this feels."

He was wrong. She knew *exactly* how good it felt, she just couldn't muster enough breath to tell him so. She moved against him, guided by the changes in the pressure of his hands. Carefully, so as not to cause him any harm, she leaned forward to press her lips against his.

They were beyond speaking now, as their bodies were doing all the communicating they needed. He lay beneath her, his eyes closed, caught up by the pleasure he was experiencing while resisting the urge to match her movement with thrusts of his own.

There was no way of knowing how long they were like that, but for Sean the gentle rocking movements brought her a tremendous sense of comfort and peace. Usually, she could be brought to the heights of pleasure swiftly, almost at will. Knowing that she was unusually blessed, she would seek these roiling convulsions of animal gratification almost greedily, clasping them into herself again and again.

This time, though, she willed herself to remain controlled, knowing that in his injured state, Christian could be badly hurt by anything more frenetic than the soothing back and forth motions of her hips. So she concentrated on him, coaxing not by wild activity but by a series of gentle internal caresses, drawing him into herself and holding him close.

When his climax came she felt such a sudden stiffening in his body that she was afraid that he would hurt his damaged ribs. His mouth opened in surprise, and she held out her arms to embrace him as lightly as she could, to let him know that she was there with him throughout it all.

When his ragged breathing subsided, she settled down beside him and laid her head on his shoulder. She felt the perspiration on his body gradually cool against her own wet skin. It was a long time before either of them could say anything.

"Are you all right?" she asked with concern. He was lying next to her, not moving, but staring up at the ceiling. Her elation was quickly demoted to despair. Regrets already?

He drew a breath. "I'm fine, I . . . thank you."

She smiled. "I don't usually get thanked for sex."

"I know but. . . . I just feel like I railroaded you into

it." The guilt and self-hate in his voice was almost tangible. "I feel like you only did it because of me."

This wasn't what she had wanted to achieve. Dammit! What had gone wrong? She hoisted herself up onto one elbow and let her fingers run through the curling hair on his chest. "Nobody railroaded me into anything, Chris. I did it because I wanted to."

"Okay." He nodded, but he didn't seem convinced. After a pause, he spoke again. "You didn't . . ." he paused, embarrassed to mention the fact that she hadn't had an orgasm.

Sean shook her head. "It's okay. It doesn't matter." Okay, it was a cliché, and not one that most smart men were willing to buy. But she meant it, quite sincerely.

He shifted slightly so that he could look at her, eyes starkly black. "It *does* matter. It matters to me. It matters to you, too."

She knew that his limited mobility galled him, and she hoped that his masculinity hadn't been offended. But he should know better, she reminded herself. A man of his experience shouldn't let one such incident daunt him. Still, she hastened to explain. "I didn't want to lose control. If I'd lost it, I might have hurt you. I'm okay, I promise."

After some thought, he seemed to accept that. "Okay."

She snuggled against him, sweetly tired. She was sure that sleep would have no more nightmares in store for her tonight. "Maybe next time," she promised sleepily. Her eyes flew open in shock. *Next time?* What in the name of Pete made her say that? She and Christian were over years ago, parted company on the worst possible terms. There shouldn't even have been a *first* time.

Maybe he hadn't heard her say it, she sought to console herself. Maybe he was already asleep. But the rise and fall of his chest, and the slight restless movements as he sought to make himself comfortable told her that he was

awake as she, and that there could be no doubt that he
had heard her rash promise.

Christian needed Sean to help him sleep. That truth embarrassed him, made him feel like a little boy afraid of the
shadows on the wall. But the fact was that only her soft,
sweet-smelling presence allowed him a full night's restful
sleep. Each night she entered his room under cover of
darkness, silently tugged off the sash that held her pseudo-
silk dressing gown together, tossed aside the soft garment,
and climbed in next to him. Her face showed no discern-
ible emotion, no desire, no fear, no resentment. But in
spite of her quiet restraint and the calm dignity that she
displayed, she seemed to need him, too, but this knowledge
did nothing to assuage his hurt pride.

By day, they never discussed the visits. It was just one
of those things that you acknowledged was happening but
never attempted to probe any deeper. Neither of them
made any attempt to repeat the lovemaking that had
taken place on the first night that she had come into his
room. Instead, they reached out to each other for warmth
and security, cuddling like children, seldom speaking. In
the mornings, at daybreak, she climbed out of bed, patting him on the cheek with something resembling affection, and went back to her room.

Christian knew that Sean believed he felt unmanned by
what had happened (or *hadn't* happened) on the night
that they'd made love, and in a way he did, but not for the
reason that she thought. His concern was not so much the
fact that he had not been able to fully please her, but her
motives for giving herself to him in the first place.

She'd done it as a sacrifice, as a pacifier offered to soothe
his pain. It was like offering cookies and warm milk to a
sick child, he thought with disgust. That stung. What was
worse was that he'd pleaded with her to do it, knowing that

she was reluctant but needing her so much that it didn't matter. He made himself sick. He hadn't had to plead or cajole a female into giving him sex since he was a clumsy, gangly teenager. He was a grown man, now, for chrissakes. Was he ever going to start behaving like one?

The circumstances in which they had parted the last time only made the humiliation of her capitulation worse. The last time he'd spoken to her, that horrible night back at her dorm, she'd told him in no uncertain terms that she never wanted to see him or talk to him again, much less touch him. But she had always had a kind heart, and felt deeply for wounded souls, injured animals, sad children. She made him feel like a sexual charity case.

So although he looked forward to her silent nightly visits, each night lying in bed listening to her as she showered and puttered about her bedroom, preparing for bed, almost frozen with fear that tonight she wouldn't come, he also accepted them with resentment. And as she clambered into the high bed and molded herself to the shape of his body with a sigh, he was tugged apart by conflicting desire and self-disgust. In the end, neither emotion won, and he was forced to be content with her closeness, her warmth, and the scent of her perfumed soap.

He comforted himself with the knowledge that the problem would soon be solved. He wouldn't be helpless much longer. In a few days he would be up and around, and wouldn't need her tender ministrations. By then the Company would have finalized his accommodations, and he could finally leave her apartment, thank her very much for her kind hospitality, and be on his own again, independent. The way he liked it.

Of course the return of his freedom would remove any excuse to be near her. He wouldn't have a reason to while away endless empty hours playing Scrabble with her or watching television at her side. The next time he saw her would be in the sterile, impersonal office hallways of

Orion, where office protocol would demand that they greet each other with the impersonal courtesy of worker ants passing each other on a trail.

And if he did find a reason to be alone with her, then the unresolved issues of their last parting would be sure to come up. She would turn her hurt, accusing eyes on him, and he would plead innocence, at least to her final and most destructive charge. Of course, she would never believe that there had never been anything between him and Elsa.

She would hurl the existence of that damn apartment lease at him like a missile, and he would acknowledge that yes, he had been paying for Elsa's apartment, and no, he had never told Sean about it. But, as he did last time, he would swear that he had never expected anything from the other woman in return, and indeed had never received any recompense from her, sexual or otherwise. And she would curl her lip in disbelief, look at him with those lovely hazel eyes that could be so damn cold and condemning when she wanted.

He'd be hemmed in by his own lies, damned by his past infidelities and broken promises. He never denied that throughout his relationship with Sean there had been other women. He'd been stupid and arrogant and childish, and he regretted his actions bitterly, more so for the hurt that they had caused her. And the one time he was truly innocent of any wrongdoing, she chose not to believe him. Whose fault was it but his own?

Every time he thought about his impending freedom, he was overcome with mixed emotions. He wanted to be far from her, so that his conscience would finally give him peace. But he both wanted and feared being alone with her again in a place where they would be both whole and healthy, unable to hide behind pain or trauma. A confrontation was coming, and he wasn't looking forward to it.

Five

The Prophetess was filled with a holy joy that only came of heeding the words of the Celestial Goddess. Her exhilaration was infectious, and as a result her followers were filled with a happiness that spilled up out of her and into them. That was the way it should be; they were fulfilled by her, and defined by her. Her moods were their moods. When she felt a holy sadness, they were sad. When she felt joy, they were joyous. When she was angry, they were all in a lot of trouble.

But they weren't in any trouble now. She swaggered back and forth along the hard-packed dirt floor of their temple, her impressive girth undulating under the flowing blood-red robes that she wore as an outward manifestation of her happiness. Her thick, gleaming, neckless face was adorned with smiles. A bright red turban was tied around her head in a manner befitting her station, with more elaborate folds and more intricate knots than any of the other women in the Family. Under heavy black brows, her large, bulbous, fish-like eyes were bright with excitement. Her flat feet thudded dully as she paced, and the sausages of fat that encased her chest and belly heaved with each step, keeping precise time with the penetrating sound of drumming out in the yard.

She had declared this a week of feasting, a week in which they celebrated their victory over the nest of usurers that called itself a bank. On her instructions, her men slit the throats of a dozen goats and roasted them in big ovens at the back of the communal home, and they served it with hot brown rice and fresh tomatoes that the young girls grew in the gardens. It was a time of laughing and self-congratulation, and after they prayed and listened to the wisdom of her inspired prophesy, they ate and sang well into the night.

Even the small children were excited; they ran around, unclothed, as all her righteous followers should be until they attained the age of ten. They played tag in the dust and flew homemade kites in the breeze. Their shrill excited cries to each other filled her heart, carrying on them the promise of a better tomorrow, making her sure that what she was doing was right.

Of course, people had died in the bombing. That was to be expected; this was a time of war. War against sin and materialism and the restrictions of society. But these deaths were not to be borne by her conscience. Those who had died with pure hearts would be dealt with kindly in the afterlife. Those who hadn't, well, what problem was that of hers?

As for the rest of the secular world, they were wasting their time speculating about the reason for the 'heinous act,' as they chose to call her warning shot. She did not allow any of her flock to watch television or to read the newspapers, all except three tried-and-true men who she knew wouldn't be swayed by the influence of these mind-distorting instruments of capitalist brainwashing. These three had informed her that people, although mourning their dead, were naive enough to believe that that one small insignificant attack was a single, isolated incident that couldn't be repeated.

The mere idea made her laugh. Fools. What fools! How dare they underestimate her? Who were they to shrug her off as if she were some harmless seer, a simple-minded woman whose community, which she had taken years to build, was nothing short of the neighborhood joke?

Isolated incident? *They* were the joke, not she. That little attack, that little insignificant bloodletting was far from over. It was only the beginning.

It was purely by the grace of God that Sean managed to survive the next ten days in close confinement with Christian Devane. Were it not for this divine intervention, she would surely have given in to the temptation to run screeching out of her own apartment, and kept on running, anywhere, until she was far away from the morose source of so much stress.

At first, when he was finally able to get out of bed for himself, she was happy, not just because it was a sign that he was healing well, but because it gave her hope that he would stop sulking in his room all the time.

He stopped, but what came next wasn't necessarily any better. Instead of being confined to his room and left with his thoughts all day, he began venturing out into the living room more and more, and from there to the kitchen, and later into the garden. The problem was, he wasn't exactly Rebecca of Sunnybrook Farm while he was doing it.

No, the man prowled around her house like a captive, bad-tempered bear, poking about her bookshelves, flicking the television on and off and sighing heavily, until Sean was ready to scream.

Come on, she wanted to yell at him. He wasn't really still brooding over the night they'd made love, was he? If he was, well, his ego was bigger than she thought. Not that his evident regret did *her* ego any good. So maybe they did make a mistake. Maybe they shouldn't have stepped over that barrier so fast (or at all, for that matter). But she was big enough to get over it. Why wasn't he?

Her nightly visits to his room confounded her; she could not explain her compulsion to climb into his bed with him, especially after a day of listening to him stomp about like a grouch. She couldn't explain it, but there was no way that she could avoid it. Every night as she brushed her teeth and prepared for bed she promised herself that she would be spending the night in her own room this time, that she was going to get a grip. If there were nightmares, well, so be it. She was a big girl. She didn't need Daddy at her side to keep the monsters of the Id at bay.

And each night, she broke her promise to herself, and went to him. Gutless! He always welcomed her, tugging her towards him and holding onto her like she was a huge, warm teddy bear. There were times when she wondered if he would try to go beyond the holding; she half hoped for it, and half feared it. But he never did. She couldn't decide if she was disappointed or not.

The only thing that seemed to brighten his mood was a visit from Delta, and these were increasingly frequent. The perky lawyer, who Sean knew as not exactly the most thoughtful person in town, had found a number of reasons to pop in. All these reasons involved Christian.

Her first act of generosity was to call up the airline and throw her legal weight at them. Obviously intimidated by her shrill threats of a lawsuit and a public exposé on their inept baggage-handling practices, they knuckled down and located his long-lost luggage in double-quick time, and offered him two free tickets to any Caribbean destination into the bargain.

Then Delta volunteered to see him settled into his new apartment, a task which Corporate Services were glad to turn over to her. As luck would have it, his new domicile was located less than a mile away from Sean's. When she

first heard of his new address, she wondered privately if
the folks at Orion couldn't have managed to site him a
little farther away, like, say, in the next borough. Granted,
the area was favored by Orion because it was twenty minutes away from the plant, and sure, the company always
saw to it that all of its expatriate staff were given the best
accommodations, and her neighborhood was certainly
one of the nicest. But she *had* been hoping. . . .

Not that it mattered; when it all came down to it, she
and he were colleagues. She'd see him every day in
Orion's hallowed halls, bump into him at the cafeteria
during lunch, sit side by side with him in strategic meetings—seeing him would be unavoidable. In short, she was
stuck with him. She was going to have to live with that.

"All packed?" Delta squeaked cheerily.

It was a moot question. Christian's two pieces of luggage, still bearing their many tags and stickers from their
island-hopping adventures without him, stood on Sean's
front steps. His trunks, books and other heavy things that
had been airfreighted to him had already gone to his
new address, courtesy of Delta, who had insisted that she
would get everything unpacked and put away for him
while he convalesced. His new place was going to be a
pleasant surprise, she promised him. Christian accepted
her gesture with the same amused grace that he had accepted her offer to bring his company car up from the
plant and drive him to his new home.

"I'm sure Sean's all tired out," Delta explained. "We
don't want her driving halfway across town to settle you in
when I'm perfectly willing to help. You're both out to work
on Monday. She'll be glad for this last weekend's rest."

Sean thought it ungracious to point out that Christian's
apartment was, after all, within walking distance of her
own, which hardly qualified it as being 'halfway across

town,' so she thanked Delta for her kindness, and she and Christian said their good-byes at the door.

As he stooped to pick up a small bag she felt a rush of panic. This was it. He was leaving. Now she was going to be alone again. Funny how someone can drive you crazy when they're around, but the minute they leave . . . you *miss* them! She wondered if her confusion showed on her face. She should have worn her stupid shades to hide her eyes, even if they would have made her look just a tad ridiculous; it was, after all, well after dusk.

He seemed to be saying something. She tried to focus on his moving lips. Big mistake! All that did was cause a tightening deep inside her, one that she didn't care to experience right now. She lifted her gaze slightly, to meet his eyes, to find that she would be a goner if she spent too much time looking at those, too. Tonight they were darker than usual, if that were possible, and filled with something resembling warmth, even a sort of sadness. As a compromise between those two danger zones, she concentrated her stare on his long broad nose. Noses were okay. Noses were safe.

". . . owe you my life," he was telling her. "I owe you everything. I wouldn't have made it if you hadn't let me stay with you. I wouldn't have stayed sane in a nursing home, or alone in a hotel. I don't know how to tell you how grateful I am. I wish there was something I could do. . . ."

Sean waved away the suggestion. "You don't have to do anything. I didn't mind having you here, you know that. And if it were the other way around. . . ."

He let the backs of his fingers move slowly along the side of her cheek. "Thank you all the same. I know I haven't been a great roommate. I've been a pain in the ass, that's what I've been. And I'm sorry for. . . ." he drew a breath and opened his mouth, unsure whether to go on.

Sean braced herself. Something, a sixth sense, told her

he was about to refer to the night in his room, *that* night, and she wasn't sure if she was ready to hear anything about it.

"Ah-*hem!*" At her elbow, Delta coughed loudly and far from discretely, as if she were hacking up a hairball. The cunning legal mind that lay camouflaged under all those layers of fluff and ditz was audibly clicking. Her eyes flickered back and forth between the two, reading the expressions on their faces with the penetration of a laser. This was not the kind of interaction you would expect to find between two colleagues who had just met a fortnight ago and who were simply thrown together by unfortunate circumstance!

Christian took the hint and shouldered the bag. "Thanks again," he said more formally. "I'll see you at the office on Monday."

"Monday, then," Sean agreed weakly. She watched as he proceeded to load his cases into the trunk of the new metallic-blue BMW that would be his as long as he was employed with Orion. The time for any further discussion was not now.

"You take care, babe." Delta put her arms around her and got up on tiptoe to kiss Sean on the cheek. The gesture held a note of compassion that bordered on understanding. *Aw*, Sean thought silently. *Don't tell me she's gone and figured it out!* Delta was her friend, but she wasn't up to dredging up any old secrets with her, especially not secrets about her and Chris.

In an attempt to hide her apprehension, Sean broke the embrace and stepped back abruptly. Far from offended, Delta didn't seem to notice. She was already hopping into the front seat of the car, waiting for Christian to start the engine. He did, and it purred like a cat having its belly scratched. The headlights flickered on and the luxurious vehicle eased itself down the driveway. In response to his cheerful good-bye toot-toot on the horn, she raised her arm and waved.

She felt anything but cheerful. All of a sudden, the house felt unearthly quiet. Funny, she'd lived in it for two years and had reveled in the peace and independence that it gave her. She'd never noticed before how the old-fashioned kitchen clock, set into a copper skillet and hung over the stove, ticked loudly and incessantly. She never noticed how her own footsteps slapped on the polished tile floor, or how pathetic a meal for one looked when you were heating it up in the microwave.

But if her waking hours were going to be so bad, what would happen at night? For the first time she would be sleeping in her own bed again, left with her own memories. Not even able to lie and listen to him shift about in the room next door. And what if the nightmares came back? Where would she be then?

Six

Methanol is a chemical feedstock, or building block, typically used in the manufacture of formaldehyde, acetic acid and methyl-tertiary-butyl-ether (MTBE) and a number of commercially used chemical substances. Its end-uses are varied and numerous, and include the production of plastics, thinners, adhesives, paints, solvents, urethane, fuel additives, silicones, urea, cigarette filters, resins, herbicides and pharmaceuticals, to name but a few. It has also shown great potential as an automotive fluid, and a number of Japanese and European car manufacturers have been investigating the possibility of introducing methanol-powered vehicles onto the mass-consumer market. In fact . . .

"In fact," Sean groaned, "it has been known to send employees of methanol factories stark raving mad." She hit the 'Save' command on her computer keyboard, closed the document and powered down the machine with a vicious punch of her index finger.

She had been working on the damn information flyer for days now, and if she wrote one more paragraph on clean-burning fuels, commodity-based gas pricing or diesel-methanol fuel blends she was going to lose the fragile grip she was holding on her very last nerve and go

screaming down the hallway. The image that flashed
across her mind of her coworkers standing there, mouths
agape as she vented her frustration, was almost entertain-
ing enough to make her consider trying it.

It was her fourth day back on the job. The first two had
passed almost pleasantly, and she was big enough to admit
that the attention of her coworkers, the huge "Welcome
Back" banner in the staff cafeteria and the solicitous admonitions not to "work too hard" were quite pleasing. It
was nice to know that there were people who were glad to
see you back out in one piece. It was nice to know that the
people she worked alongside of had cared enough to chip
in and buy her a huge welcome basket, one that featured,
among numerous other goodies, a large selection of chocolate nibbles. That alone was proof that she wasn't exactly
invisible here at Orion.

But notoriety doesn't last nearly as long as you'd like
it, and pretty soon her admiring colleagues got tired of
pleading for the gory details of the blast, and visits to her
office got fewer and fewer. So there she was, at two-fifteen
on Thursday, stuck behind the one-eyed digital monster
that stood forbiddingly on her desk, churning out company propaganda by rote.

Which wasn't bad, not in and of itself. If Sean had any
guts she would have admitted to herself that her restlessness was due in large part not to her boredom with the
more routine aspects of her job but with the fact that in
the four days she'd been back at the office, a certain dark
handsome face hadn't deigned to grace her office.

No, he hadn't dropped by, not even to say 'Hi.' Not
so much as a phone call. For a while she wondered if his
neglecting to reach out and touch her via the interoffice
lines had anything to do with the fact that some absent-
minded nitwit over at Corporate Services had forgotten
to place an internal telephone directory on the wide teak
desk that dominated that swanky new Operations Man-

ager's office of his. It took a lot of guts to admit that she was fooling herself, dredging up excuses where the truth would have sufficed. If he wanted to call her and didn't have her extension, well, he had an English tongue in his head; all he had to do was ask his secretary.

Or better yet, he could have untangled those long legs of his and taken a walk in her direction. "Now tell me," she griped aloud, "would it have killed him to take a little stroll? And to think I saved a couple of the best nibbles from my welcome basket, just in case he dropped by. The *nerve* of that guy!"

She got to her feet, tossed aside the half-dozen folders that lay on her desk, clamoring for her attention, and headed for the door. It was time to stretch her legs. Never mind she'd stretched them twice already for the day, once to the Info Center to browse through a few week-old U.S. newspapers, and once down to the car park, on the pretext that she thought she heard her alarm go off. So sue her. She was edgy.

She was barely past the palm-lined glass doorway that graced Orion's main entrance when she collided head-on with a redheaded tornado that was traveling faster than a speeding bullet in the opposite direction.

"Delta!" she exclaimed, as soon as she recovered from the blow of having her girlfriend run full-tilt into her midsection. She sucked in some air; that steadied her. Delta's mischievous, mascaraed eyes gleamed. "Sneaking out? Cool! Where we going? Did Gooding see you leave? How about the mall?"

Sean raised a hand to bring her friend in check before things began to get out of hand. "I was just stretching my legs."

Delta nodded and fell into step. "Cabin fever, eh?" she offered sympathetically. She offered Sean a crooked arm to take. "I know how you feel, girl. Let's walk it out."

Sean decided that resistance was not an acceptable option, and fell into step. She listened as Delta prattled on, ears straining to catch everything that was said in that thick Jamaican accent. She was glad for the company, and for the distraction.

They strayed about the huge property, not seeming to be headed anywhere in particular, but soon Sean became aware that in their aimless wandering they were in fact on a trail that led gradually to only one place . . . down on the plant. Dressed as they were in office drab, they were hardly geared for the site; as a matter of fact, if they were spotted walking around the production area without the regulation boots, overalls and hard hat, they would have been marched back up to the office, where the rest of the civilians were holed up.

Sean wondered if their unspoken decision to wind up on the plant accidentally-on-purpose had anything to do with the fact that this was where Christian spent eighty percent of his day. Furthermore, she wondered which of them had been subconsciously leading the other there, or whether they were both drawn to it independently.

When Delta spoke up, she realized that their intended destination wasn't as subconscious as all that, at least where *one* of them was concerned. "Did Christian tell you how much he likes it here already?"

Sean struggled to keep from pursing her lips. Christian hadn't so much as passed her a how-de-do note on a slip of interoffice stationery, much less have held anything resembling a conversation with her all week. When, pray tell, would he have found time to tell her how ecstatically happy he was on the job? "Uh-uh," she answered, and hoped she sounded nonchalant.

"He was telling me at lunch yesterday just how challenging it is here, how he loves the state of the art equipment, and the drive everyone in the plant seems to have to keep production up. He hasn't seen anything like this since he left that factory in Nigeria."

Sean barely heard the second half of the sentence, so thrown was she by the first part. She almost had to manually nudge her gaping mouth closed. *"He was telling me at lunch . . . ?"* Where had they had this lunch, pray? He'd certainly not been in the cafeteria eating red beans and rice off a Sterno heater.

"Lunch?" She tried not to let her voice go up too high. Polite interest, that was the goal.

She seemed to have achieved it, because Delta continued, unperturbed. "Yeah. You know, I've been showing him around town, where to get his clothes done, where to eat. Tuesday we had Indian food, curried lamb and saffron rice, at that place down at the bay. Yesterday we did the whole Chinese thing, you know, butterfly shrimp, black bean sauce, blah, blah, blah. Down at Liang Song's."

Sean felt her gut clench. Christian was a sucker for a good Chinese meal. Roll him the perfect dim sum, he used to say, and he was putty in your hands. It was their favorite 'pre-loving warm-up' as he used to call it. Can't make love on an empty belly, she used to counter laughingly. She declined to comment.

Delta, however, seemed to be picking up on her friend's vibes at last. She pursed her pretty mouth in puzzlement. "Wassamatter? Didn't you two get along or what?"

Sean arched a brow. "Why?" she asked, guardedly.

"I dunno. You've gone and gotten that look."

Sean feigned innocence. "What look?"

Delta gave her a patented 'Don't try to pull one over on the lawyer' glare. "You know what I mean. That look you get when your mind starts revving up, but you don't want anybody to know that you're thinking hard. I thought you kind of liked him. Last time I saw you two together, when I came to pick him up at your place, you kind of looked at him like, well, like you *dug* him or something. Like you were all torn up that he was leaving. Your eyes were moist."

"Probably dust," Sean said dryly. " 'Tis the season, after

all." Delta was still completely unaware that she and Christian had had a past life. Was she prepared to sit down and give her friend a lesson in her own ancient history? Not likely.

They had already broached the entrance to the Control Room, so the topic of conversation died a sudden and merciful death. Sean decided that that wasn't such a bad thing.

The Control Room was a large, sterile building whose stark white walls were lined with rows of metal lockers, blackboards covered with scribbled data and hastily stuck up memos and banks of computers, lights and doo-dads. The center of the floor was dominated by a curved desk at which four or five men could sit and study the dozen colored monitors that gave information on every single step of the methanol process being carried out on the plant. The super-sensitive readouts gave temperature, pressure, fluid levels in the tanks; every conceivable morsel of information that anyone would want.

Normally, the atmosphere inside the Control Room was one of sedate concentration. The handful of technicians needed to monitor the sensitive, fully computerized remote operations could normally be seen sitting at their desks, comparing the figures and levels on the screen to a number of confusing charts, sketches and jottings stuck to clipboards across their laps. Most of them sipped coffee to help them through their grueling twelve-hour shifts. They conferred in low voices, and sometimes, when things were slow, chatted and laughed among themselves.

As soon as they crossed the threshold into the building, Sean and Delta could see that today was not a normal day. Inside, the scene was far from one of muted efficiency. It was chaos. Men were huddled around a single monitor, poking anxiously at a row of flashing knobs, consulting thick operation manuals and tossing questions and suggestions to each other in loud, agitated voices. They had obviously not come at a very good time.

"Oh, oh," Delta breathed. "Trouble in Paradise."

Sean didn't even find it necessary to concur.

One tall form detached itself from the mass of frantic men and stepped forward. His solid frame was clad in the brilliant yellow flame-retardant regulation coveralls that every employee was required to wear within fifty feet of the plant, and which she and Delta, incidentally, were suddenly standing out for not wearing. Even rigged out in the hot, garish, uncomfortable outfit, which she and Delta fondly referred to as the Puke Suits, he looked good. Considering the ugliness of the get-up, it was saying a lot.

As he approached, her heart called it quits. Or maybe she was just imagining things. She certainly wasn't feeling any evidence of life within her chest cavity. She tried to smile, just to take her mind off her idiotic bout of nervousness.

Christian's gruff welcome jarred the smile right off her face. "What the hell are you two doing here?" He pointed rudely at their neat, tailored linen power suits. "And out of safety gear to boot. What, did you take a wrong turn on the way to the donut machine?"

Well, she thought, they hadn't exactly called ahead, but there was no need for him to be *that* rude! She drew her thick brows together. "We were just out for a walk, if you really have to know. We were just. . . ."

"Down at the plant? Dressed like that?" he barked. He pointed at their shoes with an accusing finger. "And suppose, just suppose, we sprung a leak? I guess you thought you'd both just trot back up to your safe little airtight offices on those spindly little high heels. What were you thinking? *Were* you thinking?"

Now, this time he was questioning her common sense, and *that* smarted! She lifted her head and looked him directly in the eye. "I think I *told* you . . . we hadn't planned to come down here. I was fed up with sitting, so Delta and I. . . ."

"Well," he interrupted gruffly, "fed up or not, you can just go *back* to sitting, before I memo you both for safety violations."

She couldn't believe what she was hearing. She knew they were wrong, but he had no right to be speaking to them like that! "Look, I know the rules as well as you do, but it was purely by accident. . . ."

"There won't be any accidents here, not under my watch," he cut her off. He opened his mouth to speak again when one of his similarly clad technicians called out to him. "Mr. Devane . . . !" His voice was tense, strained, almost scared. "Please. . . ." he was urging Christian back to the monitor, as politely as he could, as a subordinate speaking to his superior.

Christian's head snapped in the direction of the voice. "I'll be with you right away, Ricky," he answered reassuringly. "You just keep searching."

It was then that Sean's attention was refocused on the hubbub in the small room. The issue was not about their safety gear, she remembered. Something was seriously wrong. "Chris?"

Having satisfied himself that they would accept his edict and leave, he had already turned to go. He stopped with such suddenness that his heavy safety boots squeaked on the clean smooth floor. His head snapped around. "What?"

"Is something wrong?"

"You could say that. But I'm busy trying to sort things out, and I really don't have time to get into it, okay? Get back to your office."

That was it. Enough was enough. Angrily, she grasped the sleeve of his overalls and spun him to face her. "Listen, I may be on your turf, but I'm an employee too, and if something's gone wrong, I have a right to know. What's up?"

Delta joined in to support Sean. "I think you better tell us, Chris. What's the problem?"

Christian sighed gustily and ran an agitated hand across

the stubble that was finally beginning to show on his shaved head. "I don't know. I don't understand it. Our entire re-mote monitoring system has crashed. It just froze. We've been trying all morning to try to get it up again, but noth-ing doing. We haven't been able to get a peep out of it."

That was a source for concern. The computer system was the brains behind the plant's safe operation; without it, they were back in the industrial dark ages. "Software problem?" Delta asked briskly.

Chris shook his head wearily. "I wish it were that easy to identify. We honestly can't say right now. The Info Tech guys are working at it, but so far they've come up empty-handed."

"What about production?" Delta wanted to know.

"We shut it down hours ago. The whole plant's down, and we can't do anything more until the system's back on stream."

Delta's body went rigid. "We have a ship docking to receive cargo on Saturday. Will we be able to make de-livery?" On a high-production plant such as this one, any shutdown was a serious matter, and a day's losses could run into the hundreds of thousands. If they were com-mitted to a delivery, and couldn't make it, there was no telling what the repercussions could be, in terms of fi-nancial losses as well as their loss of reputation, possibly even a loss of business. The methanol industry was a highly competitive one, and there were a number of other plants that would be only too willing to step in and offer an alternative shipment to Orion's clientele. Knowing this, Delta was all business, bristling with nervous excite-ment. Sean could almost see the word 'lawsuit' written across her forehead in neon.

Sean could have kicked herself. Had she gone soft in the head? In her pique, she was missing the big picture. There she was, curdling like bad milk at Christian's tone of voice, when the company's bottom line was being threatened!

Even Delta, who outside of the office couldn't be trusted to follow a straight line painted down the middle of the sidewalk, was all business. She was ashamed.

She struggled to keep her voice calm. "Is there any way that we can help? Anyone you need notified? Is there any danger to the plant? To the people along the perimeter?"

He shook his head emphatically. "No physical danger. We've done manual checks on all the valves and the holding tanks, and everything's according to specs. But I really have to get back. . . ."

She nodded. "Okay."

He was about to walk away. "One thing, though. We've been holed up in here all morning, and we haven't had a thing to eat or drink. Can you do us a favor and have something sent down? The cafeteria's probably closed by now, but in your profession you've got to know at least a couple of caterers nearby. . . ."

A retort about Public Relations not just being about fine food and drink sprang automatically to her lips, as it would to anyone else in the field. After years of misunderstandings by other professions, it was a Pavlovian response. But she bit it back in self-disgust. Less than a minute ago she had forcibly set aside her own interests to offer to help in a crisis, and there she was, almost about to blow it again. What was wrong with her?

Instead, she nodded. "Don't worry about it. I'll get on it right away."

His black eyes were full of gratitude. "Thanks." He almost smiled.

The agonized voice of the young technician behind them broke in. "Mr. Devane! *Please!*"

Christian nodded to both of them and stepped away. "I've got to go. Ladies. . . ."

Sean and Delta murmured their good-byes and left hastily. As they stepped out of the room and into the sunshine, the change in atmosphere from the tense one

inside was palpable. They stood for a moment, staring at
the closed door and hearing for the first time the awesome silence around them. The low-pitched hum that
usually dominated the air, the sound of a thousand machines, valves, computers and generators doing their job,
was completely absent. Even the palm trees along the
fence were unmoving. The silence was almost death-like.

Delta expelled her breath and expressed her awe in a
well-chosen, drawn out Jamaican epithet. *"Raaaaawwwtiiid!"*

Sean couldn't agree with her more.

Sean couldn't sleep. The restlessness that she had experienced in her office all day was still with her when she
finally got home that afternoon, and remained with her
throughout the evening. By eleven she had reluctantly
locked up the house and was sitting in her white-painted
wicker rocker, rocking it agitatedly back and forth.

What the hell was wrong with her? She stared into the
glass of ruby-red Pinot Noir that she held in her hand,
peering down into the liquid depths for an answer, or at
the very least a good clue. The wine represented the last
of the goodies in the Welcome Back basket that her office
mates had given her on her return to work. It was a pretty
miserable thing, she discovered, to be drinking it alone.
By rights, she had intended to save it, just in case *somebody*,
and she wasn't calling any names, decided to be neighborly and drop by.

Fat chance. She clicked irritably through the thirty-
odd channels offered by her cable provider. Most of
them were American channels, and although she usually
enjoyed the tenuous link they provided with home, tonight she couldn't even concentrate. Her mind kept
straying back to a small room, miles away. A room dominated by rows of nonfunctional computers . . . and a
tall, good-looking man who not only hadn't seemed in-

terested in passing by all week, but who had unceremoniously pulled rank on her and tossed her off his turf like a bad-tempered bulldog.

"You," she sternly addressed the undulating reflection in the glass of wine, "are pathetic. No, really. You are the most pitiable. . . ." A loud knock on her door saved her hapless reflection from being further reviled. She leaped out of the rocker, and the momentum propelled her forward, sending red liquid splashing onto the stunning beige, locally made rug that lay under her feet. Well, the formerly beige, now speckled-with-deep-red rug.

She cussed like a sailor and raced to the kitchen, threw open the cupboards, and began rummaging around for soda water to pour on the stain. Not that it would help much, she thought pessimistically, the rug was woven out of dried grasses, absorbent, organic material that was eagerly sucking up the red wine as she stood. She dashed back to the living room, and the soda, now thoroughly shaken up, obliged by fizzing handsomely the minute she popped the top, spraying all over of her furniture, books and papers. Some of it was kind enough to actually land on the stain, but not much to speak of.

The knocking persisted. "I'm coming!" she yelled, still on her knees, dabbing frantically at the stain. Who the hell could be calling on her at this hour anyway? And whoever it was, didn't they know she had a rug to rescue? She dribbled the last of the contents of the bottle onto the rug, and stared at it, contemplating following the soda up with generous mounds of salt.

The loud rapping stopped suddenly, and was replaced by the crunch of heavy feet on the gravel of her driveway.

"Aw, dammit!" she expelled a gush of air and lurched toward the door. The three glasses of wine that she had consumed (all right, the two and a half that she had consumed before tossing the last half down on the floor) didn't help much with her coordination. She yanked it open and stepped out into the crisp starry night. "Yes?"

She could see Christian's brilliant yellow coveralls, glowing like a beacon in the darkness. He was in the act of levering his tall frame into that shiny blue car of his. "Chris!" she bawled, but he didn't seem to hear her. He pulled the door shut and the engine awoke.

Barefoot, but undaunted by the fact, she ran out to the car and tapped on the roof. The engine died as quietly as it had come to life and the door flew open, almost hitting her in the belly. She stepped hastily back.

"I thought maybe you'd gone to bed and forgotten the lights on," he said by way of explaining his decision to depart. He got out of the car and stood in front of her, holding her fast with his eyes. "Or that maybe you'd gone out on a date or something." This last was spoken much more softly.

Sean shook her head vigorously. "Oh, no, nothing like that." She could almost feel herself blushing. Her? On a date? *That* hadn't happened in months. But it *was* nice that he'd asked! "I had a little domestic crisis. No biggie, but I just couldn't get to the door in time." She realized that she was grinning idiotically at him, happy enough to see his face that she was willing to forget the many bruises he had inflicted on her ego earlier that day. "Come inside." She tugged him by the hand, and he followed willingly.

As they stepped into the living room, he threw himself onto the couch in an exhausted yellow heap. Sympathy rippled through her.

"You must be so tired," she observed unnecessarily.

Just as unnecessarily, he nodded. "Today was a bitch. There's no denying it."

"Did you make any headway?"

He passed his hands across his eyes. "Yeah, we found the problem. We're back on stream, thank God. But with a loss of over fourteen production hours. We're going to have to work full tilt in order to catch up in time to make that shipment on Saturday."

"So what was the problem?"

He sighed deeply, and immediately she relented.

"Oh, God, Chris, I'm sorry. You must be thirsty. Let me get you something."

His head fell back limply onto the cushions. "That sounds like a *really* good idea."

"Hungry, too?"

She hurried into the kitchen, not even waiting for an answer. She'd only cooked enough dinner for one, and that was all gone already. But there was ham, and she could nuke a few of those frozen whole-wheat rolls and a bowl of canned soup in no time. She busied herself in the kitchen, clattering pans and dishes about. "Ten minutes!" she promised loudly. The muffled answering grunt told her that if he was still awake by the time she was ready to serve him dinner, she'd be lucky.

She brought a tray laden with a steaming hot dinner out to him in half that time, and set it down on the little coffee table in front of him. He fell on it like a pack wolf. He was halfway done before he even looked up to find her still standing there, watching him.

"Gosh, I forgot my manners!" He looked embarrassed. "Aren't you having anything?"

Sean waved his question away. "I've already had dinner," she told him. She didn't bother to explain that most of it had been in liquid form.

Christian patted the couch next to him. "Well, come and sit next to me. Keep me company. I feel like a worn-out tired old man tonight; I could do with someone warm and comforting by my side. Times like this I regret I travel too much to be able to keep a dog."

She couldn't refuse such a flattering invitation. Stepping over his long legs, she squeezed herself into the space next to him and plopped down into the soft padded upholstery. There was no more conversation until he had finished eating. He pushed the tray away from himself with a sigh.

"That's the second time for the day you've saved my life," he said. "You're a gem."

She didn't answer, but his gratitude made her feel all warm inside. Then she remembered the half-full bottle next to her rocker. "Wine?" she offered, and made a move to get up.

He held her back with a restraining hand. "Lord, no. I'm wasted enough as it is. One drink, and I don't think I'd be able to find my keys, much less start the car."

It was on the tip of her tongue to suggest that even if he chose not to have any of the wine, he didn't necessarily have to go home that night. Then her guardian angel told her to shut up. She took his wise advice.

"Just stay here with me for a while," he was saying.

"Okay." That was fine with her.

They sat for a long time, appreciating the silence. Then he took her hand in his and began stroking her palm with the tips of her fingers. The result was far less soothing than arousing. She sucked air sharply into her lungs. Sensory recordings of that night they'd spent in his room, making love, began to bombard her; she could smell him, feel him, taste him, hear him. It was like a full multimedia flashback. She hoped to God that her color wasn't rising, and that the hand he was holding hadn't started to sweat. She didn't want him to start getting ideas. Not *really*. . . .

"I passed by to tell you how sorry I am for not coming to see you since I moved into my own place. I'm not usually that rude, especially not to people who have been kind enough to open their homes to me like you did. I should at least have called. But it's been hellish, just settling in, and things on the plant will take quite some time to smooth out. The backlog is tremendous, and I need time to get used to new men, a new working environment."

"I knew that. I didn't expect anything," she lied, "really. It's a strange country, with strange customs and accents and everything. You need time to yourself." She hoped she sounded sufficiently offhand about the whole matter. The last thing she needed was for him to catch on to the fact that she'd been mooning around the phone like a college freshman who'd been necking with the football star, only to have him break his promise to call.

She seemed to have pulled it off, because he nodded and moved onto other things. "I also wanted to tell you"—he cleared his throat—"that I feel like a rat for speaking to you like that earlier today. I was out of place. I'm really sorry."

Since he still hadn't let up on the circles he was drawing in her palm with his fingernail, she had to fight to bring her thoughts back to focus on what he was saying.

"I guess I was under stress," he went on, "I don't have any other excuse."

She peeled her tongue off the roof of her dry mouth and told him it was quite all right.

"I didn't embarrass you?" he inquired, concerned.

"Oh no," she said with a touch of good humor. "I've been bawled out in front of twenty colleagues before. It's no big deal."

"Good." He was smiling. "As long as it wasn't the first time." Now that his more base need for food had been satisfied, he, too, seemed affected by their proximity. Although his eyes were red-rimmed with exhaustion, they still managed to convey a message that was part restraint, part invitation. She was sure he knew just how nervous he was making her. She tried to keep a noncommittal expression glued to her face, in denial of the mild tingling that was starting up somewhere south of the border. Maybe, she decided, a slightly bored expression would throw him off.

It didn't work. His head moved toward hers, blocking

out the light from the glittering chandelier that hung
overhead, and his mouth was warm, seeking more to
soothe than to seduce. Sean tilted her head to him, willing to accept the comfort that he offered. It had been a
long week, and the light stroking of his lips against hers
was more the reassuring touch of an old friend than anything else. She felt her shoulders relax as the tension
oozed out of her.

Then the path that his intent was taking seemed to
change drastically, and the kiss deepened. Sean could feel
the increasing pressure on her lips, and in response she
opened her mouth, welcoming his curious tongue. His
name rose to her lips but was kissed away before it could
become audible.

This is getting serious, something in her warned. The gentle heat that his initial kiss had kindled in her was cranked
up suddenly until it roared in her like a blast furnace.
The horrible industrial material of his safety coveralls
rasped against the nipples that had begun to make their
presence known by poking up even through the thick
fabric of her track top. She was sure he could feel them
pressing into his chest, and, embarrassed by the loud declaration of desire that her body was making without her
consent, she tried to ease her upper body away from his
broad hard chest.

But the man wouldn't let her. His hands pressed into
the small of her back, forming a tender but insistent
prison from which she couldn't have escaped even if she
truly wanted to. Thus relieved of the responsibility to seek
her pleasure, she allowed him to coax and caress her
back, let his hands slide down the track pants of which
she had been so ashamed an hour ago, but whose fleecy
interior was now charged with the electric network that
ran along the fine golden hairs that covered her body.

Even if resistance had entered her head, she would have
dismissed it as futile. With a shuddering, expelled breath

she eased her hand in between them to tug the zipper of her top downwards, leaving her swollen pain-tipped breasts open to his touch. "Chris," she finally managed to get his name out from between her lips. "Touch me."

He did not immediately respond, and in surprise, Sean opened the eyes that she had squeezed shut in anticipation and stared at him, bewildered. He was looking longingly down at her open front, at the round swellings that she had so shamelessly offered to him.

The reluctance in his voice was manifest. "I'm sorry, baby," he said softly, and reached regretfully out to help her up with her zipper.

Stung and embarrassed, she slapped away his hands. All of a sudden her impulsive gesture seemed foolhardy and wanton.

Christian was keenly aware of her embarrassment, and hastened to reassure her. "I'm sorry, Sean. It's not you." He reached for her zipper again. "Let me help you up with that. . . ."

She wrenched out of his arms and stood. "I don't need your help, Chris. Leave me alone."

"I only. . . ."

"Drop it," she said more harshly than was necessary. The disappointment was like a pinhole in a hot air balloon; not only did it deflate, but it left her stranded in midair, and it was a hell of a way down. She crumpled her brow and peered at him from under it. Why had he stopped?

He heard her unspoken question and answered it regretfully. "I'm sorry. I'm really tired, and this thing"— he tugged disdainfully at his coveralls—"has been through quite a day. I feel really grubby, and it just doesn't feel right. Not like this. It wouldn't be all we'd want it to be, and that wouldn't be fair to you. I don't have the time or the energy to give you the kind of loving you deserve." His voice dropped slightly, holding a promise that made her tingle. "At least not right now."

Well, she had to agree that after a day of anxiety and pressure he was a little gamey, but that wasn't necessarily a bad thing, now, was it? If he insisted, she was about to tell him, her guest bathroom was still available. She would even be willing to give him a hand with the bath, even though he obviously didn't need it for medical reasons this time. . . .

"Let me just sit with you for a while, okay?" He settled back into the cushions, tilted his head back and closed his eyes.

"Okay." She managed to thrust aside her ragged feelings and to make it sound as if it didn't matter. Now she knew how high school boys felt when they encountered reluctant virgins. She was aware of an uncomfortable dampness deep between her legs, and a swollen mouth that quivered as if it were about to cry. To get her mind off the warmth that he had stirred up in her, she reached out, poured herself an ill-advised but much needed glass of wine and brought up the question she had set aside earlier. "So what was wrong with the computer system?"

"Huh?" He gave her a confused look, as if her words had dragged him back from some far place. The darkness and depth of his eyes told her that she was not the only one affected by their interrupted encounter.

"The computers," she said patiently, "at the plant. What was wrong with them?" *That's it,* she told herself as she swigged the wine down in too-large gulps. *Find something neutral to talk about.*

He shook his head. "Damnedest thing I've ever seen. It was completely fouled up. Every setting was skewed. Right down to code level. There were lines of code in there that just seemed to have fallen from the sky."

She wrinkled her brow. "Virus?"

"In a closed system? Not likely. A virus that damaging could hardly be introduced into it by accident, and my men all know better than to bring potentially contaminated material into the Control Room. It would be an atrocious violation of company policy. And if it was, I've never seen anything like it. And the kind of damage that was done, the monitoring package and the operating system were equally screwed."

"How do you think that could happen?"

He shrugged. "I don't know. I can't imagine. I've been working on the system, checking it through for a day and a half, and I never noticed anything wrong with it."

"What do you mean working on it?"

"Going through the settings, checking through the entire thing. One thing's for sure, that other guy, the guy before me, what was his name?" He snapped his fingers absently, trying to bring it back to his mind.

"Fabregas," she supplied. "Carlos." Color rose to her face, fast and furious at the mention of his name, but she hoped that Christian was too tired to notice.

He was. "Ah, yes. Fabregas," he went on nonchalantly. "He had some shoddy bits of work in there. The system wasn't running at optimum levels at all. And I'm surprised that nobody else seemed to notice it."

Her mind flashed back to the swarthy, handsome face surrounded by a glossy shock of straight black hair. She remembered the day he had been fired, the awful day when, in the presence of the Vice Presidents, she had been obliged to divulge what she knew of his foul-ups. She remembered the twist of his finely shaped lips and the hateful glint in his black eyes as he listened to her damning testimony. She'd always thought she was a scapegoat. Carlos's many faults were evident to anyone willing to look, yet the company had insisted that she speak up and tell all she had gleaned about him before they let him go. It had been humiliating, painful, intrusive and unfair. But the man couldn't stay; the continued safety and good name of Orion would have been too much at risk.

"He had a few problems," she explained euphemistically.

"I should say so! Like I said, he cost me a day and a half; that's how long it took me to unravel all that garbage he'd put into the system, and reconfigure half the settings."

"Are you sure all this didn't happen while you were changing things around?" she asked ingenuously. Before the question was completely out of her mouth, she realized she would have willingly bitten off her tongue to take it back. No such luck.

Christian's handsome face darkened. "What?"

Sean sought to explain. "All I'm saying is, while you were changing things around, putting in your numbers or whatever, maybe something happened."

"Are you saying it could be my fault?" His voice had gotten dangerously calm. The purring sensuous black panther that had so recently been lounging on her couch had dramatically been transformed into a coiled, muscled, very dangerous animal.

She put her hands up in an unconscious gesture to ward off his anger. "I'm not ascribing blame to anyone, Chris, not even you. I'm just *wondering*. . . ."

"You were just wondering if I was damn fool enough to screw up a multimillion-dollar system? One that I'm being paid a hell of a lot of money to look after? Come on, Sean. You know me. If I'd made a mistake, I'd have found it and fixed it. And I certainly wouldn't have wasted the company's time and endangered its revenues by doing anything so stupid. I know my job. I work by the book. I never put the system in jeopardy."

"Well, I'm sorry. I didn't mean to offend you. It's just that this is your first week on the job, and you've just been through something awful. And you were hit on your head during the bombing. I was just wondering if maybe. . . ."

"You were wondering if maybe I'm not fit to assume my duties? If a bump on the head and a lousy break are enough to make me forget six years of college and another six years of operational experience on three different continents?" He had shot to his feet and was already holding his car keys in his agitated hand.

Sean tried to avoid the piercing glint in his eyes as he continued. "You know, I thought the worst of the day was behind me. I thought I'd come by and get some sort of comfort or understanding. But I'd forgotten what you can be like. The way you hoard your trust like old gold, never willing to give it away, or even lend it out for a spell. Are you ever going to have faith in me? For *anything?*"

She was so pained by the rapid deterioration of events that she couldn't even answer. She just stared at him as he clomped angrily towards her door in his steel-tipped work boots. "Wait!" she yelled and ran after him.

He had already yanked open her door. "Why? So you can insult me again?" His black eyes flashed with fury.

"I wasn't insulting you," she defended herself hotly. "I was just asking a question. I'm *sorry!*"

"What's the point of being sorry? Why be sorry? You just spoke your mind. The truth as you see it. And the truth as you see it is that I can't be trusted. Not personally, that you've made abundantly clear. Lord *knows* I've heard enough about that! And now, evidently, I can't be trusted professionally, either."

So that was what it was about! Not the stupid computer or his blow to the head. It was about their painful, bitter parting, all those years ago. The crack about her not trusting him personally hit her like a slap in the face. Now *she* was getting angry. Of course, she didn't trust him personally. What had he ever done to deserve that trust? She told him exactly that.

"I made a lot of mistakes in the past," he conceded, although his anger had in no way cooled, "but that last time, when you turned me away, you owed me a chance to explain. You never gave me that."

"What would you have told me?" Her voice was high enough and loud enough to make her wonder fleetingly if the neighbors could hear, and if so, what they would think of her, but she was beyond caring. "What would you have said about . . ." the name Elsa just couldn't make its way past her throat. ". . . about *her?* Would you have told me more of your lies? More excuses? More promises not to do it again?"

"I didn't *do* anything! Not with her! I told you that!"

"You *lie!*" She couldn't stand it. Why, why, why wasn't he man enough to admit his mistakes? Why couldn't he just own up and confess that he was keeping a woman in an apartment across town? She had been heartbroken when she'd found out, and furious enough to bite, but even though she told him she didn't love him anymore, even though she gave him back the ring, part of her wanted him to beg for her to take him back. If he'd only done that, only confessed and said he was sorry, *again*, it would have been okay. But she couldn't stand his lies.

"I'm not lying, but you're so taken up with your damn small-minded suspicions and your crippled emotions that you can't even see that. You're too hard to ever give me a chance. What in the name of God did somebody do to you to leave you the way you are?"

His last words fell like a shower of bricks upon her. She opened her mouth and shut it. Then she opened it again, but no sound came out. She thought of her father, and the promise she'd made him, that she would keep his secret, even if it killed her. And the trust she'd seen shining in her mother's eyes every time she looked at him. Undeserved trust. What did somebody do to destroy her trust? He was laughably close to the truth, but that was one question she was honor-bound not to answer.

Christian was already down the driveway, tearing open the door of the car with a vengeful lunge. Bogged down by the memories that his last anguished question had dredged up, Sean couldn't move, not even to beg him to come back. Helpless, she watched as the car tore out of the driveway at a dangerous speed and disappeared up the road.

Just what the hell had happened there, Christian wondered as he skated into his driveway in a shower of gravel and dust. One minute she was in his arms, soft, warm and willing, and the next they were hurling hateful missiles at each other. Had he missed something?

Although his sudden, gut-wrenching anger had long put paid to his erection, an agonized, unsatisfied pain still dwelled in his groin. But sexual frustration could surely not be the reason for his quick flight to anger. That was the reaction of a boy; he was a man. Even so, the decision to halt what could have been an opportunity to ease away the tensions of the day by stretching himself out on her long smooth body (God, how he loved the sheer height of her!) had been entirely his. He had the opportunity, and he botched it.

He eased his long body out of the car and was at his front door in three long strides. His anger had not diminished; this was evident in the force with which he thrust his key into the door and yanked it open. So, he quizzed himself, it wasn't the sex that had his innards boiling like a cauldron of crawfish. Was it pride? Her suggestion that he himself might have been responsible for today's fiasco down at the plant was an unkind cut indeed.

He had to concede that she had asked in all innocence, but the knowledge of that did nothing to ease the sting. To think that someone who knew him as well as she could imagine him capable of such gross incompetence! But as he marched into the bedroom and peeled off the offending safety gear he knew that her slip of the lip was not what irked him, either.

That could only leave one thing, and it had nothing to do with what had gone on between them tonight. What it was, as he had blurted out to her earlier, was trust, and more specifically, her lack of it. He shook his head. How someone so kind, open and gentle could harbor in her heart such a chilling inability to give an inch where he was concerned was beyond him. Or was it just where he was concerned? Was he the only man she refused to trust?

His mind flew back to the soft toweling robe she had lent him on his first day as her houseguest, the robe that obviously belonged to a man, perhaps even a lover. There had been no other sign of a man's presence in her house, and no indication that she was actively seeing anyone, but still, he had no way of knowing, other than to ask outright, and he was damned if he was going to do that.

But whether her misgivings were for him alone or whether they were extended towards one half of the human race, he acknowledged that he was probably a major contributor, if not the only contributor, to its existence. As he had a thousand times since that awful night when he'd tossed his returned engagement ring into the bushes outside her dorm, he wished he'd woken up a long time ago and seen the damage his wild ways and selfish thoughtlessness had been doing to the bond that they'd shared.

His had never been an epiphany, a bolt from the blue that made him realize that if he didn't straighten up and learn new respect for himself and for women, no amount of academic brilliance, good looks or physical excellence would make a man out of him. He'd watched other brothers as they wept with that same realization at events like the Million Man March; indeed, he'd wept right along with them. But his maturing process had never been sudden. It had come about through agonizing years of self-examination, self-disgust and regret. He guessed that was what they called growing up.

He entered his huge carpeted bedroom without even

bothering to turn on the lights. He tore off his coveralls, and his sticky shirt and jeans and balled them up, kicking them viciously into the corner, and then his cotton boxers sailed through the air and into the basket. A perfect three-pointer. Naked, with his long taut muscles gleaming in the muted light that leaked in from the hall, he put his arms akimbo and looked down his lean torso to the organ that had incessantly gotten him into so much trouble when he was a young man.

"You and I might have been hell on wheels back then, buddy," he said softly, "but that was then. We've changed now. I only wish she'd give us a chance to convince her of that. And if she doesn't believe me, she sure as hell won't believe you." He got no response; but then, he hadn't expected any.

With smooth animal grace he walked to his en suite bathroom and began to run himself a warm bath. After the kind of day he'd had, his best chance at getting any restful sleep lay in a fifteen-minute soak. Especially since he'd gone and turned down a much more attractive offer, he thought ruefully.

The insistent beeping of his bedside phone caught his attention and summoned him back out of the bathroom. Quickly, he snatched it up. At this hour, it could only be Sean, calling to apologize for her thoughtless comment. Sometimes, she could be soft that way.

"Well, well, home at laaasssst," the usually high-pitched tones of the female on the other end were now several octaves lower, and rendered in a throaty drawl, liberally sprinkled with the spice of a West Indian accent. "I've been trying for you all night. What, are they trying to kill you on your first week here?"

"Delta," he sighed, and glanced at the mesmerizing blue glow of his digital bedside clock. It was almost one A.M. What the hell could she want at that hour?

"Just calling to see how everything went. At the plant,

I mean." Something in the sound of her voice suggested that she was lying stretched out. He had to shake his head to get rid of the image.

He rubbed the back of his neck, trying to bring some ease to the knotted muscles there. Surely she could have found that out in the morning! "Oh," he answered crisply, "we're back on stream. Thanks for asking." He hoped she'd leave it at that and let him have his bath in peace.

"You were certainly, uh, *manly* back there in the Control Room. Ordering us out like that. Threatening to throw the book at us."

He glanced anxiously across at the bath, the water level of which was getting dangerously high. "Well, I'm sorry for bawling you out like that. I was under stress. I apologize."

Low lazy laughter rippled over the lines. "Oh, don't apologize. I liked it. As I said, it was really . . . manly. It was kind of cool, seeing you rampaging around in battle gear. I like to see a man take charge, especially when he's on his own turf. It's kind of like a wolf, setting the limits to his territory. Are you hungry?"

The penny finally dropped. Sean's little girlfriend was coming on to him! How could he have been so dense! Oh, sure, he'd sensed, no, *smelled,* her attraction ever since the first day he'd met her, back when Sean had left him half naked and stranded in her bathroom. And to be honest, he'd kind of enjoyed her bold glances and sly, flirtatious comments. But this, well, this was different. He knew women well enough to recognize that tonight that little red-headed cherry bomb meant business.

"I thought you might be hungry, so I cooked up a little something. No big deal, but it's hot, and I know how hungry you must be after the kind of day you had."

It was a long, long time since he'd had a one A.M. booty call. He wasn't sure if he was irritated or flattered. Perhaps a combination of both. Before he could sort out his conflicting emotions, Delta pressed home her point. "I know you're tired. I'm only a few minutes away, you know. The streets are so clear, I could have everything into a basket and be over there in no time. That is, if you want me."

His frustrated groin tightened just a little, and it took a lot of mental effort to drag his thoughts north of his bellybutton. If he squeezed his eyes shut, he could envision the half-pint succubus curled up on some piece of furniture or other, tiny fingers twisting the devil out of the phone cord, her small, small red mouth close to the phone. If this was some kind of Divine test, well, he had to conclude that God had a sense of humor.

The gurgle of his bath water was a welcome distraction. "Delta," he said, his breath skipping just a little, "hang on a sec." Sprinting, he reached just in time to shut off the tap, and made his way back to the phone a little more slowly. In the five seconds it took him to return, his mind was whirring along at three hundred megahertz.

Delta was really coming on strong. Didn't she know that he and her best friend had a history together? Probably not. But if she did, would she have cared? And what about his reaction to the tiny, sexy creature? Two minutes ago he was gloating over how much he'd changed, and what a far cry he now was from the reckless, insensitive young man he once was. Hadn't he just sworn that these kinds of casual self-gratifying encounters were no longer for him?

Now a measly phone call later and he was actually warming to the sultry voice. Actually thinking, in some deep, shadowy part of himself, that what she had to offer would be a damn sight more relaxing than a hot bath anytime. Was he out of his mind? With staunch conviction, he snatched up the phone again. "Delta?"

"Hmmm?" The answer came from her throat. "I'm here. But not for long. I'm halfway out the door. See ya in two shakes."

"No! Delta!" For a second he thought she'd already

put down the phone, but to his relief she answered. "It's okay. Thanks for the offer, but I, uh, I've already eaten."

"What, that greasy-spoon garbage Sean had them send over for you guys? Since this afternoon?" Delta snorted inelegantly. "Be serious."

"No," Christian responded patiently. "I've just come from having dinner."

"Huh. Dinner, he says. You men'd eat cardboard and ketchup and call it dinner. I'm talking about a *real* meal."

This time, he was slightly amused. She could really play hardball when she wanted to. "It was a real meal, Delta."

"Mmm-hmmm? Who cooked it for you?" she asked, too casually.

"I passed by Sean's place, if you must know." As soon as it was out of his mouth, he was sorry he'd said anything.

"Ahh. Sean." The soft feminine sigh spoke volumes of dismissal. "Then you must be *allll* filled up."

Filled with bitterness and frustration, Christian thought but did not say. "Thanks, though," he said in an effort to end the conversation, which was beginning to get naggingly uncomfortable.

"Are you sure?" In his mind's eye he could see the full, small mouth shape itself into a sultry pout. "It's *reeeeally* good."

If the situation were not so serious, her blatant offer would have caused him to burst out laughing. But he struggled to be firm. "No, Delta. Really. But thanks."

"Be like that," she huffed. "You don't know what you're missing." She set the phone back down with an irritated click.

Delta was wrong, he thought tiredly as he stepped into the too-full tub of water. He had to pull the plug and let the water drain for a few seconds just so that the descent of his solid frame wouldn't cause the water to go slopping over the sides onto the sea-green tile floor. He *did* know what he was missing. Only what he was missing wasn't a pompek-sized ball of flame, but a tall, long-legged, spice-skinned beauty who at the moment was very, very mad at him.

It was going to be a tough night.

If he thought the next day was going to be any easier than the last, he was gravely mistaken. He let himself into his institution-white office at seven thirty, well before any-one else was in the building. What did it matter? It wasn't as if he was getting any sleep, so he might as well slip in early and continue getting acquainted with the company via the piles of records and documents on his desk.

As Operations Manager, he was in the unusual position of having two home bases, so to speak. Most of his time was to be spent down at the plant, in an office just off the Control Room, where he could be close to his men and keep an eye on operations at all times. The other, where he was now, was more formal, and would be used for stor-age of pesky paperwork, and serve as a quiet place where he could come to think when he needed to be away from the incessant hum and buzz of the plant. It also provided a safe location in which to receive visitors, rather than open them to risk by inviting them down to the Control Room.

Since he got here, though, the pace had been so hectic that he had barely popped in to Head Office, and only for a few moments at a time. Now that the plant was back on stream, he was glad to be able to direct his attention to the paperwork that had been left neglected by his ob-viously incompetent predecessor.

As he tossed aside his well-worn black leather briefcase and rummaged around for the marbled blue coffee cup he'd schlepped around with him ever since undergraduate school, a slip of yellow sticky notepaper pasted to his tele-phone receiver caught his eye. He picked it up, immedi-

ately recognizing the surprisingly masculine handwriting
as belonging to his Vice President, Angela Gooding. A single terse sentence requested that he report to her office
the minute he came in.

Sighing, he replaced the coffee cup among the stacks
of files on his desk and made his way over to her well-
appointed, luxurious status-symbol of an office. She was
seated behind the broad mahogany table that was bereft
of anything save a telephone that seemed to have more
lights and buttons than any monitor down at the Control Room, a large executive blotter that was covered
with what was obviously fine, expensive calf-leather, and
a thick manila folder. Her crisply coiffed wheat-colored
head was bent intently over her work. In the silence of
the unoccupied office, Christian could have sworn that
she had heard his approach. She did not deign to look
up, however.

At his single knock, he was invited in.

"I was sure you'd be an early riser," Gooding said approvingly, although her approval never reached the flat
blue eyes that regarded him from behind her expensive
stylish glasses. "Have a seat." It was not a polite invitation,
but a directive.

Christian eased his frame into the leather chair and
winced as it squeaked audibly. The smiling, almost coy
woman who had ushered him through the offices on his
first day, introducing him to all and sundry was nowhere
to be seen. In her place was a frosty executive who was
far from happy.

"Tell me what happened yesterday," she said without
preliminaries.

Christian nodded. He'd been expecting that he'd have
to face a barrage of questions; yesterday had been a disaster, any way you looked at it. By the unyielding look in
her eye, he could tell that as far as she was concerned,
the new wunderkind had blotted his copybook but good.

Cursing himself for being nervous, Christian cleared his throat and filled her in with as much detail as possible. Being a man of courage, he made no attempt to shift the responsibility for the fiasco onto anyone, but merely gave his superior a blow-by-blow account of all that had taken place, from their discovery of the problem to the final solution. Steeling himself, he also gave her an estimate of how much the lost time had cost the company in terms of dollars and cents, but followed it up with an earnest commitment to meet the upcoming shipment if it killed him. When he was finished, she was silent for a very long time, leaving him feeling like a graduate student defending his thesis before a one-woman committee.

After an agonizing millennium, she drew a large fabric-covered diary from her top drawer, flipped it open and scribbled something in it. "I'd like a report on the whole incident on my desk first thing Monday morning," she said without looking up.

Effectively dismissed, Christian stood and took his leave. He considered for a moment objecting on the grounds that seeing that the shipment of methanol actually left the dock on schedule after so much lost production time would be cutting it close enough, but having to divide his energies between that and paperwork would be a nightmare. But he'd been in the trenches before, and if it meant no sleep for the next twenty-four hours, well, so be it. He only wished he didn't have to contend with a third distraction that seemed to threaten to tear his mind away from the job at hand; a distraction called Sean. A distraction which he doubted would want very much to do with him after last night.

Seven

"A prophesy yet to be fulfilled?"

Those in the know are wondering just what is going
on in a large barrack yard that lies not too far from
the center of our nation's second city. Many readers
will remember a number of incidents over the years,
including the illegal importation of arms and ammunition, alleged child endangerment and land theft,
which somehow all seem to involve a certain female
whose career in the military ended in dishonor eight
years ago.

Word has it that the rumblings we have been hearing over the horizon are more than just nature's way
of warning us that it's about to rain. A mere month
ago, when a well-established local bank experienced
an explosion that had nothing to do with the capri-
ciousness of the stock market, those who had eyes
but could not see looked outside these islands for a
culprit. This reporter however understands that
when the walls of Jericho came tumbling down, certain influential government officials were conducting
their financial business anywhere else but there, having received ample warning by their ecclesiastical
friend.

What this paper would like to ask is this: if there

are people in high places who know what happened,
and who is responsible, why have they not acted? And
if we are still under threat by this overtly prayerful
community, exactly how serious is this threat? All we
can say is, beware of those that go out like lambs
amongst the wolves; their teeth may be sharper than
you think.

Sean folded the newspaper carefully, creasing it once,
then twice, but, distracted as she was, she was unable to
put it down. Instead she held the local tabloid in her hands,
turning it over and over until the dark ink stained the tips
of her fingers. Her eyes burned and the makings of a headache were beginning to take root around her temples.

Oh, the papers had been full of the bombing that had
almost torn her life apart, but in this country of nine-day
wonders it had died a natural death, with the occasional
column inch appearing here and there to remind readers
that the authorities were 'investigating the incident.'

So why this? Why now? She stared at the lurid masthead
of the cheap weekly paper. She knew the island's culture
well enough to take the weeklies with a little more than
a grain of salt, since 'news' items were often little more
than scandal-mongering to maintain sales, or mudsling-
ing between the handful of political parties that were in
a constant wrangle for power.

But as a trained Public Relations professional she also
had an eye for the germ of a truth, and was usually able
to discern a smear job, or a fictitious snippet of 'news,'
from something that contained a genuine nugget. This,
her sixth sense told her, had something in it.

As always happened whenever she was suddenly reminded of her hellish experience, her head began to buzz
as her ears filled once again with the crashing of flying
mortar and the screams of the innocent. She was forced

to pass the back of her hands against her moist eyes in an effort to calm herself.

Could it be possible that a woman had engineered that mayhem? Why? The article seemed to hint at some kind of misguided religious reason, and worse yet, backing from some politically motivated faction or other. Furthermore, the unnamed reporter appeared to think that the incident in which she and Christian had been injured was only the beginning, and that there was a greater threat in store.

What could this mean for her as a foreigner in a land that she had come to appreciate and love, but whose passions she still could not quite understand? Was she in any further danger? Ugly and admittedly ludicrous images of some sort of civil disruption rose to her mind, and on instinct, her hand reached for the phone.

Luckily, the U.S. Embassy was a mere twenty or thirty miles away, and employees there were more than aware of the presence of a larger number of Americans down in the Trinidadian oil and gas belt. As she was about to hit the number she always kept on automatic dial, her hand stilled. The last thing she wanted was to come off sounding like a green, hysterical female to her own countrymen. She was an experienced traveler, and a professional to boot, goddammit. Her two years here had been thrilling, and she had never had cause to question her safety.

Irritated by her own stupid fears, she balled up the tabloid and shoved it viciously aside on her desk. "Stupid, sensationalist hack," she snarled at the absent reporter. "Get a *real* job, willya?"

Although this made her feel significantly better, she had to admit that she was still plagued by a vague but gnawing sense of loneliness. She wished there was someone she could talk to, someone who wouldn't be discussing methanol shipments or public education seminars. She wished she hadn't been too engrossed in her exciting work to make a few real friends here, rather than just be content with nodding acquaintances with her coworkers and neighbors. Those were fine when all you wanted was someone to share lunch with, or someone to keep your company at one or the other of the endless round of parties that rocked the island every weekend. But when you needed someone you could really talk to about your fears, well, those just didn't seem to lie too thick on the ground.

She sighed. Maybe it was time for another visit back home, just a short one. But what would that hold for her? Her heart hurt at the idea of being back in chilly, ice-locked New York, but on further examination, it was not the weather that daunted her, but the knowledge of what would be waiting.

There would be her mother, Elspeth. Elspeth with the long silences and sad brown eyes, who had never done Sean any wrong, but who seemed to have lost her daughter somewhere along the way. Who, whenever Sean visited, would try to make conversation as brightly as possible, and offer her cakes and home-cooked food to the point of force-feeding her, all the while pretending that the wall between them never existed. But from time to time, Sean would glance over and catch her mother's tired inquiring eyes on her, eyes that asked the questions, *Where did I go wrong? What did I do to you to cause you to drift away from me like that?*

"Nothing, Mama," Sean gasped, and her head fell onto her open palms. How could she call to seek comfort from someone who had needed comfort from *her* for such a long time, but had never received any? Sometimes the guilt, and that awful trapped feeling were all too much for her to bear. She thought back on the ten years since a wedge had been driven in between herself and her mother, and then, before her eyes, arose the face of the man who had done the driving.

"Dad," she whispered forlornly. The apparition did not respond, but stared stolidly forward, holding her to the promise he had dragged out of her all those years ago. It was a promise which, although reluctantly given, she held onto with stoic determination, even as she saw how much it was slowly ruining her life. . . .

She had been seventeen, bright, eager to see the world, but sensible enough to know that her best mode of travel would be on the wings of a good education. Too tall, with too-long limbs and too-large feet, she had been awkward and shy, and compensated for her lack of social skills by spending time hidden away behind her favorite carrel at the public library every afternoon after school.

It had been a cool day in late autumn when she'd forgotten her mint-green sweater in the back of the bus and had had to cozy up to the radiator for the entire day. There'd been a gas strike that had been raging on for three days, and as a result, her daily trip to the library was cut short when she encountered a curt note tacked to the institution's front doors that the building had closed early due to a lack of heat.

She rarely got home before six on an evening, so her arrival at the front stoop of her family's brownstone at four-fifteen was unusual. Her mother supplemented her income as a math teacher in a nearby public school by teaching evening classes at the local community center, and her father, the loans manager at a Manhattan bank, was known to work late most evenings getting through piles of paperwork. It was not surprising, therefore, that as Sean let herself in through the front door, she presumed herself alone.

She remembered kicking off her sneakers, brand-name basketball shoes that had been all the rage that year, and which her mother had, after a little hesitation and much juggling of her weekly budget, finally bought her. Her books followed the shoes in their untidy heap behind the door, and it was thus, her feet covered in thick cotton socks, that her approach to the kitchen had been as near-silent as the padded footsteps of the family cat.

If she had only known what was to greet her in the kitchen! If she had had any idea that in innocently stepping into the fruit-scented heart of her family's home, with its bright-scrubbed copper kettles hanging on nails and long strings of garlic draped on the farthest wall, would forever change her image of her father, and by extension, all men, she would surely have retraced her steps, gathered her books, and walked out again. But in her innocence she stumbled right in.

The sounds were what first caught her attention. A chorus of groans, one set soft, high-pitched, like a fretting puppy. The other, loud, deep, guttural and urgent. The audible information that she received took a long time to reach her stunned brain, so much so that even the shocked face of her father as he spun around to greet her, grey trousers down around his knees, black leather belt flapping, she still did not realize that the animal grunts had been coming from him.

Her shock and horror had the effect of nailing her feet to the ground. She tried to turn her head from the awful sight, but even the small movement was impossible. Revulsion curdled within her at the sight of her father in this state of arousal. With clumsy haste he scrambled to pull his trousers back up, twitching fingers feeling for but not finding his zipper. His conservative button-down shirt and monochrome tie were in disarray, and the damp graying hairs of his chest clung to the thin fabric of his inner vest.

A morbid curiosity drove her forward, if only to allow her to discover the identity of the female with whom her father was defiling the kitchen table upon which her family had taken their meals all her life. The hot sudden tears that blurred her vision were unfortunately not mer-

ciful enough to prevent her from recognizing her closest
friend and next-door neighbor.

"Kaiyo!" The girl's name was expelled from Sean's
mouth in a gush of air. She stared with morbid fascination
at the naked girl sprawled on the tabletop. They had been
friends since grade school, spent weekends at each other's
houses, been away together at camp, but in all that time
her friend's deeply-rooted cultural inhibitions had prevented her from baring her body in Sean's presence as
it was now. Sean's pained gaze took in the magnolia skin
and bare, tiny pink nipples. A sexual flush kissed her
breasts like the blush on a peach.

Kaiyo's parents, indigenous Japanese, had been adamant that their only child should receive the best education possible. As a result, they sent their daughter to a
private school on the other side of the city, a school that
Sean's family had never been able to afford. It was the
skirt of her school uniform, an almost ironically cheerful
tartan, that rode up on the girl's youthful thighs.

Following the line of his daughter's gaze, James Scott
hastened to pull the skirt back down to a modest level
and help his young lover down from the table. Both girls
stared at each other, mouths slack with horror, unable to
speak. Several long terrible minutes passed before Kaiyo
gasped and threw her hands up before her eyes in shame.

"I'm so sorrrry!" she whimpered forlornly, rocking her
slim body agitatedly from side to side. "I'm sooo sorry,
Sean! You don't understand!"

The older man hastened to put his arms around the
weeping girl. Sean watched with jealous horror as her
father pulled her friend to his chest and smoothed her
hair. The image of the dark hands, sprinkled with grey
hairs, soothing their way through the glossy black mane
under them would be forever burned into Sean's mind
as a blasphemy.

The man was over fifty! And Kaiyo was a mere six

months older than Sean was herself. What in the name of sweet Christ could have prompted him to do such a foolish thing? Still unable to speak, she only stared as her father helped her 'friend' back into her uniform, smoothing down her starched white blouse with loving hands.

She couldn't believe it. There she was, his own daughter, in need of a comforting word, a glance, an apology, and her own father was more concerned about comforting the teenaged usurper in their home! It was a rejection that Sean would never get over.

She watched, with a clenched heart and trembling mouth, as the young girl fled from the kitchen with her pile of books clutched to her chest, tossing one last "I'm sorry" over her shoulder as she went. Then, Sean's glistening hazel eyes turning deep brown with emotion, she turned to focus on the man she once thought she knew.

In the interim he had managed to return his appearance to some semblance of decency, but his white shirttails still hung obscenely out of his pants waist. She held his hooded, shamed eyes defiantly, waiting for him to speak.

After too long a wait, she realized it would never happen without her prompting. "Well?" she demanded through gritted teeth. Her pain and shock had been replaced with an anger she never knew she possessed. She would have been surprised to find that she was trembling, but at the moment her physical condition was of no importance to her. "Well?" she screamed shrilly. She should have been shocked by her own actions; it was the first time she had ever raised her voice to either parent. "Aren't you going to say something?"

"Sean," the older man held up his hands as if to fend off her fury. "Sean."

"That's my name." She folded her arms tightly around her chest, just to make sure that in its violent beating, her heart would not burst through. "What do you have to say for yourself?" She discovered she was grinding her teeth.

He opened his mouth, found no answer, sighed, and shut it. "Nothing," he confessed. "Nothing to say." He lowered his head and stared shamefacedly at his scuffed feet.

Sean laughed harshly. "Well, if you have nothing to say to me, I wonder what you'll have to say to Mama when she gets in. . . ."

"No!" the shout ripped from deep within and he sprang forward to grasp both her hands. Sean tore them out of his grasp and stepped sharply back, pulling up short against the wall. "Don't," he begged. "You can't."

She snorted her disgust. "I can. I intend to."

"You can't," he insisted. "You'll hurt her."

"*You* hurt her!" she raged. "You did. Can't you see how you hurt her?"

He shook his head. He was crying now, and it was a sight that Sean would have preferred never to see. "I didn't mean to. I love your mother."

Sean indicated the kitchen table, its tablecloth and napkins in disarray, with a disgusted wave of her hand. "You have a fine way of showing it." Her stomach rolled at the thought of ever having another meal on it again. "And why her? She's my friend!"

His shoulders heaved helplessly. "I don't now. I don't know."

"And she's so young! Do you have any idea what that makes you?"

"She's eighteen," he argued, even in the face of his colossal error. "She's legal."

"She may be legal, Dad," Sean countered agitatedly. "But she's my age. She could be your daughter."

"That's different." He looked at her stubbornly.

"How different? You mean its okay for her, but not all right for me? How would you feel if somebody else, some . . ." she hesitated, and then spat out in anger, "some *old man* had me spread out on his kitchen table like a little whore. . . ."

The slap across her face sent her reeling. She had gotten her height from her father, her long limbs and solid frame, and so his blow barely fazed her. She was back on her feet in a second, continuing her taunting. "You play chess with her father. You dance with her mother at parties. Your wife and her mother go to church together. You should be ashamed of yourself. Every time you look in the mirror, you should make yourself sick!"

"I never meant it to happen . . ." he began in an effort to calm her into lowering her voice.

"How long, Dad?" she raged. "How long has it been happening?"

"Please, no more." Tears were streaking down his face. His skin was tired and gray, drawn taut over his high cheekbones.

She nodded, realizing she was going to get no more out of him. More importantly, realizing that she was too disgusted to want to hear anymore. It was bad enough being eight years old and discovering that your parents had sex with each other. It was a thousand times worse being eighteen and discovering that your father was having sex with someone else. "Fine," she agreed tightly. "Fine. No more. Until Mama comes home." With this last dire threat, she turned to leave.

She never made it to the door. With surprising agility, her father had seized her by the collar of her light blue fleece shirt and pinned her to the wall. "Listen to me very carefully," he said in a tone that she had never in her life heard before. "You listen. Not one word to your mother. Not a single word. Do you understand?"

"I'm telling her," Sean insisted. "She has a right to know that the man she so adores is nothing but a child molesting. . . ."

"She's eighteen!" he roared into her face.

"Whatever." She was willing to let her friend's age slide. "But you're still an adulterer. You're still not worth the vows you made to her twenty years ago. And she loves you so much. What will you do, Dad, when I tell her, and the light in her eyes goes out forever?"

"You'll kill her," he said softly. "If you tell her, she'll die inside. And it will be all your fault."

"Not my fault!" she protested. "Yours! Only yours! I had nothing to do with this!" Her loyalty for her mother burned bright. How could she let her loving, gentle, trusting mother continue to live with her false illusions about the man she married? Sean wasn't about to let it happen.

"But she doesn't have to know. Nobody's going to tell her. We'll both walk out of here as if this never happened. You never saw anything."

Sean was silent.

"It's for her own good. Believe me, if you tell her, you'll only be doing her more harm. If you break your mother's heart, it will be on your conscience."

"And *your* conscience will be clear?" She was incredulous.

He shrugged grimly. "What she doesn't know. . . ." he let the rest hang in the air.

Sean felt her shoulders sag, and the reduced tension in her body was signal enough to her father that he had won. He let her go with a suddenness that almost caused her to tip over, but didn't step away. His face was close enough to hers that she could feel his breath on her cheeks. "Promise me," he said.

"What?" she lifted her tear-filled eyes to the man who up to a few moments ago had been her hero.

"Promise me you'll never speak of this again, Sean."

"But my mother," she protested. How could he expect her to keep his guilty secret for him?

"Your mother never has to know. Neither does anyone

else. Promise you'll never speak about this to anyone. Not even Kaiyo."

"Are you crazy?" The first and only expletive she ever let fly in front of her father sprang from her lips before she could stop it. "You want me to not discuss it with my own friend?"

"What went on is between me and her," he insisted through tightly pressed lips. "You will talk to no one."

Sean hesitated.

"Promise me!" he commanded.

Beaten, Sean nodded. There was no more fight left in her. "I promise."

"No one," he added. "Ever."

"Ever," she echoed.

She had no way of knowing just how much such a burden would prove to weigh as she struggled to act as if nothing had ever happened. She never held a conversation with her best friend again, at least no conversation longer than one could exchange while passing each other on the stairs in front. She and her father also had little to say to each other, even though they both struggled to maintain a semblance of normalcy for her mother's sake. But the relationship they once shared, in which she was able to look up to a male figure and love him for all the sacrifices he had made and the contributions he had made to her development, was over.

Her relationship with her mother, though, was the saddest casualty. The poor woman couldn't help but notice the cessation of the once-regular visits from the petite Japanese girl next door. Worse yet, the cooling of affections between father and daughter were painfully obvious, and she would have been lax as a mother if she had not inquired about it.

Sean was never able to offer more than a muffled "It's nothing." Eventually, the defeated woman let it rest. It soon became obvious that the painful secret was preventing her

from ever looking her mother straight in the eye. Every
time she did so, she felt like a liar and a cheat. Every time
she caught her mother gazing upon her father's face with
the same love she'd always held for him, Sean's heart
ached. Shouldn't she say something, even if it was to relieve
her mother from the delusion she held? Spare her from
the stupid folly of trust? Shouldn't she, armed with her
new knowledge, let her mother know that no man was ever
to be fully trusted, and that no words of love could ever
drown out the clamoring of their lustful hearts?

But each time the truth sprang to her lips, it was beaten
down by the memory of the promise she had made. The
time she and her mother enjoyed together, shopping, popping into coffee houses for tiramisu and cappuccino, discussing the books they were reading lately, all these
pleasant interludes that kept mother and daughter together, gradually decreased. Sean always knew her mother
felt that she herself was to blame for the long silences that
grew between them, and the knowledge pained her. When
the time finally came for her to leave for college, she moved
out gratefully, even though she only went to a city univer-
sity, and could easily have commuted to her classes. The
relationship with her mother cooled to dull ash.

She resented her father for the secret he forced upon
her. Not even his death set her free. At his funeral, Kaiyo
and her family paid their respects, but her former friend
sobbed in misery, so much so that an outsider who did
not know of their clandestine relationship would have
been surprised. Sean knew that the girl had continued
to be her father's lover right up to his death, long after
she had moved away and made a career for herself. For
this, she was unable to forgive him.

At her desk, Sean returned to the present to discover
that she was sobbing openly into the cradle formed by

her folded arms. The sleeves of her fine rust peach-skin jacket were stained with her tears, and knew without having to check her compact that her face was a horrible road map of creases and streaks. She looked like hell. All she needed was for a big client, or worse yet, one of the VPs, to come rapping on her office door.

She felt like a fool, falling apart like this. She was a grown-up, for Pete's sake. But the memories that assailed her only served to remind her of the last scathing words that Christian had spat at her as he left her home a few days ago. He had, in some uncanny way, managed to hone in on the root cause of her inability to fully trust him or any man, even though she herself had never before been capable of admitting, even to herself, that the legacy of mistrust that her father had left her went so deep that even rational thought could not rout it.

She tried to think of what it had been like with Christian. She had been young and untutored. No virgin, certainly, but inexperienced enough to be taken in by the careless charm and quick intelligence of one of the most popular students on campus. The young man with the loud unbridled laugh and penetrating black eyes had lost no time in seducing her, and if she were honest, she would admit that he didn't have to expend that much effort, so entranced with him was she.

But with the suddenness and the illogic of a dream, their affair (which was what they had both intended it to be) took on a seriousness that neither could have predicted. Was it love? In retrospect, with the wisdom of hindsight and the experience gathered during the intervening years, Sean didn't think so. Sure, it was deep, thrilling, and passionate, enough to fool them into thinking that they wanted to spend the rest of their lives with each other.

Christian's spontaneous proposal of marriage came without warning, and if she had been more aware of the ways of the world, she would have realized that he enjoyed the idea of it, the glamour of it, more than the reality. He enjoyed the fantasy of having an adoring young bride, but had never been mature enough to accept the responsibility and commitment that such a covenant would entail.

Responsibilities like fidelity, Sean recollected bitterly. Responsibilities like trust. The first time she became aware of his cheating, she had reacted with shocked disbelief. Christian was her idol, her god. The realization that his feet were made of clay nearly proved to be the unraveling of her mind. Swift jagged images of her father, his clothes in disarray, modesty exposed, came to her like remnants of a persistent nightmare.

Previously, she had never made a connection between the behavior of other men and that of her father. *He* was the one who had disappointed her. *He* was the rogue, the fiend. But the next time she caught Christian out in one of his inept lies, her father's face came to her again. *Don't let it be so,* she remembered praying. *Don't let this be my lot. Isn't it enough that my mother must suffer? Should I wind up, like her, a fool and a cuckold, all for the sake of love?*

At his third infidelity, she remembered crying, not so much because she thought she had been made a fool of, or at the thought of the long, strong, chocolate-brown body mingling with that of some campus groupie who didn't know better. Not because of any of this. She wept because it finally became clear to her that all men were like that. All of them, without exception, were fallible. They wore their sexual vulnerability like a stain upon their bodies and handed it down from father to son, like the mark of Cain. And it was the women who would suffer.

That was a long time ago, Sean reminded herself. Six years was enough to change anyone. From what she saw of the man, he had grown, both in wisdom and in stature. The boyish body had filled out to become that of a man: strong, long, lean and powerful. She remembered with a hot flush the night they had made love in her apartment.

Even under those constrained circumstances, she was aware that his lovemaking had changed. There was none of the bullfighter's flamboyance or the arrogance that had tinted the sexual performance of the young boy she had known. She could sense more control, more mental effort, a greater awareness that his partner had a mind that was as much in need of his touch and attention as was her body. She had no doubt that the Christian of today did not indulge in the games and risk-taking so much enjoyed by the Christian of yesterday.

All well and good, she thought bitterly. Kudos to him. But so what? What did that mean to her? What they had was over, long dead, and buried. That one night that they had spent together was merely a means of assuaging the pain of their bodies and the anguish of many sleepless nights. They were both adults; neither of them was stupid enough to attach any further significance to it than that.

Besides, he had shown little interest in knowing the Sean she had become. She wasn't a little girl anymore. If he'd wanted to get to know her more, he'd have done something about it before now. And even if something developed between them (that is if she took leave of her senses long enough for it to happen!) what then? Sure, he was more mature, more serious, but one day the curse of manhood would lift its head, and the nature of man would rise up within him, and then, being male, and weak, like her father, he would listen to it, and act upon it.

And if she knew about it she would be brokenhearted, but resigned; if she didn't, she would remain in adoring ignorance like her poor, blind mother. What kind of choice was that?

Sean sucked her teeth in disgust. *Look at you,* she chided herself silently. *What's wrong with you? It makes no sense even thinking about it. Nothing's going to happen. What are you so worried about? Christian isn't interested. He has a*

*new job, he is in a new country, and he has more than enough
to occupy his mind. And of course, there is always Delta.*

Sean wasn't stupid. She knew her friend well enough
to smell her desire for a new man. It oozed from her
pores like a sweet, intense perfume, marking everywhere
she went, like civet from a cat. And she knew enough to
recognize that Christian, in turn, was at least curious. She
snorted. That was men all over.

Rising out of her chair, she rustled through her drawers
for a tissue to mop up the sopping mess she had made
of her face. The door swung open, and the absence of
any knock, any by-your-leave or hesitation whatsoever told
her immediately that her visitor could only be Delta. The
woman was uncanny. She had a homing device that allowed her to respond even to an unspoken thought. Sean
sat down again with a despondent plop.

"Sweet chile, what's happenin'?" Delta asked with an
overdose of good humor. Then she spied the tear-
streaked face before her and stopped dead. "What's
wrong, Sean? You sick?" Her finely tweezed brows shot
up in alarm to meet her russet bangs.

Sean shook her head. "Nothing. I'm fine." She really
didn't want much to do with Delta, or anyone else, right
now. All she wanted to do was crawl back into her shell and
nurse her pain at her own speed and on her own terms.

"You're all right, my ass." Delta snorted. She slipped
quickly around behind Sean's desk and laid a light hand
on her shoulder.

Sean's shoulders relaxed a little under the light pressure of her friend's tiny hand. "Oh, it's no big deal, really," she tried to convince her. "Just work."

"Mmmm? What you working on?" Delta's voice
sounded distant, barely with her. Her small hand kept
stroking.

"The relocation of the squatters and landowners around
the perimeter fence. It's become my albatross. The local

government isn't offering the landowners near what the land's worth, and as for the squatters, well, they aren't moving because they simply don't have anywhere else to go. The government isn't being very helpful, and these people are scared. They're beginning to get belligerent. I'd hate to see things deteriorate to violence."

"And how's Orion making out in all this?"

Sean shrugged. "What do you expect? We're the bad guys. We're the big bad Americans that came down here to take the people's land away. The company's image is taking a nasty blow, and the reporters are fanning the flames."

"That's too bad," Delta said softly. "But what about you?"

"Me?" Sean spun in her chair to face her. Even seated, she was almost eye to eye with the small woman.

"You ain't gonna tell me them tear-marks on your face are there because a bunch of poor families have nowhere to go, are you?" Delta's imagination could never stretch to embrace such a probability. This time, though, she was quite right. Her tears had nothing to do with the plight of their neighbors.

"So what's wrong?" Delta's brown eyes gleamed. "Man trouble?"

And how! But as much as Sean liked her flamboyant friend, she just couldn't see her way clear to sharing confidences, not about something so painful. She shook her had vehemently. "No. Nothing like that."

"If you're sure," Delta murmured. Then, as if the thought had just hit her, she brightened. "Tell you what, girl. Why don't you and I leave early and go to the beauty salon? We could both get massages. Do something with your hair; it's frightful. And get yourself a facial, because take it from me, sister, you look a mess."

Sean stiffened, and turned her hazel eyes onto her friend's steady, unrevealing ones, searching for deliberate cruelty. For the life of her, she could find none. Delta's comments stung. Ever since the bombing, she just hadn't seemed able to pull herself together long enough to return to her usual meticulous regime of beauty care. The best she could do was roll her thick shoulder-length hair up into a French pleat, and apply makeup as best as possible. Facials? Forget it. She just didn't seem to have the time.

The naked honesty of her friend's comments shook her, though, and coming from anyone else, she would have assumed it was a deliberate attempt to put her down, to undermine her self-confidence. But Delta had no reason to do that, did she?

Before she could answer her own question, there was a soft tap on the door. "Come in," she said resignedly to the closed door. Why not let the whole world come barging in on her, especially when, as her friend had convinced her, she looked like she'd been sleeping on park benches for a month.

A slight young woman, one of the pool secretaries who doubled as receptionist, stepped in timidly. "Miss Scott? Sorry to disturb you," she said in her soft musical Trinidadian accent, "but a delivery man left this for you downstairs in the lobby." She leaned forward and placed a long white box on Sean's desk.

Sean's eyes brightened. "Thank you, Claire." She picked up the box and held it, turning it over gingerly. It was festooned with brightly colored ribbons, a gay mixture of fuschia, purple, lavender and pink. The box could only have held flowers, and from the size of it, lots of them. In spite of herself, she was excited.

Delta leaned over her and peered at the package, trying to catch a glimpse of the card. "Oooh," she cooed. "Color me jealous. What man you got sending you flowers, girl?" The sharp look that she threw at Sean hardened her attempt at levity.

Sean shrugged, even though she knew the package

could only have come from one person: Christian. He was sorry for the mean things he'd said to her the other night, and had decided to apologize through the silent eloquence of flowers. She reached and extricated the small gold card from the tangle of ribbons. The handwriting was unrecognizable to her, and she felt a slight twinge of disappointment. It didn't mean anything, though. Most times, flowers ordered over the phone came with cards written out by one of the florist's assistants, so the absence of Christian's black, bold writing wasn't too much of a disappointment.

Still, she would have preferred to open them alone, to allow her to revel in the generosity of the gesture in the privacy of her own office. She glanced pointedly up at Delta, but the other woman was oblivious to her need. "Open it!" she insisted. "Let's see!"

Reluctantly, Sean bowed to pressure and tugged at the lavish satin ribbons, freeing the smooth white box top. She lifted the top off carefully, laid it aside and gently parted the rustling layers of delicate white tissue, and gasped. In the box lay an abundance of red roses, easily two dozen of them, tied together with a frothy white satin ribbon. They were very, very dead.

With a sharp cry of shock Sean cast them from her, recoiling as if they contained a nest of clicking, writhing scorpions. The rotted heap of roses tumbled out of their box and onto the table, disintegrating on impact, scattering wrinkled moldering petals across the files that lay on her desk.

"Rawtid!" Delta exhaled, dropping the neutral accent she usually affected while at work and in her agitation, lapsing into intense Jamaican creole. "But what the ras' clat' mih see 'pon your table?"

Sean grasped both hands in an effort to steady them. Her stomach lurched, and she prayed for the fortitude not to begin throwing up right there in her office.

"Girl, you really, *really* gone and pissed somebody off this time!" Delta regarded her, brown eyes glittering. "What you do to deserve that?"

Sean flashed her an indignant look. "I didn't do anything to deserve this! I can't imagine how somebody could be so cruel and . . . and . . ." she struggled to find a word that suited the act that had been perpetrated on her, ". . . and *vicious!*" she finished triumphantly.

But in spite of her pleas of ignorance, her belly was tight and cold with horror. How could Christian have stooped to such a low-down, foul-minded trick? How could he humiliate her, and, yes, frighten her, like that? Was he really that angry with her? Just as she was beginning to feel badly again for the things she had said to him, she halted in her mental tracks. No, Christian wasn't getting away with it that easily. He wasn't going to play games with her mind like this, do something this mean-spirited to her and then succeed in having her believe it was her fault.

"Not on your life!" she hissed aloud.

"Not on whose life?" Delta pounced shrewdly. "Do you know who sent this? Who sent it, Sean? Why? You and some guy had a falling out?"

Sean shook her head. "No. It's nothing. Don't worry about it."

"Come on," she wheedled sweetly. "You can tell me. I'm your *friend.*"

Sean nodded wearily. The headache she'd started the morning with was developing nicely into a migraine. "I know you are, Delta, but right now, if you don't mind, I'd really rather be alone."

"Fine," Delta sighed heavily. She made her way back to the front of Sean's desk. "But this afternoon, we really must go to the beauty salon. I'll tell you what, you can get your hair done on me, okay?"

Sean tried to smile and nodded. "Okay. Thank you."

As she made her way to the door, Delta stopped and pointed at the heap of putrefaction on her desk. "You want me to get rid of these for you?"

"Thank you." Sean was too tired to resist.

Carefully, Delta gathered up the mess, packed the blackened, curling petals into the box and jammed the bright, cheerful ribbons back into place. "I'll make sure no one sees me throw them out," she said helpfully.

Sean barely had the energy to voice her thanks. As the door pulled carefully shut, she let her head fall forward onto her hands. She was stunned. This was unbelievable! The Christian she had known had been reckless, maybe, and insensitive, certainly. But cruel? Never! What could have changed him so much? It just went to prove that she'd been right not to trust him all along. Christian was a dangerous man.

Sean gave an angry grunt and pulled her phone nearer to her. Dangerous or no, he wasn't getting away with this little piece of spite. With furious fingers she jabbed out his extension number and waited for him to pick up. The phone rang five times, six, then seven. As she was about to hang up with a frustrated howl, it was snatched up and a deep melodious voice was on the line.

"Devane," he answered crisply.

At the sound of his voice, she faltered. Now that she had him, just what the hell could she say to him? *I got your rotten roses, thank you?*

"Hello?" his voice clipped and impatient, as if he had the world of work before him and wanted nothing more than to get back to it.

"Happy now?" she snarled, surprised at the amount of poison that rose in her voice.

There was a brief hesitation, then, "Sean?"

"You got it. I asked you if you're happy now."

"Sean, what's this about?"

"You know what it's about." *Come on,* she urged. *You've*

*been childish enough already. At least be a man and admit to
the crap you've done.*

He sighed heavily. "Sean, if you're planning to dredge
up the other night again, forget it. We said what we had
to say, and let's leave it at that, okay?"

"No," she insisted angrily. "It's not okay, and it's not
about last night."

His own voice was beginning to take on her angry ca-
dence. "Look Sean, I haven't got the time to play games
with you today. Things are going crazy down here, and
I've got to see about them. So if you don't mind. . . ."

Before he could hang up, Sean cried out: "The flowers,
Christian. The flowers! *That's* what it's about. But then, you
already know that!" This was even more insulting, his playing like he didn't know what the hell she was talking about.
Well, she wasn't letting him get away with it.

He sounded honestly puzzled. "What flowers?"

How she hated him for his stonewalling! "You know
what flowers. Admit it."

"Honestly, Sean. I don't know anything about any flowers. I didn't send, touch or take any damn flowers."

For a second, she was hesitant. Could he be speaking
the truth? "You didn't send them?" She pulled the phone
away from her ear and stared at it, as if it would allow
her to read either innocence or guilt on his face.

"No." Far away from her ear, his voice was distant and
tinny. She put the phone to her ear again, in time to
hear him say sarcastically, "Maybe it was another one of
your boyfriends. Whoever it was, he may have misjudged
your taste in flowers, but I'm not taking the flack for that.
So if you'll excuse me, I have work to do." The line went
dead with a loud bang.

Sean sat back, not knowing what to say, do or think.
Christian had certainly been convincing. Maybe he *didn't*
know about the flowers. But if he didn't send them, who
did? She may not be chummy with everyone around here;

that was impossible. But she certainly didn't have any enemies.

Then she laughed cynically. Of course it was him. She'd
kicked him in the ego, and he'd found a way to get even.
Fine. It was a pretty crappy way to get back at her, but
so be it. She was woman enough to deal with it and put
it behind her. He wanted them to be even, and so they
were. She'd just have to watch him like a hawk from now
on, and keep her distance.

She shrugged and rose to her feet to get the kinks out
of her spine. Keep her distance from Christian Devane?
Hell, that was just fine with her!

Eight

Christian folded the newspaper over and dropped it on his desk with a hollow thud. The article that had drawn his attention stared at him, face up, from among a sea of poorly printed advertisements and scathing editorials. In the short time that he had been on the island, he'd come to have a pretty good understanding of the personalities of the various newspapers that were printed here, where they stood politically, and what kind of audience they catered to.

The weekly he'd just been reading went for the jugular. It seemed to hold no cows sacred, whether they held political office, positions in big business, or held religious sway over the polytheistic population that embraced Christianity, Hinduism and Islam, as well as a slew of other sects, cults and factions.

The article he had just read offended him to the very core. Twisting his lips at the irony of it, he stared at it again, reading the sarcastic words that were penned by some smarmy know-it-all who in spite of his fighting words didn't seem to have the guts to include his byline.

Most of us would assume that a stable is best put to use for keeping animals. Even the Savior Himself, when He became flesh, accepted that His choice of birthplace meant that He would be surrounded by cattle, sheep and goats.

Strange, then, to hear of a certain stable in Southern Trinidad, which is overseen by men and women who are faithful to a woman said to have the gift of prophecy. The talk in town has it that the woman's manger holds something other than a babe wrapped in swaddling clothes, and that somewhere under those piles of straw and cattle dung lies the entrance to a chamber that is stocked with items more dangerous than horse food.

Have our Customs and Excise Division heard, as I have, of a recent shipment of Russian arms and ammunition said to have arrived on these shores from neighboring Venezuela? If so, has this shipment, said to have arrived by fishing boat in the dead of night, been subject to the processes of examination, certification and licensing as required by the laws of the land? Methinks not.

If nothing is done about this little cache soon, it seems extremely likely that this woman, a woman of God, or at least of goddess, might soon be separating the sheep from the goats by very unconventional means.

It was beyond him. Here was a paper that claimed to have intimate knowledge of the goings-on within some sort of cult, the same cult that allegedly caused the deaths of eleven people in the bombing at the bank. As the image of death crossed Christian's mind, he saw again the smiling face of the bank clerk, Naimah, and then, superimposed upon the image, another, one with blank, staring eyes and a slack mouth. This face, the second face, was the one that kept him company as he tossed and turned alone at night. He knew deep within him that this was a face that would stay with him for years to come.

A sigh of frustration escaped his lips. What the hell was really going on here? He knew in his gut that the paper was on to something. How come nobody else was? What were the authorities doing about it? More than a month had passed, and there was no sign of an arrest, no sign that investigations were continuing at an acceptable rate. The whole affair seemed to have been swept under the carpet.

He remembered with dark foreboding the last nasty article he'd read, no doubt from the same reporter, the one that seemed to suggest that there were people in power who were aware of what was going on, but who didn't seem to be doing anything about it. His scalp prickled. This wasn't going to be the last he would hear of it. Things were destined to get worse.

But why was nobody doing anything about it? Why was this madwoman, this supposed religious leader, being allowed to continue building a cult that was so obviously dangerous? Hadn't Jim Jones or David Koresh taught anybody anything? As far as he could tell, the Southland was sitting on a powder keg, and when it blew, he hoped the authorities were able to bring things back under control.

As far as control went, he himself was having surprising difficulty keeping his, at least as it pertained to his job. There was so much that had been left hanging by his predecessor, so much that screamed out to be rectified. The plant was running at way below optimum levels, and with a handful of other methanol plants operating on the island, their weaknesses were their competitors' strengths.

The country, tiny though it was, was the world's largest exporter of methanol. This translated into hundreds of thousands of tons of the chemical being shipped out each year, and hundreds of millions of dollars up for grabs. He conducted his business each day with the knowledge that the other plants were just waiting for Orion, the newcomer on the block, to slip up so that they could step in and take their customers away from them. It wasn't a nice thing to think about.

It was late; most of the office staff had already left for the day. But Operations staff wasn't office staff; their job consumed them twenty-four hours a day in strict rotation. As the man in charge, he felt it his duty to be there with one or the other of the shifts, showing his men that he supported them fully. He wasn't an eight-to-four manager.

His feet, clad in their steel-tipped, leather-covered prison, hurt. He'd just come back from an exhaustive inspection down on the plant. All systems were go, fortunately, but it had taken the better part of the day to determine that, at least to his satisfaction. He was hungry and tired. Maybe he should call it a day, he mused. Pack it in for the evening, hand things over to his evening-shift superintendent, and go in search of dinner.

He hadn't found the time for eating out, not in any formal sense, since he had come to the island. Maybe he'd pass by and see if Sean was in the mood for a bite. . . .

Sean. He'd forgotten she was mad at him. Three days had passed since he'd been on the receiving end of her bizarre phone call, and he still had no idea what she'd been rambling on about. Something about flowers. He wondered, with a strange mix of jealousy and amusement, just what kind of man could send a woman flowers and wind up getting her so irate. Did Sean have a hate-list for flowers? Did she have some kind of allergy? He couldn't remember.

It was a good idea, though, asking her out. He'd pass by, ask her to show him where they'd find good dining in the city, and then apologize for his outburst at her apartment last week. He'd really blown everything out of proportion, and he did want to tell her he was sorry. He tugged at the snaps on his brilliant yellow safety suit and began to peel the lightweight material down off his arms, revealing a plain white cotton shirt. He was just about to ease it down over his hips when his door crashed open and one of his men stumbled inside.

Christian's head snapped up in alarm. His skin tingled as he caught sight of the pallor on the young man's face and the wide, bulging eyes. Dread filled him. "What's wrong, Khan?"

Eniath Khan was panting heavily, and his panic was so great that he had difficulty getting the words past his lips. "The plant, down at the plant. . . ."

"What down at the plant?" Christian demanded impatiently, tugging the suit back on with deft, hasty fingers. Then he relented his harsh tone as the young man flinched visibly.

"Down at the plant," the man tried again. "There's been an explosion."

Heart thumping, Christian followed quickly on his heels. The plant was huge, and lay sprawled across several acres. Snatching the keys from Khan's cold fingers, he leaped into the Jeep that had come for him, and sped away, with the young man barely having time to jump in next to him.

"Where?" he barked.

"Valve station six," Khan answered, and held on for life as Christian put the Jeep's accelerator to the test.

The valve station was one of several located at intervals along the plant's piping system, and was designed with a series of valves that shut down automatically if pressure within the valves rose to dangerous levels. Each was housed within a small structure comprising four walls, a roof and a door, resembling a security guard's night shelter, and was not much larger.

The Jeep skidded up to the valve station, and Christian leaped out without bothering to cut the engine. Khan shut it off for him, pocketed the keys, and followed close on his manager's heels.

The scene that met him was appalling. The door of

the valve station had been torn off its hinges, blown away by the force of the blast. The roof sagged sadly, and the entire structure was shrouded in a cloud of dust and debris that still swirled, getting into his eyes and his nostrils, acrid in his mouth.

Although his men had managed to shut down the pipes at stations farther down, the air was acrid with the smell of methanol. This was, for Christian, the most frightening thing. Methanol had been spilled, and judging from the smell of it, quite a large amount. He thanked God fervently that there had been no source of ignition at the time of the blast, no sparks, no flames. The idea of what methanol could do in the presence of such a spark was enough to make him shudder.

A methanol factory was, no matter how one tried to deny it, a huge bomb. The men on the plant lived with the knowledge, and did all that they could to minimize the risks involved in running it. There had never been such an industrial accident on the island, and he ardently hoped that such a thing would never happen. Methanol had one quality that made it a greater horror than any of the other dangerous substances in use among the cluster of plants in the vicinity. It was a quality that, as far as he was concerned, made it a far more lethal and insidious beast than even ammonia or natural gas.

Methanol was perfect energy. It was so fine, so free of impurities that it burned with an invisible flame; methanol on fire presented itself as little more than a shimmering wall of intense heat which could sneak up on the unsuspecting like a hellish wave of death. It was common lore in the industry that workers had been known to step directly into a sheet of burning methanol without realizing it. Without sensors, you wouldn't know it was there until you felt the heat. By then, it was usually too late.

He thought of the four holding tanks in which hundreds of tons of the deadly liquid was stored, envisioned a small fire taking hold of them, and then pictured them going up with a series of deafening explosions. Then his mind ran on the families close to the plant who had been refusing to relocate ever since the plant began construction. The things that could have happened to them if this little incident had gotten out of control. It was enough to make him giddy. He closed his eyes and struggled to regain his composure.

"Was anyone injured?" he managed to croak.

His youngest technician, Ricky Conrad, stepped forward. "There's Emory Payne. He was standing nearby, and then it went off. . . ."

"Where is he? Have you called the ambulance?"

Ricky's thin, coffee-colored face was taut with an indefinable mix of emotions. He nodded. "It'll be here in two minutes. Payne's over there." He pointed to a small group of men who were gathered around a pile of bright yellow clothing on the ground.

As Christian lunged forward, he recognized the pile of clothing as Emory Payne. The man lay in a limp heap on a blanket that had been spread for him by his anxious colleagues. They had removed his safety helmet in order to examine him for head wounds, and someone had put a rolled-up jacket under his head.

He was a horror to behold. Blood matted his longish hair, and clung to his face, already drying to a sticky red smear. One eye was swollen shut, and from the size of it, and the depth of the wounds surrounding it and on its lid, Christian had the sickening knowledge that the chances of his regaining full sight in it were slim. His mouth and lips were also smeared with blood, and the slackness of the jaw suggested that it was very likely broken.

Concern and empathy brought Christian to his knees. With light, gentle fingers he touched the man's skull, slipping his fingers around the back of his head, feeling for any bleeding or obvious crushing of the skull.

"The back of his head seems all right," one of the men volunteered. "He still had his helmet on."

"But not his goggles, evidently," Christian answered bitterly, glancing at the horrible eye wound again. Not wearing goggles while carrying out such close work was a flagrant safety violation, but Christian knew that some of the men considered it too much of a bother to be constantly putting them on and taking them off. Payne had gambled, and would pay with his eyesight.

Even though the man had made an unfortunate choice, he was still in Orion's employ, and the company was still responsible for his safety. And as his superior, Christian reminded himself, *I'm responsible for his safety. And it looks like I failed.*

The wounded man stirred and groaned painfully. Christian took hold of his leather-gloved hand and squeezed it comfortably. "Are you okay?" he asked softly, even though it was blatantly obvious that the man was far from okay.

Bravely, the man tried to nod but the excruciating pain that darted through his skull stopped him. "Don't worry," Christian began, and tugged the leather glove off so that he could make contact with the man's bare skin. He wondered if he should assure him that he would be all right, but he didn't want to be offering empty assurances. The man would very likely be blind in one eye. How all right was that?

The screeching of the ambulance penetrated the night and spared him from having to give any such assurances. The white vehicle with its flashing green lights skated up to the group and stopped short with a spray of gravel. Christian watched as two uniformed paramedics descended and quickly but carefully stabilized the wounded man and slid him on a stretcher into the back of the vehicle. The group of men stood silently, watching the vehicle as it sped off towards the plant's main gate.

Now that the injured man had been seen to, Christian

made it his business to find out exactly how the accident had happened, and why. "Okay," he snarled. "What happened here?"

"The valve blew out," one of the men volunteered.

"Obviously," he sneered. The sheer stupidity and avoidability of the accident made him sarcastic. "What I want to know is—why?"

The man swallowed hard, and his Adam's apple dipped nervously. "The valve calibrations were off, sir."

"Off—what do you mean, off?" He marched towards the twisted heap of metal that had once been a valve station, and bent over to inspect the dials and indicators. The valves were set at a certain pressure, ensuring a smooth flow through the pipes. The selected pressure was just high enough to keep product moving, but not high enough to cause a breech on the line to be dangerous. If by some accident the pressure rose to unacceptable levels, the valve would be activated, shutting down the entire system until the problem could be rectified.

"Somebody hand me a torchlight," he demanded. The methanol alarms were silent, and his own nose told him that the spill had dissipated sufficiently to allow him to use a light without fear of igniting any stray gas. A torch was slapped into his hand with the precision of a nurse handing a surgical instrument to a doctor. Christian flicked it on impatiently with his thumb and peered at the dials that had been stilled by the blast. Some of them had reset to zero by the blast; others were frozen at the figure they had been indicating at the time of the explosion. Christian read the figures and cursed out loud.

It was incredible. The flow was set at a level of pressure that no sane person would have allowed. There must have been a mistake. He shook his head. Perhaps the force of the blast had caused the dials to shift position. There wasn't a pipeline on the entire plant that was calibrated so high. Surely it had to have been an accident!

But even so, the valve was designed to shut down when it reached the designated pressure. This one obviously hadn't. "Why didn't it shut off?" he demanded.

"The valve, er, was isolated from the system. There appears to have been some kind of . . . diversion." The shift superintendent cleared his throat and looked miserable.

Christian rounded on him. "What do you mean, *isolated*? Are you out of your mind? You don't isolate a damn pressure valve! That defeats the purpose of the whole thing! How in hell is a valve going to shut down when the pressure gets too high, if the valve can't read the pressure in the first place?" He knew he was shouting. He knew that the supervisor understood the importance of the valve, but it made him feel better to shout anyway.

The man was nodding unhappily, all the while glancing back between the damage and Christian. He kept agreeing with him, saying, "Yes, yes, I know, yes."

But Christian wasn't finished. "And furthermore, what about the pressure? Did you see how high that pressure was set? How can you just sit around and allow a flow like that? That's madness! That's not a pipeline, that's a bomb!" His anger at the stupidity of the whole scenario, and the horror at what could have happened but didn't, left him panting. "Wait 'til I get my hands on the fool who set the damn thing so high in the first place!" He put his hands on his hips and faced the group of men, teeth bared and nostrils flaring. "Who's the bastard that set the calibrations on that thing last?"

There was a painful silence that cried out to be broken. The men shifted from foot to foot and glanced at each other. Some stared at their feet, others readjusted their helmets and belts.

"Well?" Christian was beside himself with impatience. "Maybe you haven't heard me. I asked you a question. Who calibrated the flow in that pipe?"

There was a leaden silence, and eventually, young Ricky spoke up. "You did, sir," he said softly. "Just this morning."

Sean gritted her teeth and allowed herself to be subjected to the stringent security search at the gates of the plant. It was eleven-thirty at night, they'd just had some sort of incident at the plant, and still security was patiently going through the routine of checking her trunk? She couldn't believe it.

"Come on, come on," she muttered as the man rummaged through her untidy heap of shoes, bags, tool kit, medicine kit and assorted junk. As Public Relations Manager she was on the company call out list, one of the vital staff members required to return to the plant in the event of any emergency. "We've got a problem down at the plant, and he wants me to declare my *running shoes!*"

Eventually the officer seemed satisfied that she posed no threat and waved her in. She found her way to the Control Office, the designated meeting place, without any problem; it was a swarm of activity. As she parked, she recognized many of the cars that had arrived there before her, among them cars belonging to most of the Vice Presidents, the President of the company himself, and Delta.

Every person there had a specific duty to perform. Sean's duty was two-fold. She was there to handle any questions from the press, which would inevitably begin coming in, if not tonight, then first thing tomorrow. She was also there to put a face on the company, especially as far as the family of the injured man was concerned. Arrangements had already been made to take his wife and parents to the hospital to be with him. In the morning, she, as well as a few selected executives, most likely the head of Industrial Safety, one of the Vice Presidents and Christian would have to pay them a visit, at which they would express the company's concern and offer their assistance in making him and his family as comfortable as possible. If there was a chance that the family would be belligerent and begin talking compensation or even lawsuit at such an early stage, Delta would have to make the trip out with them.

As she entered the room, Sean's eyes immediately searched out Christian. He seemed to be the center of attention; he was surrounded by the Safety man, three Vice Presidents, the President and Delta. A quick glance at his drawn, gray face told her that their attention was neither pleasant nor wanted.

Well, she sighed, if she was to carry out her duties in disseminating information the next day, she would have to acquire the information herself. And the best way to get that information was to stay quiet and to follow the conversation. She walked up to the tight, tense group and slipped in as unobtrusively as possible between them.

"Good evening," she greeted them, and was promptly ignored by everyone present.

"I simply can't have a report ready within forty-eight hours," Christian was saying urgently to Andrea Gooding, his immediate superior. The woman was standing before him, hair impeccable, dressed in one of her classic business suits, as if being called out at this hour of the night was no surprise to her. Sean glanced downwards at the jeans and long-sleeved cotton shirt she had dragged on the minute she received the call-out, and flushed.

"Forty-eight hours is just about as long as I can wait, Chris," she answered smoothly, her surprising use of the diminutive of his name making her sound like a teacher having her patience stretched to the limit by a bright but troublesome student. "This is easily the worst accident we've had in the two years that Orion has been in operation. I'm sure you're as anxious as we are to get to the bottom of this."

"Yes, Ma'am, I am, but what I'm trying to explain to you

is that this isn't as simple as it looks. At first glance, this *incident,* and I'm not ready to rule it an accident just yet, might in fact warrant a full-scale investigation. I don't anticipate being able to pull anything that large off in two days."

The President stepped forward. "What do you mean, not ready to rule it an accident? Are you saying that someone deliberately . . ."

Christian hastened to clarify himself. "Not necessarily deliberately. I have no evidence to support that just yet. It's just that the settings were so way off, so far from the norm, that even gross negligence stretches the imagination. And as for that valve being isolated, well. . . ."

"I don't need to remind anyone here just how stiff the competition is within the methanol market. And I'm sure I don't need to bring up the importance of guarding against industrial . . . er, tampering."

Sean felt her body tense. The President was talking about sabotage. It was a legitimate fear for any large industrial plant, with so many things just waiting to go wrong, and with so much to be gained by any other competitor if another plant were to fail. Sabotage was not unheard of, and, if it was successful, the results could mean irreparable damage to the company's good name at best, and complete ruin at worst.

But who in hell could be responsible for any act so dastardly? If it were indeed sabotage, then the culprit had gotten off lightly; all he had managed to damage was a valve station, and only one man had been injured. If Emory Payne had been standing a few inches farther to the left, or if he had contrived to be in line with that flying door, the question would not have been one of industrial sabotage, but one of murder.

"Sir," Andrea Gooding addressed the President in her most dulcet tones, "I find it very difficult to believe that any of the men working under me could even be considered capable of such an action. If I were called upon to vouch for any of them, I would, without hesitation. Why, I've known almost every man here since the opening of the plant. . . ." She stopped and caught her breath, suddenly realizing that the only man she *hadn't* known since the opening of the plant was Christian.

Her eyes flew to his face, as did every other pair in the room. His own black ones darted from face to face, reading the silent question with increasing dread. "Surely you couldn't. . . ." his voice died in his dry throat. The group continued to appraise him silently, as if waiting for him to defend himself or confess.

Sean felt rising panic. They couldn't be serious! They couldn't be crazy enough to think that Christian could have been responsible! She opened her mouth to rush to his defense, but to her surprise, Gooding beat her to it.

"Come now! I can't believe you could even imagine that a man of Christian's qualifications and reputation would ever be suspected of anything so dastardly!" She moved quickly to his side and grasped his arm protectively. "I hired this man, and I believe him. I'm willing to defend him to the hilt, even if it means staking my own reputation and good judgment on him. I'm confident that he will get to the bottom of all this. Why, it was only a week ago that we had that computer breakdown. Wasn't he right on-site to locate and fix the problem? And as for the calibrations on the pipeline, I've been told that Christian himself participated in a calibration exercise just this morning. If there's anyone capable of obtaining the information necessary to get to the bottom of this, it is he."

Several pairs of eyes widened. Christian had been calibrating the pressure flow within the pipes? The same pipes that just exploded? This was news to them. In deference to Gooding's position as Vice President, however, no one responded with so much as a murmur.

Deep inside her, Sean groaned. How could Gooding

be so *stupid?* There she went, leaping to his defense, and in the same breath reminding everyone about last week's breakdown, and bringing up the fact that Christian had been out on the pipeline, *calibrating* the pipeline no less, just this morning? She'd gone and put both feet into her mouth, at Christian's expense. The woman might be loyal to her staff, but tactful, she wasn't.

To her relief, the group dispersed, as everyone seemed satisfied that there was nothing else to be done tonight that couldn't be handled by the technical crew. Sean was about to approach Christian, their last nasty phone conversation shunted aside in her mind, when Delta fell into step with her.

"Whatta bitch," Delta breathed in her ear.

"What?" Sean asked in surprise.

"Gooding. What . . . a . . . bitch." She mimicked Gooding's smarmy Margaret Thatcher tones: " 'I can vouch for every man here, and if Christian was out calibrating the pipes, well, he should know who done it.' Jeez. She had to have known she was dropping him right in the ca-ca! What a b. . . ."

"Come on, she didn't know what she was saying. Christian is her own right hand." In spite of her dislike for Gooding, she respected the woman for being a good worker who pushed her people but always looked out for the company's interests.

Delta snorted loudly. "Huh!"

"Besides, she has no reason to embarrass him. If he looks bad, she looks bad. And as she said, *she* hired him."

Delta seemed to toss it around in her mind for a few moments, then nodded in concession. "All right, fine. I guess it wasn't deliberate. But if he wasn't a suspect before, he sure is now. Damn. Why is it that the Vice Presidents in a company are always dumber than anyone else? The *tea ladies* in the *cafeteria* wouldn't have made such a stupid tactical error!"

"Yeah," Sean agreed moodily. Christian was going to have to fight long and hard to dust himself off of the manure that Gooding had dumped him in tonight.

Delta tugged at her arm. "Let's go cheer him up."

They hastened over to where Christian was giving terse instructions to the men on shift, who were all that was left after the other officers had gone home. "I know we've all had a pretty lousy night," he was saying, "but at least everything's back on stream. The hospital called and they say Payne's doing okay. So let's just try to get through the rest of the shift, and in the morning we can think about all this more clearly, all right?" The men nodded and set about their work, but Sean noticed with some pain that none of them seemed willing to meet his eyes.

"Chris," she said softly. He looked at the two women in surprise, as if he'd expected them to have left with the others. Shadows cut sharp angles into his face, and his eyes were hooded and red. Sean wished she could put her arms up around him and hold him until he felt better.

"Oh, hi," he greeted them, looking dazed. He stood there for a while as if he were unsure of what to say next.

"Come and have some coffee," Delta said decisively, and headed over to a small table in the corner of the room. She busied herself pouring three cups of bitter local coffee and laying them out on the table. "You want cream and sugar, or you want it black?" she asked him.

"Thanks," he nodded and sat down heavily.

The two women exchanged glances. He was more tired than he knew. "He takes it sweet, no cream," Sean finally volunteered. Delta raised a fine eyebrow, no doubt wondering where she could have happened upon that information, but complied silently.

Christian accepted the coffee but held it between his hands, staring into its depths rather than drinking it.

"Things will look better in the morning," Sean said comfortingly.

"Yes," he answered, his voice laced with cynicism, "but in the morning, will I be an incompetent or a saboteur?"

She bit her lip, remembering the night she had accused him of fouling up the computers. She regretted her clumsy comment about his abilities, and wished to God she could have taken it back. "We know you're neither," she said loyally.

Delta came to her support. "Come on, Chris, we all know Gooding's an idiot. Nobody's stupid enough to even think for a second. . . ."

He let out a short harsh laugh. "Did you see how my men were looking at me? Do you have any idea how much damage was done tonight? If I don't have their trust, I have nothing. I can't function here without that." The women allowed him to brood in silence for a few more minutes, before he burst out, "Wait until I get my hands on the sonofabitch that tampered with those valves. . . ."

"Are you sure it was tampering, Chris?" Sean asked anxiously. That was a little hard to believe. What kind of person would play games with a machine that could trigger off an explosion big enough to cause the deaths of possibly hundreds of innocent people?

"It had to be. Not even a first-year technical student would be green enough to set those calibrations so high." He rubbed his face vigorously in an effort to clear his mind. He drifted off into silence once again for an endless stretch of time, then he added inconsequentially, "I like your hair, Delta."

Sean looked at Christian in surprise. As they'd planned, both women had gone off to the hairdresser after work, and while Sean had done little more than to add a warm mink-toned rinse to her naturally dark-brown hair, Delta had declared her intention to "try something a little more conventional" and had had the waist-length red weave replaced by a classic chin-length page in a rich, dark wine color. All that was well and good, but it was ludicrous to think that in the midst of such a crisis, Christian had actually allowed Delta's new hairdo to register in his thoughts. What was even more ridiculous was that she, Sean, was piqued that he'd noticed Delta's hair, but hadn't noticed hers!

"We really must be needing some sleep," she muttered.

Christian heard her and agreed. "Well, my men will be okay for the rest of the night, so I don't think it makes much sense my hanging around, especially since I need to get my strength up for the investigation tomorrow. After all, my boss just gave me forty-eight hours to prepare for my own trial." His lips twisted at the incongruity of the situation.

Reaching out, he patted Sean's hand lightly. "Sean, I don't think I've got the energy to drive. My eyeballs feel like they're drying out, I'm so tired. You don't think you can give me a lift home, do you?"

"Oh, I'll do it," Delta popped to her feet and jingled her keys.

Christian waved away her offer. "Don't be silly. Sean's a lot closer than you are, and besides, it'd be out of your way."

"No trouble," she said determinedly, with just a hint of a sexy smile. "Sean won't mind, will you?" She gave Sean an arched look.

Realizing that she did indeed mind, but knowing that she would rather have her tongue torn out than admit it, she hastily said that she didn't mind at all. This was ridiculous! It was well into the early hours of the morning, here they were in the midst of a crisis that could have career-changing implications, and two good-looking professional women were arguing over who got to drive a man home!

Eventually, it was Christian who settled the little wrangle. Planting a light kiss on Delta's forehead, he got to his feet and helped Sean up. "Thanks, Delta, but I wouldn't like to put you out of your way. Sean?"

Aware of Delta's tightened mouth and cooling eyes, Sean gathered her bag self-consciously and led the way outside. They said their quick good-byes, and Sean watched as Delta's car screeched out of the parking lot at a speed way beyond that recommended by company policy. This time, the security officer let them leave without any fuss.

Christian sat slumped in his seat without even bothering to buckle up. He looked wasted. Moved by sympathy she reached out and patted his thigh; even in his fatigue she felt the warm flesh tighten under her hand. She pulled her hand away and put them both safely on the wheel where they belonged. He saw the movement and chuckled.

"Any chance that you might have another can of soup lying around there somewhere?" he asked as she eased the car into their neighborhood ten minutes later.

She took her eyes off the road long enough to look at him in surprise. "What?"

"I was inviting myself in for something to eat. I haven't eaten in . . ." he consulted the flat gold watch on his left wrist, ". . . seventeen hours. Take pity on me."

She smiled. "I think I can find something lying about."

"Good."

She parked, fished out her keys and let him in. There was just a light burning in the hall, and she preceded him into the house, turning on the lights. "Sit down," she told him, "and I'll get cracking on dinner."

"Great," he groaned. To her surprise, he bent over right there in the middle of the hall and shucked off his safety suit, standing in just the street clothes that he wore underneath. "I've been meaning to get that damn thing off for hours," he muttered, and found his way to the living room, whereupon he threw himself down onto the couch and was immediately asleep.

* * *

Christian awoke to unfamiliar surroundings, in a room lit by just one lamp. He shot upright, rubbing his eyes, trying to take stock of where he was. It didn't take him long to realize that he was in Sean's living room, or that she was sitting on the edge of the couch looking at him.

"Is it morning?" he asked groggily.

She laughed. "No, you've only been out for an hour or so."

He nodded. Man, he was tired. He felt as if he had been sleeping for ages! He remembered having a strange dream, in which Sean was sitting in a room surrounded by baskets and bouquets of flowers, white lilies, the kind put on graves. She was angry, and was shouting into the phone she held in her hand, "Why did you send all these flowers?" even though he himself was in the room with her. "I never asked you to send me all these flowers!" Now, he thought, what kind of stupid dream was that?

Then he remembered that the last conversation he'd had with Sean had indeed been about flowers, flowers that he'd never sent, but which she seemed to think he had. He cast his sleepy eyes around the room. The wretched bouquet or whatever had to be around here somewhere.

"Where are they?" he mumbled.

Sean leaned forward, trying to catch the soft words. A smile played on her lips. Those beautiful lips.

"The flowers," he insisted, his mind still clouded with sleep. "Where'd you put them?"

Sean's head snapped back as if she'd been slapped. Her eyes widened with horror, and she stared at his face as if she'd never really seen him before. "Did you really expect me to keep them?" she asked in a high, strangled voice that wasn't her own.

What was the woman on about now, he wondered, but was too tired to ask. Instead, he chose to agree with her. "I guess not," he shrugged, and was instantly asleep.

Nine

Sean dressed carefully. The first visit to an injured employee's family was a crucial one, as it could determine the kind of response they would have from the family throughout the man's recuperation as well as the tone that the ensuing negotiations would take. She wasn't kidding herself—there were going to be negotiations; injury of that nature would naturally result in some kind of monetary compensation. Orion was not the kind of company to shirk its duties in that area, and there was never any question of evading the issue or attempting to cheat the victim out of his just due. It was simply a matter of reassuring the family that the company would stand by its commitments, and her performance this morning would in part determine whether the financial settlement would proceed amicably or whether the family would feel slighted or taken for granted and thus decide to turn to the courts.

As such, she dressed in one of her nicest morning suits: a cool professional white linen blouse with a lace collar and small pearl buttons, coupled with a warm brandy-colored knee-length skirt and dark silk stockings. Although she usually wore the matching double-breasted jacket whenever she wore the suit to the office, she chose to leave it at home this time. For one thing, the family would likely look with distrust upon people in suits, finding them too cold and corporate, and that was the last impression she intended to convey. For another, Payne's family lived in the central part of the island, a flat, arid stretch of unending canefields which would prove hot, sticky and uncomfortable, despite the air conditioning offered by her car.

Dressing herself took longer than usual; she had had almost no sleep last night, so her eyes were puffy and her face looked drawn. She stared at herself in the mirror, trying her best to cover up the dark blotches of fatigue with a concealer stick that matched her spicy tone perfectly.

"I look like hell, thanks to you, Devane," she accused him with a twist of her lips. How could she sleep, after hearing him ranting on about those damn flowers he sent her? Because after last night, there was no doubt in her mind that he had been responsible for the sick joke.

How childish could he get? Conventional wisdom was right; some men never grew up. They were just tall boys with lots of body hair. Maybe he had only seen the prank as a harmless means of getting back at her for her guileless accusation, but as far as she was concerned, it was a rotten trick to pull.

As she brushed vigorously at her mass of curls, now shiny and soft from her trip to the hairdresser yesterday, she remembered wryly how Christian, even in the midst of his distress, had seen his way clear to noticing Delta's surprisingly conservative new look. Who would have thought that Knock-'em-Dead Delta would have chosen such a traditional cut? Who was she trying to impress?

The answer came swift upon the heels of the question. She was trying to impress Christian, of course. Maybe it had dawned on her that he wasn't into anything as wild as a three-foot red weave, and was trying to conform to her idea of what he would like.

"You want him, you can have him, babe," she told an absent Delta. She patted her warm brandy-tinted lips with a tissue and straightened up. "Lord knows, *I* have no use for him!"

With her ego thus bolstered, she sprayed herself lavishly with her favorite Givenchy perfume and gathered up her purse and briefcase. She was halfway out to the living room when she heard the soft growl of a car engine outside. The crunching wheels told her the car was pulling into her own driveway. Who could be visiting her at this hour, on a workday to boot?

Before she was able to fully unlock her front door, she recognized the sound of the engine as her own. Half-fearing that a thief was making off with it, and completely forgetting that the car was moving *into* and not *out of* the driveway, she wrenched open her door and hurried outside, her heart beating madly.

Christian pulled up the handbrake and eased himself out of the driver's seat.

Before he could shut the car door, she was by his side. "What are you doing with my car?" she asked tightly.

He looked a little taken aback at her aggressive welcome, and glanced ostentatiously at his watch, as if to wonder how she could be so crabby even before breakfast. "Good morning," he said mildly, and, pulling open the fingers of her right hand, dropped her keys onto her palm.

She felt a flash of embarrassment, but then decided that she was mad enough at him to justify any amount of rudeness.

"I didn't want to wake you, and I had to get back home to shower and dress," he explained, and began moving purposefully into her place and towards her kitchen as if he paid the rent. "I picked up breakfast."

"I don't want any," she said mulishly.

"You stopped eating breakfast?" He raised an eyebrow, but began laying croissants onto a shallow wicker breadbasket.

She watched him as he worked. He fished out two small jars of jelly, a slab of butter (didn't he think she had butter in her own refrigerator?) and a round package of what looked like expensive imported cheese. It looked good.

She ran the tip of her tongue along her top lip before she could even stop herself.

"I haven't stopped eating breakfast," she answered shortly. "I just don't want any." At least not with *you*, her mind added silently.

"Don't be an idiot." He broke a croissant with deft fingers and spread a thin layer of butter, followed by a more generous layer of strawberry jelly. "Come on, have a nibble." He stood close, close enough for her to smell the clean scent of the soap he had used and the tingly cologne he'd splashed on afterwards. "Open up," he coaxed softly, and before she could protest, he had slipped the flaky morsel into her mouth.

Croissants, butter and jelly. He knew just where her taste lay. In spite of herself she sighed with pleasure and savored the sweet buttery taste. "Come on, relax and have breakfast with me." He tugged the handbag that she was still valiantly clutching under her arm and tossed it onto the eggshell-green laminated countertop.

"Don't you have to get in early to start on your report?" she asked.

She shouldn't have brought it up, she realized as he flinched visibly. "Sean, believe me, the first thing I intend to do the minute I drive through those gates is begin my investigation. But you know as well as I do that the next two days are going to be murder; I'll be lucky if this isn't my last meal before Thursday. So if you don't mind, I'd like to enjoy breakfast with you before I go out onto the battlefield, okay?"

She nodded in understanding. "Okay." She really had to admire him, she thought as he buttered up another crumbly piece of croissant. There he was, a man under fire, and an hour before he was due in the dragon's lair he was calm and collected, not even breaking a sweat. As he eased the food between her lips, she forgot she was angry at him.

"Mmmm," she sighed, and flicked her tongue out to catch a smear of jelly on his finger.

"Good, huh?" he said softly. He was standing a lot closer than he needed to.

"Uh-huh." Then she realized that she was the only one eating. "You aren't having any."

He smiled. "That's because you haven't offered me any."

She reached out and cut off a wedge of the cheese, which turned out to be cumin gouda. One of her favorite hard cheeses. Where had he been able to find this stuff at this hour in the morning?

"Private stash," he said in answer to her unspoken question.

"I see. You just happened to have heaps of my favorite food lying around, huh?"

"I was just hoarding it in case you ever gave up being mad at me long enough to come over for a meal. You haven't been to my apartment yet, you know."

If that was an apology, she thought, it was a mighty ham-handed one. "I'm mad at you because you deserve it, Chris," she said defensively.

"Why, because of what I said about you not being able to trust? I meant it. I'm sorry if I hurt you, and I didn't mean to say it in anger, but honest, honey, you need to work on your trust." He took the piece of pastry that she was offering him and laid it down on the side of the plate. Her back was to the countertop, and as he stepped forward, she took a reflexive step backward, but the counter didn't give her much room to maneuver.

She felt his mouth on her ear, soft and coaxing, and found that her inner turmoil was not enough to stop her from lifting her mouth towards his for a kiss. He tasted of jelly; he tasted of Christian. Her mouth opened to him, and swiftly and without warning the hunger in her belly transmuted into a hunger a few inches farther south.

Without even acknowledging the risk of wrinkling her neat white blouse, she allowed herself to be crushed against him. His chest was hard under the rough linen of his pale blue shirt, and as her fingers sought out the tiny peaks of his hard male nipples she felt the electricity crackle through him.

"Maybe you and I could find some time to work on this trust thing together," he whispered. "Maybe you and I can talk it out. Or *not* talk, if you like," he added suggestively, letting his hands slip around her to cup the roundness of her bottom.

Maybe it was a little too early in the morning for rational thought, she wondered giddily, but he was beginning to make sense. Or at least, the knowing probing of his tongue and the sensual coaxing of his broad hands were making sense. . . .

Under his bold touch, her entire body seemed to sigh. It had been such a long time since she'd felt the firm warm pressure of his lips, since she'd reached up to stroke his clean-shaven chin. Not since the night of the computer foul-up, in her living room, when she'd wanted him so much but spoiled it with her big mouth.

"You deserved it," she heard herself say against his mouth.

He didn't even pause from his aching kisses and kneading caresses on her warm bottom. "What's that?" he asked, but didn't stop for an answer.

It was hard to tear her concentration away from what he was doing to her ear long enough to clarify her statement. "You deserve me being mad at you, after what you did."

"What did I do this time?" he asked resignedly. His fingers, which were tracing hellfire along the line of her panties, stopped in mid-stroke. She almost wished she could take back what she'd said, just to get him to keep touching her like that.

But the spoken word had already left her lips, and she was too much woman to back down now. "I said I was right to be mad at you, after the flowers."

He tore his lips from hers and took a frustrated step away from her. "Just what is it with you and those damn flowers, Sean? Every time you open your mouth, I have to hear about these flowers. What's your problem?"

She chose not to remind him that he was the last one to have brought them up. Instead, she tried to pull her jagged senses together and answer. "What do you mean 'what's the problem'? You think I liked what you did to me?"

He looked genuinely puzzled, and seemed about to let fly an angry retort when he inhaled and tried to collect himself. Placing both hands on her shaking shoulders to steady her, he said slowly, "Sean, listen. I swear to you, I don't know anything about any flowers. Maybe the last time I was here I was a little harsh with you, and maybe I should have sent you some flowers by way of apology. I should have, honey, but I didn't. Now tell me what it was about these flowers that have you so upset."

Her brow wrinkled as she searched his face for a lie. Did he really not send them? "They were roses," she began, her stomach churning with the memory.

He smiled slightly. "And you don't like roses?"

She held up her hands. "No, no, you don't understand. They were roses, but they were dead."

His face grew serious. "What do you mean, dead?"

"Dead, Christian. Dried out and rotten. Falling apart."

His body grew tense. "Someone sent you dead flowers? Where? How?"

"They sent them to my office. By hand. In a flower box. It was all wrapped up with ribbons, and it was so pretty, and there was a card. . . ." She faltered. "I thought they were from you."

"Well, they weren't. How could you think that of me?" He looked like a little boy wrongly accused of popping a frog into his mother's underwear drawer.

She shook her head, truly ashamed of having entertained the idea. It was stupid of her to have even suspected him, much less to have believed he was guilty. "I'm sorry "

"Well, I accept your apology, but it still doesn't tell us who sent them. Who else could it have been? Just tell me, and I'll deal with him." Christian looked angry enough to go charging out to find the culprit and handle him on his own terms.

Sean tried to think, but her mind was buzzing with the surprising turn of events. This was really frightening. All the while, she believed the culprit was Christian, and was content simply to seethe with anger at him. But this was different. If it wasn't he, then who? For the first time, she was afraid.

The fear must have shown on her face, because his large hand reached up to stroke her. "Don't be scared. Think. Do you have any enemies? Have you stepped on anyone's toes lately?"

"Don't be ridiculous," she tried to dismiss the idea, but her lip trembled as she spoke. "Enemies? Why would I have any enemies?"

"Any old boyfriends?" He didn't realize it, but he was holding his breath while he waited for an answer.

She hesitated, then shook her head in the negative. "No. No one in this country, at least. I haven't dated anyone in the last few months. As for boyfriends, well, I was with someone for a while, but well, it didn't work out, so . . . that came to an end." She prayed he wouldn't probe the issue any deeper. His questions would only bring hurt to her, and shame at her incredible stupidity and poor judgment as far as men were concerned. She had done everything she could to put her last humiliating liaison behind her; why open old wounds? It was over and done with, and she had burned all her bridges as far as that accursed relationship was concerned.

Christian's eyes were on hers intently. Did he perceive

that she was being evasive? She hoped he wouldn't probe the tender scab of her last barely healed wound any farther.

Instead, he seemed to have other things on his mind. His mind went back to the dressing gown she had lent him when he first stayed here, the one that had caused him a twinge of jealousy. "The dressing gown," he muttered to himself. "In your bathroom."

"What?" she frowned into his eyes.

"Nothing. It isn't important. I was just wondering. . . ."

She finally caught on. "If the dressing gown I lent you was his? Oh, yeah. He sort of left it behind." *Don't ask any more questions,* she silently telegraphed. *I couldn't bear it if you knew the truth.* Then her hazel eyes flickered upwards to Christian's face, becoming shrewd. She'd picked up a tone in his voice that she hadn't heard before, not from him. Was he jealous, she wondered? Wouldn't *that* be different! Usually *she* was jealous of *him!*

Christian steered the subject away from her love life. "Could it have come to you by mistake?"

"I doubt it. It was addressed to me by name, and came by messenger to the office. I don't see how it could have been a mix-up." Considering the alternatives, it would have been nice to think that it hadn't been meant for her, but she was wise enough to know that such an explanation was hardly likely.

"Maybe it was just a dumb practical joke." Christian offered hopefully. It seemed doubtful, but in the face of a total lack of evidence, he was willing to grasp at straws.

She sighed heavily. "I hope so. I hope it's nothing more serious than that."

He clasped her to him and vigorously rubbed his hands up and down her shoulders. "Look, Sean, honey. It's getting late. We both have to get to work. But I promise you, as soon as we have the time, we'll get together and work on this, all right? But meanwhile, stop worrying. Think about who it could have come from, but don't worry, you're not in any danger. The person who sent them might be twisted, but I doubt they're dangerous. They might just be trying to scare you." He planted a light kiss on her forehead. "Don't worry. Okay?"

She was glad he was there to hold onto, and didn't want to let go. She had to, though, so she did, and began reluctantly gathering up her things. "We never got to finish breakfast," she said sorrowfully.

He gave a soft laugh. "Don't worry. We'll have breakfast together again soon. When we both have time to enjoy it." There was something in his voice that implied that he didn't intend to turn up at her house for breakfast, but would be content to simply wake up to it, together, with her. An answering voice deep inside her told her she wouldn't be too averse to the scenario herself.

But there was still something between them that bothered her, and she had to get it out of her system. "Chris?" she began tentatively.

He turned to look at her. "Yes, honey?"

He always used to call her honey. On his lips, the trite endearment became warm, soothing, and sensuous. "I just wanted to tell you . . ." Oh, apologies were so hard sometimes! ". . . I wanted to tell you that I'm sorry for what I said, about you causing that computer foul-up last week."

He regarded her with his jet eyes for a long time. "Thank you. That means a lot to me." He considered her for a while longer, then turned towards the door.

She put a hand out to stop him. "That's not all. I wanted you to know that I never, not for a second, thought that you might be responsible for last night's . . . accident."

The corners of his beautiful mouth curved upwards. "Thank you. Thank you for your faith in me."

She took the smile, and his gratitude, and hugged it to her chest, allowing it to keep her warm throughout the rest of the day. She didn't need to answer. Quickly, she gathered up a few large, ripe bananas and made her way outside to her garden fence.

"Feeding your birds," he observed.

"Uh-huh. They're only getting bananas this morning, I'm all out of mangoes and papayas." She impaled each banana on a sharp prong along the fence, and was immediately greeted by the chirps and cheeps of the assortment of winged creatures that populated her garden.

"I'm sure they don't mind," he reassured her. "They're just glad to know you're looking out for them."

He followed her out the front, and as she paused to lock her door, she felt him toying with a lock of her hair with one finger.

"You look different today," he murmured. "A nice kind of different. Did you change your makeup?"

She gave him a baleful glance.

"Cut your hair?" He tried again.

She smiled mysteriously and tugged her freshly colored hair out of his grasp. *Men!* she thought.

"You and your men, they done cleaned and tested all the guns?" the Prophetess wanted to know.

Her first lieutenant looked proud of himself. "Everything ready. The troops posted in the north and south, and some of the Elders busy moving the women and children to the safe houses." Like her, he spoke in the thick heavy accent of the island.

"An' the animals, what about them?"

"We leaving the animals here at the temple 'til we ready to strike. Afterwards, if we successful. . . ."

The Prophetess cut him off with a stinging slap across the mouth. She was a huge woman, even heavier than he was, and her blow, coming as a surprise, left him giddy. "Not *if* we successful, man! *When* we successful! It ain't have no ifs here! We guided by the Goddess, and she tell me our mission bound not to fail! You understand me?"

The lieutenant could feel the spray of saliva on his face as the angry woman took him to task. He was too ashamed of his lack of faith to answer with more than a slight nod.

"We is the chosen ones! We is the ones to bring them infidels to they knees. This government going to feel we power. When we bring them down, and when the President dead, they will know who we is! Let the fools and them laugh at us and say we crazy. Let them call we cultists, or freaks, or whatever they want. When we in control they will know just how mighty is the name of the Goddess!"

The lieutenant shivered in the face of her anger. Everyone feared the Prophetess, including him. Even her *consorts* feared her. She was capable of crippling a man with a simple curse. He had heard rumors that she could make goats stop in their tracks and fall over dead at a word from her. She wasn't a woman to cross. She was certainly not a woman to anger.

The huge dark woman wiped sweat from her face with a flap of her head-wrap and began stomping along the length of her reception hall. Her heavy flat feet thudded on the unpolished wooden floor.

"Get your men into position. I want final confirmation that you ready to bring down the television and radio stations . . . all of them . . . at my command. Make sure the safe houses stocked with enough food for a month. If you don't have the money for that, thief it."

"Yes, Prophetess." He nodded vigorously, anxious to make up for his *faux pas* by proving his efficiency.

"And the young men you planted in the city, let them know this . . ." She paused and drew in a sharp breath through her broad, flat nostrils.

"Yes?" He waited. The men in the city were the crucial ones. They were the linchpin of their attack; they were the ones who were being prepared to put their plan into action and bring down the President.

"Let them know that the time is right. Tell them for me that we going to strike in three days, on Friday afternoon, when the President giving a speech at the new wing of the orphanage."

He faltered, eyes bugging with shock. "But Prophetess, Friday so early! Why not wait a few more weeks? And the orphanage, it full of children, one of them could get hurt. . . ."

She stilled him with an angry glare. "The children of the infidels isn't no concern of mine. And besides, I thought you said your men ready?" The steel in her voice told him he was treading on very dangerous ground.

"Of course, of course we ready," he faltered. "But a week or two more, just for practice, can't do we any harm!"

"A few more weeks and we purpose might get cold. Plus he will be a' easy target at the orphanage, is not like there going to be any heavy security or nothing. Is the perfect time to act. Tell them we strike on Friday. If you not prepared to work with me. . . ."

There was no need for her to enunciate her threat. He had seen what she was capable of doing by watching her effect punishment on other young men of the Family. He shuddered. "No, no. Friday will be the day. I will tell me men."

She nodded and turned her back on him in dismissal. "Let it be so," she said, and did not speak again.

Christian was tired. He rubbed his eyes and looked over his personal copy of his report. *If you could call it that,* he thought derisively. After two days of investigation, of questioning every single man in his department whether he was on shift on the day of the accident or not, all he could come up with was a mass of speculation and conjecture.

All of his hypotheses led inevitably to one possibility: sabotage.

Even the word left a bitter taste in his mouth. Infiltration of the plant by an outsider was impossible; security and safety measures made sure that no unauthorized person got past Head Office without the knowledge and consent of the company. That could only mean one thing: someone within Orion had betrayed him. Out of an employee field of over a hundred people, finding out who it was would be close to impossible.

He dropped the report on his desk. He had come in at dawn and e-mailed it in its entirety to Ms. Gooding, and had also taken the precaution of personally placing a hard copy on her desk in a sealed envelope addressed to her eyes only.

Then he had begun to wait. The day moved slowly, and by midday he was going out of his mind, sitting in his office and staring at the clock. In order to get his mind off the wait he had gone out with his men on a routine testing exercise, which involved removing samples of methanol kept in the huge tanks down at the plant and sending them for testing. He had done some of the tests himself, lowering small empty bottles into the tanks and drawing them out, sealing them and sending them for analysis. It was hot, strenuous work, but it was better to be out of the office than remain inside, sweating.

Now, at almost quitting time on Friday afternoon, he hadn't heard anything from her. Her prolonged silence left him uneasy. He considered calling and inviting himself into her office to discuss the report, but his instinct told him that this was a woman who liked to call the shots; she wouldn't take kindly to an underling deciding when and where she would meet him.

"Call, dammit," he said to the silent phone. It was the weekend, and taking into consideration the bitch of a week he'd had, all he wanted to do was get their little interview over with and go home. Maybe he'd take Sean out.

As the image of her came to his mind, a soft smile crept up on his face. He missed her. He couldn't deny that in spite of her prickly response to him, he was growing more and more fond of her. It was funny, after having spent so many years putting her out of his mind, shoving her somewhere into the dark reaches of his memory where she couldn't do him any harm, it was now as if he were meeting her for the first time.

It was a first time for both of them, he realized; the adults they had become were almost different people from the children they had been. When he looked at the new, grown-up Sean, he liked what he saw. He wondered if she liked what *she* saw. Was there any way to find out? Maybe this weekend they'd have a little time to talk things over. He wasn't ashamed to admit that he wanted to be with her, but he only wanted her if she was willing to come to him with a trusting heart. The fact that she was willing to believe him on the issue of the industrial accidents was good, but if she would only be willing to believe him on the more painful issue, the one that had caused their breakup, well, that would be a little harder to achieve.

The phone obeyed his command and began to beep obligingly. He snatched it up. "Devane," he said.

"Chris?"

It was Sean. She didn't sound good. "Sean?"

"Yes." She sounded like a lost child, and the fear in her voice was evident.

"What's the matter? Is something wrong?"

"My birds," she began, and then disintegrated into sobs.

His entreaties for her to explain were drowned out by her crying. Instead of pushing her, he let her cry, murmuring soothing words into the phone and wishing he could be there with her rather than hanging on inadequately to a stupid phone, twenty miles away. After an awful eternity she quieted down.

"Tell me," he urged gently.

"They killed them. My birds. All of them."

His mouth dried. "Who killed them?"

"I don't know. I just got home and went into the garden. And they were lying on the grass, all over. Dead."

"How, Sean?" His imagination conjured up for him images of bloodied, butchered carcasses.

"I don't know. I think it's the fruit. They poisoned it. My poor babies. . . ." she disintegrated into more sobs.

Christian stood to his feet and began shoving papers into his briefcase. This was nonsense. He wasn't about to sit around and wait on Gooding to deign to call, not while Sean was in such obvious pain. She had his pager and his cell numbers, dammit. She could find him when she wanted him.

"Sean, honey, I'm on my way over. I'll be there in ten minutes, okay?"

She sniffled like a little girl. "Okay." Her voice was distant and muffled.

He hung up and began shucking off his safety gear. The phone beeped impatiently at him again. Snatching it up, he began to offer his assurances that he was on his way. "Sean, baby. . . ."

"Andrea Gooding." The cool, clipped voice cut him dead.

He plopped back into his seat. *Great timing, lady,* he thought dryly. "Yes, Ms. Gooding."

"Christian, when I hired you, I did so with every good intention. Your resumé and references were impeccable, and your reputation preceded you."

He frowned, not liking the woman's warm-up. What was she getting at?

Before he could ask, she continued. "But I would like you to know that I am not in the least bit satisfied by your performance recently. It's bad enough that the company seems to have suffered some terrible mishaps under your watch. This, I can understand, even if I don't like it. Accidents will happen. . . ."

This was no accident, he wanted to say, but instead continued to listen, mesmerized by her frosty voice as he would have been by the flicking tongue of a venomous snake.

"But if there is one thing I will not accept, it is insubordination. You and I had the understanding that you were to have delivered the report I requested to me at the open of business hours this morning. I've been patient enough to allow you several more hours today, without bothering you, but really, Christian, your failure to deliver has me wondering about the wisdom of the company's decision. . . ."

Christian recovered from the shock enough to interrupt her. "Ms. Gooding, are you saying that you haven't received my report?"

"That's exactly what I'm saying. And I wish to advise you that the President has been notified of my dissatisfaction. A copy of that memo has been forwarded to you."

His shock caused him to raise his voice, even though she was his superior. "Ms. Gooding, I e-mailed that report to you at seven this morning. I placed the original hard copy on your desk! Haven't you received either one?"

"I'd appreciate your lowering your voice, young man." Her voice traveled across the line on a puff of frosty air. "I've received nothing. I asked my secretary repeatedly today if anything had arrived from you. I called for you and was told that you had gone jaunting off down at the plant."

Jaunting? He recalled the sweaty hours he had spent up on top of a tank of fluid as explosive as dynamite, and would have liked to protest, but instead said in a calm voice: "Ms. Gooding, just give me a few seconds, I'll e-mail you another copy."

"If you insist," she said in tones that made it clear that she didn't believe that there had ever been a first e-mail.

He quickly brought up his e-mail software and opened his Sent Mail folder, with the intention of simply sending off the report a second time. It wasn't there. He sucked his breath in sharply.

"I'm not seeing anything coming up on my screen, Christian," Gooding harped.

"Ms. Gooding . . ." he searched frantically through his mail folders. Nothing. He opened up his word processing software and called up the file. 'File not found,' the wretched machine taunted. He checked his file manager. Nothing.

"Christian." The single soft word spoke volumes of threat.

"One moment, Ma'am. I can't seem to locate it."

The response was sarcastic. "Oh. You can't seem to locate it. Are you sure it actually existed?"

He couldn't believe what she was accusing him of. He set the phone down on his desk with a silent apology, in order to let himself concentrate. Clicking open his computer's recycle bin was his last hope: if someone had deleted his data, a copy of it would automatically go there. The bin was empty. He sucked in a sharp breath.

"I'm waiting," a tinny voice reminded him.

He snatched up the phone. "Ms. Gooding, something seems to have gone wrong with my data. . . ." How was he going to explain this?

"More computer trouble?" she asked softly.

"No, I mean the document has been deleted. Nothing else, just this. It's been completely erased from my drive."

The woman gave a skeptical snort. "Come now, you don't expect me to believe . . ."

"That's exactly what I do expect you to believe, Ma'am. Someone was in here while I was down on the plant and erased my report."

"And now you have nothing," she provided softly, seemingly undisturbed at the idea of an intruder.

"Actually, I have a copy right here." Thank God he was fastidious enough to keep personal copies of everything that passed through his hands! "I'll be over in five minutes with a copy of that."

"You have a copy?" she sucked in a breath, evidently surprised that the document existed elsewhere than in Christian's imagination.

Christian smiled tightly in satisfaction, imagining the look on the woman's face. For some inexplicable reason, she had been willing to sentence him without a trial, but he'd survived her attack in one piece. Deftly hanging up, he strode over to the copier and tore the report viciously out of its bindings. He didn't like what his mind was telling him. All along, ever since he became aware of the reality of sabotage, he had been convinced that the perpetrator had been holding a grudge against the company. Now, he had evidence to the contrary; there was a saboteur, alright, but the person was bearing a grudge against *him*.

But why? He'd been in the island less than two months, and a few weeks of those he'd been in bed, wounded. That left less than a month in which he'd obviously ticked someone off. Who, he couldn't imagine. But while he was figuring it out, he thought grimly, he would have to watch his back.

He delivered the photocopy of the report to Gooding with a curt nod. She took it without looking at it, dropped it in her bag and murmured darkly about getting back to him on it. As for that memo she'd sent to the President, well, they'd sort it all out next week. After the damage had been done, Christian thought sourly. He held the door open for her as she left without another word.

He churned out of the parking lot and sped onto the highway. It was a full twenty minutes since he'd told Sean he was leaving. He didn't like the idea of her being home alone, not as frightened and upset as she sounded on the phone. His able BMW easily ate up the undulating highway, speeding through the miles of towering cane. All he could hope for was that he didn't encounter a navy blue and white highway patrol car on the way, as they had a reputation for taking a speeder to task, humiliating him even before giving him a ticket.

As he drove his mind churned with resentment. He'd grown up in poverty, one of two sons. His brother, the elder child, had struggled his way through life to become a dentist. His brother's generosity had gone a long way towards helping him make it through school, but he had had to rely on brains and determination to pit himself against thousands in order to earn the many scholarships that had seen him all the way through to graduate school. His grinding stint as an army engineer and the years that followed as he moved from one private enterprise to another had allowed him to gain the knowledge and skill that ensured that his reputation in the industry was one of the best, even for a young man of thirty-two.

And now some unidentified person, for some absolutely inexplicable reason, was trying to take that all away from him. Why? And what about Sean? First, a box of dead flowers, now dead birds. They were both under attack; that was certain. But were their plights related or had they made separate enemies? The puzzle confounded him.

The buzzing of his cell phone drew his mind back to the present. He flipped it open, wondering if Sean was despairing of his ever coming. "Hello?"

"Hey, big man." The Jamaican on the other end of the line was in a playful mood. "You finish that big bad report yet?"

"Delta." Damn. Not now.

"That's me. I was thinking, you must have been working so hard all week, poor baby, I was thinking you might be in the mood for a little relaxation. How about you and me go somewhere out west for a drink? They have the best nightclubs out on the west coast. You haven't been there yet, have you?"

Was she joking? Since he'd arrived, he hadn't had the chance to be *anywhere*. "No, but I can't make it tonight."

"Don't tell me you have other plans, you hear!" the voice sounded petulant, with a germ of anger.

"That's just what I do have, Delta. I appreciate the invitation, but. . . ."

"But what? You can't change your plans? Just for tonight?" The voice dropped an octave. "We don't have to go *out* if you don't want to, you know. . . ."

At any other time the unsubtle invitation would have been amusing, if not titillating, but today, the only person on his mind was Sean. "I've got to go see Sean," he said, wondering why he was explaining his actions to Delta. "She needs me right now."

"Why?" Delta asked acidly. "Someone sent her more dead flowers?"

Christian felt the hair on his scalp prickle. "That's unkind," he chastised her.

"What's unkind is you leaving me on a Friday night without any company," she whined.

"I've got to go, Delta. We'll talk tomorrow, okay?" All he wanted to do was get the woman off the phone.

"Don't blame me if one day you wish you hadn't," she cooed. She hung up.

He skated into the driveway of Sean's apartment, pulling up next to her Volvo and had barely locked the car door when Sean pelted outside and took hold of his arm. Streaks marred her makeup, and her beautiful eyes were swollen from crying. Her soft curls were escaping the barrettes that tried to hold them back, flying wild about her shoulders. The sight of her pain and distress moved him deeply.

"Come here," he said softly, and she went willingly into his arms. He let his fingers roam in the dense forest of hair until they found the vulnerable nape of her neck, which he cradled like a wounded animal. At his gentle touch, her tears began anew, and he held her, feeling their warm wetness as they soaked through his shirt and met his shoulder. He held her for a long time until her crying subsided to breathless shudders.

"Let's go into the back yard," he coaxed. "You can show me what happened."

She stared up at him with wide eyes, not seeming to absorb what he was saying.

As he looked into their wet hazel depths, his heart expanded. The reaction was so sudden and so violent that at first he was afraid that he would never be able to draw another full breath. It was as if all the hardness and bitterness that he had shored up within him for this woman suddenly burst up and out of him, and all that was in him was tenderness, desire, and an urge—no, a duty—to protect her. Driven by the power of these emotions, he bent his head and kissed her lightly on her trembling mouth.

Her lips were like petals, soft, velvety, moistened by the dew of her tears. A sigh escaped him as he slid his hands under her chin to tilt her head gently backwards so he could better explore her mouth. Her taste was different, her scent was different, the feel of the delicate skin under his tongue, the softness and the shape of her lips . . . it was as if she had been transformed into a whole new woman.

No, he reminded himself. She hadn't been transformed. He had. In the few short moments that he had held her to him his perception of her had radically changed. The innocent, defensive young girl that he once knew and the vexatious, confused woman that he later saw her to be had been changed in his own perception into a woman who was desirable yet defensive, self-possessed yet childlike, strong yet fragile. He was seeing her as his soul was telling him that she was a warm, beautiful, lovable woman. The thought took his breath away. He stopped kissing her and just stared at her face.

"Come out back and see," she said, breaking the spell. "See what somebody did to them."

He allowed himself to be led by the hand, glad for the distraction. His confused thoughts were a little too much for him to deal with right now. The light was just beginning to fade. The swiftly falling Caribbean sun tinted the peach of her apartment walls, the gray flagstones of her path, and every bush and every plant a sweet warm rose hue. At the far end of the garden, along the same fence where she used to stick fresh fruit for the birds to come and eat during the day, a small sad heap lay on the ground.

He dropped to one knee. A dozen birds were laid tenderly side by side along the fence. There were a few ground doves, one brown, one speckled russet and white, and one slate gray. There were larger black ones with brilliant yellow breasts; their vibrant colors mocked the death that had them in its grasp. These he knew to be keskidees. There were some he couldn't identify, small black and yellow birds with fat round bellies and bright black eyes.

"Bananaquits," she said sadly. "And that's a finch. And two parakeets."

Gingerly, he lifted one of the tiny bodies. A small crimson jewel of blood spotted the beak. He was no vet, but he was sure that bleeding through the air holes in its beak was almost a certain sign of poison. The birds had died horribly.

"I found them all over the garden," Sean informed him. "And there's no telling how many died outside the fence."

"What did you feed them?"

She reached out and handed him the shell of a large papaya. It had been hollowed out by the ravenous birds which, tempted by the succulent flesh, had literally eaten themselves to death. The inside of the fruit should have been a bright salmon-pink; instead, it was tinged with black, and a slightly chemical smell emanated from it. Sadly, he set the fruit down.

She was watching his face anxiously. "What do you think?"

He nodded in agreement with her diagnosis. "Poison."

She was still staring at his face, as if she were waiting on him to make it all better. The hope in her eyes hurt his heart. He could do many things, but as for making her feel better right now, right here, he just didn't see how that was possible. He wasn't Superman.

"I'll bury them before it gets dark," he offered. He got abruptly to his feet in an effort to avoid her pleading gaze. "Show me where you keep your shovel and pitchfork."

Silently, she walked off to a corner of the garden to find him the tools he needed. As she did so, Christian spotted a tiny object on the part of the flagstone path that veered close to the fence. It was so small that by rights he should never have seen it, but the bright orange glow of the setting sun glinted on it, drawing his attention to it. He picked it up and held it in his hand.

It was a small piece of gold foil, imprinted with a red crest. It could have been anything, a candy wrapper, a bit of decoration from some bauble or the other, or piece of the wrapping off a cigar. He sniffed it, but it was so small that he wasn't sure if the smell of tobacco was part of the foil or part of his imagination. He slipped it into his pocket. He'd ask Sean about it later.

He made quick work of burying the tragic corpses in the soft earth. When the poisoned fruit had similarly been disposed of, he put the tools away and coaxed her inside.

She clutched his hand childishly. "The garden will never sound the same," she mourned.

He pulled her to him and gave her a hug. "There'll be more birds, Sean. They'll wander into your garden, just like the others did. In a few weeks, you'll never know it happened."

"I'll always remember it happened," she countered. "Who could have done this to me? Why? What have I done?"

He'd been wondering the same thing for both their sakes, but he thought it wiser not to bring the subject up in her present state. Instead, he led her upstairs to her room. "We'll put our heads together and work something out later," he promised. "Right now you need to relax."

She followed him meekly into her bathroom, where she allowed him to begin tugging at the buttons on her blouse. "Come," he said softly.

Obediently, she allowed him to slide her blouse down her shoulders, even let him unhook and unzip her skirt and ease it down her hips, so that she was standing only in her underwear. Instinctively, though, she balked as he reached for the clasp on her bra.

"Take it easy," he whispered. "I only want you to feel better."

Her hesitation melted away and he undid the small clasp at the front of her bra. As he did so, the backs of his fingers encountered the soft spice-toned skin of her breasts, causing her to draw her breath sharply inward. He eased the creamy satin material out of the way and then the weight of her full breasts was against his hand. He slid his palm under the left one, reveling in the wonderful weight and firmness of it, admiring the brandy-hued tip which, under his awed gaze, began to tighten and sharpen as if by magic.

"Ah, beauty," he sighed heavily, and dipped his head to take it between his lips. Her skin was like velvet, her nipple like a diamond in the rough. His tongue swirled around it, drawing it tenderly in, bathing it as he sucked ever so slightly. Then, reluctantly, he released it and allowed his lips to move upwards along the soft topside of her breast. Her heart thumped rapidly, reverberating through the soft flesh to beat out an impatient tattoo against his mouth.

He looked up at her face, hoping against hope that he would see the desire and longing that he felt for her mirrored in her own eyes. The recognition of her mute desire caused a joyful leap in his chest and a tightening in his groin. *Slowly,* he thought. She was like one of the poor birds in her garden, beautiful but frail and easily frightened. He needed to proceed with extreme care. For all he wanted to grasp her by the arms and sink down onto the bathroom rug with her beneath him, he knew he had to pace himself, soothe her and win her confidence, so that she would come to him willingly. If he forced the point now, she would very likely give in to him, but it would be a hollow victory. What would it profit him to win her now, only to lose her as she woke in the morning to face her regrets?

He eased around her and turned on the bathwater. She watched him silently, not bothering to draw her hands up to cover her exposed breasts, as he rummaged through her collection of bath salts, lotions and oils until he selected one of her aromatherapy bath gels, a combination of sage, rosewood and mandarin whose label promised relaxation. Well, he thought, relaxation was what he was looking for. He poured a generous amount under the stream of hot water and watched the suds form.

"Come," he said comfortingly. "Let's get you in the bath." Kneeling before her, he hooked his thumbs into the waistband of her panties and then looked up at her inscrutable face, searching for signs of resistance or encouragement. Finding nothing, he took her silence for consent. The panties were made of the same creamy satin material as her bra. They were trimmed with tiny ribbons, and cut high on her smooth unblemished hips. He remembered with fondness the cotton briefs the girl of yesterday had worn in college; the woman of today had more refined tastes.

He slid the panties slowly downwards, like an artist unveiling a piece of work; it was too delicious to be done quickly. As his fingers brushed her haunches, they quivered like a filly's. Over her hips, they went, past her knees, until his tingling fingers let them fall in a glossy pile at her feet.

His mouth was suddenly dry. The plump triangle that stood precisely within his line of vision mesmerized him. The dark brown curls that modestly covered it glistened with a hint of moisture; proof positive that she was as affected by being touched as he was by touching her. Her scent wafted towards him like delicate fingers, teasing his nostrils, causing him to flick his tongue out to wet his lips.

She was enchanting. He longed to bury his face between her smooth thighs with a groan, tilt his face upward and feed on her. *Easy,* he cautioned himself. *Not so fast. Don't spoil this.*

In spite of his own admonitions, he was moved to place a light kiss upon her silky lips, felt the electric crackle of her dark hair, and it was all he could do to prevent himself from grasping her glorious round bottom and pulling her close enough to fully engulf her with his mouth.

Her breath came in sharp stabs. "Chris," she moaned. Her thighs quivered under his hands.

"I know," he groaned.

"No," she panted. "It's the water. The tub. . . ."

The water had long passed the high mark and was threatening to spill over, as the overflow valve was overwhelmed by the pace at which the tub was filling. He sprang towards it, ignoring the sharp pain that such an action caused his painfully engorged crotch. He turned off the water and motioned to her to step in.

"Come, get in and relax. You don't have to do anything. I'm here."

Sean seemed only too willing. She slid into the warm

water with a grateful sigh. Christian rolled up his sleeves
and busied himself with the delightful task of soaping her
all over, hands lingering at her throat, her breasts, her
delicious round belly and her slippery thighs.

The warmth of the water was itself a caress. Not trusting
himself to let his hand rest too long between her legs,
he reluctantly moved farther down her legs, only to be
surprised by her own hand, which grasped his firmly and
led it back to the crux of her thighs.

Her head was tilted backwards, her neck resting against
the pale lemon porcelain, hair twisted up out of the reach
of the water, except for a few tendrils that floated among
the suds like seaweed. Her eyes were squeezed tightly shut,
as if she refused to acknowledge what her hand was doing.

Christian could feel the pulsating warmth of her desire,
could hear the slight irregularity of her breathing, and
wanted nothing more than to give her what she wanted.
What he wasn't prepared to do, though, was to allow her
to shut him out, reduce his caress to a localized stimulus
that would bring her pleasure, even release, without having
to acknowledge him. He leaned closer to her, close enough
for his mouth to brush her ear, and as his hand insinuated
itself between her tautly muscled thighs, he whispered:
"Open your eyes, Sean. You have to look at me. It's not
much good if you try to forget I'm here, too."

Her dark-lashed eyelids fluttered open, and eyes that
were now more dark brown than hazel held his, first shyly,
then, as his questing fingers began to work their magic,
with more boldness. Her gaze drew him in as surely as the
slick, muscled sheath drew in his large fingers. He experi-
mented with the pace of his probing until he hit upon a
speed that made her hips buck under the water, and her
belly came up hard against his forearm. "That's right," he
encouraged her, "just lie back and take all you want."

He was almost as soaked as she was, as he leaned even
farther over the tub to position his hand so that his

thumb found and applied pressure to the throbbing bead at the apex of her entrance. As he touched her she let out a sharp, surprised cry. He never gave her the chance to prepare herself for her orgasm; he drove home his advantage with dexterity, and her cry turned into a musical wail as her entire body stiffened and lifted itself almost fully out of the water. He watched the gamut of emotions race across her sweet face: surprise, resistance, delight and joy. The tremors went on and on, and Christian knew that she wouldn't cease her trembling, and that her wonderful sheath wouldn't stop its convulsive clasping of his fingers until he himself took mercy on her and stopped the movement of his fingers.

By the time he eventually withdrew his hand, her breathing was labored, and her color heightened to a deep flush that made her face glow with a fire from within. Her body, which was arched as though electrified, grew limp and flopped into the water with a splash that wet the carpet, and whatever parts of him that were still dry.

He put both arms around her and held her as she struggled to breathe regularly again, kissing her damp brow and her wet, swollen lips. He held her close, murmuring endearments against her damp hair until the water began to get cold, then he helped her out of the bath and wrapped her in a big spongy towel.

He patted her dry with infinite care, squeezing the water out of her sodden hair. As he did so, he realized they were standing in front of her full-length mirror. He turned her by the shoulders until she faced it.

"See how beautiful you are?" he told her softly.

Sean lifted her damp lashes and took in her reflection. Her body was lush, and taut with excitement. Her skin glowed with pleasure that had not quite been satiated. She stared as if she were seeing herself for the first time, and then slowly her lips curved into a smile. It thrilled him to see her own appreciation of her nakedness.

The excitement that she had aroused within him climbed even higher. While she had achieved some measure of release, he had not, and he could feel the tension in his loins as the hot blood throbbed there. He pushed his hips forward so that the rough tented material of his trousers brushed her round behind.

"You're wet," she observed.

"That I am," he smiled.

"Well, why don't you get out of those wet clothes before you catch a cold?" The sly look that she gave his reflection from under her long dewdrop-laden lashes told him that concern for his health had played only a small part in prompting her suggestion. He did not hesitate.

As soon as he was naked, he returned to his place behind her, slid his arms around her and watched their reflection intently. His deep bittersweet chocolate skin threw her lighter spice tones into contrast, but together they melded into a glorious landscape of hills and valleys, shadow and light. Her eyes were on the bulging muscles of his arms, shoulders and chest, and he found her unabashed appreciation of him delightful.

Of its own accord, his erection, heavy with anticipation and long abstinence, found its way between her thighs, probing like a curious and insistent serpent. As the smooth rounded head brushed against the tight curls between her legs she quivered, but parted her thighs ever so slightly.

Christian needed no more encouragement. He let the towel drop to the floor and gently guided her hands to the bathroom countertop so that she could brace herself for him. She shut her eyes against the onslaught to come, and obeyed. As her head dipped forward, he could look down at the now naked nape of her neck. He ran his tongue along its curve, flicking lightly at the short, soft, baby curls there.

Below, his questing organ echoed his movements,

searching and finding. From his position behind her she was unbearably tight, but her slick wetness made it easy to slip into her. When they were fully joined, pressing skin against skin, there arose in him such a sudden and violent tremor that he was forced to remain completely motionless, and to lean forward and rest his hot cheek against her back in order to contain himself.

He lifted his head and caught sight of them in the mirror again, and urged her to do the same. "Look at us, Sean. Isn't it beautiful?"

She raised her eyes and met his in the mirror. Her face was the picture of rapture. She was just able to gasp out her agreement before her body took over. Christian was almost thrown back and out of her by the sudden force of her backward thrusts. He felt the firm muscles of her bottom hitting his thighs and the grasping of her insides which closed around him like a determined fist, and responded by joining with her, picking up her urgent timing. All the while their eyes were locked in the mirror, each in silent competition to out-hold the other's gaze even to the final moment when their movements became so frenetic that bottles and cosmetics were sent crashing down from the countertop.

When the surge of power hit them, it was like a blow to the head, he realized he wasn't breathing, but the prolonged, anguished cry that forced out from between his lips would let no breath past. His heart hammered in his chest, and with his hand over Sean's breast he could feel that she was also experiencing the same turbulence. A gush of warmth from within her soaked his thighs, and her inner grip grew even tighter than he had thought possible. He was convinced that to remain joined to her like this would mean certain death, but so help him, he didn't care. All he could do was cling to her and hope the storm would pass.

Eventually, it did, and she became limp in his arms. It

was difficult enough bearing his own exhausted weight, but to bear hers as well was a manful task indeed. Giddily they sought refuge in her bedroom, and the handful of yards' distance seemed almost impossible to cross.

They flopped onto her bed, among the books and papers that she had scattered there, too tired to brush them aside. They were silent for a long time. Sean slept. As he hoisted himself up on one arm and watched her, the ebbing of his sexual tension allowed him to think clearly again. What he realized startled him.

He loved her. Not in the way he had loved her before, when they were both dumb kids with no true knowledge of the world. Not with simple sexual desire or admiration of her pretty face or the supposition that she would make a good wife and give him pretty babies. That was the old Christian's thinking.

The man that he had grown into loved her spirit, her fire, her vulnerability, her generosity and her warmth. He loved her even when she was mad at him, even when she doubted him. It was a love that went above and beyond even those serious but reparable complications. He traced her damp brow with his knuckle, then kissed it. Her nose wrinkled in her sleep but she did not wake.

Christian sighed heavily. Okay. He loved her. Now what? In spite of what they had just shared, how did she feel about him? He was worldly-wise enough to know that good sex did not translate into love, and that even a woman as particular about her mate as Sean was would not immediately interpret sex as love, or expect him to do so. What to do? He knew that somewhere inside she carried a wound that prevented her from fully trusting anyone. How would he convince her to at least give him a chance?

Beside him on her bedside table, the phone rang urgently. Sean stirred. Not wanting her to wake so soon, Christian reached down and yanked the plug from the wall. Then he curled his body around her, cradled her head in his hands, and drifted off.

Ten

Sean awoke to almost total darkness. Only a silver blade of light slashed through the dark from the crack of her bathroom door. Beside her, almost on top of her, actually, Christian slept. She lay in silence, feeling the weight of his head and shoulders rise on her breasts with every indrawn breath. Although her right arm and shoulder were cramping from the pressure that had long cut off her circulation, she was reluctant to move him if there was any chance that such an action might cause him to wake.

She stretched her legs out languorously, and tried to encourage the flow of blood into her arm by opening and closing her fist. All around them was the dizzying smell of sweat, sex and scented soap. Her bare skin vibrated with an electrical charge that ran right through her and around them both. She glanced down at the top of Christian's head with a slight smile. There was no doubt that what they had just shared was the most unbelievable sexual experience of her life.

The chill of despondency did not hesitate to fall upon her at that thought. So what of it? The sex had been transcendental. But what else was there between them? Good sex did not necessarily mean what one hoped it meant. She had no doubt that a man like Christian would have acquired more than a few sexual flourishes in his life. She had not objected when he had used them on her, but to tell the truth, that was pretty much all that it was: good sex. With all the sincerity of his words and the intensity of his touch, she knew that coming from him there was no greater emotion involved than a desire to possess her and, perhaps, a need to stroke his own ego by bending her body to his sensual will.

She shrugged, forgetting that he was still resting on her shoulder. In his sleep, he moved obligingly aside, freeing her. Taking advantage of her liberty, she sat up, feeling the blood course into her arm with the prickle of stinging nettles. She almost laughed at her own disappointment. What did she expect? Love?

She had loved him once, a silly little-girl love that she suspected he had never really returned, except on an equally juvenile footing. True love, true unselfish God-inspired love had never played a part in that, so why should she expect any of that now? And besides, she had no intention of loving him back, even if he did. She'd promised herself, hadn't she? There was no one she could rely upon to protect her; her protection lay in her own hands.

She threw her legs over the side of the bed; the mixture of satiation and exhaustion made her limbs feel like sandbags. With her wide hips gently swaying, she walked like an animal who had just eaten a satisfying meal into the bathroom where she pulled on her brilliant rose-covered satin kimono, avoiding the reflection of the sleepy-eyed, sexually sated woman in the mirror. The evidence of their abandon was scattered all over the bathroom floor. She gathered her bottles, bath salts, makeup and hair ornaments and tossed them carelessly onto the counter. She'd arrange them later.

Her thoughts had just begun turning to food when she became vaguely aware of a shrill buzzing in the room below her feet. It finally dawned on her that it was her phone. She frowned. Why wasn't her bedroom extension ringing? Not even thinking to check the phone by the bed, she sped barefooted out of her room and down the stairs, snatching up her living room phone on what must have been the hundredth ring.

"Yes?" she managed to say breathlessly.

"Where the hell have you been?" Delta shrieked.

Sean stared at the phone, more than a little taken aback. What right did Delta have to inquire so imperiously as to her whereabouts? She was about to tell her so when the high-pitched voice went on. "I've been looking all over for you! I've been ringing you for ages! And I've been calling Christian, and I can't find him, either."

"Christian is with me," she said, before she could ponder the wisdom of the revelation.

There was a pause. "I see." She could hear Delta's erratic breathing into the mouthpiece.

"Delta?" The woman still hadn't stated the reason for her call.

"Turn on your TV," Delta said abruptly, and clicked off.

Sean held the dead phone in her hand and stared at it. Why had Delta seemed so insistent on tracking them down? And why was it so important to her to know if Christian was with her? There was no doubt that she was attracted to Christian. He was a man of varied tastes, she remembered wryly; in all likelihood, he returned the compliment. But Delta had sounded almost distraught.

Could it be that the unspoken (and barely acknowledged) rivalry between them for his attention had finally pushed the high-strung Jamaican woman over the edge? Images flashed across her mind in quick succession, over and over, like a strobe. One image featured a box of dead roses. The other, a dozen dead birds, laid out in a row.

Sean sat down abruptly with the phone still clutched to her. Was she going mad, or could Delta have been the one responsible for those atrocities? Could she really have meant to take revenge for Christian's obvious interest in such a ghoulish manner?

"No," she whispered. Delta was her friend. It was impossible. Sean pushed the treacherous thoughts from her mind and set the phone back in its cradle, as it had already begun its annoying off-the-hook beeping.

There must have been some other reason for Delta's call. Dimly, she remembered her friend had told her to turn on her TV. She did so, clicking to one of the local news stations. The image blurred for a moment, and then sharpened. What she saw made her holler for Christian at the top of her voice. She didn't stop calling until she heard the thump of his feet on the stairs.

He raced into the room, still naked, eyes bright from being so suddenly yanked from sleep. His body gleamed, tense and alert, ready to protect her from whatever had caused her to shout out for him. "What is it? Are you hurt?" He grasped her by the shoulders and spun her violently towards him. Wordlessly, she pointed at the TV.

On what was supposed to be the set used for the nightly news, a familiar anchorwoman sat glumly at her desk. Instead of holding the sheaf of papers that she habitually ruffled as she read the news, she sat with her empty hands placed flat on the tabletop. She wasn't speaking, but stared at the camera, her face pale. A tall, coal-black masked man held a rifle against her temple, while another stood in the far corner of the screen, standing at ease with an automatic weapon resting on his shoulder.

Behind them, a hugely fat woman heaved her girth back and forth, ranting at the camera and occasionally shaking her fist to the heavens in a gesture of triumph. Her rotted teeth gleamed blackly as saliva spurted from her mouth as she spoke. The woman was clothed entirely in crimson cotton, voluminous masses of it that swathed her huge breasts and gathered in folds about her hips, doing nothing to disguise her girth. On her head she wore a length of red cotton that had been fashioned into an astoundingly elaborate head wrap. The entire scene looked like a very bad play.

But Sean knew it was real. In her deepest heart, she knew without being told that this was the woman who was behind the bombing of the bank, who had caused her, Christian and countless others so much pain and grief. She also knew that something was terribly, terribly wrong.

"The government of this country has been overthrown!" The atrocious woman spat. The frightened anchorwoman flinched. "Your President dead, your Ministers dead, and we have liberate you from their oppression! We in charge! We will have a government run by the poor people of this country! We will take back from the rich every penny that they owe us!"

"Jesus," Christian breathed.

Sean nodded. What the woman was saying was sheer madness. Was the Trinidadian President really dead? How could this have happened? They watched in silent horror as the woman continued, spewing venom towards every individual and organization within the island that she perceived to have offended her or to be a threat to the existence of her 'Family.' The woman condemned the Church, as well as Hinduism and Islam, successfully denigrating the three major religious bodies within the country. She raved against the parasitic rich, the banking system, organized business, the educational system, and the law. For a full half-hour Sean and Christian stood side by side, unable to move, even to sit, as she outlined her hell-driven plans for reform that stank of fascism and violence.

Sean found that she had been clutching Christian's hand so tightly that her short curved nails had punctured his skin. He didn't seem to notice. The phone rang frantically, startling her out of her skin. "I'll get it," Christian assured her, as she was too shocked to immediately respond. With two long steps he was on the other side of the room, and he picked up the phone.

"Chris!" Delta squawked loudly enough for Sean to hear. "Do you see? Do you see?"

Sean watched as he talked tensely with her for much too long. She didn't like the expression on his face as it grew more and more grave. She hated the way he kept glancing at her every now and then. Finally, when he put down the phone, she waited for him to convey the information.

Tiredly, he rubbed the back of his neck. "She's been in touch with a few of her friends in the local Legal Affairs division. The woman, this Prophetess, is lying. Delta says the President isn't dead. She says two Jeep-loads of young men, boys, really stormed an orphanage in Port of Spain where the President was opening a new wing. A couple of government Ministers were there, too, together with social workers, guests, and about a hundred kids."

Sean gnawed at the inside of her cheek. It all seemed too awful to contemplate. "So what happened? Why couldn't the authorities stop it? Doesn't he have bodyguards? And what about the police?"

Christian shook his head. "Delta says they created a diversion by driving a Jeep loaded with explosives into the police headquarters in Port of Spain. They have no idea how many policemen and civilians were killed in that one. While everyone was responding to that incident, they took their hostages."

Sean inhaled sharply. This would mean that right now, any number of government workers and small children were under the gun. This was insane! But she could tell that there was more. "What else?" she demanded, steeling herself.

Christian sighed. "It seems that they've got one or two

of the television stations, a few of the radio stations, and the two major power stations. They pretty much have their bases covered."

Sean turned to stare again at the obviously demented woman who was still strutting up and down before the cameras, spouting her doctrine to her captive television audience. The anchorwoman, still with a gun to her head, looked as if she were about to cry.

"Do you think we're in any danger?"

Christian shook his head. "There's no telling. I have no idea. Right now most of the action seems to be taking place up in the capital, and that's a good distance away. But remember, the rumors said she and her men were from right here in San Fernando, so that can't be good. There's likely to be some activity here that we don't know about."

"So what do we do?" She was anxious, but determined to ride out the storm, whatever it took. Somehow, the knowledge that Christian was by her side gave her strength and courage. Then she hesitated. He was going to stay by her side, wasn't he? "Will you stay with me?" she asked timidly.

He put both hands on her shoulders. "Of course. I'll be here as long as you need me. I won't let you go through this alone. Did you really think I would?"

She wasn't sure how to answer.

He looked down at his nakedness as if he hadn't realized before that he wasn't clothed. "First, I think I'd better get dressed," he said lightly. His smile made her feel much better, in spite of the seriousness of the situation.

Then she slapped her hand to her mouth. "Oh my gosh, Chris, the clothes you came in are all wet! They're still on my bathroom floor!" She hurried up the stairs. "I'll have to tumble them in the dryer for a few minutes."

"Please," he said gratefully. He had only two other options of clothing. One was his safety suit, which was still in his car, and which, being flame-retardant, was bad enough over regular clothes; against bare skin it would be hell. The other option was the dreaded maroon bathrobe, and given his knowledge that it had once belonged to another man who had shared her body and her bed, however fleetingly, he wasn't keen on wearing *that* at the moment.

As he waited for her to reappear with his clothes, he busied himself in her kitchen. It was almost midnight, and he was starving. They might as well dig down deep and wait this thing through, he thought. It was going to be a long night.

Christian and Sean piled cushions in the middle of her living room floor in front of the television, and settled down for an uneasy night. They agreed that the TV would remain on, whatever happened, as it was their only source of information. The madwoman had long tired of her ranting, and upon her instructions the station was now showing the brilliantly striped test pattern while soothing, nondescript music played in the background. All the radio stations played similar music, even those that hadn't been captured. It was as if everyone was attempting to keep the frantic population as calm as possible.

Sean lay passively in Christian's arms, listening to his reassurances that everything would be all right. At the sound of his deep comforting tones, she almost believed him. She dozed.

At some point during the night she woke to find him staring intently at her face from a distance of just a few inches. The probing gaze disturbed her, and she struggled from out of his embrace. His arms tightened, discouraging her from moving.

"Sean, there's something I want to talk about."

She didn't like the sound of that. She looked at him

from under her thick curling lashes. "What?" she asked suspiciously.

"I want to talk about why we broke up. About what happened with Elsa."

This time, she successfully broke from his grasp and pulled away. She folded her arms across her chest. "Why?" she asked, hostility showing on her face. "We're in the middle of a crisis. We don't even know which way is up, or how long this mess is going to last. Why do you want to talk about this now?"

He sighed and reached for a hand that she refused to give him. "Because it's important to me. The country might be in crisis, but so am I. There are things we never really discussed, and they've been hanging over our heads for too long. I want us to get it all out in the open."

Sean still wasn't giving in. "What for? What's the point?"

"The point is," he searched her eyes for a reaction, any glimmer of encouragement, and finding none, pressed on manfully, "the point is I want us to try again. We're older and smarter now, and we still . . . care for each other," he paused, giving her the opportunity to contradict him. She didn't. That was a good sign. "So I was wondering if you and I could try to work things out."

Sean got to her feet, shaking. She didn't need this. Didn't want any of it. Work things out? She never wanted to return to the place of sheer vulnerability that she had been with Christian. She spun around and began to hasten to her bedroom.

He overtook her in a second and pinned her against the wall. He was no longer tentative. He was angry. His large fingers were biting into the fleshy part of her upper arm as he tried to haul her back to the living room and the piled cushions on the floor.

"The least I can expect from you is the courtesy of an answer, Sean."

"My answer is, don't ever manhandle me in my own home!" she stormed back, and wrenched out of his grasp. "Who told you you could bully me around like that?"

"Right now, baby, I'm beyond caring." He thrust her roughly back onto the cushions and sat facing her, tucking his legs under him. His face was a mere three or four inches from hers. "Look, I don't give a damn if you don't want to listen to this or not. I don't care if you believe me or not. Knowing your selfish heart, you probably can't find it within you to believe me."

That stung!

"I can't force you to try again, but I can force you to listen. You owe me this. You owe me the fair hearing you never gave me. So I'm not letting go of you until I've said what I have to say, understand?"

Mutely, she nodded. Fine, let him say what he had to say. It wouldn't make much of a difference. She would listen, and then go to her room.

He drew a large breath into his lungs, as if he were powering himself up for the task, and began. "There was never anything sexual between me and Elsa. Her brother Tony and I were high school buddies back in Texas. I knew her as a little girl; she never really had much to do with us, but she liked to hang around when we were studying, bring us soda and sandwiches. She was kind of sweet on me, but she was only about fourteen or so at the time.

"She was kind of fragile, the kind of girl you always sensed was destined to be roughed up by the rest of the world. When I was in college, Tony got sent to the Gulf War. He never came back. By that time, Elsa was out on her own; she'd broken off with her parents because she'd fallen in with a man they didn't approve of.

"I'd promised Tony I'd keep an eye on her. I searched for her for years, called up everyone Tony and I knew to see if she'd ever made contact. It was like she'd disappeared. Eventually, I didn't have to find her; she found me. She tracked me down to New York, to my college residence. She needed help.''

He paused to see if his narrative was having any effect on Sean. It was impossible to tell. She was listening, but her face was emotionless. He scratched his head and went on.

"By the time she came to me, she was strung out on heroin, and her man had left her in an apartment with an eviction notice on the door. She'd been in and out of rehab, and every time she came out, she fell into the same old trap. She told me she knew that if she stayed alone one more time, without support or guidance, she'd be back on it in a week, and that this time, it'd kill her. So I did the only thing I could do. I couldn't let her stay on campus with me, because it was a single occupancy room, and I could have jeopardized my grant. So I found her a place nearby.''

Sean found that her eyes were locked in with Christian's. The full weight of her mistake was beginning to descend on her. She knew without question that what he was telling her was the truth. But why didn't he tell her sooner? Why all the secrecy? She asked him as much.

"I couldn't tell you. I was ashamed. I'd just asked you to marry me, and I couldn't even afford a decent ring. You can't imagine how low I felt when all the money I could scrape up was barely enough to buy a ring with a fly-speck on it that passed for a diamond.''

"You explained that to me," she protested. "I understood. I told you it didn't matter.''

"But there I was spending money on a lease for another woman's apartment. I felt guilty, but I knew I'd have felt worse if I'd denied Elsa at the time she needed me. I didn't have a choice. Putting her out on the streets alone would have been murder.''

Sean remembered the heated visit she'd made across town to the address on the lease she'd found secreted in

Christian's apartment. She'd been almost blind with jealous rage, promising herself that this time would be the last, that if a woman answered the door to the unknown apartment, she and Christian were through.

The face of the woman who responded to her furious knocking came to her. She had been small, deathly pale, with limp, tangled dishwater hair that could have done with a shampooing, wet eyes that were so pale they were almost colorless, and lips that held no blood but which instead had the bluish pallor of a corpse.

She remembered that her reaction had been not so much one of surprise, as she had already known that the apartment would contain a woman. But what a woman! As she made her way back to her dorm, the wound to her ego had been more real that the wound to her heart. Christian had cheated on her countless times before, but his choice of mate had always been one of superficial good looks. This she had almost come to accept as her fate.

But this limp, sallow woman who looked as if the life had been sucked out of her, had Christian really found her attractive? Enough to lie to the woman who loved him, and to hide her away in an apartment that he could ill afford? The knowledge that he'd chosen a woman so dull and sexless to perpetrate his latest crime of infidelity against her burned deep. It slashed at her confidence in her own good looks. That was the sting in the tail of the scorpion; what he was implicitly saying about Sean's own looks hurt most of all. She hung her head.

Christian went on. This time, his voice was laden with bitterness and remembered hurt. "If only you had let me in the night I came to your room. The night you stood me up in front of my family. I'd have told you everything. But you never let me in."

She protested hotly. "Could you blame me? You'd lied to me before! You'd promised it would never happen again. You promised you would go straight, that there'd be no more women."

"I kept that promise, Sean. Once my ring was on your finger, I kept that promise. There was only you. You have to believe me."

Her eyes dropped. Believe him? What man deserved to be believed?

He reached out gently and nudged her chin upwards. He seemed to have let go of his anger, and there was only tenderness there. "Sean, the other night I asked you who had hurt you so badly that you weren't willing to give your trust anymore. I said it in anger, but in the heart of me I meant it. You have a wounded soul, and I know that my own carelessness contributed to the damage, and from the core of me, I regret it, and if I could take my actions back, I would. But I know that there's another hurt in you, a deeper hurt, and it will only heal once you start to let go of it. And letting go of it begins with telling someone else."

Hesitation and pain clouded her eyes, darkening them. How could she tell him? Her father had made her promise. She shook her head.

"I want to listen, Sean. Just talk. I won't interrupt, and I won't judge. Just get it out into the open. Once you do that, the hurt will start to go away.

She resisted. "My father. . . ." she protested. Her father's spirit would never forgive her.

Christian's eyebrows drew together. "Did your father touch you?"

The horror in his voice was enough to cause her to hasten to deny the inference. "No! No! He never laid a hand on me. It wasn't that."

He pulled her towards him and cradled her trembling body like a child. "Talk," he urged her. "You don't even have to look at me. Just talk, like you're talking to yourself aloud. I won't interrupt you. I'll just be here, holding you and listening."

Tentatively, and with a whispered prayer for forgiveness to her dead father, she began. Once she opened her mouth, the story tumbled out. She talked about the little girl who lived next door, who came over to play records in her room because her Japanese parents were too restrictive in her choice of music. Then she told about the day she came home early, and about the sight that met her in the kitchen. Her friend, half-nude on the kitchen table, her father, ignominiously aroused, with his pants around his ankles. About the promise he'd forced out of her, never to tell another soul. About her shattered friendship with Kaiyo. Finally, there came the most painful story of all; she recounted how the burden of the secret forced a rift between her and her mother, as her shame and inability to look her mother straight in the eye grew into a chasm which, ten years later, couldn't be breached.

Christian listened solemnly. When she was finished, he kissed her gently on the forehead. "Not all men are like that, Sean. You can't tar every man on Earth with the same brush. You aren't destined to live the same fate as your mother."

Her mouth twisted wryly. That was what *he* thought. She thought of her last bitter encounter with romance, and of the heavy casualties that had followed—to her heart, her ego, her sexual confidence and her professional life. But that was more than Christian needed to know. Instead of contradicting him, she remained silent.

"It's time to tell your mother," he suggested. "Your father's dead now; the relationship that's important is the one between you and her. When all this violent mess going on outside is over, and when you can think again, you need to call her and talk to her. Explain what came between you all those years."

She was aghast. "Tell my mother? I couldn't! I promised!"

He shook his head emphatically. "Some promises are meant to be buried with the dead. The most important relationship right now is not the one between you and your Dad but the one between you and your mother."

Sean's hands flew to rub her pounding temples. "I can't. Not now."

He sighed. "Okay. Not now, but soon. You've lost a father over this, don't lose a mother, too. As for your own personal life, well . . ." he bit his lip and hesitated for just a moment. "You need to rebuild your faith. I'm offering you the chance . . . I'm asking you to rebuild it with me."

Her eyes widened. What was he saying?

In answer to her unspoken question, he said, "I still love you, Sean. In fact, I love you more that I did then. I don't know if you still have any of those feelings for me, and after what you've been through, I wouldn't blame you if you didn't. But we can work on that. Just give me that chance. Come to know me again; I think—I hope—you'll like what you see." His voice was thick with emotion.

Christian loved her? The possibility of it made her heart beat madly. She covered her confusion with a contemptuous snort. "And what do you base that love on, Christian? The fact that we can have good sex?"

"No. Of course not. It's more than that. Why can't you accept that you can be loved just for you?"

She didn't have an answer to that, so she remained silent.

He lifted her hand and kissed it tenderly. "I'll let you think about it, my love. I only ask one thing: just give me a fair chance. Open your mind long enough for me to prove to you that I can give you what you deserve."

Tears stung at her eyes, so she squeezed them tightly shut to keep him from noticing.

Christian coaxed her into a lying position, and for a moment she was afraid he was going to try to prove his so-called love by attempting to seduce her, so her body stiffened defensively. "Relax," he soothed. "It's getting light outside. We've caught nothing but a few hours' sleep all night. If this coup, or whatever it is, is as serious as it sounds, we're in for a rough few days at least. So let's get some sleep, okay?"

Numbly, she settled down next to him, and soon was aware of his gentle, rhythmic breathing. It's all right for him, she thought. He can just drop his 'love' bombshell on me, and then drift off to sleep. But there are so many complications, so many reasons for things to go wrong. Too many things she couldn't bear to tell him. If Christian knew of the shame and hurt she'd brought upon her life with her stupidity and poor judgment, would he be so eager to declare his love?

Mind whirring, head thumping, Sean lay next to Christian. She didn't sleep.

Eleven

"What did the Embassy say?" Sean hovered worriedly over Christian's shoulder as he set the phone down into its cradle with unsettling care. He let his cool black gaze settle on her face, taking in the taut anxiety that etched itself around her mouth and eyes, before answering.

"They're just telling all U.S. citizens to sit tight for the time being. They really don't expect that any of us are in immediate danger, but they're monitoring the situation. In the meantime. . . ."

She interrupted, aghast. "Monitoring the situation? What a load of bureaucratic bull! This isn't a bunch of schoolboys throwing eggs at the neighbor's houses! This is a *coup!* People are rioting in the streets!"

He laid a gentle hand on her shoulder. She was right; by mid-morning, reports of riots in both the northern and southern cities had come flooding in. Rumors were flying thick and fast by phone, over the Internet and on the radio stations that hadn't been captured. By the early hours of the morning the capital was in chaos as panicked citizens rushed about, trying to gather up as much food and water as they could.

The unsavory elements had also come pouring out, happy that the attention of the police had been diverted towards the hostage situation. Hundreds of impoverished young men stormed the elite shopping districts, smashing plate glass to get at what they wanted. What began as a panic for food and necessities degenerated into a looting frenzy that saw everything from jewelry to televisions being carted off. By sunrise, many of the stores were on fire.

Although it was far from the scene of the coup, the south was also suffering from civil unrest. As the police and military were engaged in the drama playing out in the north, many southerners took advantage of the absence of authority. As a result, San Fernando was in a state of equal turmoil.

Living just four miles or so out of the city, Sean wasn't very happy. In the distance, from her gently elevated suburb, she could see spires of black smoke curling upwards into the azure Caribbean sky. The reassurances of the Embassy struck a hollow note deep in her belly.

Christian strove to reassure her. He kissed her gently on the crown of her head; because of their similarity in height, he had to tiptoe to do so. "The Embassy is here to protect us; that's why we pay taxes. But there's no need to panic. We don't have to leave the island, not yet. Besides, the ports and the airports are all closed. But don't think our people aren't doing anything; there's a ship filled with Marines already on its way down from Barbados. By nightfall, they should be entering the Serpent's Mouth." He paused, and then added for clarification, "That's the gulf."

"I know what it is," she said, irritated. Her sleepless night hadn't sat well on her. "I've lived here longer than you have."

He ignored her testiness and went on. "There are other Marine contingents as close as Puerto Rico. If there's the slightest indication that we're in danger, they'll be here."

"But why don't they just. . . ." She didn't finish the sentence.

"Just what, Sean? Invade? You can't just rush into a friendly territory with guns blazing like that. Diplomacy has to run its course. Let the Trinidadian army handle it. If they need assistance, there are allies throughout the Caribbean islands who are perfectly willing to step in. They'll have everything under control in awhile. Promise."

Sean sighed. She hated the fact that Christian was seeing her so rattled. She had always thought of herself as being so strong in the face of danger. Now here she was, falling apart at the first smell of trouble. Smoothing her mussed, tangled curls, she rolled the mass of brown hair into a twist and fastened it on top of her head with small clips. Half her unease had to do with the fact that she hadn't had so much as a moment's restful sleep last night, she reasoned. At least, if she took the initiative to clean up and look less like a heap of rags and hair, maybe she'd feel better, too.

Besides, Christian had a point. She wasn't really expecting the U.S. troops to blast their way into the country with John Wayne at the fore. The country would soon have its affairs under control; it was best to allow them to do so. She remembered the invasion of Grenada, and the effect it still seemed to have on the psyche of the islands. Caribbean forces had been preparing to deal with the military coup that took place there back in the eighties, but the U.S. got there first. After fifteen years, many Caribbean people hadn't forgiven them for what they saw as an affront to their sovereign rights. Military action now would be a colossal public image *faux pas* that her country could ill afford.

I guess there's nothing left to do but wait, she thought moodily. She started gathering up the cushions that they'd scattered on the floor the night before. The television still displayed the monotonous, brilliantly colored test pattern, accompanied by the drone of whatever music the harried hostage media workers could dredge up from their archives. The female lunatic responsible for the entire debacle had not shown herself onscreen since last night. There was talk on radio that she'd already been shot by one of the hundreds of soldiers who had surrounded the station, but that was speculation that couldn't be substantiated, as few had the courage to venture into the zone of fire to see for themselves, and all telephone communications within the station had been cut.

"Sean, come here."

Instinctively, her deeply rooted rebellion kicked in. She stopped her cleaning and looked at him across the room, one large cushion still clutched tightly in her hand.

"Come on," he encouraged. "There's something I want to say to you." His face was serious, but there was emotion ebbing and flowing under the surface.

"Why don't *you* come *here?*" she countered inflexibly. She knew she was being boorish, but as her mind cast back to the night before, when he'd also had something to say to her, she felt great reluctance. He'd already told her he loved her; that was hard enough to swallow. What other bombshell was he going to drop on her, especially at a time like this?

Humoring her, he left the wall he'd been propping up and walked over until he was within inches of her. He took the cushion from her hands and tossed it accurately onto the couch. Noticing that her hands were unsteady, and finding nothing to do with them, Sean clasped them behind her.

Christian reached out and held her jaw between index and thumb, firmly, in spite of her resistance, forcing her to look at him. "I told you I love you, didn't I?"

She nodded. Sure he did. But she was taking that with a whole *handful* of salt.

He could read the doubt in her eyes and in the taut

resistance of her body as she held it carefully away from him. "I know you don't believe it," he said, with such sadness that Sean almost believed he was sincere. "But it's true. And I'm promising you, Sean, on my honor as a man, that I'll do whatever it takes to protect you, now, through this, and through anything else that's to come. So don't fret. Whatever's going on out there, you'll be safe as long as there's still breath in me. Okay?"

Sean could feel the sting of tears, and prayed feverishly that they wouldn't humiliate her by spilling over onto her cheeks. The timbre of his voice, the deep emotion that ran through it, had the ring of truth, but it was more than she was willing to accept. She couldn't bring herself to answer.

Christian wasn't letting her go that easily. The pressure of his hand on her chin increased. *"Okay?"* he insisted, black eyes searching her face as if her response meant everything to him.

Hesitantly, but more out of a desire to get him to leave her alone, she nodded.

He read the doubt in the gesture and passed a tired hand over his face. "I just hope I never have to prove it to you," he muttered as he turned abruptly and walked away.

With the unerring accuracy of fate, the opportunity presented itself that very evening. The apartment, indeed, the entire neighborhood, was shrouded in the eerie silence that came from a mixture of fear, impatience, and the impending darkness. Electrical power had gone late in the afternoon, as the rebels seemed to have decided to play one of their trump cards, the surrounded power stations, in their battle against the armed forces that out-manned them fifty to one. There was little the soldiers could do to restore power without risking the loss of the power stations by fire.

As Sean rummaged around in a drawer for votive candles, her only alternative source of light, the shriek of the phone jarred her. "Yes?" she snatched it up before it could ring a second time.

"Is Christian there with you?" Delta demanded without preliminaries.

Sean instinctively looked up to lock eyes with Christian, who had raced downstairs to the living room at the sound of the phone. "Yes, he is. Do you want to talk to him?"

"No. I want both of you to get out of there right away. You're in serious danger."

The blaze of fear in her eyes brought Christian to her side. He leaned close to the phone, trying to pick up on the conversation as well as he could. "Why?" Sean choked. Please, God, she prayed. *Don't let it be getting worse.*

"The looters are fanning outwards from the city into the suburbs. They're all out of control, and the handful of officers left in the south can't do a thing to stop them. They're fed up with the stores, and I've heard they're robbing houses."

"That's ridiculous!" Sean protested. "Everyone's at home; there are people in the houses. It's not like breaking and entering."

"No, it's not. It's robbery. They're a couple of gangs; they're armed, and they're whipped up into a feeding frenzy that won't make them easy to reason with."

"So where do we go? The Embassy?"

"Don't be stupid, Sean. The Embassy is an hour away. You might never make it. Even the army could be a threat to you. They're patrolling the highway in droves. The acting President has declared a state of emergency, and that means martial law. You can be arrested and held on mere suspicion, without probable cause; all you have to do is be seen outdoors. The jails don't have enough room for the people they've arrested so far. And there's a full curfew on. If they see you out in the open, you could be shot."

"We're American citizens!" she protested.

Delta snorted. "Tell that to the soldiers. *If* they give you a chance. Two black people wandering around a declared military zone, you could pass for anyone else on the island. And I doubt anybody's going to ask to see your passport before he draws his weapon."

"So what do we do? We can't just sit back here like cornered rats and wait for the bandits, and we can't seek sanctuary. What do we do?"

"Come here," Delta said firmly. "Come to my place."

"Why? What's so safe about . . ." She trailed off. Delta had been living in Trinidad for ten years; she hadn't needed to make use of Orion's expatriate housing. The condo she'd bought was in one of those exclusive walled colonies that offered twenty-four-hour armed security. Access to her apartment involved passing through two sets of electric gates, and a weapons scanner, and only on her invitation. There was no way that a bunch of renegades was penetrating *that*. She was right. Delta was their only chance.

Then something clicked. "But there's a curfew on. We aren't allowed to leave our houses. You said the army'd shoot if they spotted us." What she was suggesting was madness!

"That's why you have to come now. Forget packing. I've got enough food for a few weeks. Get your valuables, get a few changes of clothes, and get the hell over here. If those young men ever reach your neighborhood, consider everything else lost."

"But Chris has no clothes. . . ." she blushed at the admission that he'd spent the night.

"Tough. He can't stop by his place to get them. Get the hell out of there, Sean! How much time do you think you've got, dammit?"

Christian snatched the phone out of Sean's tight grip. "I heard, Delta. We're on our way."

"Be careful," she advised. "Avoid the crowds, and stick to the back roads as far as possible. Hurry!"

Sean was already gathering the few small items she didn't want to lose; her passport, some jewelry, cash and credit cards, as well as a few items of clothing. The idea of leaving behind all her belongings twisted her heart, but she knew that her very life would be at risk if they dallied much longer. By the time she made it downstairs with a single duffel bag on her shoulder, Christian was already in his BMW, warming up the engine by forcefully applying pressure to the accelerator.

She gave a last look around to ensure that her place was locked as securely as possible (fat lot of luck that'd do, she thought grimly) before joining him. Gravel sprayed from under the wheels as he sped from the driveway.

"Oh God, my paintings! My books!" She clutched her head with the pain of imagining her tiny but precious collection of West Indian art lost to a band of violent thieves.

Christian took one hand off the wheel and placed it on her knee. "Don't worry about that, love. These people are in a hurry. They're looking for cash and jewelry, not art. You'll lose your stereo equipment, and probably your food. But your art should be safe. And if the Army is out rounding everyone up like Delta says, the looting can't last for more than a day. We'll be back by Monday for the latest, and then, if you need me to, I'll help you put your life back together."

"And what if the Army tries to round us up?" She wasn't comforted.

He set his jaw grimly and returned his hand to the wheel. "I'll see that that doesn't happen."

In the growing darkness, the back streets were eerily quiet. Terrified residents who had also heard the talk of approaching bandits had literally battened down the

hatches. Many of them had nailed planks across the doors
and windows and set their dogs loose. The pale flicker
of candlelight could be seen behind drawn curtains.

"All these frightened people," Sean lamented. "Does
this madwoman know what she's done?"

They passed few cars; the occupants of those they did
see had the determined air that said they were on the
same mission: seeking out safety. Delta's apartment lay
on the other side of town, and there was no choice but
to brave the burning city, just for a few moments.

As they approached, the orange glow and smell of
smoke spoke of the violence and panic that was going on
around them. Sean watched in horror at the dozens of
scurrying individuals who were carrying everything por-
table from the smashed and pillaged downtown shopping
area. Men, women, and even small children ran with ra-
dios, televisions, clothing and food. Cases of rum and
scotch were passed hand to hand, bucket brigade style,
to small vans and vehicles that were parked anywhere,
filling up with illegally gotten gain.

"They don't even seem to notice us here," she
breathed in awe as people skirted the car, so intent on
their looting that they paid no attention to anyone else.

"Good. We're almost out of San Fernando. The roads
beyond should be clearer." Christian was forced to slow
to a crawl as he navigated the panicked, delirious throngs.
As they inched past a shattered supermarket, Sean saw
three or four men exiting with shopping carts full of loot.
As they made their way gleefully down the sidewalk, a
small, thin boy who was barefoot despite the broken glass
shattered all around him, passed in the other direction.
With the skill of a practiced thief he lifted what appeared
to be a large frozen leg of lamb from one of the men's
carts and ran off.

He was instantly spotted by the man closest to him,
who raised the alarm. Two of the men took off in hot

pursuit, while the other stood grimly by their goods with
the self-righteousness of someone who had forgotten that
he himself had stolen them a few moments earlier.

Sean watched as the two men caught up with their
quarry and brought him to the ground. Even above the
chaos and din she heard him squeal in pain as they
wrested the leg from him, and, using it as a club, proceeded to rain merciless blows about his body.

"No!" she shouted, and threw open the door. Before
Christian could stop her, she was out and running towards
the scene.

"Let him go!" Sean demanded, and held onto a man's
upraised arm with the tenacity of a pitbull. The man tried
to shake her free, but her height was greater than his,
and this gave her enough leverage to hang on. His partner was not so disadvantaged. With a quick hand he
snatched onto her hair and yanked her head back, pulling it painfully until it was close to his own.

"You can't mind yuh own business, bitch?" He
breathed a gust of foul air into her face. Sean released
her grasp on the other man and brought both hands up
to her hair to try to free herself from the mean grip.

Her original target laughed, reaching out for her and
grabbing both her hands, twisting them brutally behind
her. The pain made Sean sob; the fear and the stench of
smoke made her gag.

"Hold she there, man," the other gloated, "we go
teach she that cockroach have no right in fowl party."
Sean grimaced at the local dictum that meant that for
people who stuck their noses into other people's business,
the consequences would be dire. Before she could wonder what form those consequences would take she felt
the man's rough, fetid tongue drag its way up from her
chin, pausing at her lips before proceeding to disgustingly
explore her nostrils. The bile rose to her throat, but before she could make one last bid for freedom her assail-

ant was lying on the ground with Christian's foot on his neck.

"I'll break it," Christian promised. "Don't doubt me."

Unable even to breathe, much less put such a threat to the test, the loathsome creature lay still. His tiny, pig-like eyes held Christian's like those of a cornered animal. Leaning forward, Christian increased the pressure of his steel-tipped boot at the apex of the man's Adam's apple. The man's breathing became a hoarse rattle.

The sharp prick in her abdomen drew a gasp from Sean, and Christian's head whipped around to see the man who still held Sean holding a small blade to her. "Let he go," the man snarled. "Let he get up, or I going to cut she. *Real bad,*" he emphasized, and to prove it he forced the tip of the blade into the soft flesh of her belly.

She grated out her pain through her teeth as the warm gush of blood that spilled over the blade and began coursing down towards the waistband of her jeans told her that she was cut.

"Sean!" Christian reacted in horror. With one move he let up on his fallen opponent, only to grasp him by the shirt and slam his head against the concrete sidewalk. His eyelids fluttered shut.

Before his partner could react, Sean had obeyed Christian's shouted order to duck. The bulk of Christian moved past her like a charging bull as the hand holding the knife was wrenched away from her belly. Sean threw herself out of the fray, rolling herself into a tight ball. She could only hear the crunching of fist against bone, and then a clatter as the knife went spinning away.

Then Christian was dragging her to her feet. "The car," he barked. "Run!"

They ran. The second man was close on their tails, one eye spurting blood from the blow Christian had dealt him. Her heart pounded, and her disgust at what they had done to her still rested heavy upon her. But there

was no time even to reflect on that. Several of the crowd
had seen the fight, but none of them seemed to have
followed the drama from the start. The child Sean had
tried to save had long scampered, leaving only the evidence of a fight.

There was misplaced outrage, and shouts of "Hold she!
Hold she!" and Sean felt clawing hands at her hair, arms
and breasts. The car was swamped by a pulsing crowd of
people who knew only that one of their own had been
attacked. Christian overtook her and began to clear the
way, shoving people aside as he fought his way to the car
door. She stayed close to him, following in the small space
in the crowd that he had left in his wake.

They were inside. The engine obediently roared to life,
and Sean almost sobbed with relief as they began to move
forward, inch by inch. "Oh, Jesus," she cried, tears beginning to roll, "thank you."

Her gratitude was premature. The infuriated crowd,
egged on by the bleeding man and his friend who had
stayed back to watch the carts, surrounded the car, refusing to let them leave. There were shouts of "Stop them!"
and then rough angry hands were on the car, pushing
and shoving. The obvious value of the BMW, unattainable
by most of them, only served to infuriate them further.

The rocking increased, as the car began to sway violently. Short of running over a dozen people, there was
little Christian could do to escape. "Get your seat belt
on!" he shouted at her.

She watched him, puzzled. They'd come to a complete
stop, and it was evident that they wouldn't be moving
anywhere anytime soon. Why did she need a seat belt?
The answer came swift on the heels of the question. Just
as she clicked the belt into place, the angry crowd gave
one final heave, and the heavy car turned up and over,
landing on its side with a crash.

Glass sprayed as Sean's side hit the asphalt. The force

of the impact reverberated through her body, sending shock waves that rattled her teeth. A kaleidoscope of light played before eyes she didn't know were open or closed. As the babble of the crowd dimmed to the mere humming of bees, she felt anxious hands on her.

"Sean!" Who could be calling her name? She tried to lift tired hands in protest but they were tangled in the thick restraining belt.

Christian called her name again, tugging himself free from his own belt while doing his best to ensure that, once released, he didn't obey the pull of gravity and come crashing down upon her. She felt him tugging urgently at her belt, and then his strong arms went around her as she slumped sideways onto the smashed side of the car.

"We'll have to climb out the door on my side," he told her. "Can you do it?"

She nodded numbly, but still didn't move, paralyzed by the fear of having to contend with the angry crowd once outside. Miraculously, though, the destruction of the car seemed to have satiated the crowd's appetite for vengeance, and most of them had returned to the business of looting. There was a very good chance that they could walk away unmolested.

"Hurry," he urged. Opening his door, which now formed the roof of the car, was a task in itself, as the heavy slab of metal had to be pushed up rather than out. But in a matter of seconds Christian was up on the car's side, offering a helping hand down to Sean. With every bone and sinew in her body protesting the injustice, Sean followed his lead and climbed out. The leap onto the road was brain-jarring, but, she shrugged inwardly, significantly less painful than anything she had endured for the evening. Christian reached in to snag the canvas bag that held her passport and valuables and together they peered through the smoke and mayhem to get their bearings.

"We're going to have to walk it, love," he said. "You can make it." He took her hand and she let herself be led away from the center of activity. By her estimation, they were maybe three or four miles away from Delta's neighborhood. With the soreness of her brutalized muscles, her spinning head and her still bleeding knife wound, Sean knew that the walk would not be a stroll in the park.

Christian seemed to read her mind. "How's the tummy?" he inquired gently.

"I can handle it," she answered grimly, determined not to let him see her fall apart.

"That's my girl."

They walked in silence, making their way slowly away from the besieged shopping area. Total night had fallen long ago, making it difficult to navigate. The sudden flash of headlights cut through the black blanket like a broadsword, and for a second Sean had a vain hope that the owners of the vehicle would stop and offer them a ride. She raised an arm frantically to get their attention.

Christian's full weight was upon her, knocking the air from her lungs and bringing her to the ground like a sack of vegetables. Before an angry protest could leave her lips, he forced her head down into the dirt. "Army!" he hissed. "Lie still!"

A huge green van was roaring out of the night like a renegade rhino. A handful of men leaned out of the sides, and at every opening in the canvas canopy poked the long deadly nose of a rifle. There was no doubt that they were headed into town to round up the looters; as they approached, they squeezed a few rapid warning shots into the air. A searchlight like a monster's eye clicked on, turning night to day.

"They can see us!" Sean panicked.

In wordless response Christian lifted her bodily and lowered her into the deep drain that ran beside the road.

She obeyed his prodding, moving farther along, away from the open segment to a closed culvert that bridged the gap between the road and someone's driveway. Her heart beat so fast and so high in her throat she felt that if she didn't strive to take deep, measured breaths she would surely vomit it up. Dank black water swirled around their ankles, and the stench of stagnant water and rotting garbage was thick enough to make them gag.

"I can't take this," Sean gasped, then closed her mouth as the stink of their surroundings seemed to enter it.

"Just a few moments," Christian soothed. "Just lie still, my love. They'll be gone in a few seconds."

The few seconds that he had promised felt like infinity, but then the road above them trembled under the weight of the passing van. The brilliant light sped past like a moon gone mad, and finally, the thunder of the wheels began to diminish and eventually fade.

"They're gone," he assured her. "Come, let's get out of here."

He didn't have to ask her twice.

It was an exhausted, bedraggled pair that emerged from the tertiary roadways close to Delta's colony more than an hour later. They'd been forced by passing military vehicles to ditch three more times, and Sean was on the brink of deciding that if the decision faced her again she would give herself up, be arrested or shot, and be damned with it.

But the glow of lights powered by the colony's private generator, was reassuring. It promised clean water, food, and most importantly, safe shelter. But as they stepped into the circle of light offered by the guard's booth, another problem presented itself in the shape of two burly guards, each of whom held an ugly pitbull in one hand, and an unholstered weapon in the other.

"Not another step," the bigger of the two grated.

Sean almost dropped to her knees in despair. They'd

traveled through so much chaos for just this security from the outside mayhem, only to find it turned against them. The small click that followed the order could only be the sound of a safety being eased off.

"Listen," Christian began, and the attention of the dogs and the muzzle of both guns followed the sound of his voice. "We're guests of Miss Chase. Delta Chase. She's in apartment. . . ."

"I know what apartment she's in," was the barked response. "Get out of here." His gaze moved over their filthy appearance, wet clothes and hair, and mud-encrusted shoes.

"I know what we look like," Christian persisted, tone neutral, although Sean knew him well enough to know he was itching to light into the guard with a few choice words, if not an honest-to-goodness punch. It was only sanity and the evil gleam of the outstretched weapon that prevailed. "If you'll only call her. . . ."

"I ain't calling her for shit," he ground out. "There's a curfew on, you two breaking curfew. If the army truck come around and ask me if I see anybody, what I going to tell them?"

"If you call her, she'll tell you to let us in," Christian added reasonably. "Then we can go inside, and we won't be breaking curfew anymore."

The logic of the argument seemed to strike a nerve within the man. "Watch them," he instructed his companion brusquely, and he turned to go into the booth. As he went, the hound gave a last regretful look at Christian's solid thighs before following his master.

The man emerged in a matter of seconds. "Let them through," he grunted at the other guard. The huge electronic gates swung open, and as Sean and Christian entered, they could feel the rueful eyes of the first guard on them, as if he'd been denied the opportunity for a good honest shooting. They made haste for Delta's place.

She met them at the door, arms wide open, hands flailing agitatedly. "Come in! Come in!" she repeated. She seemed electrified with worry; her perfect page was ruffled and tangled, with bits of hair sticking up at odd angles. "Didn't you guys leave two hours ago? What are you trying to do, give me a heart attack? I was dying in here! Look at you two! What, did you take time out to go sightseeing? Where's the car! Jesus, you're bleeding!"

Sean let the reassuring babble wash over her like warm water; answering Delta didn't seem an option. Safe at last, and weak from the loss of blood and the agony of their trials, she let herself slip down onto Delta's plush cream carpet, and the lights went out.

She became dimly aware of standing barefoot on cold wet tiles, with Christian holding her securely by the shoulders and Delta plucking at her shirt buttons. The shower gushed just inches from her, so much so that she could feel the warm splashes against her face.

"You look like you been rolling in the gutter," Delta grumbled like an old schoolmarm. "Look at yourself. You got mud up to the eyeballs." Her shirt peeled from her skin like wet muddy leaves. Somehow, as cool air hit her, she realized she was now down to her bra and panties, and irrationally, she didn't want Christian seeing her like this.

She wriggled from his grasp. "Go away," she complained. "I can shower myself." She thrust his restraining hands from her.

Christian renewed his grip. "Shower yourself, nothing," he retorted. "Five minutes ago you were dead cold on the floor. I'm not leaving you here."

"I'm *naked,*" she countered, whining like an infant. "Go 'way." Sean was tired and miserable. She longed for the soothing arms of her mother, which hadn't surrounded her since she was a child. She longed to be clean again, and to be able to lie down and close her eyes to the nightmare. What she didn't want, was for Christian to be a witness to her misery.

"She's right, man." Surprisingly, Delta came to her support. "Thanks for helping me get her upstairs, but maybe you ought to leave us girls alone."

Sean countered Christian's raised, defiant eyebrows with a smirk of triumph, feeling like she'd just won a schoolyard squabble with the class bully. Reluctantly, Christian climbed out of the shower, sighing like a martyr.

"You can use my shower and get yourself cleaned up," Delta told him by way of compensation. "And if you're lucky, I just might find a jogging suit that'd fit you hanging around. You're lucky I like my men big." She backed up her statement with a broad wink that didn't escape Sean.

Christian smiled in gratitude. "Thanks, babe. I owe you dinner sometime." He left with a brief nod in Sean's direction.

I owe you dinner sometime. Damn the man. He'd flirt in his sleep, if he could. Sean gritted her teeth and stepped under the stream of the water while Delta busied herself gathering up the muddied clothing. Sean would have loved to have luxuriated under the hot steamy stream for hours, but the reality of the situation was that they were running on a generator, and continued power could not be guaranteed. Too soon, she stepped from the water and accepted the thick golden towel that Delta offered.

She allowed Delta to examine the wound left by the madman's knife. "It's not so bad, really," Delta announced, swabbing it with a cotton pad. "The muscle of your abdominal wall wasn't penetrated. It's just cut in to your tummy fat. It bled like hell, but the bleeding seems to have stopped. You need painkillers?"

Sean shook her head. She was so tired that sleep would be all the painkiller she needed.

"Then we'll just have to keep it clean and dry. If it

doesn't look better by morning, we'll get you to a doctor.'' As Delta deftly taped down a square of gauze with sticky surgical tape, Sean shuddered at the idea of having to go out into that mess and seek out a doctor. She'd *better* feel okay by morning!

"Here's one of your T-shirts," Delta said with mock severity. "Get it on, and get your sorry ass into bed. You're not leaving the room until morning."

Sean wasn't arguing about that. She crawled gratefully into the huge bed, glad for the simple luxury of fresh smelling sheets.

"Hold on, sit up. You ain't draping all that wet hair all over my pillow, girl. Sit still." Delta perched on the edge of the bed, just behind Sean, and clicked a little blow dryer on with the flick of her thumb. Sean felt small, gentle hands move through her hair as Delta ruffled it under the warm current of air.

"I can do it," she protested, trying to wrest the instrument from her friend.

Delta slapped her hands sharply away. "Don't be an idiot. You tried to get yourself killed tonight. Least I could do is dry your hair for you. Don't be so prickly. You don't have to be in control every second of the day, you know."

Sean was too tired to argue. She submitted to the gentle ministrations.

"So you and the hunk really getting along, eh?" Delta said after awhile.

Sean's spine stiffened so suddenly she almost injured herself. She tried to seek out any hint of jealousy in the lushly accented voice.

"Hey, that's cool with me. I was just askin', girlfriend."

That's cool? Delta had showed nothing but enthusiastic interest in Christian from day one. Was she really willing to give up the fight just like that? Sean's tired mind stumbled back to an image of a box full of dead flowers, followed by the painful vision of a dozen dead birds. She contorted her torso in order to see Delta's face; there was only concern and mild curiosity.

"Is it?" Sean had to ask.

"Is it what?"

"Cool with you."

Delta laughed. "Look, girl, I won't lie to you. If he wanted me, he could've had me in an instant, whether you were in the picture or not. I never made any secret about how I operate. You know me, you seen me in action a dozen times. I like men, and they like me. But this one, I'm telling you, he barely sees me. I mean, he's nice to me and all, but there's never been any question who he really wants, and believe me, I'd try anything. But I could tell from the look on his face tonight, and the way he leaped for you when you pulled that fainting stunt downstairs, that I just didn't stand a chance. He's a goner. Hell, I could run butt-naked out there right now, and he'd tell me to take care I don't get a chill." Delta laughed loudly at the idea.

Sean watched her face, searching for signs of deceit. Delta didn't seem to notice, and went on speaking. "So like I said, he's gorgeous, but it looks like he's all yours. I ain't going to kill you for him."

"Would you kill my birds for him?" Sean blurted without thinking.

"What is your ass talking about, girl?" The high whir of the blow dryer slowed and died. Delta had a scowl on her that made her look like an irritated pompek.

Sean floundered. "My birds, I . . . someone killed them."

Delta's eyes popped. "No! What, like strangled them or something?"

Sean shook her eyes; the memory alone was enough to cause her throat to constrict. "Poison," she managed to gasp.

"And you thought it was me?" Delta was incredulous.

She hopped off the bed. Even standing, she was barely eye to eye with a seated Sean, but nevertheless, she looked dauntingly ferocious. Sean felt miserable. It was a fine houseguest who fainted on her host's floor, trailed mud all over her bathroom, wet her sheets and then called her a sadist.

She floundered. "I'm sorry, I just thought. . . ."

"You thought I do it? And why the *boomba clat'* you never call me on it?" In her anger, her dialect became more pronounced. "Look, if I wanted to fight you for a man, you bet your ass I'da fought you to your face. I'da scratched your eyes out, or pulled me out a couple handfuls of your hair, but I never woulda killed your birds. Or send you them damn rotten flowers, if that's what you were thinkin'. "

Sean put her hands to her flaming face. The gentleness she had witnessed in Delta tonight, and her outrage at being accused, were all the proof she needed that her suspicions were misdirected. "I'm sorry," she apologized sincerely. "I couldn't think of any other reason for someone. . . ." She realized that Delta's innocence still left no pointers towards a guilty party, but somehow, seeking Delta's forgiveness was more important than pointing fingers elsewhere. "Forgiven?" she asked timidly.

"I'll think about it," Delta sniffed, but she was smiling. She clicked the dryer back on and resumed her handling of Sean's hair.

"So where are things going with you and your man?" Delta said when she was calm enough to resume their conversation.

Sean shrugged. She wished Delta wouldn't call him *her* man. Christian Devane wasn't any woman's man. "I don't know. It's kind of hard for me, right now."

"After what you went through the last time you got led down the garden path by a member of the opposite sex?

I'm not surprised. Your last heartthrob left you in shreds."

Sean felt a muscle in her jaw twitch. Her last brush with romance had left her so badly hurt and humiliated that she hadn't been able to talk about it with anyone, not even Delta. She felt the temperature of her skin drop several degrees. Delta didn't seem to notice, but went on blithely.

"But I'm sure Christian has been very supportive, even though it touches him so close to home, too."

Sean didn't answer.

"Isn't he? He does understand, doesn't he?" Delta twisted her body around so that she was peering into Sean's face. Her stricken look and evasive eyes told her all she needed to know. "Omigod."

"Delta, don't go there. . . ."

"Sean, are you saying that you've gone and gotten involved with Christian. . . ."

"Delta." Sean's tone was sharp. "Cut it out."

"And you haven't told him . . ."

Sean threw her hands up in front of her face, trying to shut out her misery. "I can't!"

". . . that you and Carlos Fabregas were lovers?"

Twelve

For the second time tonight, the hair dryer grew silent. Delta clambered onto the foot of the bed so that she and Sean sat face to face. "You lived together!" she said almost accusingly. "You got him fired. You two were the talk of the whole Company. And now here's Christian, taking up Carlos's old job, working with his staff. Don't you think he's going to walk into his office one day and hear a bit of gossip and put two and two together? Do you really want him to find out that way?"

"I don't have a choice," Sean protested unhappily. "I can't tell him. I'm so ashamed of letting a man like Carlos into my life. And my home. How could I?"

Delta shrugged. "Damn, girl, you remember what he was like. He could charm the panties off the Wicked Witch of the West. You were alone and far from home, and God knows it's not like you have male company crawling all over you. You were ripe for his play, and you fell for it. You can't blame yourself."

"But he was such an awful person! He's nothing I would ever have dreamed of letting close to me in any circumstances."

"But you did."

"Yes," Sean agreed dully. "I did. And I pay for it with regrets every day of my life."

Delta patted her on the cheek kindly. "We all make

one tragic mistake in our lives. We're only human. Forget him. Put him behind you. He's five thousand miles away, and I bet wherever he is, he isn't sitting around agonizing about *you.*"

Even the idea that he wasn't thinking about her, when his ghost haunted her hallways every day, stung. Delta was right. The self-absorbed bastard had probably sailed on to greater challenges long ago. Lord knows he was doing quite a bit of that, even while he was with her.

Delta's face grew grave. "But I still think you should tell Christian before things get out of hand. He's a man of the world, and he's probably got a few skeletons under his bed himself. So you should. . . ."

"I'm really tired," Sean interrupted. She didn't want to, didn't need to hear anymore. All she wanted was to be left alone.

Her friend took the hint and got to her feet. "Fine, honey, but you think about what I said. Chris'll be in soon. You sleep well."

"Thank you," she whispered, and then she was alone in the dark.

Sleep well. Easy to say, but not necessarily to do. In her exhausted state, her will was not as strong as it could have been. Memories she had been struggling to suppress for months were bubbling up to the surface, forcing its way through her layers of defenses until they got to a place where she had no choice but to acknowledge them. In distress, she tossed about on the bed, but whatever physical position she tried to settle herself into, her mental turmoil remained just the same.

From somewhere across the sea, Carlos laughed. Even with her eyes squeezed tight, she could see him, broad well-defined shoulders shaking with malicious mirth, handsome, carefully chiseled Latin features alive, olive skin glowing. Carlos had been a sensation in Trinidad from the moment he'd arrived, she'd been told. He was the kind of man who commanded attention wherever he went, from men as well as from women. He was the kind of man who overshadowed everyone else, just by walking into a room. He was intelligent, wily, flamboyant and seductive. He was also dangerous, especially where women were concerned. He had the kind of sexuality that drew them towards him, almost against their will. She'd collided with him like a bird hitting the windshield of a Ferrari, and had broken both wings on impact.

Of course, she'd been fully aware of his track record with women; nobody working within Orion could be *unaware*. His sexual antics were a source of amusement among the Control Room staff, who recounted the stories he told them like boys recounting winning plays by their basketball heroes.

Knowing that, she wondered bitterly, how did she allow herself to become one of his victims? It was as if she accepted it to be her family curse, her *womanly* curse, to be attracted to men like that. But still, she was a grown-up; she was responsible for her own decisions. It was all right for Delta to wave her mistake away, saying that 'everyone makes one big mistake in her life,' but she had had the option to say no, and she hadn't taken it. Citing loneliness, or homesickness or the simple longing for male company as excuses, no matter how valid they were, just wasn't enough. She'd blundered in with her eyes wide open, and as far as she was concerned, she deserved everything she suffered afterwards.

Carlos had pursued her with almost idle interest. In retrospect, he was like a boy who, bored with everything offered on TV, clicks through the hundreds of channels and then decides to sit and watch one chosen at random, merely to fill the time. Her unapproachable air had only provided a tiny element of challenge, which he must have enjoyed quite a bit.

Some challenge, Sean reflected wryly. A master of seduction, he'd known just which buttons to push; he'd feigned interest in her work, flattered her, sent her trinkets, flowers, cards. She'd taken the bait willingly, and Carlos had reeled her in like a marlin, but with much less of a struggle.

It was what happened next that truly amazed her, truly shamed her. The night she let him into her bed, she had been swept away by his skilled lovemaking. Her loneliness and unappeased sexual hunger encouraged her to throw away caution and open herself up to him fully. He pressed home his advantage, and when he was through she clung to him, helpless, unable to hold back tears of anguish and need. After that night, he never really vacated her apartment.

At first, she was flattered that a social butterfly such as he could have deemed her worthy of all that extra attention. And she would be lying if she said they never had fun together. Although her tastes ran more towards nature walks through the island's lush countryside, and his towards yachting, parties, and social events at which one could be seen, they managed to strike what she had believed to be a happy medium—until she realized that the 'happy medium' entailed her bending to his will and always going where *he* wanted to go.

Although he spent most of his nights with her, at least at first, he never fully moved in. Over time a few articles of clothing appeared in her closet, a few shaving items on her bathroom counter, a pair of safety boots in her hallway. He maintained his own apartment, and was just as prone to be found there as at hers. Give him time, she consoled herself. He's the kind of man who needed to have his own territory closely defined. At the end of the first month, he made no move to assist with the groceries and miscellaneous bills, but, having been paying them all along herself, she never saw it as an issue, and continued paying them without complaint.

But then it became apparent that the locker-room stories making the rounds of the company hadn't stopped. *Surely they must be old stories,* she'd been naive enough to think, as somewhere deep inside her she still nurtured the hope that she would be able to hold the sole attention of a man, if only just for a little while. Then he began wandering in at odd hours, smelling of smoke and alcohol. This, too, she had been able to dismiss, as Carlos had always been a partying man. It stung that he had chosen to find his entertainment without her company, but in her desperation not to rock the boat and thus upset the fragile balance of her life once again, she said nothing.

Then he wouldn't come in for many nights, and she was forced, in spite of herself, to admit that he had gone back to his old ways (or maybe he had never left them!) with other women. Her confrontations and tears were met with soothing kisses and denials, cemented with sex that was so passionate and so absorbing that he left her doubting her own suspicions. It was only in her sober moments, when he wasn't inflaming her senses with his touch, that she was able to see clearly what Carlos was doing to her, and every time she decided to do something about it, her anger and disillusionment ended up being silenced in bed.

In the darkness, Sean's mouth twisted wryly. Good sex? That was easy. The good sex she'd had with Christian a mere twenty-four hours ago might have somehow convinced him that he loved her, but she knew better than to misinterpret a few orgasms as signs of love everlasting. Allowing herself to be suckered into that kind of thinking just wasn't worth the heartache.

With Carlos, it was only a matter of time before the painful dilemma that was facing her took on proportions far beyond the scope of their pathetic relationship. As his drinking increased, his vigilance on the job became

sloppy. There were accidents. Sean suffered the humiliation of walking into a room to find her colleagues discussing the latest near-miss down at the plant; at least,
that was what she surmised they were discussing, because
her presence was always a signal for the room to fall silent. Delta had once told her that Sean's commitment to
the company's health and growth had been questioned
in higher circles; she had been tried and condemned
purely by association.

The crunch with Carlos's job performance came, coin-
cidentally, right after she had decided she couldn't take
it anymore. One evening, after waiting hours to have a
promised dinner with Carlos, he had come in plastered.
She asked him to take the few items he had scattered
about the house and leave. What followed was a vitupera-
tive argument in which she called him a womanizing
drunk, and he called her a desperate woman who was so
pathetic and starved for sex that she would lick up any
crumbs of affection off a man's table. He called her clinging, insecure and old-fashioned. Furthermore, he informed her ruthlessly, he had been with her only as a
matter of convenience, because he liked having his food
cooked and his clothes washed, but lately, she hadn't
been worth it. Her tears in bed were irritating and laughable, and her infantile insistence on fidelity, whatever *that*
meant, was more of a strain on him than he was willing
to endure. He ended by informing her that she was never
to believe that she had thrown him out, even though she
had spoken first. *He* was leaving *her,* he told her harshly,
and left without even bothering to collect his belongings.
He'd have one of his workers pass by and pick them up
when he was ready.

With his departure, she was left numb, unable to even
shed the tears he had so denigrated. With a chilled heart
and firm resolution, she picked up a large cardboard box
and began moving through her apartment, putting his

stray belongings into it. In the bedroom, she stumbled upon an item that was to prove the undoing of his career.

His checkbook lay on the dresser, open, leaves flapping, stuffed with receipts, tabs, and cash register tapes. Idly, she glanced at it. As Operations Manager, Carlos's salary was almost twice hers, even though they were both at the level of Manager. Somehow, the powers that be had deemed his work in the provision of the company's core product was more valuable than her tireless protection of its image. Throughout her career in Public Relations, and as a working woman, Sean had become almost accustomed to the bias. Her curiosity in perusing Carlos's documents was therefore motivated by a need to confirm that his refusal to contribute financially to the running of her home over the past three months was motivated by sheer selfishness, as there could certainly not be a financial reason.

His balance came as a shock. As U.S. citizens, they were all paid in U.S. dollars, which was held in a special foreign account to be converted into Trinidad and Tobago dollars as necessary. With the local job market being what it was, their salaries, when converted, was enough to allow them an almost extravagant lifestyle, and Sean had always been aware that the amenities she could afford here were far superior than that which she would have been able to afford back in the States. Even so, Carlos's account was thousands of U.S. dollars in overdraft.

Sean was taken aback. Like hers, his car and apartment were paid for by Orion. There was little he actually needed to pay for to survive. Then a quick look at his check stubs told the story; several thousand dollars was being paid out every month to two men who worked directly under Carlos at the plant. In total, Carlos seemed to have handed over a few months' salary to these men.

She set the documents down and tried to think back to every conversation and every rumor that had ever passed along the company hallways about Carlos. The reality came over her like a slow-breaking wave. There had been jokes about Carlos's increasing inefficiency, and speculation about how he managed to keep production together in spite of his erratic behavior. Some even speculated whether he'd had help from his two right-hand men in keeping the ship afloat. Couldn't it be possible, she mused, that he'd been paying them both to handle his duties, just well enough to keep him out of trouble?

By morning, the improbability of it had become a certainty in her mind. She went directly to the President with Carlos's documents and her suspicious, and was obliged to recount her story over and over before a panel of Vice Presidents, all of whom had by then heard the story of how Carlos had 'left her,' and all of whom regarded her with deep suspicion and not a little contempt. Andrea Gooding, Carlos's direct supervisor, was more than a little hostile. She condemned Sean for fabricating atrocious stories about "such a brilliant man" who "was in the process of sorting out certain problems" and who "had been invaluable to the company from the very beginning."

But in the end, investigations bore out the truth, and Carlos was dismissed without ceremony. He left spitting fire, swearing to his innocence in spite of the physical evidence, and blaming his downfall on her. She became known around the company as a woman scorned, and suffered being the butt of vicious jokes. In spite of it all, she endured.

Her painful reverie was broken by the sound of the bedroom door being opened. The rest of the house had grown dark along ago, but Sean hadn't noticed. Her ears followed Christian as he progressed haltingly across the utterly black room.

"You don't have to worry about waking me if you turn on the light, you know," she informed him dryly.

A bedside lamp clicked on and she felt the far side of the bed bowed down by Christian's weight. "I was sure you'd be asleep by now," he said softly. He reached for her and turned her gently over. With one hand, he tugged the covers down past her waist.

Startled, she slapped him away. "What the hell do you think you're doing?" Was he serious? Just because they were obliged to share a bed didn't imply that he could paw her at will. She turned abruptly from him.

"I was just trying to have a look at your knife wound." He sounded hurt.

"Well, you can't see anything. Delta already bandaged it up."

He was quiet for a time. "Does it hurt?"

"Yes." Why didn't he just leave her alone? Didn't she have enough on her mind already?

She could hear him breathing behind her, but he made no move to lie down. She could just feel his black eyes penetrating the back of her head, and could sense his mind ticking over. Finally, he broke the silence. "What's wrong, love?"

"Don't call me that!" she bit out.

"Why not?" his voice was heavy with hurt.

"Because you don't mean it." He *couldn't* mean it. He was just a man who, tired of sowing his oats, had decided to assuage his guilt over the wild life he'd led by rationalizing his sexual urges, making them more palatable to him by calling them love.

He lowered his head and pressed a soft kiss into the exposed skin of her shoulder. "I do mean it. Why wouldn't I mean it?"

Because I don't deserve it, she wanted to retort. Instead, she remained resolutely silent.

The mattress shifted as he eased into bed. He stretched himself against her turned back, and she could feel the warmth of his bare skin against hers. He was surely naked. "Can't you put something on?"

He laughed softly in spite of his tension. "The only thing I have, sweetie, is hanging over that chair over there. Delta was able to dredge up a jogging suit belonging to one of her old beaus, but that's about it. And until all this unrest is over, and I'm able to make my way back to my own place for some reinforcements, I'm afraid that that and what I came in wearing is about all I have to my name. So if you don't mind, I'd rather save it for tomorrow."

"But you're naked," she persisted prudishly.

His fingers caressed the length of her arm. "I was naked last night, too," he reminded her gently. "And you didn't complain."

The fact that he was absolutely right left her without a suitable retort, so she settled for closing her eyes and trying to will sleep to descend upon her. But the force of his presence, the feel of his skin against her, the strength of him, the length of him, were too great a distraction. She felt something inside her being drawn towards him, even in spite of her resistance.

It wasn't her heart, she asserted. She had shored up her defenses too well for that. It was just her body, playing her for a fool again. If she ignored the craving, it would eventually get fed up and go away.

"If you told me what was wrong, we could work it out, whatever it is," he suggested.

"We don't have anything to work out," she reminded him sharply. He didn't say another word, but instead, settled down next to her. She didn't sleep, and although she strained her ears throughout the night, she had no indication whether he did or not. He remained motionless beside her.

* * *

The rioting was quelled by morning. Both the northern and southern cities had been flushed of looters, and the maliciously set fires had been put out. What came after was almost as terrible: a silence that lay over them like a shroud. A merciful shower of rain rid the sky of its blanket of smoke, but left the gutters and streets filled with mud, soot and the debris left behind by the looters.

The army reclaimed the power stations in dawn raids that left dozens of casualties and incurred serious damage to the infrastructure; it would be a while yet before power was fully restored. The radio stations were the next to be reclaimed, but the television station housing the so-called Prophetess and her cohorts, and of course the orphanage, were still under siege, as the few dozen zealots managed to hold the army at bay purely because of the valuable hostages they had placed at unknown points throughout the buildings. Water and electricity had been cut off, and so far they had managed to deny the demands for food, so the probability of the young men being driven out by thirst and hunger was great. The hostage takers had agreed to release all the children under five, who were herded, too shocked, hungry and exhausted for tears, into waiting ambulances. The nation waited.

Christian had more immediate concerns. Half a dozen of his men had opted to remain on site at the plant on Friday when the insurrection had begun. Together with a skeleton security staff, they had managed to keep an eye on the Company's assets. Although the plant generator was just enough to keep its vital signs going, there was nowhere near enough power to run any of the processes. The moment he heard that the army had lifted the twenty-four-hour curfew just slightly, to allow citizens to leave their homes between noon and 6:00 P.M., he knew he had to go to them.

"Take my car," Delta urged him. "I'm not going anywhere. Take Sean over to her place, and see how much damage has been done by the looters. I heard they were pretty thorough in her neighborhood."

Christian's eyes fell on Sean. Since last night she had been silent, almost absorbed into a world of her own. It made him uneasy. It didn't seem to be a symptom of the shock she had been through, or a reaction to the wound in her belly. She seemed to have descended into a world of introspection that was sucking her deep into despair.

"Sean? Are you ready to go home?" he inquired gently.

Her hazel eyes were dulled to a sad brown, and the blankness within them frightened him. He longed to pull her closer and beg and cajole until she told him what was bothering her, but she had made it quite clear the night before that she didn't want him touching her.

"Sure," she sighed. "Whatever."

He bit his lip, considered speaking, and then nodded. "At noon, then."

She wandered off to the window without answering, and stared out into Delta's courtyard with the air of someone who wasn't really seeing anything.

At twelve o'clock the transformation of the neighborhood was startling. The very second the curfew lifted, the parking lot and streets came alive as every car within the compound hummed. Tired of the fear and confinement, and more than a little curious to see firsthand the damage that had been done, people streamed into the streets. Christian had to admire the resilience of the Trinidadian people.

With Sean silent by his side, he eased the car carefully into the suddenly thronging street and covered the short distance between the two neighborhoods. On an impulse, he took the same route they had passed the night before, to see if there was anything left of his car. It was gone. Whether it had been removed by the police or stripped by the rioters was something he would have to investigate later.

Right now, he was bracing himself for whatever damage had been done to Sean's apartment, and for the reaction she would have when she saw it. He remembered the pride she had in her small collection of local paintings, sculptures and books, and was sorry now that he hadn't allowed her the few extra seconds it would have taken to pack those.

Her driveway was silent, but seemingly undisturbed. Eerily, though, people living in neighboring apartments were busy cleaning up debris, damaged fences and broken glass. Some of them looked up from their labor long enough to cast strange glances in their direction; none of them spoke. Christian's brows drew together in puzzlement. It was obvious that others had suffered at the hands of the rioters; how come Sean's seemed to be the only apartment that was unscathed? It was almost as if some malevolent angel had spread his wings of protection over it.

"Stand back." He motioned to Sean to wait as he opened the door for her.

"You don't have to be a hero, you know," she informed him tiredly. "It's my home, I can. . . ."

"It's weird," he insisted. "It's too quiet." They stepped together into the hallway, prepared for the worst, and found every item in its place. Sean's relief was palpable, and she rushed into the living room and ran eager fingers along her bookshelves.

Christian wasn't convinced. Why had Sean escaped? "I still want to search the place," he insisted. "You stay here, I'll go look upstairs." He didn't believe in guardian angels, and believed even less in the luck of the draw.

For the first time that morning there was a light in Sean's eyes, but this was a light of anger and resistance. "Look, Christian, I don't know what you're trying to prove, but I don't need you to look after me. I don't need you prowling around upstairs like a hired body-guard. Whatever old-fashioned values you've suddenly discovered about the protection of women, don't seek to exercise them on me."

He flinched, perplexed at the source of her venom. He felt driven to explain that he wasn't being old-fashioned or chauvinistic; far from it. He just needed to know she was all right before he left. But her defiant posture stopped him.

He gave in. "Okay, sweetheart. Have it your way. I'll leave you alone . . . for now. But I'll be back before curfew's over, and you and I are going to talk." He wished they could talk now, wished she'd drop the prickly armor she'd assumed for some inexplicable reason, at least long enough to let him hold her. The longing inside of him to make things right between them almost made him dizzy; it was like a ringing in the ears that wouldn't go away. He needed to make her believe in him as she'd believed in him once before, but his duty to his men was pressing, and he had to leave.

"Talk about what?" she bristled. Was it his imagination, or did a flicker of guilt pass across her face? "We have nothing to discuss."

"That's where you're wrong," he answered brusquely. An anger surged up within him like an awakening animal, shaking its head and roaring. He watched her standing in front of him, eyes level with his, stubbornly daring him to outstare her, and he wanted to reach out and shake that attitude out of her, grasp her shoulders until she squealed out in pain.

The sudden violent impulse stunned him. He'd never lifted his hand to a woman, but goddammit she had him so mad at her, with her closed face and steel barriers, that he wanted to launch into a full-scale attack, tearing away at those barriers until they were down and she opened herself up to him again.

He shuddered, drew his savage impulses back under control, and made his way to the door with great effort. Did he trust himself to speak? He opened his mouth to try, and was surprised when an almost normal-sounding voice forced past his lips. "I'll be back by six. Don't go anywhere, and don't let anyone in." Enough was enough; if he tried to say anymore, he would become unglued, and Lord knew what he would say next.

She didn't answer, and made no effort to see him to the door. With one backward glance, Christian stepped back out into the brilliant noonday sun, leaped into Delta's car, and left for the plant.

Sean felt ashamed of her behavior. The hurt and puzzlement in Christian's eyes cut her deep—but what was she supposed to do? What could she tell him? She was a coward; didn't he know that?

She went into the kitchen and stood in front of the open door of the fridge, ostensibly seeking out a morsel of blessed nerve-soothing chocolate to pop into her mouth, but in reality needing the blast of cool air on her heated skin. Finding a bar, she snapped off the first few rows with the fervor of a true addict, needing the reassuring hit of sweetness to penetrate her body and calm her soul as it always had in the past.

The torment that had kept her awake last night was nothing compared to the agony of indecision that was tearing her apart right now. Last night, she was worried about her pride, her self-worth, and her fragile emotions, and how they might be affected if she ever drummed up the courage to confess her shameful relationship with and dependence on Carlos Fabregas. This morning, with one simple discovery in Delta's washroom, the ante had shot up. Everything at stake now included her sanity, and, without a doubt, Christian's career.

It was a natural act of courtesy to firmly take the dirty clothes that she and Christian had arrived in from Delta's helpful hands and insist that she wash them herself. It was the least that Sean could do. Nothing could have prepared her for the shock that such a simple deed had brought upon her; it was a shock too great to be carried by something as tiny as a red and gold foil cigar wrapper.

In her own kitchen, with the chilly breath of the open fridge curling around her face in visible tendrils, she withdrew the tiny item from her pocket. She had found it at the bottom of Christian's pocket, along with mundane items such as his penknife, wallet, house keys and gum. A cigar wrapper. A Cuban cigar wrapper. The brand Carlos Fabregas smoked.

The image associated with the name brought a chill to her that had nothing to do with the icy fridge. It was a shiny new wrapper, slightly worse for the wear it had suffered at the bottom of a pocket, but a *new* wrapper. Where he had found it, or why he had found it significant enough to warrant keeping, was anybody's guess. What it said, though, was clear enough to her.

Carlos Fabregas was here, in Trinidad—and he wasn't on vacation. Sean's head hurt as the dizzying array of bright spiky images flashed through it: rotting flowers, dead birds, blackened, poisoned fruit. Then more came, and these were worse because they were images she might have been able to prevent if she had been alert enough or astute enough to foresee them and speak up: stalled computers, and men frantically trying to get them back in working order while the company lost money at a rate of thousands of dollars per minute. An injured worker, and his dazed family trying to come to terms with the loss of one of his eyes. A dozen tiny things gone wrong on a huge plant, and all of them pointing to the incompetence of Carlos's replacement.

Sabotage. Why hadn't she thought of it before? It was so like Carlos, so malicious, so cruel, so cowardly. He was never a man to fight his battles face to face, but was happier standing far back while others slipped and slid in muck laid down by him, while he remained dry, clean, smelling of roses.

And now Christian was his newest target. When Carlos left, he'd left in a rage, under a cloud of shame and disrepute. For a man with his ego, it was an injury that unquestionably could not go unpunished. Carlos was not, Sean reasoned, the kind of man who could look within himself for the source of his problems and seek to make things better. He had to find a scapegoat, and that scapegoat was the company that had fired him, and the man who replaced him, and who, in his eyes, would make him look even worse simply by being efficient.

She slammed the fridge door shut and left the kitchen in haste. She had to call Christian at the plant and tell him that he was in danger. Carlos was a man whose behavior escalated drastically; he'd already caused one man to be injured with his insane schemes; the next time he struck would only be more devastating.

She grabbed the phone and frantically dialed the number before even putting the receiver to her ear. She listened for a ring, but encountered only an eerie silence. Frowning, she disconnected the call and tried again. This time, there was no dial tone.

Maybe sometime during the mayhem of the past few days the phone had been affected, she reasoned, and took the stairs to her bedroom two at a time to access the extension. At the top of the stairs, she halted. Something was wrong. The same eerie presence that surrounded her apartment from the moment she arrived at it, the presence that seemed to have wrapped her home in a cloak of malevolent protection, keeping it from being harmed by the looters while somehow doing some invisible harm itself, was there. She could sense it, smell it, feel it, as a small fish basking in the shallows can feel the ripple of an approaching predator hundreds of yards away.

The chocolate she was clutching in her hand offered Dutch courage. She brought it to her mouth, hoping that the scent and taste would take away the taste of dread that now coated her tongue. It was no use; the paltry comfort offered by the candy, once so dependable, failed her now. She stared at the bar in her hand almost in surprise, like a woman using a gun in her own defense, only to find in a time of dire need that the clip was empty.

"I see you still eatin' that shit." The voice coming from her bedroom doorway was gravelly, almost hoarse, but full of enough menace to send bolts of shock through her entire body. Rigid with fear, she stared, unable to spin around and bolt back down the stairs as her instincts begged her to do.

"Carlos," she exhaled. The useless chocolate fell to the floor unnoticed.

"Baby," he said, in a masquerade of intimacy. "Nice to see you. You look good."

She couldn't say the same for him. The almost unbearably handsome man, who six months ago had succeeded in coaxing her to throw every reservation to the wind and join him in a relationship that was nothing but folly, was a strained, pale caricature of himself. His swarthy Latin good looks had paled to a sallow, puffy dullness. His hair, once crisp, jet black and impeccably cut was limp, greasy and overlong. Several strands of gray seemed to have sprouted among the black, shocking Sean. What the hell had he gone through to leave him looking like that?

The man took a step forward. At the top of the stairs,

Sean was helpless; there was nowhere for her to go, even if her reluctant body was capable of movement. He didn't stop until he was within a foot of her. At this proximity she could see the lines of fatigue around eyes that were once crackling with sexual energy and charm. Redness delineated them now, and soft bags of skin hugged their undersides.

"Glad to see me?" he asked softly. There was something in his voice that could have been sarcasm, or it could have been genuine need.

Sean thought fast. The crazy flicker in his dulled eyes, coupled with her foreknowledge of the kind of man that he was, told her he was dangerous; even more so than he had been when they were together. She searched for an answer that would keep her safe without compromising her.

"Although I guess you're not." He answered his own question with something resembling humor. "Considering the pretty boy who dropped you off just now. I wouldn't think you'd be all that glad to see an old friend, now that you've got yourself a new friend." He smiled creepily.

Sean couldn't help but flush. He was perceptive, if nothing else. She didn't need to answer.

"Who was he? Ah, don't tell me, my replacement, the miracle worker. Heard he's known all over the industry for his many skills. Supposed to be some kind of engineering genius." He leaned forward, showing unbrushed teeth as his lips peeled back in a shark-like grin. "Tell me, has he been living up to his reputation?"

The bastard, Sean thought. She had been right. Carlos had been doing everything possible to make Christian look like a fool. He was tearing Christian's reputation to shreds, and enjoying every minute of it. "Stop what you're doing," she warned him. "When Chris finds out what you've done, he'll come after you."

" 'Chris' is it?" the shark-like grin came again. "He's replaced me in more departments than one, has he?" He turned and leered pointedly at the bedroom behind him.

Her stomach reeled. The memories of her allowing this cruel grinning pretender to coax her body into flame shamed her. Again she felt swamped by self-loathing. Carlos recognized the look, and his grin shut down and was replaced by a thin straight line. "What, now that you've found some new stud, you want to wipe out the memory of the times we had"—he jerked his head towards the room—"in there? You want to forget all those things I did to you?" He took her arm in his hard hand, shaking her at the precarious edge of the stairs. "Just remember everything I did, everything we did, was because you wanted it. I never had you by force." He shook her once more for good measure and added, "Never."

Before she could reflect on the shameful truth of his words, he was dragging her into her room without gentleness or care. Sean stumbled to keep up. With a rough shove he tossed her back onto the wide bed in which she had dosed after making love just two days before, and moved to sit next to her. He was smiling the smile of the insane.

"When it's dark," he was saying, "we're gonna pay Orion a visit. We're gonna take a little ride in your nice expensive company car and run up a few miles on your nice cushy gas allowance . . . you know, the stuff I had myself, before you got me fired."

"I didn't get you fired, Carlos," she protested. "You got yourself fired. You weren't functioning. You were putting other people's lives at risk. It was you. . . ." Her words were cut off with a blow that seemed to send her brains slamming against the back of her skull. The shock and the pain was nothing compared to the brilliance of the colors that pressed savagely against her eyeballs. When she could see again, she struggled to focus on his hand, amazed that his fist, although huge, could cause so much pain. It hadn't. A small, dark grey, deceptively toy-like pistol nestled comfortably in the palm of his large hand.

Carlos saw her reaction, and laughed. "Did you think I'd come all the way back here without a little friend?"

She struggled to get her aching mouth to form words, but her swollen lips were hard to manage.

Carlos wasn't waiting for more from her; he seemed perfectly willing to keep up the conversation on his own. "You should be grateful. Me and this little baby stood guard over your miserable place all night. Kept them stinking looting bastards from out in the ghetto from touching those cheap-ass paintings you like so much. They were all over the place, trying to get in through the front, the back, the side windows. One shot was all it took. They scattered like crows off a telephone wire." He smiled proudly.

He leaned forward, kissing her brow. She could smell his breath; it wasn't pleasant. The gun's snub nose stroked her brutalized cheek.

"Tonight, babes, we're going in there. Back to the place we met. We're gonna have us a party."

"There's a curfew," she managed to say. "If we're seen, we'll be shot."

"I won't let you get shot, my darlin'," he whispered with a parody of gentleness. "I'm reserving that honor for myself."

Through the haze of pain she thought she recognized the sickly, sweet smell on his breath. With horror, she realized that he was fueled by more than vengeance and rage. "How long you been using, Carlos?" she asked painfully.

He laughed. "Using what?" He pretended ignorance, but the red lines in his eyes couldn't be denied.

"Coke, hash, whatever."

"None of the above," he said with ghastly cheer. "What I'm into is much, much sweeter." His heroin-crazed eyes almost tinkled with humor as he toyed with the gun just inches from her face. "It's just me and the Dragon, baby," he said and gave a ghoulish grin. He looked mighty proud of himself.

"The bottom line, Mr. Devane, is that you're suspended." Andrea Gooding seemed to enjoy the shock written across Christian's features. The office in which they sat was eerily quiet, as only a handful of staff had braved the unrest-ravaged roads to make it out to work. Out of a staff of more than a hundred, barely twenty people were present on location. Christian was beginning to wish he wasn't one of them.

The confusing change in Sean's behavior, beginning from the moment when he'd confessed he loved her but degenerating sharply ever since they turned up at Delta's house last night, had weighed heavily on him all the way to the plant. The problem, he had decided, was that she obviously didn't want him anymore. She'd never trusted him, but at least for a while she'd desired him, even loved him back. That was over; her coldness to him had been enough proof. And to his surprise it hurt, deeply and sharply.

He had parked in his usual spot down at the control office, his mind so filled with Sean that he was barely aware of his surroundings, when he was met halfway to the building by one of his favorite technicians, Ricky Conrad. The young man was dressed in safety gear whose condition made it obvious that he hadn't had the opportunity to change clothes since the insurgence on Friday. He looked tired, and suddenly older than his twenty-two or twenty-three years. Grime smeared his face and his longish black hair clung limply to his nape. It was Ricky who, very sheepishly, informed him that Gooding wanted to see him right away.

And now he was here, with the older woman, immaculately made up even in this time of crisis, at one side of the huge desk, and him, gray with horror, on the other. He attempted to reason with her. "Ms. Gooding, I understand why you should assume the culprit to be me, but in all fairness, why in the name of God would I want to sabotage the plant?"

Her lips drew back into a thin smile. "Deducing your motive is not my responsibility, Mr. Devane. All I know is that the plant's production has been gravely affected since your arrival, you have put your men at risk more than once. . . ."

He interrupted hotly. "I have never put my men at risk . . . at *any* time. Emory Payne's accident was the result of a deliberate act of sabotage, as I outlined to you in my report. But as I said, I don't have a suspect. Until we find the guilty party, the incident is still under investigation."

Gooding raised a well-manicured hand to stop him from going any further. "It may be under investigation, Christian, but I think it's my duty to inform you that you will not be part of the investigating team, and that we do have a suspect: you."

He was launched to his feet by sheer outrage. "That's ridiculous! How the hell could I be suspected of. . . ."

"Have a seat, Christian!" Angry, Gooding had risen to her own feet and was glaring at him across the table. "It has gone far beyond even that accident now. When you're talking about a quarter of a million dollars' worth of the company's product"—she pointed wildly at the sheets of paper that Christian clutched in his hand—"you have to realize that this has all gotten more serious."

Christian stared down at the paper in his hand. They were lab results from the last round of testing he had done on the methanol stored in the huge storage tanks on the compound. He remembered giddily that he had gone out to assist with the testing on Friday, while he was awaiting Gooding's acknowledgment of his last report. The storage tanks were several stories high, and the only method of testing was to climb to the top, and lower small sample bottles into the volatile liquid through a small opening. Then they were sent to the labs for routine quality control testing. In spite of the unrest, it would seem that the testing had gone on as scheduled.

This time, the results came back with a bombshell. The contents of tank four were contaminated—with salt. Christian shook his head. He'd been neatly framed with a trick that was so easy, it was almost laughable. He'd heard reports of it being done in methanol plants in Nigeria, where he'd last worked. It was simple; the person lowering sample bottles into the methanol simply had to pour a few ounces of salt dissolved in water into the sample bottle before letting it down into the tank. The tiny amount was all he needed to contaminate the entire tank of methanol, render it useless, and cost the company a horrendous amount of money.

Someone had either contaminated the bottles he and his team had used, or arrived before them and somehow managed to pull his prank unseen. But it was more than just a prank, he reminded himself. It affected the company's resources, it was a tremendous waste of manpower, it would throw their delivery schedule off, and, tragically, it pointed to him as the saboteur.

Gooding was smiling. She had him nailed. Christian felt his stomach churn as he took in the sheer malicious delight on the pinched face. He'd always found her cold; everyone in the office found her cold. She was the target of more spiteful nicknames than anyone else on staff. And he'd always sensed she didn't like him very much, but never bothered to dwell on the suspicion, nor to try too hard to find a reason for it. But this reptilian pleasure hit him hard. It was as if she delighted in seeing him fail, even if as his supervisor it could quite possibly reflect badly on her, too.

"Why would I do this?" he demanded.

Gooding shrugged. "You know what the market has been like for methanol these past few years. Competition is stiff. I'm sure quite a few of our friends in the business would benefit from stealing some of our clients. So less costly than going out there and finding them yourself. . . ." Her lips peeled back over her teeth in a snarl that tried to be a grin. She had him in her sights; all she had to do was pull the trigger.

Well, he wasn't about to let that happen. With a snort of disdain, he was on his feet, shoving his chair roughly aside and striding for the door.

"I want you to gather your personal belongings and be off the plant in half an hour, Christian," she screamed shrilly at his departing back.

Out of the plant? She must be joking. He wasn't leaving until he had the information he needed to clear himself. He stormed down the corridor and into the smaller office he used in the main building for administrative work. His career, his reputation and his future were on the line, and there was one person whose expertise would be crucial to him at this juncture. He snatched up the phone and dialed viciously, punching out the numbers with a pressure that almost hurt his fingers.

"I need you," he said without preamble.

"Come pick me up," Delta said. "I'll be outside waiting."

"This is crazy," Sean protested. She could barely speak the words. Her mouth had ballooned up from the blow Carlos had given her, until it felt as though it was filled with sodden cotton wool. Try as she might, she couldn't rid herself of the metallic, salty taste that plagued her, threatening to torment her stomach until the bile rose out of it.

"Just drive," Carlos snapped. The blunt-nosed weapon that had done so much harm to her face nudged her in the ribs. Between his feet lay a mysterious canvas knapsack that clinked loudly whenever they hit a pothole in the road. Sean hadn't dared ask what was in it; but whatever he had insisted on carrying with them, she knew wouldn't be anything good.

As she drove, her eyes wildly scanned the highway for passing military vehicles. The roads were as dead as a lazy Sunday afternoon, but their quiet desolation had a far more sinister cause; the vast majority of people had done whatever they needed to do after the lifting of the curfew, bought provisions and gas, ensured that relatives were okay, and returned to the relative safety of their homes well before the fall of curfew. Now, by late afternoon, only the brave or the determined were still on the roads.

Adrenaline surged as a deep green Jeep veered into view on the horizon. Soldiers! She shot a quick glance at Carlos to see if he was relaxing his vigilance. His crazed idea to go down to the plant promised nothing but trouble; besides, if they did as he threatened and entered after dark, there would be no one, with the exception of one or two security guards, around to help her. She would be alone on a vast plant, hazards on every side, with a madman bent on vengeance.

Carlos took his eyes from the road and let his gaze catch hers. "Don't even think it," he warned softly.

Her fingers, reaching for the headlights that she had intended flicking as they approached, relaxed. It was no use. Her best opportunity so far was going to hurtle clear past her at a hundred miles an hour, and there wasn't a hell of a lot she could do about it.

"That's better," Carlos said approvingly. "That's a good girl." The nose of the pistol caressed the side of her breast with a lover's insinuating touch.

Despair tore at her. The Jeep was close . . . so close! It rushed past with such speed that the draft rocked her car.

"Stay calm now," he warned. "We wouldn't want anything to happen to you before we can drop in on your boyfriend." He was smiling with the promise of malevolent delights to come.

Christian! What was Carlos planning to do to him? Sean thought of Payne and the explosion that almost killed him. She had no idea how Carlos had managed to pull that one off, but she did know that Christian, being the target of his twisted hate, would suffer so much more if she didn't do something to stop it. With determination and sudden fire, she turned the wheel sharply to the right, sending the vehicle skittering off the paved highway and onto the grassed depression that separated the northbound and southbound carriageways.

After a few teeth-jarring, metal-grinding moments the car came to a dusty halt. Panting, she steeled herself for the retribution that would come. She didn't have to wait long.

"Bitch!" Carlos sprayed spittle in her face with the force of the word. The flat palm of his free hand descended on an already tender face, tearing a cry of agony from her. "There's more to come if those soldiers stop," he warned.

Her fate was sealed; almost out of sight, the Jeep ground to an abrupt halt, veered to the shoulder, and reversed towards them almost at the same speed with which it had passed them. With a squeal of its huge ribbed tires, it pulled up on the roadway just above them and a number of armed men leaped from under the canvas canopy and began skating down towards them.

"I'm warning you, you little ball-breaker, what I was going to do to your boyfriend before ain't nothing compared to what I'm gonna do to him if you squeal on me now. Let me talk our way out of this one, and maybe he'll still be alive to find himself a new career when I'm done with him. Screw this up now, and his blood will be on your head."

It was already on her head, she decided miserably. It was her stupid mistakes and her neglect that had allowed things to progress as far as they already had. If she brought anymore misery upon Christian now, she would never survive the guilt. She said nothing.

Carlos had just enough time to slip the gun into the front of his pants and pull his jacket closed before a soldier came around to his side of the car and leveled a sleek black self-loading rifle at his head.

"Get out," he barked. "Slowly." In the late afternoon heat, even his deep green felt beret couldn't keep rivers of sweat from running down his gleaming black forehead.

"What's the problem, Sir?" Carlos asked with elaborate surprise.

The man picked up on the American accent immediately, and his eyes narrowed calculatingly. He tilted his head just a little, peering inside, trying to size up the couple. His job was to keep the streets clear of looters and troublemakers, not tourists. Satisfied, he lowered the gun. "Are you okay?" he asked after a few seconds' deliberation.

"We're fine," Carlos lied easily. He was playing his American accent to the hilt, recognizing it for the formidable diplomatic weapon that it was. "We musta hit a rock back there. Skated clean off the road."

The soldier signaled to a few of his colleagues, who immediately began inspecting the car for damage. "Looks okay," one called out. "Y'all get out of the car, and we'll pull it back onto the road for you."

With a single nasty glare at Sean, Carlos got out. Sean descended gingerly out her side, landing in soft springy grass. The soldier who had first spoken immediately noticed her bruise. He fingered his weapon again. "What . . . ?"

Carlos stepped forward, schooling his features into a concerned expression. "My girlfriend and I ran into some looters back there. They hit her."

The soldier winced. "You okay?"

"Doctor says she'll be fine," Carlos interjected before Sean could answer. The soldier gave them both one long, sharp look. Sean kept her features deliberately bland, casting her eyes downwards at her shoes. Much as she longed to escape from the untenable position into which Carlos had forced her, the last thing she wanted was to stir up more trouble for Christian. She trembled under the inquisitive gaze of the huge, muscled soldier.

"Get the rope!" he turned and yelled to one of his men. "Let's get these people back on the road."

A mixture of relief and foreboding shot through her.

Under normal circumstances, security officers at Orion's gates carried just a nightstick and perhaps a small pistol for protection. Considering the current social climate, their supervisors had seen fit to supply them with heavy, mean-looking rifles as well. The surly young guard who confronted Christian and Delta looked as if he hadn't used one before, but was itching to try it at least once.

"Ah have mah ordahs," he was saying loudly to Christian in his thick Trinidadian accent. "Miz Gooding say you not supposed to be here, so you can't come in."

Delta wasn't the least bit intimidated by the weapon, even though it was almost as long as she was tall. "I don't care what your orders are, mister." She stuck out her jaw aggressively. "We're coming through."

The safety clicked off with the ease of a well-oiled catch. Delta didn't flinch. "You ain't coming in. An have mah ordahs, and dat is dat."

Christian watched in admiration as Delta struck a threatening courtroom pose, pointing directly at the man's badged chest. "This employee was wrongfully suspended. He has work to do. You will let us in, or I'm going to sue Orion. . . ."

"Orion don't sign my paycheck," he countered gleefully.

". . . I'm going to sue your security firm . . ." she went on, undaunted.

The guard was enjoying the game. "I don't care. It have plenty other work out there." He patted the rifle for punctuation. "Plenty, plenty."

". . . and," she delivered her *coup de grace* with triumphant malice, falling into her own vernacular for emphasis. "I'm gonna sue your ras' so hard and so fast, you never gonna know how you gonna feed any of your pick'ney ever again."

The threat of personal litigation might have had no basis in law, but the guard was none the wiser. He flinched. She'd hit him where it hurt. Grudgingly, he stepped aside. "I ain't getting into trouble for the likes ah you," he growled, allowing them access.

She'd dazzled him with bullshit; Christian smiled with awe. She'd got him inside. Now to dig up the evidence that would clear his name.

The defeated security guard couldn't resist a parting shot. "Goddam Jamaican," he hissed as she sailed gleefully past.

"Rawtid Trinidadian," she countered jubilantly, and led the way into the administration building.

Inside, Christian took charge. He threw open his filing cabinets and tossed files onto his desk. Some were easily six inches thick. "We've got to find out two things; first, exactly how all this has been going down. Second, who's been doing it. I'm not taking the fall for this."

He began flipping through the piles of papers.

"You won't take a fall," Delta promised. She laid a tiny hand lightly on the back of his neck. "I won't let you."

The sincerity in her deep brown eyes made him ashamed that he'd ever suspected her to be a part of this whole mess, for now he was convinced that the person who was targeting him and the one who was tormenting Sean was one and the same. He was glad she was on his side. He let her put her arms around him in a comforting hug, and for a fleeting moment he remembered the attraction he'd felt for her before Sean had obliterated every thought of any other woman from his mind. He returned the hug gratefully, hesitating just a little as he felt her slight frame pressed against him, and then she pulled away. Somewhere in her liquid eyes, she recognized his attraction and acknowledged the reason he couldn't give in to it. She smiled, patted his cheek one last time, and picked up a file.

"I wish she was here," he sighed. It was a dark hour for him, and although he hated the idea of exposing Sean to risk, he wished she could be at his side, fighting for him. Even if today she didn't seem as if he and she had anything to fight for.

"Don't worry," Delta comforted. "We'll put our heads together and solve this problem, even if we have to ride out the curfew hours in here. By morning, you'll be in the clear, and then you can go home to Sean. She's safer where she is, anyway."

Christian nodded uneasily.

The water was cold. It soaked into Sean's jeans, penetrating her underwear, making her wrinkle her nose in disgust at the idea of the filthy water, brown with effluent

from the towering industrial plants around them and the
ragged shanties nearby, touching her naked skin. It was
a recipe for infection. She shuddered.

"I think you'll be happy to know that the gun works
as well wet as it does dry," Carlos said with a touch of
humor. "But don't make me prove it to you."

Sean wouldn't dream of it. In the past few hours Carlos
had taught her he meant business. He had forced her to
ditch the car a mile or so from Orion, whereupon they
had clambered down the uneven rocky hillocks that
sloped towards the muddy beach running past the plants.
His gun was hidden, but Sean was acutely aware of its
existence. The knapsack that he forced her to carry was
heavy, and it cut into her shoulder as they made their
way under the brutal afternoon sun.

As they waded along the mudbanks, facing the incoming tide, curious eyes followed. The handful of squatter
families whom Sean had been bent on persuading to
move had stubbornly dug in their heels, in spite of the
horror of living in the shadow of dangerous chemical
plants. As she passed, she wondered if they recognized
her, disheveled as she was. Her long thick hair was a messy
tangle, its burnished tone dimmed by a fine powder of
dust. Sweat, grime and fear distorted her face, and her
clothes were torn and filthy. Fat-bellied, naked children
gaped as they passed; adults eyed them silently. Any penetration into the tiny mudflats they called home was a potential threat.

They walked past the clumsily constructed clapboard
houses without so much as glancing at the inhabitants.
Finally, as they continued on without stopping, the squatter families were satisfied that they posed no threat, and
so returned to the business of eking out a living on the
harsh land.

"Stop," Carlos barked.

Battered and browbeaten into obedience, Sean stopped.

Grasping her arm with unwarranted force, he shoved her into the shadow of an ugly gray sea wall that supported the farthest side of Orion's land. "Sit down," he commanded. Sean looked dubiously down at the stones lining the base of the wall, where moss grew side by side with an unidentifiable gray slime.

"What are we doing here?" she asked instead of complying.

"Waiting."

She looked at him from under the damp muddy clumps of hair that fell over her face. He was implacable; the rage she'd seen in him back at the apartment had been replaced by something resembling serenity. She wasn't sure if she should ask, but did anyway. "Waiting for what?"

He spat on the ground and took his own cool time withdrawing one of his long, slim Cuban cigars from his breast pocket. Unwrapping it with his teeth, he bit savagely down on one end, tore it off, and lit it. Sean's hopes sank; he was making himself comfortable for a long siege. "What are we waiting on?" he asked rhetorically, and forced her into a sitting position with the pressure of one hand. "Darkness, my dear." He blew a foul cloud of smoke in her direction.

Something wasn't right with Sean. Christian was sure of it. He let the phone fall back into its cradle. "She's not home," he said dully to Delta, who hovered anxiously over his shoulder.

"Maybe the lines are down," she soothed. "There were an awful lot of fires out there. Maybe the looters unplugged it."

He shook his head. "They never came."

She turned her sharp eyes on him. "What?"

"The looters. They never came to her place. They hit

everyone else in the compound, it seems, but not her place."

Delta shook her head. "That doesn't make any sense. The house was empty. It would have been like Christmas to those guys."

He rubbed his eyes with a weary hand. There was too much that just didn't make sense. He plopped heavily back into his chair. Delta recognized his fatigue and sought to comfort him by winding her arms around his stooped shoulders. "Come on, let's just get through these manning reports, and then you can go home to her. The way I see it, the same crew was on duty every time something went wrong on the plant. All we have to do is figure out who could have been stationed where, and we can narrow it down even more."

Christian tried to concentrate on the papers again, more out of a desire to please her than out of a need to solve his mystery. For the thousandth time he was thankful for Delta's support, glad to have her there. But his thoughts kept going back again and again to another woman, one who had possessed him so thoroughly that he was sure he could hear her breathe, knew when her pulse quickened or slowed, and when something weighed upon her heart, even when she was miles away. And the sadness—no, foreboding that he felt now left him with an acute sense of impending disaster.

What was wrong with him? He knew something wasn't right with her; every nerve within him was screaming out for him to get up, find her, help her, save her . . . from what, he didn't know. He stood abruptly and began searching for his things. What purpose did it serve to expend his energies trying to save his own career when his career would mean nothing if harm came to Sean?

That was it. She needed him, and he was going to her. With a growl, he encircled Delta's fine wrists with his hands, removing them gently from his shoulders. Delta straightened, confusion written on her small features. "Christian?"

"I'm sorry," he started to say, before the door to his office imploded.

"What the hell are you still doing here?" Gooding had stripped herself of all pretense of corporate decorum. She stood in the doorway like a hellion, eyes ablaze with a pale fire, skin inflamed with anger. Her neatly combed hair bristled with energy, coming alive like Medusa's serpents. The sight of her was enough to cause his bowels to twist.

He struggled to master the situation; he wasn't allowing her to gain the upper hand, not now. "I'm in *my* office, going through *my* files," he answered with quiet determination. He let his black eyes hold hers with a steady stare.

His calm only served to anger her more. "Your files? *Your* files? The aren't yours anymore, are they? You're suspended. As a matter of fact, you're fired. Get out!"

"A member of Management can only be fired by the Board," Delta reminded her pleasantly.

Gooding chose to pretend she didn't hear that. "Are you leaving or what?" she snarled, her eyes never leaving Christian's face.

Christian was almost swayed from his recent decision to leave, just so that he could set Gooding's teeth a little further on edge. Instead, he said calmly, "I'll leave when it suits me, Andrea. I have a saboteur to find."

She blinked rapidly, then found her voice. "Go ahead, blame it on someone else. That'd be just like you. I know you're guilty. And believe me, the Board will take my word for it."

He sighed wearily. "Whatever. Now, if you don't mind. . . ." He waited for her to leave.

She glared at them both, taking in Delta's close proximity to Christian with a satisfied smirk. "I'm not leaving this compound unless you do," she warned him darkly.

"Curfew starts at six," Delta reminded her with forged innocence.

"Then I guess I'll have to spend the night," Gooding snapped and made her way noisily down the hall, footsteps echoing in the empty building.

"She hates you," Delta observed unnecessarily as the woman rounded the corner.

Christian shrugged. "I suppose she thinks I've embarrassed her in front of the rest of the company. She is my supervisor, and I seem to be the villain of the place."

"Not for long," Delta said loyally, and returned to the piles of papers. "Come on, let's keep digging."

He couldn't keep on working. Standing next to her, he laid a light hand on her shoulder. "I'm sorry. I'm sorry I dragged you out here and wasted your time, but I can't stay. Something's wrong with Sean. I can sense it."

"B-b-but we have to keep looking through the papers!" The sweep of her arm encompassed the mess on his desk. "Your career's in trouble, and we have to get to the root of this. This might be our last chance to get you into the building. Didn't you hear what Gooding just said? And once you leave on suspension. . . ."

"Screw that!" he exclaimed forcefully. His patience was stretched thin. "We've been looking for hours, and we've found nothing. I have no enemies here, I've stepped on no toes. Besides, the person targeting me is bound to be the same person taunting Sean. Who could possibly want to harm us both? Nobody. We're chasing after a ghost."

In frustration, he gestured wildly, the office keys clutched in his hand jingling like small bells. As he threw his arm out, the keys slipped from his hands, sailing across the room and impacting against the glass of a small cabinet against the far wall. The thin glass shattered like fine crystal.

Delta moved quickly, hooking the key ring with a little finger and picking it up without risking a cut. Christian stretched his hand out for them, saying, "Come on, I'll take you home, then I'll go to Sean."

Instead of responding, Delta seemed engrossed in the heavy bunch of keys, her face a screen on which emotions flitted too rapidly for him to identify. "You do have an enemy," she exhaled finally. "You both do."

Christian was incredulous. "You can't be serious! I've been here a matter of months. Part of that time I was recuperating from a goddamn bombing. Where would I have found the time to make an enemy?"

Delta waved away his protests. "You inherited one, even before you got here," she answered cryptically. Holding out her hand, face up, she forced Christian to take a second look at his own keys.

His face grayed with shock. The keys to his office, locker and other rooms were linked together by a standard office-issue metal tag, stamped with the name of the Operations Manager. The only thing was, nobody had thought to have a new key ring made for him when he came, and he'd never seemed to mind carrying around a bunch of keys that bore the name of his predecessor.

"Carlos Fabregas," he breathed. It was like a light switching on.

"You took his job. . . ." Delta began quietly.

"He forfeited his job!" Christian protested, "through incompetence and endangering his own men."

". . . and you took his woman," she finished. She didn't look up at him.

"What?" he asked weakly.

"She never told you," Delta stated.

Christian was giddy. "No."

"It wasn't for long," she apologized on her friend's behalf. "It didn't last. It couldn't last. He wasn't right for her, and she realized it fast enough."

"You're damn right he wasn't for her! From what I heard, that bastard was a womanizing drunk! Why him?

What did she see in him?" He was shaken. The first part of him that took a slug was his ego: if she could see her way clear to sleeping with a bastard like Fabregas, then what did it say about how she saw him, Christian? And if she gave of herself to that man, what kind of value did it place on the loving she had so recently given to *him*?

Delta gave an 'it was one of those things' shrug. "She was lonely. She was far from home, and I guess she needed someone. It happens."

Christian could feel a pain in the depth of his abdomen, slicing up under his ribcage like a fine hot blade. He wasn't prone to jealousy; he didn't think he'd ever felt enough for any other woman to justify such a primitive possessive instinct. But he recognized the emotion now, and his first taste of it was galling. But the aftertaste, which tinged the savage emotion like the putrid metallic edge that coats the tongue after a taste of blood, was anger. He wanted to find Fabregas, search him out, drag him out of his lair like the worm that he was. He wanted to feel his fists connecting with that bastard's flesh, make the ground beneath them hum as he pummeled away his hurt.

Then there was Sean.

She'd had an affair with his predecessor, a man whom he'd never met but for whom he'd held nothing but contempt. For him, not telling was as bad as lying. "She could have told me." He let out a ragged breath that hurt as it escaped him. "All she had to do was say. I'm not a monster, I would have understood."

Delta rose to Sean's defense. "She was afraid! She didn't know what you would say!"

"She's always been afraid!" he spat in frustration. "She's always been afraid of something or the other, too scared to trust. She's never trusted me. I'd be fooling myself to think she ever will, and I can't live in a relationship like that."

"What, so you're just going to give up on her? Just like that? Because she slept with someone you don't approve of?" Delta was rounding on *him* now, her fine nostrils flaring. Her fierceness almost frightened him.

"Not because of the man," he answered brokenly. "Because of the lie." Maybe Sean had been right this morning. Maybe there wasn't anything to talk about. He'd gone and overrated the sex they'd had, that's what. He and his army buddies used to say "hard in the crotch, soft in the head." But he'd never expected that sort of thing to happen to him. He snorted out of contempt for his own idiocy.

Delta watched him for a long time. "She still needs you," she said at last. "You sensed she was in trouble. She probably is. Carlos isn't a man to be toyed with."

"Fabregas isn't here," Christian grunted. "He's thousands of miles away, back in the States."

Delta shook her head. She could now feel the same cold dread that Christian was feeling, a sureness that something awful was about to happen. The unknown impending evil frightened her. "Think again," she told him.

"Climb faster, dammit." Carlos poked Sean's bottom viciously, trying to force her up and over Orion's back fence. She dangled, clutching the chain link with hands that were slick with nervous sweat. Her sneakered feet were too big to fit into the small trapezoids formed by the linkages, so Carlos had forced her to discard them at the base of the fence, where the incoming tide now lapped. Now, the harsh wire cut into her delicate soles, making every foothold agony.

Having Carlos coming up behind her did nothing to make the faltering climb any easier. The darkness that deepened around them with typical tropical suddenness made it all the worse. Hanging precariously at the top, she could barely see the menacing razor wire that festooned the upper rim within inches of her face.

"Climb over! Climb over!" he urged her roughly, punctuating his words with a flat palm that pushed up on her bottom again. The loathsome intimacy of the gesture made her gag.

"Razor wire!" she panted in protest. Her mouth was as dry from fear as it was from the hours she'd spent cowering at the cliff base, pressed flat against the clay promontory to ensure they wouldn't be spotted.

"Pretend it isn't really there," Carlos retorted, and laughed.

The emptiness of the laughter chilled her heart; the muddled hopes of somehow attaining salvation by biding her time and playing along with him was beginning to fade. She was in serious trouble, and she had no idea how she was going to get out of it. Carlos was getting worse, veering between sadistic coldness and incoherent mirth. A usually fastidious man, he would never have dreamed of getting his feet wet in the nasty water they had traversed earlier, much less gone clambering up over sharp wire fencing that could tear into flesh like claws. The fact that he could so easily contemplate inflicting such pain on himself made her realize, if she hadn't before, that he was off-balance enough to prove lethal, if she made the wrong move.

Where was Security when you needed them? Probably out front, sipping coffee, she thought contemptuously, instead of patrolling like they were paid to do. Still clinging to the top of the fence, she peered anxiously through the loops of sharp wire. The plant was dimly lit, as power had not yet been fully restored. It was silent. The accustomed hum of a thousand machines carrying out a thousand processes was replaced with a ghastly silence. But somewhere in there was Christian: she knew it in the depth of herself.

"Go over!" he barked again, all patience lost. The insistent patting of her backside was now replaced by a more sinister prodding that could be nothing other than his gun. The reappearance of the dreaded object made her whimper.

"The wire," she protested, embarrassed by the piteous tone of her own voice, "I can't get over it."

"Here," he said in a macabre parody of kindness, "let me help you." With a surge of strength that only the insane possess, he shoved her mightily, and Sean felt herself clear the twisted curl of razor wire—almost. As she descended on the other side, some of the teeth seemed to reach out for her, like claws on something alive. She felt a shredding of her skin, along her arms and legs, as the wire sliced into her so cleanly that she didn't begin to bleed until well after she hit the ground.

She lay there sobbing as Carlos landed beside her in the dark, dragging his heavy canvas knapsack over with a thud. Her head hurt; she was sure she had hit her already painful jaw. Her pelvis was twisted and her arms and legs lay in a tangle. As she struggled through the molasses of her thoughts, she felt him tugging impatiently at her tired body.

"On your feet," he ordered. She had no idea how she found the strength to comply. Each step hurt. He half-led, half-dragged her past the looming, silent methanol tanks that stood like round gravestones in a gigantic cemetery. Their gray forms were shrouded in shadows, and their silence, in contrast to their usual activity, frightened and disheartened her.

They passed the last of the tanks, into an area reserved for other processing operations, where a variety of oddly shaped buildings and installations gleamed dully by the little light there was. A few hundred yards away, the Control Room stood wreathed in shadows, pale light showing through its windows.

He was in there! Her heart thudded against her bruised ribs. Chris was there; all she had to do was get to him, break loose from this monster and run like hell across the plant, shout and wave until he heard her and came outside. Then she wouldn't have to worry anymore, because he would be in control, and Chris would make things right.

She didn't stop to think, plan or reflect. Action followed swiftly upon the heels of thought, and before she realized it she was free from his unsuspecting grip and running, bare feet thudding down onto cruel gravel, lungs fighting for air, just running. She heard, sensed, and felt him hard behind her, heard each expelled breath like that of an enraged animal, footfalls huge and echoing, closer. . . . She was within yards of the Control Room, screaming "Chris! Chris!" sure that he could hear, when the heavy hand of her tormentor slapped against her open protesting mouth, covering her nose as well, cutting off her air.

She struggled wildly, twisting and bucking, like a shark that refused to be reeled in. Sharp teeth sank into his hand, drawing blood and curses. In the few seconds that he was distracted, she sought to cry out the name of her savior again, hoping that he would hear and respond. Then, with a tackle worthy of any football game, she was down.

"I'm sorry," she heard him say, his voice like a penitent child.

"For what?" She was confused. He had forced her out of her home and into a hellish march through mud and waste, was torturing her, taunting her with a gun and an uncertain future, and now he was saying he was sorry? She moved her swollen lips again, forcing out the words. "For what?"

"For this," he said, sounding weary of the game, and his hands closed against her carotid.

Light . . . or something resembling it. Sean peered

through gummy eyes. Wasn't heaven supposed to be better lit than this? Maybe she had overestimated her final destination. She tried to move, and the jarring pain that shot through her destroyed any misconception she might have held about her spiritual and corporeal selves having parted company. She was still very much earthbound, and very much a prisoner.

"I'd advise you to do that slowly," Carlos cautioned.

Understatement! The range through which she could move her head was surprisingly limited. It seemed be swathed in something sticky that crinkled as she moved. She put a hand up to her forehead, tentatively touching what seemed to be bandages. Running her fingers along the wide rough band, her hand encountered something that made her wish she was unconscious again. It was Carlos's gun, and it was taped to her head, with the barrel of it pointing firmly at her right temple. To make the nightmare far worse than she could ever have imagined, Carlos's left hand was taped to the other end of the gun, and his finger was on the trigger. Now she knew that one of the items he'd carried around so purposefully in the bag was tape.

"You haven't got a *clue* how hard it was to rig that up single-handedly," he observed conversationally. He sounded as if he was admiring a room he had decorated all by himself, or an engine he'd scrapped down and put back together without consulting a manual.

There was nothing she could say.

"Up," he instructed. Then he added needlessly, "Very gently."

She took his advice. Gingerly, they rose together. Responding to his prodding, she walked beside him, taking careful steps, ensuring that her foot was firmly planted before she lifted the other one. Sean was painfully aware that if she or he were to trip and fall, his hand would convulse around the trigger. . . . She couldn't think beyond that.

She didn't even want to ask where he was taking her next. Anywhere on the plant would be a hazard zone, once he had a loaded weapon. The risks were higher than her own shooting death: a stray bullet hitting almost any fixture on the plant would result in a methanol explosion that would tear the entire plant up out of the ground and toss it into the air like a divot.

Carlos seemed to be rambling about, almost as if he wasn't quite sure what lay where anymore. A thought hit her: he was a heroin addict, that much he'd admitted. What if he was aching for a fix? That would account for his disorientation, his near incoherence. It made him even more unpredictable.

Wildly, she struggled to control her racing pulse as they inched past the Control Room. Christian was sure to be in there with his men. Knowing better than to call out loud for him, she sent out frantic mental messages, bright hot balls of energy that she launched, picturing him being bombarded by them as they sailed towards his head on waves of psychic light.

Nothing. They passed the Control Room and were once again surrounded by darkness. The sound of her feet hitting asphalt told her that they were on their way towards the Flare Knockout Drum, a grotesque bullet-shaped structure where highly volatile impurities like ethanol were removed as part of the process. Its contents were so dangerous that they were piped a full quarter of a mile away before they could be harmlessly burned. Usually, at night, the flare of burning ethanol stood against the skyline like a small version of Lady Liberty's torch. Tonight, there was no flare. The Drum sat silently in the darkness and hoarded its lethal contents.

As Carlos stopped, Sean's heart sank with disappointment and dread. As perversity would have it, he'd chosen one of the most frightening places on the plant, outside of the methanol tanks themselves, in which to play out the next step of his little game.

"This'll do just fine," he murmured.

She had to find out. Keeping her tone level and non-confrontational, she asked, "For what?"

"For this," he replied, and reached out and yanked down the fire alarm.

The shriek slammed into her like a physical force, causing her to jump back in sudden panic. The bandages around her head tugged, and in horror, thought processes moving almost in slow motion, she realized that her reflex action had caused a tugging on the hand that held the gun.

"Don't move a muscle!" Carlos barked above the scream of the alarms, which had been set off all across the entire plant. Her guts turned to liquid when she realized that her movement had put pressure on the trigger, which was now halfway depressed. She knew very little about guns, but she knew enough to picture the hammer now half cocked, poised and awaiting a signal to fall, sending a bullet slamming into her brain. Breath eluded her.

Carlos lightly, gently, gingerly inserted a finger of his other hand between the hammer and the pin, preventing further movement. With infinitesimal movements, he eased up on the trigger, allowing it to move forward, and lowering the hammer softly back into its resting position. "Next time, I'm not stopping it from going all the way," he warned.

Sean took him at his word. It had been a close call, but she knew better than to mistake his gesture for kindness. He saved her only because it fit into his plans. But at least she was alive. She hoped to God she hadn't wet herself; in her numbed state, she had no way of telling. Not that it mattered; she was damp and filthy enough as it was.

There were shouts and running feet as the few souls still housed within the building after the fall of curfew came running in response to the alarm. She searched desperately through the darkness, searching for the silhouette of broad shoulders and a thick, solid chest. She recognized Christian immediately, leading the pack. Her relief was close to hysteria.

"Chris!" she shouted his name, fearing that for some reason he wouldn't hear her, or run right past her, unseeing.

He was running, tailed by a handful of men, two Security Guards, Delta and Andrea Gooding. The second he was close enough to see her predicament and understand it for what it was, he stopped short, spraying gravel under his boots.

"Goddamn!" he expelled, eyes round with shock.

"Chris, please," she begged. She could see only him, was aware of only him. Everything else was shoved into the peripheries of her vision.

"Shut up!" Carlos dug her in the ribs.

Cowed now, completely at his will, she shut up miserably. Her only hope was Christian. Her only lifesaver was Christian. She laid her trust at his feet and waited dully.

"Let my woman go, Fabregas." Coming from Christian, it was a calm order given by a man who was accustomed to being obeyed.

Carlos snorted. *"Your* woman?" He threw a sidelong look of contempt at her. "Gets around, doesn't she?"

Sean cringed with shame as Christian flinched under the other man's mocking taunt. She saw that pain in his eyes, a hurt that rimmed the fear for her safety. She was guilty of never having told him about her disastrous affair with the man whose gun was now aimed at her temple. She had, in effect, lied to him by omission. She looked at Christian, so beautiful and noble, even under these circumstances, and then thought of how she must look, wet, dirty, bruised and beaten on the outside, and a deceiver on the inside. She was ashamed.

"Let—my—woman—go," Christian repeated, enunciating every word deliberately. Sean felt a surge of joy that was immediately dampened by Carlos's response.

"Kind of hard to do, under the circumstances." He indicated the tape, and the gun, with his free hand. Then, with a sudden movement of the head, he turned to look at the two security guards, who were taking advantage of the situation to inch closer and unholster their weapons.

"Don't even try," he snarled. "Drop 'em, and kick 'em over here."

Sullenly, the two guards threw their weapons to the ground and kicked them towards him.

"You, Delta, come over here and pick them up."

Delta complied, but her entire small body screamed defiance. She picked up the two weapons, holding them gingerly by the barrels. Even in such a potentially inflammatory situation, she refused to be cowed. She approached him slowly, glaring unabashed at his face and muttering under her breath, "You strung out . . . ."

"Don't even consider using them, Shorty. Lemme tell you how this works. You draw on me, I pull the trigger. You shoot me, I fall, and as I fall, my hand squeezes down on the trigger. Either way. . . ." he shrugged. There was no need for him to finish.

"What do you want?" Christian fought to take control of the situation.

Carlos seemed to hesitate. He didn't seem able to answer that one. He closed his eyes for a while, thinking. "I don't know. Quiet, lemme think." He was definitely slowing down. His voice was becoming slurred.

"You can have my job back," Christian offered.

Carlos laughed. "Aw, come one, you know as well as I do that nobody in their right mind will ever hire me again. My career is over. I'm done as an engineer." He turned his head accusingly towards Sean. "Thanks to a bitch who just didn't know how to shut up."

"She had nothing to do with it," Christian countered. "You know that. You lapsed in your responsibilities. It was always your fault." He was taking a chance, but deflecting Carlos's anger seemed like the only option open to him.

"Don't tell me that she got you so bamboozled you don't recognize a jealous, paranoid bitch when you see one." Carlos spat on the ground. "She had a real problem with insecurity, you know: what was I doing when I wasn't with her?, who was I out with?, was there someone else?, you know, woman shit. 'Til one day she decided to get even with me over the chicks, and went squealing to the President. Got me fired. Now she pays."

There was a silence that nobody seemed to know how to fill. Finally, Carlos filled it himself. "So, I hear you aren't doing too hot on the job yourself, Devane." He gave a smile of deadly satisfaction.

Christian nodded in exaggerated agreement. "It's been tough."

"Why? Because you didn't turn out to be the wonder everyone said you were?" Carlos gloated.

Christian didn't even bother to acknowledge the sabotage that Carlos himself had launched against him. Instead, he continued playing along. "Them's the breaks," he said affably, and waited for Fabregas's next gambit.

"I'm getting tired," Carlos commented, as if he'd just realized it. "My hand hurts. It ain't easy holding it out to my side all this time, you know." His voice was petulant, almost accusing, as if it was Christian's fault he had his hand taped to Sean's head in the first place.

"Then maybe we could help you. We could get that tape off, then you can put your hand down." Christian's voice was silky, cajoling.

Carlos reacted with startled cynicism. "You screwing

with me, man! What do you take me for? A damn fool? Maybe I should pull the trigger now, get it over with."

Sean cringed, a cry went up from the crowd, but Carlos made no move. He was pale as a headstone now, face gleaming like gray marble, sweat springing from his hairline and flowing downwards. He looked seriously ill.

When Gooding spoke up, all heads turned in surprise. "Carlos, it's time to stop." She took several steps forward. She was as pale as he, hair disheveled, linen suit hanging limply from cowed shoulders. Carlos's eyes became riveted on her. She spoke softly with a quaking voice that was a far cry from her usual authoritative bellow. "Darling, please, you've gone too far. Let her go. You're sick, you need your medicine. Let her go, and we'll get you some, okay?"

Carlos hesitated. He turned his head to look at Sean's strained, terrified face, then turned again to look at Gooding, who was still approaching slowly, step by step. "Don't come closer, Andie!" he warned.

"Love, let me help you. Don't let this go any further."

Shock waves rolled through them. *Andie? Love?* Gooding and Fabregas, lovers? It boggled the mind. Sean thought about Gooding's irrational mistreatment of Christian, and it all clicked into place; Gooding had been aiding and abetting the deliberate destruction of Christian's career all along. It made sense. Carlos had to have had inside help; his face was well known on the plant— he'd never have been able to have pulled off all that he did on his own.

She was still approaching Carlos, one arm outstretched. When she got within ten feet, Carlos commanded her to stop. Sean could see the tears on the woman's stricken face. Even in her present dire straits, and although Gooding was a woman she had never liked, Sean pitied her.

Carlos sighed, and his body seemed to deflate. Either Gooding had somehow managed to make him see reason, or he was simply too tired to go on. "Get this tape off your girlfriend, Shorty," he said to Delta without even looking at her.

Delta grinned jubilantly and immediately set about trying to gingerly peel away the strips of duct tape stuck to Sean's head. It only took her a few seconds to realize that it was so firmly stuck to Sean's hair that it wouldn't budge. Tugging was not an option.

Christian recognized the problem. With slow deliberate movements he extracted his penknife from his back pocket and kicked it towards her. Delta flicked it open and gingerly began snipping away at Sean's hair.

"Sorry, babe," she whispered into her friend's ear.

"Be my guest," Sean almost managed to smile, in spite of the thick chestnut clumps that fell at her feet. Finally free, she bolted from Carlos's side until she slumped sobbing into Christian's arms. The feel of his hard chest and the smell of him were more comforting than she had ever imagined. His big hands moved up to cradle her head, and he showered kisses of relief all over her face.

"That's enough!" Carlos couldn't stand to look at them. He was still holding the gun, and Delta still worked diligently at snipping away the tape that fixed it to his hand. He was tired, swaying like a drunk. The ordeal wasn't over yet.

"Why don't you put it down now, Fabregas," Christian suggested gently. "There's no harm done. We can go inside, have some coffee, and then we can get you to a hospital."

"I don't want to go to no hospital," Carlos slurred. "I'm fine."

"Whatever you like," Christian promised, still holding Sean to him. "Just put it down, and walk away. You've done no harm, and we can just forget it."

Everyone waited. Slowly, he bent forward and laid the gun at his feet. Delta kicked it a few feet away, and it lay close to the two guns belonging to the security guards.

Gooding closed the distance between herself and her lover, putting her arms around him in an uncharacteristic gesture of warmth. Everyone exhaled.

"Let's go to the Control Room," Christian suggested. "It's over now."

Slowly, and dejectedly, they turned to leave. They hadn't gone more than three paces when a broken voice behind Christian and Sean piped up.

"I didn't mean for it to turn out like this."

Everyone turned and stared. Young Ricky Conrad, Christian's favorite technician, was lagging behind, hanging his head. His dark, long-lashed eyes were filled with glittering tears. "I'm sorry man, I respect you. I'm sorry. I didn't know it would go this far."

Gooding let go of Carlos and turned on the slender young man. "Shut up, Ricky!" she hissed. There were signs of the serpent within her coming awake again. "It's over. Shut up!"

Ricky shook his head. "It's not over, Andrea. I can't let it end like this."

"For Pete's sake, don't say another . . ."

Carlos shoved through the crowd and stood aggressively before Ricky. "Andrea, who is this child?"

She waved her hands dismissively. "Just a technician, love. He's nothing."

Carlos wasn't being so easily deterred. "What did he mean, about being sorry? Why did he call you Andrea?"

"It's nothing," she insisted firmly. "Let's go inside."

"We are not going anywhere until you tell me. . . ."

"He's just the boy I got to handle the details on the plant," Gooding blurted. "You didn't expect me to go shinnying up the side of a methanol tank to toss salt inside, did you? I'm an executive, not a field worker."

Carlos examined the cowering boy with slitted eyes. "Fine, but why did he call you Andrea?"

Ricky was sobbing openly now, his resistance broken by

guilt and shame. "She made me. She made me. I didn't want to do it."

"Did she pay you?" Carlos growled.

He shook his head, unable to speak.

"Then how did she make you?"

Ricky didn't answer.

"Bitch!" Carlos rounded on Gooding, taking hold of her by the throat. "You slept with him, didn't you? He's half your age, what did you think you were doing?"

Gooding had returned to her serpentine self. "What did you think, I gave him money and liquor like you did your own staff?" She threw this at him with venom. "Sometimes it takes more than that."

"That's disgusting!" Carlos spat at her.

"Not all the time," she countered snidely. "Sometimes, it was almost a pleasure. But you wouldn't remember about pleasure, would you, since you and the bottle came to be such good friends."

Hell hath no fury like a man whose manhood has been challenged. His hands tightened about her throat like a snare.

"I did it for you," she managed to gasp out, before the pressure on her throat became too much to allow her to speak.

Christian had seen enough. He let Sean go and sprang forward to part Carlos and Gooding. It took a hell of an effort to prize the madman's hands away, as his insanity and rage had given him the strength of a demon. The two men rolled in the dirt, trading punches. Christian, slightly taller and unimpaired by months of drug abuse, managed to dominate, but Carlos was a street fighter, slick, wily, and fueled by blind rage. He broke a hold and started running. Christian followed, body low to the ground, muscles coiled, running like a panther.

To Sean's horror, she watched as Carlos made it to the pile of guns they'd stupidly, stupidly left lying in the dirt.

One seemed to leap into his hand, and he drew it to eye level, taking a bead on Christian.

"Chris!" She shouted out a warning. "The gun!"

Instinctively, he dropped onto his belly as Carlos fired off a shot. It whizzed overhead, disappearing into the night. The stakes had gone up again. A gun had no place on a methanol plant. One burst pipe. . . . "Run!" he shouted.

The crowd looked around in panic. The Control Room was too far away; Carlos could pick off at least a few of them before the others made it inside. The nearest structure large enough to hide behind was the Flare Drum, filled with flammable contents. It wasn't much of a decision.

Human nature being what it is, they made for the Drum, which was closer and darker, hoping to at least draw cover from the bullets. Carlos fired wildly. There was a 'thunk' and a scream as one of the Security Guards was hit. Sean dropped to her knees, grabbing the man by the shoulders and trying to drag him to cover.

By now Christian had seized one of the other guns and was leveling it at Carlos, trying to take aim, but the madman was dancing wildly, darting from side to side as he fired off shots. Unlike Carlos, Christian cared where his bullets went, so he had yet to squeeze off a single round.

The Security Guard was heavy. Sean was slowed down as she tried to half lift, half drag him behind the drum. Seeing her thus encumbered, Carlos grinned cruelly and took aim. The bullet hitting the guard in the back of the thigh entered so hard he felt bone shatter. A scream of agony burst forth from his lips as he pitched forward, one last round exploding from his gun as he went down.

Sean heard a high-pitched whistling sound close to her head, almost like a huge angry bee. The bullet impacted on the metal housing of the flare drum, penetrating with a shower of sparks, bursting through to the contents inside, and suddenly Sean felt a heat she had never before experienced.

Flammable liquids or gases under low pressure, once released, go up in a fine mist, forming a cloud which, if ignited, explodes in a ball of fire that will consume everything in its path. Under high pressure, though, the same substances will jet forth like water from a garden hose. In the presence of a spark they will not explode, but will burn like a torch or a Bunsen burner. The contents of the Flare Drum were kept under very high pressure; they were saved by a miracle of physics.

The realization that the Drum did not explode as she had expected was replaced instantly by a hideous pain in her eyes. The flare had erupted within inches of her face, its brilliant orange flame spewing forth with the force of a rocket at takeoff. Sean dropped the Guard, clasped her hands to her eyes and staggered away from the flame. Then arms were around her, Christian's strong arms, clutching her close. She could hear his panicked questions about whether she was all right, she could smell the stench of fear clinging to him and the stink of her own hair being singed, and as he gathered her into his arms and made toward safety, she could taste the roughness of him as he folded her face into his chest. All around, there were sounds of people reacting as they had been trained, struggling to put out the fire.

With wonder she realized she could hear, feel, smell and taste. The only thing Sean couldn't do was see.

Thirteen

Nurses, doctors, attendants, everyone was gossiping. Everywhere he looked, people were huddled together in small groups, whispering. New arrivals turning up for change of shift were greeted with joyful shouts of "Have you heard? The insurrection is over!" People who had seen the live coverage on TV regaled those who hadn't with stories of how the army had finally ground down the resistance of the hostage takers in the orphanage by starvation and water deprivation, and how, just hours earlier, after five torturous days, they'd released the hostages and given themselves up.

Above his head, a television caged in by wrought-iron blared, as the same newscasters showed the same footage over and over. There were grainy images of the hostage dignitaries and children being escorted out of the besieged building by a phalanx of soldiers. They looked tired and drawn after their ordeal, and many of them had tied handkerchiefs and scarves over their faces to ward off the stench of the bodies that had lain on the ground for almost a week. The children seemed to be the worse off, many of them so exhausted from their ordeal that they had to be carried. Most of them had the blank, empty stare of children in war-torn countries far away, as if the horror that they had witnessed at the hands of the monsters was forever etched in their consciousness

and would forever be a part of them. As he watched them
being swept up in the arms of waiting social workers and
community police officers, Christian felt tears sting his
eyes. The murders and lawlessness unleashed by the cult
was one thing, but the destruction of young psyches was
something the people in this country would never forgive
them for.

The motley bunch of insurrectionists emerged last,
hands behind their heads, each one escorted by a soldier
holding a rifle to his back. They looked astoundingly serene, even nonchalant, as if the mayhem, bloodshed, terror and loss of property they had caused had all been
justified by their zealous religious motivation.

As they walked into the sunlight, soldiers hastened to
surround them, as enraged crowds of onlookers surged
forward, shouting obscenities and threats. Some among
the crowd had to be restrained as in their righteous in-
dignation and grief they sought to force their way past
the soldiers and attack the people responsible for such
destruction.

The camera cut to a shot of their loathsome leader
being forced out of the television station, her huge body
seemingly undiminished by the lack of food and water.
Her slick, gleaming face held no sign of remorse, no recognition that what she had instigated was wrong. She
calmly climbed into the back of the police van and took
a seat.

Christian had had enough; he didn't think his stomach
could take any more of the garish display on the screen.
He was happy that the torment was over for the small
country, but at the moment, his fears and concerns were
directed at the shape that lay in the bed at which he
stood. For a tall woman, Sean looked surprisingly small,
as if the anguish and physical hardship she had endured
all day had somehow caused her to dwindle.

The noise emanating from the television was beginning

to grate on his last nerve. For the tenth time he cast around for the remote control, but somehow it was an amenity that seemed to be missing from the room. The television itself was an ancient relic with twist knobs instead of touch controls—and the knobs had long been lost. Eventually, cursing with frustration, he strode across the floor, reached above his head and tore the cords clean out of the wall. Finally, blessed silence reigned.

The noise hadn't disturbed Sean from her exhausted sleep, but somehow, the quiet penetrated. She stirred, groaning and flailing her limp, sallow hands. Instantly, Christian reached out to clasp them in his own.

"Sean," he whispered. "Lover."

She struggled to yank her hands from his, reaching up frantically to touch the cool bandages that covered her eyes. As she touched them, she flinched and let out a scream. "He's got a gun, Chris! Help me, I can't move!"

For a second he was confused, and then he realized that she thought that Fabregas's gun was still taped to her head. He forced her hands down to her sides and leaned over, trailing his lips gently along her brow, lightly grazing the white gauze, careful not to cause her tortured eyes any pain. Her frantic gasps abated, and slowly she came to her senses.

"It's over," she sighed.

"Yes," he comforted. "It is. They've taken him away, and they've put the fire out."

"The plant didn't go up."

"No, it didn't. We were lucky. The standoff with the hostages is over too."

She let her breath out. "Then everything will be like it was again."

He stroked her cheek with the backs of his fingers, lightly. "Yes, it will."

She was silent for a long time; he could see her jaw twitch and knew that she was turning things around in her mind. He hurt for her, because he knew what she was thinking. He waited patiently, letting her voice her fears for herself.

"Everything back to normal, except for me, right?"

He struggled for something to say. He wanted more than anything else to speak a lie and make it become the truth, tell her that her eyesight would be back any time now. But the truth was that he didn't know how or when that would happen. Nobody knew. He didn't have time to come up with anything comforting to tell her before she went on.

"I can't see."

"Not at the moment, no," he admitted.

"What's that supposed to mean?" she snapped.

He tried to make his tone confident, convincing. "Not right now. But you'll heal. The doctors examined you; it was a flash burn, you were too close to the Drum when it caught fire. There's a little heat damage, and the light, well, it was a little too much for you to handle." He watched as her lips began to tremble, but Sean, bless her stubborn heart, was refusing to give in to tears.

"And . . . ?" she prodded him.

"And your chances look pretty good."

"Not from where I'm standing," she grated.

He sighed. "The chances are good, love. You'll see again. I promise. It will just take a while." He hoped he sounded confident enough to allay her doubts, because he damn well wasn't allaying any of his.

"*A while* can be anything," she replied sarcastically. "Just how long is this 'while' going to take?"

He couldn't bear to hear the frustration and apprehension in her voice. He strove to offer comfort, even if all he had was a doctor's vague approximation. "Weeks, maybe. They don't know."

"And in the meantime I just lie here and pretend it isn't happening."

"No," he answered firmly. "In the meantime I take you home. I'm moving in with you to help you get around. I'll look after you, don't worry."

"Just what I need." Her lips, still swollen from Fabregas's brutality, twisted. "For you to play nursemaid to me. What, did you suddenly acquire a conscience, or are you trying to buy your way into heaven?"

She really stepped on his corns that time. In spite of his sympathy and concern, he felt himself bristle. "Why is it that it's perfectly okay for you to take care of me when I'm wounded, but against the natural order of things for me to return the favor? Why is it that all the things you did for me when I was hurting came naturally to you, but when I try to do them, I'm trying to buy my way into heaven? Give me some credit, Sean. Have some faith in me for a change. Give yourself time to find out the kind of man I really am. You'd like him, if you let yourself know him."

She shrugged petulantly and refused to reply.

He knew that her irritability was caused by pain, fear and the results of a long and traumatic day, but still this knowledge didn't prevent him from cursing in frustration. "You're really trying to make this difficult, you know, Sean. All I want is for you to let me love you."

She laughed, a harsh, grating, humorless sound. *"I'm* making it difficult? It doesn't get any more difficult than this, pal." She turned her body painfully onto her side, so that her back was to him. It grieved him that she had not even acknowledged his last sentence: even a contemptuous rebuff would have been preferable to her complete dismissal of his declaration of love.

"I want to sleep now," she said baldly. Her words were like nails driven into his heart.

Wordlessly, he rose to his feet. He turned off the light, even though in her condition she was incapable of knowing or caring whether it was on or off. He knew she would have preferred it if he were to just leave the hospital, go home and give her a break; but he was sorry, that just wasn't going to happen. He found a large battered armchair a short distance down the hall and dragged it along the grungy carpet until it stood just outside her door. The woman he loved was inside in great pain, and he was damned if her rebuffs would be enough to deter him from standing guard over her and making sure she wouldn't want for anything while she was at the clinic. It was bad enough that he had been too preoccupied with his own troubles to protect her from the danger that Fabregas had put her in today, but he was damned if that was ever going to happen again. With a determined scowl that warded off anyone who would have been tempted to approach her room, he folded his arms and settled into the chair for the night.

The state of emergency remained in effect for two more weeks. The curfew moved gradually back to eight P.M., then nine, ten, and midnight, before being completely lifted. This enabled the authorities to swoop down on the other cult members with a vengeance, seizing their assets, razing the illegal structures that had been erected on state land, and consigning the children into foster care pending the prosecution of their parents. The country licked its wounds, sought to make sense of the tragedy, and did their best to help their lives return to normal.

For Christian, the period was just as difficult. Sean put aside her hostility after a while, and concentrated on learning how to adapt to her visual incapacity. She accepted his assistance with quiet reserve, allowing him to walk her through her own apartment as if for the first time, making sure she knew by touch where the furniture was, where the faucets, refrigerator and radio could be located, and how many steps there were between her bed and the bathroom. She learned fast, but was determined that the knowledge she acquired would not have to be hers for a lifetime. Every day she touched her bandages lightly and informed him that the pain was less, and predicted that her sight would return sooner than the doctors said.

"Any day now," she promised with certainty.

"Any day," he echoed sadly, but his heart was heavy.

They spent their evenings together in the quiet living room, sometimes listening to CDs, other times with the TV on, whereupon he faithfully described every action to her as they followed a program together. Occasionally, though, they sat out on her porch and listened to the sounds of the birds that he had managed to entice back into her garden as she always had, with fruit speared on the spikes of her fence. These were quiet times, in which he burned to broach the subject of their relationship, but never dared. The stony wall that she set up to keep him out of that part of her life was so solid he was afraid that if he tried to kiss her he would collect a nasty bump on his forehead as he came up against it.

Delta made it a point to visit every day, and it was only when the little firebrand was there that he saw any change in Sean. The endless stream of chatter helped her to relax, and even when it was apparent that she wasn't really listening, the company still comforted her. It was when she was alone with Christian that she seemed saddest.

Then one evening, she surprised him. They were sitting closer than they normally sat, out on her quiet back porch, sipping a bucolic flame-colored concoction of mangoes, pink grapefruit and papaya that they had both become addicted to, when she set her drink carefully down on the floor and held out her hand in his general direction. "Chris," she said softly.

His head shot up. She almost never used his name anymore. The sound of it on her lips sent a tremor through him. "Love?" he answered softly, then almost bit his tongue off . . . it had been an effort to avoid that word, which he was sure would send her into another fit of surliness.

To his surprise, she smiled uncertainly and wiggled her fingers, communicating to him her desire for him to hold her hand. He took it. It was warm and dry, and felt smaller than it really was. He didn't want to short-circuit whatever she had in mind by speaking, so instead he waited for her to make the next move. The muscles under her fine facial skin worked agitatedly as her internal battle raged, and then she said, with a hint of her former humor, "I was thinking maybe I need a little help washing my hair this evening."

His brows shot up. Since that evening on the plant, when Delta had been obliged to cut off clumps of it to free her from Fabregas's tape, she had refused to have anything done to it. It hung raggedly around her head, cut short in some places, and singed in others. Even Delta had been unsuccessful in convincing her to allow a hairdresser to come in and even it off. It was as if Sean had been so distressed by the damage done to her crowning glory that she refused to admit that it had ever taken place.

Besides, she had made it very clear to him that she needed no help with any of her intimate needs. The first day he'd brought her home she'd all but shoved him out her room when he'd tried to offer his assistance, informing him tartly that she knew where to find all her body parts. But who was he to argue with good fortune?

She laughed for the first time since that awful day at the plant. "Can't exactly wash my own hair without getting my bandages all messed up, can I?" she added, as if letting him know that she meant her request simply as a matter of hygiene, rather than as a concession to him.

"Besides, when you were sick, I helped you with your cleaning up, so it's time for me to get my pound of flesh."

He couldn't contain the grin that split his face. "My flesh is all yours, Shylock."

She was about to get unsteadily to her feet when he stopped her.

"No, stay. It's a nice sunny afternoon, I can bring the things out and we can do it right here. It'd be like a spa."

She didn't protest.

He set about warming a kettle of water, making trips back and forth until he had laid out her shampoo, conditioner, towel, comb and the largest bowl in her kitchen. With a practiced hand he adjusted the level of her lounge chair so that her poor tattered hair could rest in the bowl of warm water. Docilely, she allowed him to begin to work up a lather on her scalp.

"Funny how everything, the sound of your feet on the tiles, the smell of the shampoo, all seem so much more profound when . . ." she hesitated.

"Not for much longer," he promised.

"I know," she said. For the first time, she sounded almost serene.

As she closed her eyes and let him attend to her, he was able to get a good look at her face. As he did so he realized just how much weight she had lost. The bones on her throat stood out painfully, and he longed to press his lips against them. Not succumbing to the impulse took a powerful act of restraint.

"Your touch feels . . . good," she observed, and swallowed hard.

Just being this close to her was making him giddy. He didn't trust himself to speak. There was nothing but the scent of chamomile between them.

"Nice," she said, inhaling deeply.

"Nice," he echoed. As he poured clean water to rinse her hair, some of it trickled down her neck, soaking the thin cotton housecoat she wore. He swore at his clumsiness.

"Don't worry about it," she waved it off, and to his astonishment, she shrugged out of the top of her coat, and her round soft breasts came into view. He gaped, then checked himself. She couldn't see him ogling, and somehow, it didn't seem fair; it was like a violation of her privacy. Still, as the rose-tipped peaks rose and fell gently before him, he was forced to look away.

They said nothing else as he busied himself working thick, creamy conditioner into her damp locks. She sighed as he combed it through, working from her forehead and gently making his way along the tangled curls. He gave a rueful smile. She might be comfortable, but he was in torment; he had a hard-on that was threatening to drain the last drop of blood from his brain. *Concentrate, Devane,* he advised himself. *Don't let that mind of yours wander, now.* When the conditioner was all washed out, he patted her hair dry as he would that of a small child, and waited, trembling, for her next move.

Playfully, she asked him to shave her legs for her. Without a word, he rose and returned with her shaving kit and another set of towels, and obediently lathered her up. He popped the cover off a new razor and began moving over her legs with long, deliberate strokes. It took a tremendous effort to keep his hands from roaming from the finely defined bones of her ankles to the swell of her calves.

Sean cleared her throat and began to speak. "About Carlos," she said, and the name itself was enough to deflate him, quite literally. "I'm sorry."

His brow furrowed. "For what?"

"You know," she said impatiently. "For not telling you. For not warning you about him."

"It's okay." He'd long given up hope of her ever broaching the subject.

"He tried to ruin you. Him and Andrea Gooding. And Ricky. If I'd said something earlier, told you how he really lost his job, maybe you'd have been able to figure things out earlier, and your good name wouldn't have been at stake."

"My good name is still mine," he insisted. "And as for the others, between the Board and the police they'll all be dealt with. Ricky breaks my heart, though, because I liked him and trusted him. But as for Fabregas," he shrugged, and then remembered she couldn't see him. "We don't really need to talk about him."

"But we do," she insisted. "I can't stand not talking about him anymore. I'm so ashamed of having been with him. I look back on it and I can't believe I was so stupid. I have no idea what was in my head. And every time I think of the fact that he and I actually . . ." She broke off and wrapped her arms around her breasts, as if hiding them from Carlos's absent view.

Her anguish caused his restraint to collapse. He put his arms around her and pulled her against his chest, not caring that the soapy water was penetrating the front of his pants. "Sean, honey, listen. Whatever you did, you shouldn't have to hit yourself over the head with it for the rest of your life. Maybe you were lonely. Maybe you needed something at the time, and he just happened to be the one who was able to provide it. But whatever it was, you don't have to carry it around. Just set it down on the ground and walk away."

Her face showed nothing but pain and remorse, but she seemed to be listening intently. "We all make mistakes, and the ones we make over love and sex just happen to be the ones that hurt the worst. Lord knows I've made enough of those, especially when I was with you. But all I want to do is set it aside, and if you'll set it aside, too, we can start to move on from. . . ."

She didn't give him a chance to finish. She was scrambling, half nude and splendid, up from the lounger, water streaming down her legs and onto the patio tiles, agitation written all over her face.

Christian could have kicked himself. He'd gone and broken the great taboo, and mentioned the one thing she wasn't able to forgive him for—his breach of her trust. He was angry with himself, but mad at her, too. It always seemed to boil down to this in the end. She placed no faith in him, and never would, either, because she believed he simply wasn't worthy of it.

He was determined not to let this scuttle the only real progress he had made with her in weeks, so he gathered up a huge towel and intercepted her at the door. "You've got shaving cream all over you," he said briskly, as if nothing had ever happened. "Let me dry you off."

She let him, and then allowed herself to be led into the living room and towards her couch. "What do you think you're doing?" she demanded suspiciously.

"Just finishing Madame's toilette. Relax." He left the room. He knew she could hear that he was no longer there, and knew that the anticipation of what he was going to do next was agony for her, so he did his best not to prolong his search unnecessarily. In a matter of moments he was on the couch next to her, and as his weight caused the cushions to sink, her body rolled towards him. The rest of her dressing gown fell away, and he inhaled sharply.

She laughed nervously. "Chris, I asked you what you're doing."

In response, he let his hand run lightly down her body, from the cool skin of her breasts to the abdomen that tautened under his touch, then farther down past the soft curve of her belly to the powder puff of dark springy hair underneath. Under his fingers, the fluff of hair crackled with electric tension.

"Just seeing to *all* your grooming needs, my dear," he

said wickedly. In one hand he grasped a small comb, and in the other he held her nail scissors. "Relax and enjoy it," he advised her. He combed through the fine hairs, gently, but even so the contact of the comb brought a delighted anticipatory gurgle from her throat. For several moments nothing could be heard but the careful snip-snip of the scissors. As each lock fell away, her thighs trembled, partly from the delicious sensuality of the experience and partly from an instinctive fear of such a sharp object coming into close proximity to such a delicate area.

Christian smiled. It was a long time since he'd performed this little service for her; it had once been one of their favorite precursors to a long night of lovemaking. She used to call him her little barber, and joke that if he ever decided to change careers that this might be just the one for him.

"Careful where you snip," she gasped. By now her entire body was atremble, and his every movement was being met with an involuntary quiver of her hips. Eventually he was obliged to set the comb down and use his left hand to exert gentle pressure on her abdomen, to prevent her from shivering so violently.

"Don't worry," he assured her softly. "I'd cut off my right arm before I do any damage to such a precious gem."

At this, she laughed, and the resultant reverberations through her midsection were enough to cause him to set his scissors down as well.

"How do I look down there?" she managed to ask him.

Christian didn't even have the breath within him to answer. He stared at his handiwork, fascinated by the fine, well-groomed pelt that now replaced the unruly curls. He had to admit that he had done a damn good job. Under his ministrations her nether lips were engorged with blood, swelling literally before his eyes, and the pink, moist excited tongue protruded between them, begging for, demanding attention. With a gasp he tossed both scissors and comb overboard.

The first contact of his tongue on her hyper-sensitized flesh tore a startled yelp from her throat. Her fingers dug into the cushions under her as she sought desperately to withdraw from the excruciating torture of his caress. Determined not to have her wriggle out from under his assault, he grasped her firmly, heaving his upper body up onto his elbows so that he could gain more leverage.

She tasted of wild honey, and he was a hungry bear. He delved into her, drawing her sweetness up from her depths, pausing from time to time only to graze along the banks of her upper thighs, letting his tongue explore the crease where the mountains of her legs met the valleys. His rough day-old stubble rasped against her, drawing yelps and protests, but he was determined that this was a battle that he would see to the end.

Too excited for the side dishes laid out before him, he returned to her center, where he feasted, alternately being egged on and then loudly discouraged, until a firm hand at the back of his neck made a lie of all her protestations. His eager fingers joined his probing tongue, cranking up her cries several notches, until a prolonged delirious shout tore from her, and he was engulfed in the wondrous wetness and sweetness and scent of her.

Shaking, so agonizingly aroused that it was painful for him even to move, he got up from his kneeling position beside the couch and crawled next to her. It was a tight fit. He laid his wet cheek against hers, drawing her to him, feeling her heart pounding as hard as his was.

They didn't speak, she because she was bereft of the power of speech, and he because he was mortally afraid that if he opened his mouth the result would be such an outpouring of words of love that, as skittish as she was, she would be scared away for good.

It cut him to the quick, this silence that he was forced

to impose upon himself. Here he was, more deeply and irretrievably in love with a woman than he had ever been in his life, with a need within him to shower her with words of love every day, to make that verbal connection, and yet he could not, because her stubborn refusal to acknowledge that he was capable of such love made him afraid to press the point and risk losing her forever. It was cruel, as if he were locked in some black existential play, paying for his past sins in the manner that it would hurt most. The worst thing was that there was no way to solve his problem, no magic bullet, no quick fix. The only solution was a judicious combination of time and patience, and he was not a patient man.

Her breathing slowed, although he knew from experience that she was far from satiated. He himself was still rock-hard, excruciatingly so, and all he wanted to do now was throw himself upon her, sink into her depths and find the release that he needed, but he knew that to do so would be a lethal mistake. His mind cast around for every trick he knew, every Zen thought that could possibly help him to bring his body under submission.

Eventually, slowly, his blood fell back, and his breathing fell in with her rhythm. She still hadn't spoken, but her hands had come up to grasp his. After a short time the softening of her body against his told him that she was asleep, which made her luckier than he: it was quite a while before he joined her in sleep.

In the morning he rose early; he hated leaving her alone, but the plant was now fully back on stream, and needed his attention. Besides, today was the first day of the Board tribunal at which Andrea Gooding and Ricky Conrad would be judged. That they would lose their jobs was almost a foregone conclusion. The Board had been irate at the way in which they had been manipulated by the scheming woman, and justifiably embarrassed at the manner in which they had been so easily tricked into believing Christian to be the culprit. However, the other question of whether to hand the issue of sabotage over to the police remained, but since the sabotage had involved serious damage to company property and the injury of one man, it wasn't hard to predict that the Board would also choose to go that route.

So Christian did the only thing he could do. He kissed Sean lightly on her forehead, at the place where her bandages met the hair that flopped forward from her brow, and left for work. But throughout the day, a sense of edginess prevailed within him, and he knew himself well enough to be aware that his anxiety had nothing to do with the unpleasantness of having to spend hours in close quarters with a defiant Gooding and a broken, penitent Ricky.

Something kept drawing his eyes to the window, where he could stare out towards the southern hills where Sean's apartment lay, almost as if he hoped that he could see something, a warning signal or even a sign of reassurance, written across the brilliant blue Caribbean sky. But there was nothing.

The same cold dread was with him as he sped home, eating up the miles of highway without a care for the possibility of flashing blue lights appearing in his rearview mirror. He stopped the car at her door, not even bothering to park properly, and with trembling fingers undid the locks, and, leaving the door wide open, sped through the house, calling out her name in a voice that was getting more and more desperate as each room proved empty.

His search ended fruitlessly in the bedroom, and as he slumped to the bed, deflated and suddenly bereft, he was painfully aware that his instinct had been dead right all day. A large portion of Sean's clothing and personal items was missing. So, unhappily, was Sean.

Fourteen

For a New York cabbie, the man was surprisingly patient. In thick accented tones, the Si'ikh who smelled strongly of incense spoke soothingly to Sean, placing her hands firmly onto the knocker at her mother's door, allowing her to announce her presence to the woman within. She could feel his cool rough hands encircle her wrists, and as he carefully and haltingly described the small apron of a garden out front to her, just to reassure her that he had indeed taken her to the right place, she sent up a prayer of thanksgiving that there were still a few people left in the world who could take the time to lend a hand to someone in need of it.

"I wait," the cabbie offered, "until your mother is coming."

There was no sound in the house. Sean began to worry that maybe Elspeth wasn't even in. She hadn't bothered to call from the airport. Grasping the doorknocker, she rapped again, more frantically. "You don't have to wait, you know," she told the driver, even though she was aware that chances were pretty good that she might be needing him again, to take her to a hotel. Somehow she was embarrassed to have another human being, a stranger, sense her dependency.

"No, no," the man patted her hand. "I wait."

"Well," she conceded, "as long as it doesn't inconvenience you."

"No, no," he assured her again. "No inconvenience. The meter, it running still. No problem."

She laughed aloud at his frank and pragmatic response. As the laughter burst from her, the door was torn open from under her hands, and Sean could sense the presence of her mother.

"Jesus," Elspeth breathed, and put a hand out to gingerly touch her bandages.

"Mama," Sean replied, and fell into her mother's arms.

Around her there was activity, as she heard her bags being dragged inside, and the faint rustle of money as the cabbie was paid and generously tipped. Then fine, gentle hands led her down the hall that she had traversed a million times throughout her lifetime. She felt herself being ushered into a room, and the smell of the carpets, curtains and upholstery told her that she was not in the family room, where she and her parents had spent their evenings, but into the formal sitting room, where her mother entertained her lady friends and distant visiting relatives. The formality seemed to underscore the distance that had grown between her and her mother, and this awareness only served to make Sean sad.

She felt the crinkle of thick curly hair against her cheek and smelled her mother's cologne and talcum as Elspeth bent forward to embrace her daughter. She was sure that the moisture that touched her face was tears.

"Look at what they've done to you," Elspeth lamented.

"It's nothing," Sean tried to assure her, even though she thought that the loss of her sight was definitely something.

"Nothing, Sean? You can't see!"

"Just a few more days, Mama, and then the bandages come off." She didn't tell her mother that even when they came off, there was a very good chance of them going on again, if her eyes had shown no sign of improvement.

"But still, that man, that Carlos man, he hurt you."

Sean reacted with surprise. It was true, the fault had been Carlos's, but somehow her immediate injury seemed less damaging than what he had done to Christian, and what the shame and hurt of their ill-fated relationship could do to her hopes of a future with Christian. It was as if she resented Carlos less for firing at her than for the thorn he had placed in her conscience.

She quickly reassured her mother. "Don't worry. He's in custody, and he won't be hurting anybody else again." *Not even me,* she realized, and the liberating thought almost made her smile.

Quiet fell upon the room. It was one of those times when Sean most hated not being able to see, because she knew she was missing a thousand nonverbal clues from her mother, half of which would have gone a long way towards helping her through her difficult mission. Instead she just sat there, clasping and unclasping her knees, until her mother got to her feet and offered to fix her something to eat.

"I'd love something, thanks," Sean said politely, as if she were making her annual visit to a maiden aunt rather than sitting in the house she grew up in.

"Beef stew?" Elspeth suggested hopefully. "You always liked that. With lots of carrots and snow peas."

"Lovely, Mama," Sean said, and listened as her mother bustled out of the room. To tell the truth, she wasn't hungry, it had been hard enough forcing down the dreary airline food earlier that day. But it was good to have the solitude in which to prepare her mind for what was about to come.

She sat in the darkening room, deep in thought. She wondered what Christian must be doing. By now he must have come home from work and found her missing. Fool, she thought. *You should have at least left him a note.* But in her haste to leave before she was intercepted, it was all she could do to feel her way through her packing and call herself a taxi to take her to the airport.

Christian. His face floated before the eye of her mind. Less than twenty-four hours ago she had pressed herself against him and felt the love and desire flowing from his body into hers, and she had wanted so much to turn around, open her arms and let him in. She knew the effort it had taken for him to keep silent when all he wanted to do was talk of love and a future. He may have thought he was masking his desire well, but she wasn't stupid.

She knew, too, that his reticence was her fault. God, she was so ashamed of how she'd treated him these past few weeks! She hated her own surliness and her own standoffishness. The knowledge that every day she had rejected the love of such a good man made her feel like a criminal against her own heart. It didn't make her feel any better to know that she loved him as much as she knew he did her, and that this time the love she felt was a huger, deeper, stronger, more wonderful love than anything she had felt for him in college.

But that love deserved a chance to grow in clean air, with all the sunlight and water it needed. To even attempt to plant it in the garden of her heart, so choked up with weeds and tares, was an injustice. This was her mission in returning home; to clear away her own garden by yanking out all her years of guilty secrets and mistrust by the root. And home was the only place to start. She couldn't truly allow herself to love and be loved by Christian until she set things right with her mother, and put her father's sins to rest once and for all.

Sean got up, and with arms outstretched and fingers questing, felt her way out of the claustrophobic sitting room and inched uncertainly down the hall to the kitchen. She was greeted by her mother's startled yelp and the sound of rushing footsteps. "Sean! What's the matter! Are you in pain?" Elspeth was frantic.

She let herself be placed in one of the kitchen chairs and urged her mother to do the same. "I'm fine, Mama, I just want you to listen to me."

"But I'm slicing the carrots," Elspeth began.

San almost laughed in her nervousness. "Forget the carrots. Just sit down and listen to me."

Elspeth sat heavily.

"There's something I want to talk to you about . . ." she began.

"God, you're hurt worse than you told me, aren't you!"

"Will you listen? I'm not hurt worse than I told you. It's just that we have to talk. We haven't really talked in a long time."

"No," Elspeth said slowly. "We haven't."

Sean took a deep breath. "And that's my fault. I want you to know that what's been happening between us these past years, all these years, has never been your fault. It was me all along . . ."

"Sean. . . ."

"Mama!" If Elspeth didn't stop interrupting, she'd never be able to get the right words out.

"Okay, I'll be quiet. Go ahead. Speak." She folded her arms in her lap and waited.

Sean licked her lips. "Thank you. I came back today because there's this man I love. . . ."

"Christian," her mother supplied. "I remember how much you loved him back in college. You never stopped."

"I never stopped," she agreed, "but this time it's for real, and forever. Only I can't let myself love him or place my faith in him, not fully, until I talk to you about something else."

Elspeth was quiet for a time, then prompted her daughter to go ahead. Hesitatingly, and with a quick mental prayer for her father's forgiveness, she began to tell the story, about the afternoon she had come home late to find her father in the very same kitchen in which they sat, at the very same table, half-naked and making love to the young woman who as a girl had once poured pretend tea for him at his daughter's tea parties. She had to force her voice to remain steady as she explained how her father had browbeat her into keeping her silence, using her love for him and loyalty to him as a weapon. She told her mother of the disgust and disappointment she felt, and how her father had left her a legacy of mistrust that could only now be broken, now that Christian had shown her that he was worthy of her trust, and that she deserved his fidelity in return.

Finally, she explained how she had allowed her heavy secret to come between her and Elspeth, and begged her mother's forgiveness for letting their relationship deteriorate as much as it had. Then, out of breath and shaking with emotion, she stopped and waited for a response.

Elspeth didn't say anything for a thousand painful heartbeats. Then, with an obvious effort to steady herself, she said gently, "Sean, darling, did you really think I didn't know?"

Sean was floored. "You *knew?*"

With quiet dignity, her mother answered, "I lived with him for thirty-five years. There aren't many secrets a man can keep from a woman in all that time."

Sean didn't know what to say. As she sat there, dumbstruck, her mother went on. "Do you remember, she was at the funeral, crying so hard, and everyone was touched, because they thought she was crying because her old girlfriend had lost her father? I remember the ladies in the neighborhood saying what a dutiful child she was, what a good neighbor. I knew better, but I never said anything. My loyalty to my husband just wouldn't let me. She even had the gall to kiss me and offer her condolences." Elspeth gave a short barking laugh. "I actually felt sorry for her, in a way. I suppose she must really have cared for him."

"A lot more than she cared for you," Sean snarled. "Or me. She lied to me. She used me. She came over, pretending to visit me, all those years, when what she was really doing was coming to see *him!* And she did what she did, knowing she was destroying my family. She was my friend first, but in the end, she never cared about that. She just took what she wanted! And as for him, my father, your husband, he showed you no respect. He lived under this roof, carrying on with a child next door, and never once looked ashamed of himself. He made a fool of you!"

"Sometimes you just can't tell the workings of the human heart," Elspeth said almost dismissively.

Sean had had enough. "Mama! How can you be so calm about this? I've carried this around like a crown of thorns, and you just seem so . . . cool about it."

"I'm not cool. Don't think for a moment your father didn't hurt me. It hurt like hell. It wasn't easy knowing he was taking me for a fool all these years, and keeping quiet about it. Accepting all his stories about late meetings and out of town conventions. But I kept my silence."

"Why?"

"Because after all, he was the man I loved, and I wanted to keep my family together. And somehow, I thought it was my lot in life, to have to put up with infidelity. I accepted it as just something women had to do."

"So did I," Sean whispered.

"Well, we were both wrong," Elspeth answered emphatically. "It's not our lot as women. We deserve more. It's our right to *demand* more."

Sean thought about this. She thought about the man she had left so hastily that same morning, and knew deep down that her mission had been completed; her garden was finally free of weeds, and ready to accept any seed she and Christian decided to plant there. There would be no need to demand anything of Christian; he'd tried to prove to her all along that he was ready to give her all she wanted, and more. All she had to do was accept. "Christian is ready to offer me more," she said, knowing it to be true.

"So why are you still here?" her mother asked.

She couldn't get a flight back to Trinidad for four agonizing days. During this time her hand itched to pick up the phone and call Christian, but each time she did so, her courage failed her. She'd run away without a word; somehow a phone call just didn't seem adequate now. What she had to say to him had to be said to his face. So reluctantly, she bided her time, and instead grasped the few precious moments she could spend with her mother—the first that were unclouded by guilty secrets for many a year.

The day before she left, they took her bandages off. Her mother was with her, holding tightly onto her hand. As she waited while they worked on the yards of gauze, she found herself praying hard, although she knew that with or without her sight, she would always be able to rely on Christian. She still wanted to be able to see, so that their future together could be the fullest it could possibly be.

Then painful light seared into her unaccustomed eyes. She blinked and felt the prick of tears. What welcome pain! The fact that she could see made up for any discomfort. The redness that filled her vision softened to a brilliant orange, and then from the hot mist her mother's face appeared, worried, anxious, but smiling. She reached up and touched the lined face with awe.

"I see you," she whispered.

Elspeth was too overcome to respond.

With gratitude, Sean accepted their warnings about wearing sunglasses and avoiding bright sunlight until her eyes were completely healed. Having to spend a few days with shaded eyes was a small price to pay for the return of her vision.

At the airport she kissed her mother good-bye, with reassurances that they would never again be apart so long. Elspeth waited in the terminal until Sean's plane took to the sky.

The flight seemed to take forever. In her desperation, she had taken the next available seat, a bargain fair that stopped at no fewer than five islands on the way down. The flight took the better part of the day. But finally the deep green forested peaks of the Trinidadian mountain range came into view, and Sean's entire body quivered throughout the entire landing.

Even the humidity and sultry island heat was welcome. She left the airport and urged her taxi on toward Christian's house, begging the driver to go faster along the endless strips of sugarcane-bordered highway until in exasperation the white-shirted man reminded her that speed limits still applied.

"I know," she apologized. "I'm sorry. I'm just anxious to be home."

"Going to see the husband?" he nodded knowledgeably. "Y'all youngsters never learn patience."

"Something like that," she admitted, and turned to stare out of the window, wishing the miles of canefields would whiz past even faster. The trip seemed interminable.

Christian's apartment was dark and silent. Sean stood outside, with her hands hanging dejectedly at her sides, knowing that ringing the bell yet another time would make no difference. He simply wasn't here. It was too late for work, although God alone knew that Christian had never allowed boundaries of time to get between him and his business. The scene of joyful welcome that had played out in her own imagination so many times fizzled like opening night at a bad play. She felt like crying.

"You want me to take you somewhere else?" the driver asked with the patience born of decades of pandering to the caprices of the tourists. He was leaning against the hood of the car, arms folded, watching her with a look that said he was willing to sit around all night, if she wanted to.

What else could she do? "Take me home," she whispered, and gave the address.

She could see the light in her apartment before they even made it into the driveway. Christian was still there! Had he been waiting at her home all this time? She needed to find out, and she needed to find out now. She threw the door open and leapt from the slow-moving car without pausing to wonder what would happen if she somehow fell afoul of the wheels.

"Miss!" The driver skidded to a halt and stuck his head out the window.

She'd forgotten to pay him. She stopped in mid-dash and threw a handful of American bills through the window onto the seat next to him.

"That's too much!" he protested.

"Whatever," she said. She was rummaging in her purse for her house keys. The driver didn't argue. "And your luggage?" he asked the back of her head.

"Just leave it in the drive," she told him impatiently. Couldn't he see she had a man to apologize to?

With exaggerated sighing, the driver stopped, got out, and set her small bags gently onto the gravel driveway. "These Americans mad, yes," he muttered as he eased his way back onto the road. Even in her agitation, Sean had to smile. It seemed to be her destiny to meet patient, beleaguered cabbies!

Her nervous fingers finally located the keys, but as she attempted to penetrate the first of the locks, the door was wrenched from her hands. A familiar shape filled the dimness of the doorway, and the scent of the man that she loved entered her nostrils. She whipped off the shades that she still wore, in spite of the late hour, and then there he was. The sight of his beloved face, after all these days of anguished waiting and hoping, made her gasp out his name.

His face was inscrutable. There were lines of exhaustion around his eyes and mouth, and his skin seemed almost sallow. Sean let her purse drop to the floor and stood, reluctant to even draw breath, eyes anxiously searching for some clue as to what he was thinking, and how she would be received after her sudden flight. She knew that after the way she had treated him, she would have a hell of a lot of begging to do before he forgave her and let her back into his life. Sean didn't mind; she was prepared to plead, promise, and ask for his forgiveness for as long as it took—just as long as the end result was being in his arms again.

His name fell from her lips a second time. "Chris," she sighed. She sounded exhausted. Before she could speak again she felt herself being swept up into his strong arms and was overwhelmed by the assault of kisses that rained down over her face, neck and hair. As tall as she was, she was hoisted up as if she were a child, and Christian made his way carefully down the hall and into the living room, where he set her down upon the sofa like a wounded bird.

The change in his features was awesome. A smile played on his mouth and the dark somber eyes that had first taken her in were full of light. He inhaled and opened his mouth several times, as if he wanted desperately to say so many things that he didn't know what to say first.

"You can see again," he said at last.

Sean could only nod blithely. A smile of pride danced on her lips.

"I knew you would." He leaned forward and let his lips gently brush her soft lids.

Sean almost laughed at that. Too many times she had heard in his voice the fear and doubt that she would never regain her sight, but, typical male that he was, he would never admit to being so frightened. She didn't challenge him on that one.

"Got my hair evened off, finally." She put a hand up to pat the results of two hours of salvage work at a Manhattan hairdresser. It was now much shorter than before, the ends evened off, the singed bits gone forever.

"Beautiful," he breathed, but he wasn't looking at her hair.

They stared at each other for a long time, both waiting. Sean decided that now would be as good a time as any to broach the subject that stood between them like a wall. She pulled him down beside her and took hold of both his hands. "Chris," she began.

He headed her off at the pass. "I love you." He was smiling like a child, with the sheer pleasure of saying the words. "I don't care if you don't want to hear it. I'm done holding my peace. I love you and I'm going to say it until you start to believe that it's true." He held her chin steady with one hand and stared into her eyes. "You got a problem with that?"

His smile proved contagious. "Yes. I mean, no, I don't have a problem with it, I mean, keep on saying it. I kind of like it."

"So you believe it, then?"

"Oh, Chris, of course I believe it. It's just that there were so many barriers to the truth. My barriers, not yours. My fault. I just couldn't let it happen until I kicked my own demons out. That's why I left. I needed time."

"You left so suddenly. I came home and you were gone.

I thought that I'd chased you away by what we did the night before. . . . I wanted you so much, I got a little carried away. I thought I'd pushed you, too far, and that you'd gone home because of it."

She reached up to touch his cheek. It had never occurred to her that he would blame himself for her disappearance. "No! No! It wasn't that. It had nothing to do with that night. I needed to clear out all the old rubbish inside me, so I could make enough room for you."

At that, he smiled. "Did you talk to your mother about your father?"

She nodded.

"And how did she take it?"

Sean looked down at her lap. "She knew all along."

Christian listened but did not say anything.

"I let myself suffer for so long over this, all this time, carrying around a secret that didn't need to be kept. For nothing."

He was still waiting.

Sean plunged right in. "Chris, I know I let my own personal suffering get in the way of our happiness once before. I let it prevent me from giving you all my trust."

He wouldn't let her shoulder all the blame herself. "There was a time when I wasn't worthy of that trust," he reminded her gently.

"I know, but that's all in the past. I know that you've changed, and I know that you're a good man, somebody I can put my faith in. If you don't mind, I'd like for us to put everything aside, everything—Elsa, Carlos, our past engagement, our college days, everything, and start over. We can have a bright new clean canvas to paint on, and we can make damn sure that everything we paint on it will be what we both want to see." She waited. He seemed to be thinking hard, and a rush of emotions were reflected on his face. *If he turns me down now,* she thought, *I'll die.* The breath stilled in her lungs.

"You still haven't said what I want to hear," he chided.

How stupid of her! "I'm sorry," she said sincerely. "Truly, truly sorry for doubting you this time around. Forgive me."

His laughter surprised her. As he threw back his head, his huge torso shook. She scowled at him. There she was, spilling her guts, and he was laughing? Briefly, she considered socking him one.

"That's not it," he informed her. "Try again."

Sean racked her brains. Hadn't she apologized? She'd admitted that she'd been an idiot. What more did he want? Then it hit her, and she, too, laughed.

"I love you," she said. The unfamiliar words were wondrous on her lips. "I love you, Christian."

"Now you're talking." He lowered his head and kissed her as if he were tasting the words that had just fallen from her mouth. The light silvery kisses turned a deeper purple hue of passion, and for a long time there was nothing to be heard but the increasingly agitated murmurs and sighs of a pair who had been apart too long.

Sean came up for air long enough to realize that he was clenching her left hand firmly in his grip. "What are you doing?" she untangled her tongue long enough to ask.

"Just checking to see if your ring size has changed," he said mildly.

It took just a few nanoseconds for his meaning to sink in. She raised an ironic brow. "I thought it was customary to pop the question before going on about ring sizes."

"Oh," he let his tongue draw a band of fire around the fourth finger of her hand. "I thought from the way you were kissing me back just now, that asking was redundant."

"It never is," she insisted stubbornly. "Trust me, I'm a woman, I know."

He sighed elaborately. "Well?"

"Well?" she mocked. "You're proposing, Christian, not asking me to the movies. Do it right. I'll make damn sure you'll never have to do it again."

With ostentatious gallantry he slipped off the sofa and onto the floor at her knees. "Sean Carol Ann Scott," he said in a Shakespearean flourish, "will you marry me?"

She pretended to think about it. Unwilling to wait, Christian yanked her down so that she was sprawled full length on top of him. "Hurry," he warned. "This offer may expire at any moment."

She punched him in the arm. "Yes I will, Christian No Middle Name Devane."

"Good," he sighed. "Because I hadn't figured out what I would do with the rest of my life if you didn't."

"It would have been a sad, barren existence," she said with mock seriousness.

"You're telling me!" The laughter rumbled through his chest.

For a while they stared at each other, like gleeful children sharing a private joke, then their mouths seemed more interested in talking through sign language than words. The world around them melted, dissolved and fell away, but they neither noticed nor cared, because all they needed was each other. And that, they both thought, was good enough.

Dear fellow romance lover,

In my first BET/Arabesque romance, *Night Heat,* I was excited for the opportunity to show off my beautiful home, Trinidad and Tobago, by taking my characters on a tour that found them strolling along miles of warm coconut-lined beaches, driving across the lush countryside, and witnessing the miracle of the leatherback turtles nesting at night.

In *Mesmerized,* my second romance, I have chosen to show another side of my country, the industry, the diligence and the technological excellence that has made this tiny Caribbean state a center for industry, and the largest exporter of both methanol and ammonia in the world. I felt that as a West Indian, it was my responsibility to show that the Caribbean is more than one endless beach holiday. We do play, but when we work, we work hard, and we work well.

However, *Mesmerized* is not a report on world economics; it is a love story. As always, passion and desire, sacrifice and dedication, come first. If there is one thing that I would like my readers to remember after finishing this sexy and adventurous novel, it is this: none of us deserves to be badly treated by careless lovers. Hurt is not synonymous with love; joy is. We deserve to be loved and respected, and if we demand it, we will get it. Why? Because we're worth it. Happy romance reading.

ABOUT THE AUTHOR

Roslyn Carrington, who also writes as Simona Taylor, believes that the lush multicultural Caribbean islands of her native Trinidad and Tobago provide the ideal setting for nurturing the creativity of a young writer. There she juggles a hectic career in Public Relations, a weekly op/ed column in the country's most established newspaper and a blossoming career as a novelist.

Her extensive travels and avid curiosity combine with her passion for the delights of the English language to lend wings to her writing. During the many late-night hours that she spends writing, she is encouraged by the company of her cat, Simona, from whom she borrows her pen name.

She would be delighted to hear from her readers, and can be reached at:

Roslyn Carrington
4405 N.W. 73rd Avenue
Suite #011-1241
Miami, Florida 33166-6400

Or visit her website at www.roslyncarrington.com or e-mail her at:
simona@roslyncarrington.com